THE ADVENTURES OF DOD

CONFRONTING THE DREAD

Also by Thomas R. Williams:

The Adventures of Dod,
Dark Hood and the Lair

THE ADVENTURES OF DOD

CONFRONTING THE DREAD

THOMAS R. WILLIAMS

Zettai Makeru

This book is a work of fiction. All characters are fictitious. Any resemblance to real
people, living or dead, is just a coincidence.

Publisher's Cataloging-in-Publication Data

Williams, Thomas R. (Thomas Richards), 1971-
The Adventures of Dod : Confronting The Dread / by Thomas R. Williams ;
illustrations by Christine Coleman.

p. : ill. ; cm.

Summary: After his father goes missing and his grandfather just died, fourteen-
year-old Cole finds himself inexplicably transported to the world of Green, a place
where he must use his special abilities and unique friendships to solve mysteries and,
ultimately, try to stop an evil villain named The Dread.
ISBN: 978-0-9833601-0-0 (hardcover)
ISBN: 978-0-9833601-1-7 (pbk.)

[1. Adventure and adventurers—Juvenile fiction. 2. Imaginary places—Juvenile
fiction. 3. Magic—Juvenile fiction. 4. Schools—Juvenile fiction. 5. Adventure and
adventurers—Fiction. 6. Magic—Fiction. 7. Schools—Fiction. 8. Adventure fiction.
9. Fantasy fiction.] I. Coleman, Christine, 1975- II. Title.

PZ7.W6683 Ad 2011
[Fic]   2011923133

Printed in the United States of America

10   9   8   7   6   5   4   3   2   1

For my wife and kids,

who have stubbornly insisted

that I publish this series.

TABLE OF CONTENTS

PROLOGUE

It's hard to believe anyone, much less an insignificant boy, could change the future for everyone. But it happened!

The story of how it all transpired is something no less than amazing. It's filled with mystery and intrigue, loyal friendships and blackened betrayals. It's a tale to be told and retold until the clues fit snugly together and the truth arises, shocking as it is, that one boy saved millions of people—and all of us, too. We may not know of hidden realms and their triumphs and fears; nevertheless, they're more important to our survival than we could ever imagine.

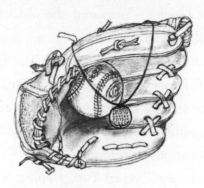

STRIKING OUT

"WHERE'S MY SON!" boomed an angry man, huffing as he pointed his glimmering sword. The flicker of one lonely torch caught the blade with just enough light to reveal its beauty.

"You're a fool, Pap—nothing more," mocked a hooded man, cloaked in black like the moonless night around him. His face was half shrouded by a frightening mask, but his gleeful smile showed plainly his pleasure in taunting. "You're getting old—so it looks like you'll die wondering."

"TELL ME!" demanded the angry man, his face reddening with frustration. "You owe it to me! I have to know—is he still alive?"

"What do you think?" scoffed the veiled intruder, calmly working his way toward the edge of a stone balcony. He waved his hand and pointed jeeringly at the cluttered chamber they had just exited, gloating over the four downed men he had already defeated. "Why do you think they call me *The Dread*?"

"F-Finish him, Pap," called the muffled voice of a wounded teen. His speech was garbled by his pain.

"You're not leaving—" insisted the older man. His steps were solid, but slowed by age.

"Haven't you had enough?" barked The Dread, his cloak licking the night air as he spun back toward him. "Your men have all fallen. If I stay another minute—you die! Wouldn't you rather keep bumbling around? I enjoy watching you, Pap. Foolish as you are, you're a curious man to me."

"Then watch *this*!" yelled Pap, leaping forward with his sword stretched out. He plunged the tip of his blade into the swirling cape, but drew it back empty.

"So you want to play?" laughed The Dread, smiling as he drew his gleaming rapier. "I warned you."

The clanking of swords cut into the stillness of the night; even the breeze stopped to watch the rivals battle. Back and forth—left and right—The Dread was wicked with his weapon, and for the first five minutes, the grin on his face suggested he was merely amusing himself.

"Tell me the truth!" begged Pap, cringing after a steady thrust of his opponent's blade had sliced his left arm. He no longer sounded as forceful as before.

"You're too old to stop me," taunted the hooded man, leaning one hand against a marble statue of a beautiful woman holding a baby. "And you're too young to be so old."

"Wisdom comes with age," huffed Pap, repositioning himself to continue the duel.

"Then I'm wiser than you!" growled The Dread. He bent over casually and dusted off his leg, where the scuffle had dirtied his pants. "I know where I'm headed," he continued smugly, "but look at you—you're little more than a weak extension of Bonboo's feeble arms—and you're always searching for your lost son. It's pathetic! You faithfully serve the very man who deceives you."

CLASH! CLANK! CLASH, CLASH, CLANK!

The men swung and jabbed, pressing upon each other. The hooded man, with his evil, mocking eyes and his eerie mask seemed to dance a cruel masquerade as he moved upon Pap, driving him toward the Hall of Death; a few moans were all that bid him come and join the lifeless men there. But their frail cries did little to aid Pap.

CLANK! CLANK!

Blade against blade, the men pushed at each other. Once The Dread found his footings, Pap didn't stand a chance; the old man flew backward, tripping at the opened entry. He landed on his back, breathing heavily, tasting blood that ran from his nose.

"I told you, Pap. You're no match for me," gloated The Dread, sauntering his way over. He shook his head, pretending to care, and added, "You really should clean up your face. It's a complete disaster."

"B-Beat him!" mumbled someone from the floor of the hall, a distance away.

"You still have a fan," sighed The Dread, burying his left hand into his cape. He looked down at Pap and laughed gleefully, pleased with the plan that was filling his twisted mind.

Instantly, as quick as a nimble youth, Pap rolled to the side, seized an apple from the cluttered floor, and launched the piece of fruit into the dark air; it met a flying dagger, ten feet out, causing both objects to fall recklessly to the ground.

"How do you do that?" raged The Dread, resembling an angry lion that had just lost its kill. "It's not possible!"

"Yet it is!" bellowed a reenergized Pap, hopping to his feet. "Now where were we?"

"But your face—it's just not possible!" screamed The Dread, stepping back. A small bag fell from his cloak as he retreated.

"I took your advice and cleaned it up," said Pap, pointing his sword at the hooded man. "Now get out! You've done enough to these boys!"

As The Dread moved to retrieve his sack, Pap lunged at him with lightning speed, grazing him as he stumbled away.

"But you were spent!" shrieked The Dread. "It's just not possible!"

"Then surrender!" ordered Pap. "If I can do the undoable, I can certainly end this now." He paused at the entry, fiddled with the handle, and swung the solid oak door closed—causing it to lock behind him.

"My prize!" fumed The Dread angrily. "You'll pay for taking what's rightfully mine!"

The men rushed at each other, their swords blazing in the dim light.

CLASH, CLANK, CLANK!

Pots and statuary and patio furniture were employed by both fighters, desperately seeking the advantage over the other, yet neither prevailed. Up and down the terrace they flew, performing the most amazing feats with their swords.

"You've been practicing," conceded The Dread, as he gave as much ground as he took. "You've been spending time with Pious—fighting with Clair and his lot—or perhaps the Red Devils."

"Give up!" ordered Pap.

"Or maybe that arrogant fool from Raul has been showing

you his sloppy moves—*The Great Sirlonk*—I can see the resemblance in the way you fight."

"Just give up!" demanded Pap, not dipping into pleasantries. He knew The Dread was trying to occupy his mind with conversation in hopes of making him lose his focus.

CLASH, CLANK, CLANK!

"That one's from Tridacello!" burst The Dread, staggering backward. He attempted to steady himself when Pap kicked with one foot, while cleverly stabbing his sword inward. "And that one's got Youk's name on it," added the hooded man, swinging frantically to deflect the blow.

Pap plunged to the ground and rolled, slicing one of The Dread's legs.

"I felt that!" grumbled the masked man, his eyes glowering at Pap. "You've even been trained by Bonboo!"

"They're my friends," admitted Pap, beginning to feel his age; after tumbling, his back ached.

"If they're your friends," chided The Dread, repositioning his mask, "then why do they lie to you?"

"They don't," said Pap, driving in again. This time he didn't even try to go for The Dread's body; instead, he twisted his sword as he caught the end of the villain's cape and tugged mightily. The action jolted both men, sending them to the stone floor.

In the chaos, Pap and The Dread rolled back and forth, thrashing and jabbing. By the time they moved apart, both men were in agony.

Haltingly, The Dread pulled himself up with the railing. His legs were injured, leaving him terribly sluggish. When he bent to grab his sword, the tip of Pap's blade pierced the top of his hand.

"No more fighting!" yelled Pap, mustering his strength to

stand. He kicked The Dread's blade to the side and pointed his own weapon menacingly at the villain. "Your reign of terror is over!"

The hooded man was silent at first, and then he began to bargain. "Join me, Pap. I've always admired your skills. With your help we can obtain the secrets."

"IT'S OVER!" thundered Pap. He yelled as though his strong voice would hide the blood that dripped from his center, beneath his trembling hand.

"No it's not," said the masked man, his eyes darting around. "I know what happened to your son; and if you join me, I'll tell you everything."

"NEVER!" boomed Pap, beginning to stagger. He jabbed his sword in The Dread's direction, pointing it at his throat. "TELL ME WHAT YOU KNOW! — TELL ME OF MY SON!"

"I can't speak of such things with a blade to my throat," insisted the hooded man. He tipped his nose snobbishly at Pap. "But perhaps if you join me—"

"NEVER!" blared Pap, stiffening up. He held his shoulders regally, pulled his bloody hand from his stomach, and said carefully, "I'll give you to the count of five to start talking—and if you don't—mark my words, right before your eyes this wound will be healed and you'll reap such wrath from me that the remainder of your life in Driaxom will be pleasant by comparison."

"Ridiculous," scoffed The Dread.

"ONE...TWO..."

"A bloody nose is one thing, but that?" said the hooded man, glancing nervously at Pap's injury and then back to his determined face.

"THREE...FOUR..."

Six years later...

"Hurry and get a couple of these orange wedges," hollered Coach Smith in his enthusiastic sales voice; his wavy blond hair danced in the evening breeze. He raised his muscular arms, brandishing his red cap in one hand, and gestured for his team to huddle around him. As the boys slowly complied, the grin on Smith's face grew to a Cheshire cat smile, and somewhere, hidden behind his bright-blue eyes, was a line to sell; it was the look he gave when he was feeling clever.

"These won't last long," he said, picking up two bags of cut oranges. "I hear superheroes eat 'em all the time: Superman, and Batman, and uh..." he paused for a minute to think of a really exciting one. "Oh yeah, and those Ninja Frogs, too. We better eat these before they use their froggy-laser things on us. I think oranges give them their super powers."

Some of the boys gave Smith a sarcastic laugh, while others rolled their eyes. It was obvious their coach hadn't spent very much time watching cartoons. Saturday was one of his best days for selling cars at Smith's Super Saver Slick Wheels, which was just a fancy name meant to hide the truth about his dealership. It probably could have been reasonably called Smith's Almost Dead and Leaking-Oil Junkers. However, that wouldn't sell very many cars.

"Come on, boys," Coach Smith continued, pausing to smell the dry, desert air. "Liven up. Next time we'll get 'em." He wiped sweat off his tanned brow and resituated his cap. "Besides, you can't beat a sky like this one—perfect blue. Breathe it in, boys—breathe it in."

Coach Smith tried hard to rally the team out of their post-game slump after a disappointing loss, though most of what he said was better suited for kids, not teenagers. He was stuck in a rut, having coached many of the same boys since they were in third grade. Each year he hoped his son, Bobby, would get on track to become the next Babe Ruth. Perhaps if Bobby had gotten his father's perfect, manly figure, it might have been possible—Smith looked like a professional baseball player.

Regardless, 'Bumbling Bobby,' with his slippery hands and knock-kneed, gangly physique, was the worst player on the team—that is, if you didn't count Cole Richards, which is exactly what some teammates did! Cole played so poorly that it was said a one-legged, blind cat could reasonably wear the team's jersey with more respect than he deserved; of course, the boys that said it were heartless and didn't know anything. Had they the slightest clue about who Cole truly was, they would have held their tongues and been much kinder—if not out of common courtesy, out of fear.

Three days before, on Cole's fourteenth birthday, he had made a few wishes as he blew out the candles on his cake. It had felt like cheating to make more than one wish, but Cole was a realist; if you wish for more, you might get one. Anyway, three of his six had already fallen through, and two of them were basically impossible, so that left only one wish: He wanted his mother to stop dating Coach Smith!

It wasn't that he didn't like his coach—he liked everyone—he just didn't want another father in his life.

"Come on, Cole," said Smith, walking up beside him. "How about a few wedges before they're gone?" He held out a limp bag that contained the last five and nudged Cole with his elbow. "I know you love oranges. Your mom says you go through them so quick at home that your brothers hardly know what they taste like."

"Right. No thanks," mumbled Cole, looking embarrassed; Bobby busied himself with tying his shoe. It was awkward for both boys whenever Smith mentioned Cole's mother around the other guys.

Cole looked down at the ground and kicked the dust with his feet, waiting for a polite moment to disappear.

"I'll eat his," said one teammate greedily, wiping juice off his lips with his shoulder. "Everyone saw I played his share of the game."

A few boys chuckled while Coach Smith shook his head.

Years before, when Cole's dad went missing, the family had been forced to move out of their nice home in Salt Lake. Presently, they shared a duplex on the outskirts of Cedar City, Utah. The small town was quaint, and having Cole's Grandpa and Aunt Hilda in the other half of the duplex had been helpful for years; unfortunately, since Cole had developed such a close relationship with Pap, as he called him, when his grandfather died, it was like losing his father all over again.

Now, twelve weeks later, everything seemed dismal for Cole. All five-foot-eight of him yearned to see his grandpa and couldn't help chasing him in his dreams, only to awaken in the morning with the pain that comes from realizing reality is sometimes miserable.

Cole had straight brown hair, with a slight wave in the front, penetrating, milk chocolate eyes, a stocky build, and a reputation as a computer geek. He'd prefer spending time with his high-tech gadgets to being around anyone, unless his dad or Pap could come back—those were the two hopeless wishes he had included in the six.

The three other broken wishes were all ruined at about the same time. Cole had earnestly hoped he wouldn't strike out for the rest of the season. Nevertheless, just barely, in his first game after wishing, he had struck out twice. And he had hoped the Blazers would win their game against the Wolverines to settle a personal grudge with Greg Sye. But Cole's last out had killed that one, too, with a final score of Wolverines 7, Blazers 6—bases had been loaded and the batter after Cole was their team's shining star, Jon Cameron.

Cole had begged his coach to fudge the lineup in order to save the game, claiming his arm was injured, but his pleadings were useless. Coach Smith wouldn't even consider it. "Do your best and believe in yourself," was what he had said to Cole, along with a lot of hype about winners never quitting and the team supporting him if it was a good effort.

Whatever, thought Cole.

His third wish had been for Jon to stop teasing him. However, after losing the game for everyone, it seemed fair grounds for Jon to have his fun. Few teammates could put orange wedges in their mouths without choking because of laughter from jokes Jon told at Cole's expense.

"Come on, guys," said Smith bleakly, bending down to pick up the peels some of the boys had carelessly dropped on the grass. "You all did your best today. Don't judge a player by one bad game."

But somehow their best wasn't good enough when all of the players took turns batting, and Jon really rubbed it in.

"Hey Cole," said Jon, his wiry blonde hair sticking out from under the sides of his cap near his ears. He smiled wickedly, poising for another joke. "At least you can help us next week against the Seagulls." He looked at the other guys and began to chuckle as he added, "—if you stay at home!"

Everyone laughed.

"—or better yet, you can join their team. We'd win for sure!"

Cole didn't say anything. It was futile to stick around. He didn't want orange wedges or post game mumbo-jumbo about being a losing-winner, and he definitely didn't want to hear everything Jon had to say. He just wanted to go home and play computer games for a while. It usually did the trick.

Cole had wanted to give up baseball for years, but due to a promise he had made to his grandpa, he kept playing.

"Remember your dad," Pap would say encouragingly.

A lot of stories had been told about Cole's father. He had struggled for six seasons as a poor player until one day it clicked—like magic. Pap loved to tell that story about his son. He went from being a nobody to starring on his high school team. They even nicked him 'Homer' because he hit so many homeruns.

Later, he was offered the job of a lifetime, a great contract to play Major League Baseball. Everyone saw he was a rising star with unbelievable talent. That's usually where Pap would end the story when he told it. He knew Cole didn't like the real ending.

At home, Cole's mother, Doralee Richards, was the first to greet him. Her blond curls were held back with a clip, and her light-blue shirt and white pants indicated she had the night shift again. She smiled sweetly, but didn't ask how the game went. She had learned it was better not to bring it up. Rather, she quickly hugged him and moved straight on to something else. If Cole had tales of success, he would obviously share them, so it didn't make sense asking questions that would only end in pain while answering.

Doralee was a great mother, the kind that always sacrificed for her kids. She cooked them breakfast and dinner when she was able, made them special lunches before school, and did her best to help them as much as possible with their homework. The rest of the time, unfortunately, she had to spend working long hours at the Truck-Stop Diner around the corner to make ends meet. It was a hard life for her as a single parent; and though she never complained, there were many times she wished Cole's father was still around to help her out.

Josh and Alex were Cole's younger brothers. Everyone called them twins, yet they weren't real twins. Eleven months separated them, which was enough to keep them a full grade apart in school. In fairness, however, they did look strikingly similar. Both had bone-straight, brownish-blonde hair, an olive complexion, and dark-brown eyes. They resembled their father and looked very little like their mother, who had curly blonde hair, creamy-white skin, and bright-blue eyes.

Cole also looked like his dad, to the extent that people, who had known his father when he was younger, made claims he had come back from the dead with a new, 'handsome' nose—that part was from his mother.

No sooner had Cole walked into the kitchen, than his little brothers started to needle him, as younger siblings often do, hoping he'd grace them with his company that night.

"It's finally Friday!" blared Josh obnoxiously the moment he saw Cole. Josh flipped his finger back and forth, playing with the peeling end of a strip of lemon-yellow wallpaper near the fridge. It was obvious he was bored-stiff.

"Let's do something really exciting," he continued, looking at Cole with pleading eyes, "—like toilet paper Jon's house."

Josh knew that Jon caused problems for Cole on ball days, and it was no secret that he wished Cole would fix it. He certainly would have if he were fourteen instead of ten. As a result of his feisty nature, the principal at Riverside Elementary School knew Josh quite well.

Earlier in the year, on the first day back from Christmas break, the school bully had picked on eleven-year-old Alex in front of the flag pole. He had shoved him around until Alex's backpack had spilled open, littering everything all over the ground. And when Alex had bent down to gather it up, the bully had kicked him face-first into the mud and had made comments about a hole in his shoe, suggesting Santa didn't dare go near Alex for fear of contracting fleas. It was humiliating and done in front of everyone.

Josh wouldn't stand for it, he wouldn't allow a bully to pick on his brother; so he promptly set the boy straight with his fists. By the time he had finished, there was plenty of blood for the whole student body at Riverside to feel fully avenged for all of the wrongs they had suffered at the bully's hands.

Later, as Josh was being expelled for fighting, Principal Lloyd did his best to get Josh to express remorse, saying that it seemed Josh had something he probably wanted to tell the boy, and the rest of the school, over the intercom.

"I do," declared Josh confidently, and then he said what he wanted to share: "I popped him in the nose—and well—it's not bad, considering he's twelve and I'm only ten."

Josh's mom did the real apologizing, by making a loaf of banana bread for the injured boy; but even then, after being drug to the bully's house by Cole, Josh still wouldn't hand over the bread until Cole compromised by allowing him to remove the sappy note, because he wasn't sorry, on the contrary, he was proud of what he had done!

Cole was the exact opposite. He was built well enough to stick up for himself, yet he chose to be friendly to everyone, even those who picked on him. It felt like the right thing to do, not to mention the logical thing; Cole had plenty of acquaintances but no real friends, so he knew if there was ever trouble, he was on his own.

"Come on! Let's go toilet-papering!" insisted Josh, shadowboxing in the air around Cole like a prized fighter. He was only armpit high to his brother. "I know of a few people we can call. You're not the only one that thinks the Camerons ought to be taught a royal lesson. If we each bring three rolls, we'd plaster the place."

Cole smiled at the thought of decking Jon's house, even though he knew he would never do it.

"I don't think so, Little Buddy," said Cole, trying to look away from his brother's disappointed eyes. He glanced around the small kitchen and settled on the stairway. "Not tonight, anyway. I've got some things I need to take care of."

"Oh!" groaned Josh miserably, letting a few of his playful punches connect. He stepped boldly in front of Cole, preventing his escape to their bedroom. "Come on, Cole! Don't be gaming all night!" said Josh defiantly. "Let's do something *real* together. It's Friday!" He then took a quieter tone and begged shamelessly, "Please." The look on Josh's face was like a locked-up puppy that had just found out it was in the pound.

"Uh, I've got this thing—" Cole began, when he was interrupted by Alex, who couldn't stay out of the conversation any longer. Peanut butter dripped down his chin as he poked his head up from behind the graying, splotched kitchen counter. He hadn't eaten much dinner—freezer-burned fish wasn't his favorite—and now he was attempting to make up for it in secret.

"Let's go sleep by the creek," blurted Alex cheerfully, his good-weather dimple appearing momentarily. He knew Cole loved camping, or at least he had enjoyed it when Pap was alive.

"I don't know," said Cole hesitantly. "It's not the same without Pap. Besides, don't you get scared when the wind blows through the willows?" Cole fixed his eyes on Alex and raised his eyebrows ominously.

"I'd be okay if you go," responded Alex nervously, peering at Cole, then Josh. He licked his spoon clean before adding it to the mountain of dirty dishes in the sink.

The answer took Cole by surprise. In the past, not only did Pap have to go in order to convince Alex it was safe, he usually had to connect their sleeping bags together before Alex would stay the night.

"Really?" asked Cole in a doubtful sort of voice.

Alex looked down at the floor for a moment and shuffled his barefoot back and forth, pushing breadcrumbs into a little pile. Thoughts of the wind whistling did sound scary.

"Don't worry," said Josh, as he read the look on Alex's face. "You can zip your bag to mine and then no dumb willow in his right mind would dare whistle at ya."

Cole couldn't help feeling proud to be their older brother.

"I guess my stuff can wait 'til tomorrow," he responded, grinning, still waiting for Alex to kibosh the plan. "You guys get the flashlights and pack up some food. I'll change and go next door for the sleeping bags." He stalled and glanced at his brothers.

"All right!" said Josh, clapping his hands together. "Now we've got a plan." Alex smiled and didn't cave in, so Cole went to change out of his uniform.

"Will you be safe?" called Doralee up the stairs as she searched a cluttered cabinet for her purse. It was almost time for her to go to work.

"Of course!" said Josh, a few feet away, eager to answer for his older brother. He fumbled through the remaining odds and ends of silverware in the nearly-empty drawer, hoping he'd missed a clean knife. When the same eight pieces didn't evolve, he finally resorted to prodding Alex into washing one.

"You know we'll be fine, Mom," answered Cole, rumbling down, two steps at a time. "I'm going with them, and I may not be very athletic, but I'm pretty good at being safe." He stopped at the base of the stairs to kiss his mom on the forehead.

A quick memory flashed through Cole's mind that had inspired the comment. A few years back, some boys on his baseball team had teased him mercilessly when he had refused to slide into first base for fear of dirtying his pants. He had figured there wasn't much use in breaking a kneecap for the game, especially considering how poorly he played anyway, though some teammates had suggested he was 'too safe' to play ball at all—of course, those were the kind of teammates that would have teased him about something else even if he had taken first base.

Cole sighed and gave his mom a squeeze as he glanced at his brothers, who were working frantically to find anything edible to take with, for the fridge and cupboards were mostly bare.

"It's the second Friday, boys," said Doralee apologetically. "I'll get my check tonight when my shift's over."

"It's okay, Mom," said Cole. "We've always got peanut butter."

He walked out the front door and across the cracked-cement porch to the other side of the duplex. Recollections of happier days filled his eyes with tears. Friday night fun with Pap had been a tradition for so many years that it felt natural banging on the screen door—the bell was always in need of repair—and marching in with a loud 'Hello.'

"Well, Cole," announced Aunt Hilda with a smile on her face. "Where are you boys off to?" She sat in an easy chair, near the corner of the room, knitting what looked like a present for some lucky person.

Cole could hear music playing quietly from an old stereo, positioned right behind Hilda's chair, and the words fit her situation well enough that it distracted his concentration for a moment. The song's lyrics spoke of a woman who kept falling in love, yet couldn't ever make it to the altar. Finally, at the end of the song, it proclaimed something about how the Queen of Hearts was the Old Maid.

Hilda knew plenty about falling in love, and as she sat alone in her chair, Cole felt like she was a bit of an old maid. At fifty-three, she wasn't really old. Her long, curly brown hair seemed almost magical. It was a mystery to him why nobody could catch her and keep her. Pap had often joked that she'd be able to marry if only she could choose two or three good suitors. Regardless, since Cole's grandma had been dead for years, Pap had been very grateful for Hilda's company and cooking.

"So, where is it that you're off to?" asked Aunt Hilda a second time. "I assume, on a Friday night like this, you've come for gear."

Cole realized that he had been so fixed on listening to the song's quiet lyrics that he had entirely ignored Hilda's question.

"Oh, we're going down to the river for the night," responded Cole quickly. He hurried past Hilda, through her kitchen, and up the stairs to a room full of Pap's treasures. "We just need a couple of bags," continued Cole in a loud voice that could be heard throughout the little duplex, though it trailed a bit when he buried his head into a closet. "I'm trying to help Josh and Alex….You know…be a good friend to them."

"Sounds fun," said Hilda, startling Cole. She had set her project down and had followed him without catching his attention. "Do you need me to come along?"

"No," said Cole, embarrassed. "We'll be fine."

It was nice to have Hilda around. She had become a second mother to Cole and his brothers, filling in when their mom had strange hours at the Truck-Stop Diner. Hilda was also great at keeping things under control, despite Josh and his crazy ideas.

Cole grabbed three sleeping bags and headed for the door.

"Why don't you take this," called Hilda, digging through a box of trinkets. "It's Pap's good luck charm. You know he wanted you to have it. He was wearing it the day he died."

"Now that you put it that way," said Cole playfully, with a twinkle in his eye, "how can I possibly refuse? After all, he *died* wearing it."

"Yes, he did die wearing it," quipped Hilda, "but he died peacefully in his sleep. You can't beat that!"

Whether Cole wanted to take the luck charm or not was unimportant; Hilda had made up her mind to put it on him.

"Thanks," said Cole. His eyes panned across the small gold coin which dangled from a chain. It looked expensive, though only about the size of a quarter, and had intricate designs on the front and back. Time had worn the symbols down so they weren't very clear. "Now let's see," said Cole, straining to remember. "Where did Pap get this from, anyway?"

"Your dad gave it to him," said Hilda, "or at least left it to him with his note…said it was for never giving up on him when others did."

Cole looked at the floor somberly, trying to hide his feelings.

"It's yours now," added Hilda, still working the clasp that held it together. "I'm sure your father would want you to have it now."

"Thanks," said Cole again, pulling an uncomfortable smile.

"Your dad was wearing it the day he hit his first homerun," continued Hilda cheerfully, patting him on the back as though she wished he could look straight forward with her and see the memory. "I'll never forget that hit. Wow! You should have seen the ball fly. It nearly nailed the biggest front window of the red farmhouse across the street from the old field, where they used to play ball. I don't think I've ever seen anyone else hit one like that."

"Well then, I should've been wearing it today," joked Cole. He tried to act happy. Hidden inside, the truth was different. Just mentioning a note from his dad made Cole's stomach turn. Each family member had received one when his father went missing; and despite Cole's occasional curiosity, he hadn't ever opened the sealed envelope that contained his. He knew the words, though complimentary, would be too painful to read.

"I'll bring these back tomorrow," called Cole to Aunt Hilda as he hurried out the door with the sleeping bags.

Josh and Alex were both waiting on the front porch, poking

and stabbing at the ground with a butter-knife. One of them explained that they had seen a spider, at least twice the ordinary size, heading straight for the house; and when they had tried to squash it with a shoe, the spider had cleverly ducked into a crack, leaving them no choice but to use the knife.

"C'mon, don't muddy it," exclaimed Cole, "or I'll clean it off with your peanut butter sandwiches. Besides, if that thing comes back out, don't expect me to get it. You know how much I hate spiders!"

Josh laughed as the two boys quickly hopped up and chased after Cole, holding their small bag of food and supplies. It didn't take long before Josh took the lead and directed them down a road, through a hay field, and across a few acres of sagebrush. It was a short distance to the river, but by the time they arrived, Cole could feel his arms aching. Holding three sleeping bags was awkward enough that it strained his muscles.

Josh and Alex immediately started playing tag in the large willow trees with Cole resting on the bags at their base. It wasn't much of a contest. Josh was like a crazy monkey, jumping and scampering instinctively up and down as though he had lived in the tops of the branches for his whole life. Alex, on the other hand, struggled; it brought back memories for Cole to watch Alex play.

A long, thick rope dangled from one prominent branch, displaying Pap's triple-cinch-double-loop-knot. Pap had tied the knot so Cole could swing on the rope, while hanging below it, with both hands grasping loops. For many years it had been the pinnacle of fun in his wonderland of branches and leaves.

"Look at me!" yelled Josh, swinging back and forth precariously with his feet in the loops. "I can do this without hands, too. Watch me!" He began to let go when Cole rained on his plans.

"Keep holding on!" he demanded, sitting up momentarily to boss his younger brother. "I'll walk you home right now if you don't! We promised Mom we'd be careful." He waited to see that he was obeyed before settling back down to watch the sky turn purple and the North Star peek out.

The eight giant willow trees that grew in a cluster on the creek's bank were in stark contrast to the hay and sagebrush fields that surrounded Cedar City. Large trees only grew where they were planted because of the desert heat and rocky terrain. The spot was an oasis of sorts, planted by early Mormon Pioneers who had settled the desolate land, and for Cole, it was heaven. The sounds of the trickling creek and chirping crickets were soothing; they seemed to possess magical powers that could effectively wash troubles and cares away with their hypnotic rhythms.

As Cole lay musing, he watched his brothers and couldn't help feeling at peace, like the cruelty of the world was far behind him; nevertheless, it wasn't more than an hour before the tranquility of memory lane was cut short. Alex dropped his pocket knife in the tall grass, and once flashlights were used to find the knife, it was pointless to try to go back to seeing without the lights.

Moments later, Cole, Alex, and Josh had their sleeping bags zipped together, with Alex sandwiched in the middle. They originally tried zipping just two bags together, with Josh and Alex sharing, but Alex complained that one side would be too scary. It was almost a camp killer.

At that point in the evening, Cole considered walking

home in the dark to spend the night in his bed. It sounded nice; however, the refreshing and nostalgic smell of the bubbling rivulet, with its moist air, convinced him otherwise. As he closed his eyes and headed off to sleep, the past danced in his mind. It was almost as if the setting brought it back to life.

Morning came sooner than any of them would have chosen. It was still mostly dark when the wind brought rain in big drops. Cole didn't want to get up, so he advised the others to curl deeper in the bag. He hoped the storm would blow over quickly before dropping very much rain.

His advice seemed to be sound, especially for someone half asleep. Unfortunately, that advice became the subject of a heated discussion over breakfast—at home!

"But I didn't know it was raining harder in the mountains," exclaimed Cole irritably, hardly able to swallow. He attempted to defend his position in a losing battle against Doralee. Alex barked croupishly next to him, doing his best to gag down breakfast. Josh was standing at the counter to eat rather than sit on the broken chair he was left with; he quietly cheered for Cole, while washing his food down with tap water.

"That doesn't matter," insisted Doralee, putting her foot down and one hand on her hip, the other hand waved in Cole's face. "I'm your mother and I'm telling you that you'll stay in your room today and think about what just happened!" She walked back over to the place where she had been working and finished drying a pile of plates.

"Besides," she continued, clanking a stack of dishes into their proper spot on an empty shelf, "I need you to help Hilda keep an eye on the boys while I'm at work." She spun around and examined Cole's face as she carried a discolored, dented pot to the stove. "I know you didn't mean any harm, and you thought you used your best judgment, but it wasn't good enough, son."

Doralee took off her wet apron and hung it on the corner of a cupboard door that was always incurably ajar. She rubbed her red hands that begged for lotion; they were horribly chapped from days and nights at the Diner and her most recent labors at the kitchen sink.

"Okay," sighed Cole, glancing away guiltily. He watched Hilda warm up the last of her taco leftovers from an engagement she had helped cater a few nights before. As breakfast food, they were slightly better than starving.

"One more, anyone?" Hilda asked cheerfully. She looked at the three boys with no indication of embarrassment over being in the same room as her sister-in-law, while the rumblings played out.

"I guess," responded Cole sullenly, feeling ripped off. He didn't like thinking about what had just happened. After ducking down deeper for shelter, the rain had slowed, and they had all fallen asleep—that is, until a flash flood picked up their sleeping bag and washed it away.

Alex had swallowed a lot of water before escaping, so his lungs sounded really congested, hence the coughing. Cole and Josh had managed to get out okay—just wet.

On the way home, Josh had actually thanked Cole for the exciting time and had insisted that if he could do it all over again, he wouldn't change a thing—even if it cost him a year's savings to replace the sleeping bags. "After all," Josh had said excitedly, "it was the adventure that was irreplaceable."

Cole completely disagreed. He wouldn't have gone at all if he were given the chance to do it over, so it seemed more than a little unfair that he was the one being grounded.

On any other Saturday it might not have been much of a punishment, but this particular Saturday was special—Cole had two tickets to a technology convention at the University. Thinking of his loss made him furious.

As Doralee left the house, Cole positioned himself upstairs in his room, sulking quietly. He didn't like the ruling, nevertheless he wasn't about to disobey his mother.

It rained and rained all day. Every drop that hit Cole's windowpane reminded him of how stupid he had been to sleep so close to the stream. He thought about Pap and how he had always insisted they sleep farther back. It had never occurred to Cole that Pap did it for a reason until the flood came.

In the end, Cole was left to spend his afternoon doing what he thought would be relatively boring, especially compared to the convention. And his agony had to be kept to himself since Josh and Alex were so tired from the morning's excitement that they napped the day away in their bunk beds.

Not much was happening—until it all happened!

CHAPTER TWO

MYSTERIOUS CIRCUMSTANCE

Cole looked out his window and viewed the dreaded rain. His eyes carefully followed an unusually large drop of water, all the way down the pane. As he watched, something strange happened—something that had never happened before—something that was so unexpected and wild, Cole couldn't believe it—something that made no logical sense at all—and regardless of the fact that he didn't believe it, it still happened!

Without any warning, Cole found himself precariously attached to an extraordinary rope contraption by a ripped harness of sorts. One of his legs was caught in the straps, while his other dangled freely. The broader, belt-like rigging, that should have been cinched around his waist, was tangled in a knot and sagging near his feet. The only thing that kept him from plunging headlong to a bloody end was his death-grip on the swaying rope.

Terrified and confused, Cole hung on for dear life and did his best to inch his way upward. He was motivated by what lay beneath him. A quick peek revealed that he was nearly at the top of a jagged cliff wall, some five hundred or more feet tall—or at least that was how far he could see, because fog engulfed the bottom. Two strange bodies were busily working their way upward, attached to the same four-rope device as he, with one of them trailing close behind, and the other fumbling much farther below.

Metallic pulleys glittered in the afternoon sun, catching Cole's attention momentarily. They were fastened at various intervals along the lines, aiding the climbers in a way he had never seen done before, despite having rappelled plenty with Pap.

A distant, low-pitched groaning of waves crashing against rocks hinted at the terrain that was hidden by the haze. The sound also muffled a disgruntled conversation between the lowest visible climber and someone else that remained out of view.

The circumstance appeared terribly dangerous. Cole did his best to shimmy and scamper up the last part of the cliff; however, he found it difficult to climb, as though he had been at it for a long time. Each tug made his arms ache horribly, like the muscle-burn of a final, feeble pushup. And as he struggled to move, the faulty harness additionally hindered him, slowing his sluggish ascent. Meanwhile, a sharp pain intermittently shot up his back, joining the constant throbbing in his head.

"Hurry now. Up the bank like a good lad," bellowed the closest climber, who was quickly encroaching on Cole. The mystery man had cut the distance between them down to a couple of yards, making his face clearly visible. His wrinkles from age doubled with concern across his broad forehead as he yelled at Cole.

"Another two blanks and you'd be fishing for flies with

your toes, and we'd be right behind you! This is hardly the place to play around! We're not out of sight yet. Don't slack on the trilang—fasten it up to the post—or Dungo and Bowlure will lose it for sure. You should have cleared the top ages ago!"

Faintly, Cole squeaked a concerned cry, only audible to the old man, "Uh, I'm not able to—"

"QUICK! TIGHTEN YOUR END!" responded the man, punctuating his words with greater conviction, much like the captain of a boat commanding young shipmates.

Miraculously, Cole's hands instinctively obeyed.

"Yes, like that," continued the man. "For a moment, I thought you'd lost your freshy-mind—swinging around harnessless. Just because you didn't head back down with Dungo doesn't give you liberty to dawdle."

Cole heaved a leg up and caught the ledge at the top, the moment he was close enough, and spun his body around until he was positioned on his back, with dirt comfortably beneath him. Still tangled in the riggings, he stared up at the sky and attempted to catch his breath.

"Keep it up, boy!" yelled the old man, chiding Cole for taking a moment to rest. "Don't let the lines slack 'til we're all clean of this cliff. With the cords twisted and rubbing, we're certain to pay!"

The seasoned climber continued to grumble until he finally reached the top and pulled his gangly body over the lip. He staggered back and forth, breathing heavily, while clearing rope and gear from between his legs. As he did, he added an unusual stretching dance that made his six-foot-six-frame block the sunlight momentarily from reaching Cole's face. Eventually, a prominent cracking sound burst from his middle back.

"Ah, that feels better," he confessed, glancing disapprovingly at Cole before poking his head dangerously over the edge of the cliff.

"Dungo, did you get it?" he bellowed anxiously.

From hundreds of feet down, a muffled response wafted back, unintelligible.

Cole stared in amazement and disbelief. He couldn't understand where he was, or how in the world he had gotten there, or why his clothes were different. Instead of Levis, his pants were made of rough cloth, and his shirt was a matrix of black-leather wrappings. He also had on a loose, deep-maroon jacket that had been constructed of a thicker hide.

When he attempted to rise, in order to help the elderly gentleman with the gear—for Cole was prodded by a dozen cross looks from him—the world spun around until Cole had to resort to a crouching position on the ground in order to avoid passing out. A sideways glance revealed that the old man's mood had shifted from annoyed to slightly concerned when he saw Cole collapse.

"Are you solid, boy?" he asked, sensing something was wrong; but his pressing concern for the difficulties, which were unfolding farther down the cliff's face, hindered him from pursuing deeper. Before Cole could respond, the man had already wholeheartedly turned his attention back to readjusting the ropes and studying the progress of the other climbers.

Bathed in sunlight, the aged gentleman's hair was a bright white, or at least the hair he had left. Most of the top of his head revealed sunburned, shiny skin. And his body was as skinny as the wind blown trees lining the cliff's edge, interrupted occasionally by muscles that rippled under his wrinkles. He wore a worn, short-sleeved shirt and tan pants—nothing special—and appeared very ordinary, except for one distinguishing feature: a browning, reddish, round band, much like a garden snake, encircling his lower neck, characteristic of...a tredder!

Cole didn't recognize everything all at once, but things did seem to fade in and out of his memory, like bits and pieces of a past dream. Information about the tredder people and their customs filled his mind as though he had known them all of his life. Even the old man was no longer a complete stranger. It was like someone had flipped on a light switch, making it possible to see much of what had been hidden before.

The seasoned climber, standing before Cole, was named Tridacello. He was a lover of freedom and a man who had spent much of his life doing good for other people, or so it seemed. That's what the blurry memories suggested.

As Cole processed the situation, he tried to retrace his bizarre entrance; however, before he had time to so much as think of his bedroom, the old man yelled to take cover and jumped to the ground. Two rocks, each at least the size of an apple, cleared the cliff's edge and whizzed a distance beyond them into an adjoining forest. One stone hit a twenty-foot birch tree and split the tree in half, sending pieces of flaky white bark into the air like confetti; the other landed in a nearby bog and produced a fountain of mud and weeds.

"That couldn't have come from the dogpaddler," complained Tridacello. He looked at Cole and added, "How many ships did you see while we waited?"

"Me?" muttered Cole. "I didn't see any."

"Not even in the distance?" replied Tridacello skeptically. "Whoever's firing at us is certainly floating on something bigger than the hundred-man ship Dungo and Bowlure just visited. I'd say it's Dreaderious himself, judging by the height of those balls."

"How many did *you* see?" asked Cole, turning the question back at him, for despite Cole's general knowledge of the world around him, he didn't know anything about the sea or the ships down below.

"I stayed above the fog-line," said Tridacello quickly. "Remember? I was guarding our retreat." He crawled over to the cliff's edge and peered out carefully. "Dungo! Do you still have it?"

Faintly, yet clearly audible this time, a voice responded, "Oh, I have id, bud all da sduff in da air bumped Bowlure indo a glandor's pid. I dink his line is clean cud. And don' ask me do head down righd now eider. Dreaderious is in da open wid ad leasd dree hundred poorlings—maybe more. Id's nod word my skin for his. Besides, we can come back when id's quied and dry do redrieve him. If he can handle da glandor's sding widoud doo much fuss, he jusd mighd sday in one piece."

Dungo's voice faded for a moment into a muffled noise. The sound of cracking branches made it clear his ascent was quickly nearing the higher, wooded part of the cliff wall.

Tridacello stood back up and shook his head, still cautiously peering over the gulf. It was evident that he didn't like a plan going south on him, and Bowlure's line breaking was definitely in that category.

"Glantors!" he muttered to himself. "I'd take a bath in red ants before spending the day sitting in a pit of Glantor-Worm slime. That stuff—" His voice trailed off as he recalled past experiences with the burning chemical created by Glantor Worms. The worms themselves were small and harmless; however, their slime was painful.

Cole slid closer to the edge and peeked out, watching for incoming debris. A volley of stones, flung from somewhere below, pierced the blanket of fog and pelted the cliff wall. Fortunately, this time they didn't rise as high as they had before, so all of them failed to clear the top.

"Dod," grumbled the climber that was now nearing completion. "Whad was your problem back dere?" His cold black eyes were sternly looking at Cole, who could now see, from where he sat, that Dungo was a monstrous creature, not a man.

Dungo glared between two rugged trees that were lodged in a crack, both jutting directly horizontal for about ten feet and then vertical for another ten. He grabbed at the branches and pushed them out of his way with two hands, while using two more to work upward on the rope; his two legs moved quickly below the foliage, clawing at the rocky wall with his massive feet.

"You mean me?" squeaked Cole apprehensively, once again trying to stand up. He held the trunk of a baby pine, to steady himself, as he poked his head over the edge far enough to get a better look at the four-armed thing. Dungo made eye contact with him for a few quick seconds before Cole pulled back.

"No, I mean da udder Dod!" roared the creature, agitated. "Of course I mean you! All of a sudden id was like you never scaled up cliffs wid a drilang in your whole freshy-life. Danks do you, I had do go back down do help Bowlure. We could have all been yurflo feed."

A few mangy, scavenger yurflos floated on the rising breeze just yards away. They were mostly talons and beaks, making Dungo's point more poignant. One carried the remains of a dead fish, with two more pursuing vigorously, trying to steal it.

"Well, to be honest," squeaked Cole, "I don't know where

I am." In his mind he continued, *or who any of you are.* His thoughts drifted to the immense pain in his back. It was nauseating and caused his eyes to blur. He clung tightly to the young tree at his side and tried to stay conscious, taking deep breaths of the briny breeze that blew in his face.

Cole thought to himself, *there must be a logical explanation—maybe I fell asleep and was just dreaming that I almost died on a cliff with a—* Cole's mind trailed as he shuddered, but unfortunately, his mouth mumbled his thoughts quietly:

"—couple of ugly things—I must be dreaming."

Dungo's tail announced his completion of the ascent, smacking Cole's aching back squarely in the middle, sending him to his knees.

"Ouch! Ahhh," yelped Cole in pain.

"Dungo! That's enough!" ordered Tridacello. "Dod's not well."

"Yeah, you musd have been dreamin' back dere," continued Dungo, towering over Cole threateningly. The smell of his sweaty fur was disgusting.

"And danks do your dreamin' we have do come back for Bowlure lader. Besides, who you callin' bugly? Your pale whide skin and puny arms look like a tiny bug do me. If you hadn'd been da besd poind man ad da drials, dere is no way you'd be on a mission like dis. You definidely weren'd chosen for your sdrengd. Ha-hgg, Ha-hgg—"

"I didn't call you bugly," choked Cole, looking away. He hoped the monster wouldn't eat him.

"Den whad was dad you muddered—"

"Stop it and quiet down—both of you!" chimed Tridacello,

with the voice of a father scolding two disobedient sons. "I'm sure Dod just got a little flush in the head, while we waited for you and Bowlure. It took quite a bit longer than the hour you promised."

"You can'd blame us for unwanded company," rebutted Dungo, spinning around to face Tridacello. "Dreaderious was supposed do be oud do sea, remember? Jus' da dogpaddler in da bay. Dad's whad you said. Id's quide a bid differend raidin' a wired ship. Wid da Magellan docked close by, we're lucky do be alive."

"The Magellan!" groaned Tridacello. "I knew it! Only Dreaderious's vessel has the platforms and decks to support a hailstorm like that. Did you pull the lower leads?"

"I did," said Dungo. "Nobody will be climbing dese ropes from down below." He poked at the lines with his foot.

"Good," responded Tridacello, looking a bit relieved. Still, worry cloaked his face like a mask.

Cole slid backward, up against the baby pine, and wished to be farther away from Dungo. Part of him hoped that another tree-chopping stone would come flying through the air and send 'Stinky' to his knees. The pain Cole felt was bad enough that he could only watch; running away to hide wasn't an option, since he knew he'd likely pass out before he hit the forest.

Tridacello tugged at the latches of a small bag he wore at his waist. His long, wiry fingers looked like the legs of a spider, spinning a web, as he finished the lengthy process of unhitching. Once the mouth of his compartment was gaping, he turned to Dungo, opened his hands wide, and asked for the triblot.

"Here you go," responded Dungo slyly. He faked handing him the triblot by rolling it from one hand to the next. He chuckled as he showed off his agility, moving all four hands at the same time, and said gloatingly, "You have do pick a hand, bud dink careful because you only ged one chance."

Tridacello scolded him, saying, "We don't have time for games, Dungo! Besides, my chance to choose a good 'hand' ended before we started on this journey, didn't it?"

Dungo quickly relinquished the triblot and began amusing himself by squishing blue-and-red swamp beetles with his enormous feet.

The triblot was a round stone, about the size of a baseball, with three distinct dimples equidistant on the sides. It glowed a mystical yellow as the sun crept through the almost transparent sphere.

Cole watched Tridacello carefully tuck the triblot in his bag. The stone was treated with such caution that Cole knew it had to be important. He couldn't imagine anyone treating a whole bag of emeralds or diamonds any differently.

After the treasure was stowed, Tridacello nudged Dungo into action, and both of them busily packed gear into a coffin-sized box.

Dungo was not only tall, he was massive. From the rear, he resembled a very large, golden-brown hyena, but with a longer tail and four ape-like arms. He stood upright in a hunching sort of way, with such bad posture that his head was nearly concealed from behind, allowing only his two little horns to show, protruding from between his ears. His face, however, was not entirely different than that of a hairy man with a thick beard.

When the job was done and the ground was cleared of everything but the four ropes, Tridacello constrained Dungo into hefting the container into a nearby hedge. Logs and branches were then used to cover the box until it was completely concealed from view.

Surprisingly, despite Tridacello's repeated commands that made it clear he was eager to get moving away from trouble, when the moment came to pick up and leave, he looked hesitant.

"Do you think Bowlure will be all right until later?" he asked, looking at Dungo.

"I don' know," grumbled Dungo, his fur bristling along the ridge of his backbone. "Bud dere's no way I'm goin' back down. Da cloud's melding from da sun so we'd die for sure drying do help him. I nearly didn' escape before. Widoud da fog, da driblod would sill be back dere; and my arms and legs would be all over da deck, my dail would be dacked do da wall, and my beaudiful glidzzers would be fassened do someone's necklace."

"Don't kid yourself, Dungo. Nobody would want your horns around their neck," protested a wearied, hairy creature as it crawled out of the bushes on the cliff's edge. He was as massive as Dungo, only built differently—more like a giant, licorice-black gorilla, with a clean-shaven, human face.

"Bowlure!" exclaimed Dungo, looking surprised and concerned. "I dod you were sduck way down dere. Id's gread do see you made id up anyway. We were all so worried—"

"Hey, thanks for helping me," interrupted Bowlure sarcastically. "I appreciated you taking the time to throw me an extra line since mine broke."

Bowlure's voice was punctuated by numerous displays of physical animation—his waving arms and feet seemed to make the story come to life—and the smirk he wore indicated that he was jovial, not malicious. Despite his seven-foot stature, he wasn't scary—at least not to Cole. On the contrary, he was like a rescuing angel; he was someone that stood taller than Dungo and could clearly hold his own with him.

"When you abandoned me," he continued, creeping in the direction of Dungo, "I miraculously managed to stay alive by dragging against the cliff wall, trying to slow my fall, and was finally fortunate enough to land in a Glantor pit!"

Bowlure's posture straightened, showing his muscular physique. "Do you know how hard it is to work your way up the rocks without a line? I nearly didn't make it to the ropes. And all the while, I had the pleasure of dodging stones hurled by Dreaderious and his junky poorlings, who somehow managed to notice me, while missing to see you, the four-armed-wonder-on-a-string."

Dungo backed away from Bowlure, who was approaching him.

"Oh yeah," Bowlure added, pausing to glance at Cole pleasantly before focusing back on Dungo. "Did I mention, Glantor-Worm slime is remarkably good at burning? Do you know what it feels like? Let me give you a hint!"

Bowlure faked a stumble, seized one of Dungo's legs with his right arm, and proceeded to wipe his left arm up and down it until green slime oozed out from between the struggling limbs.

"Sdop! Sdop!" whined Dungo. "Wipin da sduff on me doesn' ged us do High Gade any fasder. Besides, id was Dod's gread moves back dere dad led you down, nod mine."

"Oh, not Dod!" said Bowlure confidently, releasing Dungo's leg. He then began wiping the slime on the grass. "I've seen Dod work, and trust me, all of that back there wasn't because of him; it was because of you, Dungo!"

"It doesn't matter," interrupted Tridacello, joining the conversation. "The important thing is that you're safe now—so let's get moving."

A barrage of stones cleared the top and narrowly missed hitting Dungo. They pulverized trees and sent dirt and mud flying in the air. It was a real battle zone. Cole slid to the edge and peered down. The wind and sun had melted the fog into a light haze, revealing two ships in the bay and three more approaching. One of them was gigantic.

"We've got to get out of here!" said Tridacello, standing over Cole. "Now that everyone on the Magellan can see where they're shooting, they'll be a lot more accurate—and one of those ships could have flutters."

"You saw what happened down below," said Bowlure, addressing Tridacello, while helping Cole to his feet. He was careful to aid Cole with his arm that wasn't messy.

"It doesn't matter," repeated Tridacello, pointing toward the forest. He was ready to be done with talking about what had gone wrong, though by his refusal to condemn Dungo, he was suggesting that he had a conflicting opinion.

When Cole staggered wearily, Bowlure picked him up and swung him onto his shoulders.

"But he didn't even flip me a spare line!" complained Bowlure, petitioning Tridacello earnestly. His tone had become less lighthearted and more serious as he futilely sought redress. He wanted Tridacello to at least acknowledge Dungo had participated in the fiasco by acting cowardly, however, his needling didn't work: Tridacello turned a cold shoulder and marched swiftly toward the forest, followed closely by Dungo; and the only things he said had nothing to do with the cliffs.

"We'll have to move faster than we originally planned," he

ordered, when he noticed Bowlure looking longingly at the pond that fed the bog. "Maybe you can wash in a little while, once we're deep enough in the thickets."

It wasn't what Bowlure wanted to hear. The Glantor-Worm slime was still clinging to his legs and left arm, and there was a fair patch of it on his posterior, too. All of the wiping and rolling hadn't cleared it off. Water was needed. Nevertheless, Tridacello wasn't about to concede in the slightest. He was bent on keeping the triblot safe and was willing to do whatever it took.

The group fell into line with the old man taking the lead. He hunched under the weight of an overflowing bag that was filled with items he hadn't stowed in 'the coffin,' though it didn't stop him from moving quickly. He took large strides through the bog that separated them from the safety of the trees.

Dungo scurried close behind Tridacello, hunching as he walked, but without a bag. His enormous feet noisily clopped against the sludge.

Bowlure followed with a relaxed stride. He stayed relatively in line, though he purposely stepped in the deepest-looking patches of mud, hoping to ease the burning sensation on his feet and ankles.

As Cole sat on Bowlure's shoulders, he searched for answers: *What's going on? Why are they calling me Dod? Why am I here…and where is here?*

Cole thought carefully and retraced his steps. He remembered sitting in his bedroom, over by the window, watching drops of rain paint pictures on the glass pane. His computer was humming quietly in the corner, displaying sea life as a screen saver. Josh and Alex were napping in their bunks.

The last thing Cole could remember was watching a large raindrop.

"This must be a really bad nightmare," he mumbled to himself. His voice got louder as he went on. "And I'm having a hard time waking up, thanks to not getting enough sleep last night! This must be one of those nightmares, the kind Josh has all the time, the kind where Mom sits for ten minutes with Josh, trying to wake him up, before he finally stops crying. I bet I'm thrashing around and everything."

Despite telling himself that it was a dream, Cole had plenty of doubts in the back of his mind. Everything seemed too real. And the pain, in his head and back, was worse than anything he had ever experienced before.

"It's got to be a dream!" Cole continued. "It's a crazy one summoned by Aunt Hilda's zesty tacos."

Bowlure lunged through a sticky part of the bog and slipped. He regained control before falling, but not before nearly dumping Cole into the mud.

"You might want to hold on a little tighter," said Bowlure, tipping Cole back onto his shoulders. He then pointed at a mushy, greenish-black oozing spot in the swampy ground and said, "That one's a real dipper. You'd hate to put your head in it, wouldn't you?"

The jovial Bowlure had returned. It had only taken him a matter of minutes to seemingly forgive Dungo and Tridacello and move on to happier thoughts.

"Thanks," said Cole, feeling grateful Bowlure had caught him. He looked around at the surroundings and tried to change them with his mind. *If this is my dream*, he thought, *I ought to be able to get us out of this putrid place, or at least make my back stop hurting.*

Cole strained and strained. He squinted his eyes and

furrowed his brow. But it didn't work. Nothing happened. His back still hurt and the mud still stunk.

The bog turned out to be much larger than it had originally appeared from the cliff's edge. It continued deep into the forest. Willows and various water-loving trees cropped up, right out of the mire, while other less-resilient trees and bushes grew in dense pockets on small islands of rockier soil. Together, they turned the landscape into a maze.

While enduring the bombardment, Cole had wished to stroll through the woods; however, now that he was doing it, he realized it wasn't very pleasant. Aside from not needing to worry about the sky raining rocks, there were few benefits. Flies and bugs came in waves off the muddy foliage, looking for places to land. They particularly seemed to enjoy swarming around Cole's head, which greatly irritated him, especially the pesky gnats!

I've gone mad, he thought, shaking his hands back and forth through his hair to disrupt the landing visitors. He smacked and whacked until the buzzing temporarily stopped.

Of all the places I could have chosen to dream about, it had to be a bog! And with the likes of him! Cole glanced at Dungo, who continued to plod behind Tridacello, rigidly keeping pace.

"Are you all right up there?" asked Bowlure, tilting his head around. He had heard Cole's whacking and wondered what was going on.

"I'm fine," lied Cole, looking down at Bowlure. He suddenly realized that he didn't know anything about him, which was unusual, considering Cole's dreamlike memories had already shed plenty of light on Tridacello and Dungo. So feeling like he'd jilted the kindest of his dream's participants, he set out to create facts about Bowlure.

Nothing came.

Minutes passed by with plenty of flies and plenty of sloshing, but still nothing about Bowlure. Finally, giving up, Cole nudged him.

"Why don't I know very much about you?" he asked, feeling dumb.

"I suppose it's because we haven't been *properly* introduced."

Tridacello halted his march in a particularly smelly part of the bog to interrupt. "Shhh," he said. "If you must talk, at least drop it to a droning whisper like the buzzing of flies or rustling of grange weeds. I'm terribly concerned about making it over the big hill before Dreaderious knows which way we're headed."

"Fair enough," said Bowlure softly, lowering his booming voice to a whisper. "You lead and I'll drone back here with Dod."

When the procession started again, Bowlure began to explain. "As I was saying, I'm Bowlure of the driadons. You don't know very much about me because we've only just met this morning. But I know a little of you; I watched you compete in the trials a while back. You're impressive, especially considering how young you are."

"I'm fourteen," argued Cole, defending his age.

"Right," chuckled Bowlure. "Anyway, where did you learn to yarn and cut with your rod? Don't only noble billies use one like that?"

The change in conversation to billies lit a fire, deep down in Cole.

"Noble?" he said scoffingly. "They are hardly noble. After eight years in route with a band of billies, you learn a few tricks.

I guess some skills are gained when you're fighting to survive. They're all thieving pirates—the whole lot of them. I haven't met a noble one yet."

Waves of memories faded in and out of Cole's mind. Billies were mean and had treated him poorly—or was it someone else? That element was foggy.

"So you've seen them?" asked Bowlure, kinking his neck to make eye contact.

"Seen them?" barked Cole. "I saw plenty of them—I saw them every day, while I served them aboard their ships—until—well, until—"

Cole's voice settled as he strained to recall how the memories fit together, leading up to where he was, but they didn't; and before he could figure them out, they faded.

"I—uh—ended up with Tridacello," he finally croaked. "He's the one who took me to the trials."

"Oh," responded Bowlure. He turned around and noticed that they were falling behind, so he picked up his pace and focused on jogging instead of talking. At times, he had to sprint to keep up.

Tridacello's physical abilities were impressive; his capacity to cut through the swamp, seemingly with ease, clearly surpassed anyone Cole had ever met; and he wasn't just running knee-deep in mud, there were vines and branches to duck under. Not to mention, the old man regularly found that they were boxed-in, necessitating he lead them, clawing and squirming, through the densest of debris. The slough was treacherous terrain, to say the least. No one in their right mind would follow them through it.

During the ordeal, Bowlure couldn't chat, even if he wanted

to, since the vigorous exercise made him pant. But Cole didn't mind; he spent the hour-and-a-half deep in thought, trying to piece together a logical explanation for everything, while hanging on tightly to Bowlure's fur. His brief conversation with Bowlure, regarding billies, had given him plenty to think about. The feelings he harbored toward them seemed genuinely raw, stemming from mysterious memories. It was baffling. Where did the information come from?

And then there was the nagging issue of the name Dod. It sounded familiar, like it fit him, but why?

It wasn't that Cole felt like abandoning his own name, yet for some strange reason, Dod also felt right. It was just one of his other names. After all, Cole did have multiple names; at home, he was Cole or Big C; among some childhood acquaintances, he was Coley; at the barbershop, he was Mr. Richards; and at the ice cream parlor, he was Buddy Big Scoop. Now, in this strange situation, Dod was his name, and it fit perfectly.

"Dod," whispered Cole to himself. He did feel like a Dod. He nearly said it again, but was interrupted by Bowlure, who poked at him and pointed at Tridacello.

"He's quite an old, steady mast of a tredder, isn't he?" said Bowlure, almost reverently; his tone hinted that he was working on a joke. "I like him like a father. He seems to have a really keen eye for planning, and that's pretty good for someone old enough to hardly see where he's headed with the two eyes he's got."

"I heard that," chimed Tridacello, as he climbed a small embankment out of the bog. His pants were muddy up to his knees and his shoes were caked three layers deep, but when he turned around to face Dungo and Bowlure, he cracked a faint smile—a first of the day. Exiting the swamplands and having successfully left the troubles of the cliffs far behind gave him grounds to ease up.

"And for your information," Tridacello continued, speaking factually, "a tredder's vision gets better with age, not worse."

"Then I'll remember that the next time you lead us into a thorny mess of swamp briars like you did shortly ago," teased Bowlure. "Dungo and I took pity on your poor sight and followed quietly anyhow."

"If you call that quiet," returned Tridacello, nearly cheery. He stopped by a trickling stream and began to wash his pants and shoes. "I don't remember your exact words," he continued, "but I think they were something like, 'OUCH, this little, tiny-weenie thorn has damaged my big toe.' Yes, I think that's what you said."

"Well I think you got it right when you said you didn't remember exactly what I said," quipped Bowlure, swinging Dod carefully to the ground. "But we'll forgive you. After all, forgetfulness is something you've earned at your age."

"Then don't forget it, just in case I do," responded Tridacello. He scrubbed until the mud was gone and then perched on a log, while he changed his socks and shoes; he had spares in his larger pack.

Dungo and Bowlure both worked, side-by-side, at the water's edge, trying to clean up, though Bowlure's earnestness was unsurpassed. The Glantor-Worm slime had certainly done its miserable job of tormenting him.

Dod took the chance to sprawl out on the ground by the brook. He hadn't even walked an inch of the journey, however, just staying on Bowlure's shoulders had been difficult for him in his current condition, especially while enduring the waves of dizziness that came and went; they, along with the pain in his head and back, made life unpleasant.

When Tridacello had finished lacing his dry leather boots, he drew a slender vial from his open bag and approached Dod.

"Here you go," he said, popping the cork off before handing Dod the container. "I warned you about eating sweets this morning. That kind of folly will poison your day just as readily as an enemy's hand. Remember it!"

Dod hadn't the slightest what Tridacello was talking about, but if he thought the medicine would help, Dod wasn't about to refuse it.

"Thanks," said Dod, propping up on one elbow to drink it down. The flavor was nasty, like cough syrup mixed with rotten fruit.

"It'll settle your stomach," added Tridacello, somewhat piously. "Two hours of scaling is enough to sicken anyone unprepared. You're just lucky we had Bowlure to carry you. Next time might be your last if you don't start learning what *I've* got to teach you. The nudging and whispers won't warn you to pack clean shoes or eat well, and as far as I'm concerned, things like that are just as important as being the fastest at climbing."

Tridacello drew three heaping sandwiches from his bag for himself and Dungo and Bowlure, before returning to Dod's side; he wasn't done scolding him for the list of things that Dod couldn't even remember. Tridacello vented like an angry parent, who had been saving up for a long time.

Bowlure sat in the creek, cooling his backside while eating; nevertheless, his occasional glances made Dod feel better about the lengthy reprimand—like someone else thought it was a little too harsh. Dungo, on the other hand, didn't even seem to notice the fuss. He devoured his food and then interrupted the womping-session, hoping for Tridacello's leftovers or Dod's uneaten lunch.

After the lecture, Tridacello announced that he would be leaving for a few minutes to scale the biggest tree in sight, in order to check for Dreaderious's possible deployment of flutters. He grabbed his noculars, two grappling hooks, and a length of coiled rope and headed off. Though a few minutes later, he returned to recruit a second climber.

Dungo protested at first, when chosen, suggesting that he wanted to stay by Dod's side to make sure his condition improved, yet the moment Tridacello snapped his fingers, Dungo hopped to his feet and trotted along obediently.

Bowlure waited until the twosome was far enough away before laughing. "I don't know, Dod," he said happily. "I think some people are too intense. If you can't eat pie for breakfast when you're young, the world's really in a load of trouble, the kind you and I can't fix."

"Is that what I ate?" asked Dod, looking at Bowlure. "I don't remember—"

"Good for you!" he responded, chuckling. His dark brown eyes were friendly and caring. "It's best to forget it. Tridacello spoke his mind out of concern for you, so dwelling on the particulars isn't necessary, is it? Why be mad when you can choose to be happy?"

"Right," said Dod hesitantly. He really had wondered what 'sweets' he had supposedly eaten that had 'poisoned his day,' but Bowlure's angle was just as good. It didn't matter either way.

"Thanks for carrying me," he added, truly grateful. "If I had tried to walk through that bog, I wouldn't have made it."

"That's all right," insisted Bowlure. "You couldn't possibly weigh a pound over two hundred. Carrying you is like hefting a picnic lunch for my family back home."

"Oh," said Dod, imagining a gunnysack full of fried chicken. "Where is home for you?"

"Up north," responded Bowlure. "My family herds sheep and cows. You know—animals don't seem to mind the way we look."

"Why would anyone care?" asked Dod, perplexed.

"Are you serious?" choked Bowlure. "You're weirder than I thought, kid!"

"And crazy, too," added Dod, feeling somewhat delirious from the medicine, which still hadn't stopped the pain. "I think my brain has flipped—I mean, look at me. Here I am, off helping Dungo steal a sparkly thing—"

"You mean me," corrected Bowlure. "Dungo wouldn't even get in the water. And I didn't steal it, I just retrieved it. If Dreaderious gets his thieving hands on another four or five triblots, we would all be in big trouble. He'd have the ability to create an impenetrable stronghold."

"Oh yeah," sighed Dod, catching glimpses in his mind. "Has anyone ever told you your fur is softer than it looks."

"What?" asked Bowlure. "Are you calling me feminine?" He let out a restrained chuckle and splashed water at Dod. "My fur may be soft, but it's macho-soft, not girly-soft."

"Okay, right," said Dod, not quite sure why he had brought it up, other than the fact that he was feeling extremely tired. "I just thought it looked more like the coarse hair of a guinea pig I once had."

"A guinea pig? What kind of creature is that? It must be from one of the other realms."

"All right," said Dod. "Now you have me confused again. What do you mean, *other realms?*"

"You know, Raul and Soosh," responded Bowlure, pulling rocks out of the creek to make a bigger hole to sit in. "I've lived all of my life here in Green, so I don't know very much about the others, but they say there's a lot of untamed ground in Soosh—plenty of space for weird creatures and stuff. Just look at Dungo—that's where he's from."

"No wonder," sighed Dod, glancing over his shoulder toward the towering tree that Tridacello was scaling. Dungo was hidden from view, on the opposite side.

"And Soosh is where the last of the driadons came from, too," Bowlure added. "They were fleeing war—bloody tredders in Soosh! Only about two hundred of us are left now—mostly my family. We owe our escape to Bonboo."

"I'm sorry about that," said Dod, trying to be polite. His eyelids were so heavy, he closed them and felt himself drifting off.

Perhaps if I sleep, I'll awaken, he thought, and then he was out.

HIDDEN TROUBLE

"Dod, Dod," whispered Bowlure. He had hopped from the creek and was nudging Dod's arm.

"What?" asked Dod, startling to full consciousness; his heart pounded with adrenaline. He had only just barely closed his eyes, hoping to rest.

"Shhh," said Bowlure, putting a finger to his lips. He pointed at a thicket of bushes about fifty feet off. Something was coming.

A small herd of deer bolted from the undergrowth and bounced away, as suddenly as they had appeared. They were led by a large doe and trailed by a well-antlered buck. Bowlure's concerned lips melted into a sheepish grin. "Oops," he confessed, shrugging his shoulders. "It wasn't what I thought." He eagerly returned to his soaking.

Dod blinked and took a deep breath. The shock of being startled had chased his sleepiness away, even though his body was still horribly tired. He continued to lay on the ground, while gazing up at the patches of blue sky that splotched the otherwise multi-green canopy. The sky reminded him of outings with Pap, which were easily his best memories.

However, such thoughts were abruptly dispersed by Bowlure's voice.

"I heard that you're aided by a swapper," he said. "Is that who you were talking to?"

"Huh?" mumbled Dod, tilting his head toward Bowlure. With one ear to the ground, he could still hear the thumping of the fleeing deer.

"You know—on the way over," prodded Bowlure. When Dod didn't say anything, Bowlure assumed 'yes.'

"I've always wondered about them," he continued, flipping a bug off his smooth cheek. "Does your swapper connect you to the experiences of others, or is he the only one that's connected? How does it work, anyway?"

Dod hesitated. The subject of swappers drew an empty cabinet in his brain, or so he felt; but his silence didn't stop Bowlure from plowing on.

"Swappers only mentor people who are positioned to do a lot of good. You sure are lucky."

"Right," mumbled Dod sarcastically. He didn't feel like luck was on his side, especially after the scathing lecture he had just received from Tridacello.

"So tell me," said Bowlure, rambling on while digging more rocks out of the water. "Does your swapper only get help from your family members when you're in a bind, or does he talk with them all the time?…Or uh…I don't know. To be honest, Dod, the whole system doesn't make very much sense to me. But I'm a driadon; we don't have any golden family chains or swappers among us—none of that whispering stuff."

"Oh," sighed Dod, distracted by two silver-striped beetles that were fighting over the same twig, a few inches from his nose. When he realized that Bowlure was waiting for a response this time, he quickly added, "What makes you think I have a swapper thing?"

"Dungo said so," replied Bowlure. "If it's not true, you can chew on one of his arms; he's got four to choose from. Besides, I watched you perform at the trials. Without help, you couldn't have competed so well—I mean, you are just a lad, and a human at that."

Dod meant to respond, yet not with the answer he gave: He burped loudly and had to resort to a sitting position in order to swallow the nasty medicine that attempted to creep back up his throat; not only did it taste bad, it still hadn't done any good.

"Perhaps half human and half bullfrog," joked Bowlure, surprised by the noise. It was louder than their voices and carried far enough to draw Tridacello's attention from high up in the tree; he looked down with his noculars to assess the fuss.

"What do you know about swappers?" asked Dod, still swallowing. He preferred listening to Bowlure talk, over answering questions.

"Not much," said Bowlure modestly, scratching at his neck; his fur grew sparse toward the top of his chest and faded into a smooth, shaven look on his neck and cheeks. If only his head were showing, Bowlure's handsome haircut and charming face would easily sell him as a character worthy of Hollywood, the kind that women would swoon over.

"You must know something," prodded Dod, trying to hand one of the beetles a new twig, but neither would take it; they liked fighting.

"I've never met anyone, before you, who was coached by a swapper," admitted Bowlure. "But I've heard a little. A friend of mine, up north, once told me that swappers are connected to golden chains, similar to staying in touch with the occurrences of the individuals in a large family—magically all at once."

"Facebook," chuckled Dod under his breath.

Bowlure raised an eyebrow before continuing. "He also said that some swappers are able to draw on the skills of the group and then pass them along when they're needed. It all sounded pretty wacky-shmacky to me. Is any of it true?"

"I don't know about swappers," said Dod honestly. He felt bad letting Bowlure down.

"Oh, I see. You're new at it," conceded Bowlure, disappointed. "I've always wanted to hear more about them, ever since I read the tales of Donis and Bollath. *Victory at Rocky Ridge* and *Defeat of the Trajillans* are two of my favorite books. Both of those guys were aided by swappers, and think of what they did!"

At the mention of Donis and Bollath, Dod cracked a smile, recalling their heroic stories, each ending in glorious victory. Though, no sooner had he found the memories, than he wondered where they had come from: The cabinet had been empty just moments before, completely void of anything about swappers.

"I'm confused," admitted Dod. He blearily glanced around before resting his eyes on Bowlure's face. "If I were being aided by a swapper, as you say, then wouldn't I know more about them, or at least recognize when I was being helped by one—like hear the voice of this mentor guy—or know something of his swapping, or mentoring, or whatever he does?"

"Are you pulling my leg?" asked Bowlure, beginning to rise.

"Of course he is dricking you," grunted Dungo, approaching quickly from behind Dod, with Tridacello at his side. "Look ad him."

"I'm serious," said Dod, feeling irritated at Dungo.

Bowlure repeatedly brushed his hands down his legs and arms, forcing water out of his fur, while asking Tridacello what he'd seen.

"Not much," was his curt reply. He walked straight to his overflowing pack, plucked it from the log as though it weighed nothing at all, and stowed his gear.

"Do you want your sandwich now?" asked Tridacello. He held it in Dod's direction.

Seeing the food made the medicine in Dod's stomach jump; the vial of cure-all wasn't sitting well.

"No thanks," said Dod, rising to his feet with Bowlure's aid. Dungo lunged at Tridacello and begged shamelessly for it, reminding him that he had climbed the cliffs twice and, therefore, needed double the lunch.

"It's Dod's," said Tridacello calmly, holding it back. He drew near Dod and held it out. "Are you sure?" he asked, looking guilty; his face oozed regret for having reproached Dod excessively, though he didn't attempt an apology for what he had said earlier, other than to defend the sandwich from Dungo.

"All right, thank you," said Dod, taking the triple-decked, meat-and-cheese delight. It was two feet long and weighed nearly as much as a small child. Dod's plan was to give it to Bowlure in return for Bowlure's continued service of carrying him.

However, Bowlure declined, assuring Dod that he was stuffed from his own lunch, along with a whole roasted goose he had eaten while back-floating away from the Magellan. He had taken the bird from Dreaderious's table to reward himself for dutifully raiding both ships in search of the stolen triblot.

Dod glanced at Dungo, whose eyes were hungry and

disappointed; his bulky beard was matted in some places, giving him the appearance of a homeless wanderer. Dungo didn't even ask for the food from Dod, recognizing that he had been mean enough to not get it. His tail sagged pathetically as he sulked, turning to line up behind Tridacello.

"Dungo," said Dod, momentarily remembering his mother's repeated examples of kindness. "Here you go. You can eat it." Dod held out the feast.

The creature's face turned more human than it had been all morning, as he gingerly approached Dod to accept the food. His eyes revealed torment, like a real person was caged inside the grumpy beast that everyone else knew.

"Danks," he grunted tentatively, gulping the offering down. He took such big bites that Dod had to look away, sensing the sight was more than his queasy constitution could take.

Shortly thereafter, Bowlure swung Dod onto his shoulders and they were off, heading southeast up a steep, wooded hillside. Tridacello led in the front, as he had done in the bog, though now that the ground beneath their feet was dry, they rushed like horses bolting for water. It was all Dod could do to hang on; more than once he lost his grip and was saved by the snake-like agility of Bowlure's quick hands.

The territory they dashed through was beautiful. The trees towered above the ground, like giants, with sturdy roots clinging to the sloping terrain; and the wind gently swayed the rooftop of leaves and needles, a hundred feet up, where the canopy of greenery almost completely blocked-out the blue sky. Between the twig-littered ground and the bushy tree tops, an outdoor auditorium gave flocks of birds room to fly freely, displaying their feathers for each other as they burst from one part of the forest to another; their chirping chorus joined the running threesome's heavy breathing, like flutes and piccolos with the drums in an orchestra.

After hours of toiling their way up the seemingly endless hillside, Tridacello slowed the team's pace to a comfortable trot, allowing them to catch their breath.

Eventually they came to a colossal tree, whose trunk was more than twenty feet across, and whose roots reached out another hundred in every direction, like giant serpents. Dod shifted back and forth nervously on Bowlure's shoulders as they climbed over and ducked under the web of wood. Something wasn't right. A cold feeling of fear and dread seized upon him. It was like knowing a horrendous thing was about to happen, but not able to recall what it was. The feeling grew until it burst Dod's capacity to contain it.

"WATCH OUT!" he yelled frantically, looking over his shoulder in anticipation. "Bowlure, it's right behind us!"

Dod's sudden cry made Dungo trip and fall headlong into Tridacello, knocking them both down. Bowlure swung around recklessly, yet still managed to stand in a fighting position; he searched the ground and sky for threats, expecting something to come rumbling out of the roots they had just cleared.

Nothing came. Even the chatty birds hid from view.

"Where?" asked Bowlure anxiously, still searching. "What do you see?" As a few moments passed, his look faded from concern to confusion.

Dungo began to berate Dod. "I jusd don'd ged id, kid. Dis whole mission is doo indense do sdard playing games wid us."

Just then, a large beast came crashing through the canopy, right where Bowlure had been looking. Its wings were massive, each about fifteen feet across, with feathers that appeared to be made of black rubber; and from beak to tail, the bird spanned another twenty feet. It dove at Bowlure, with it's banana-sized talons out, followed immediately behind by a second of its kind.

Everyone scattered in separate directions. Dod hung on as Bowlure tried to make his way back to the safety of the mammoth-tree's roots. Dungo stumbled again and scampered into a thicket of bushes. Tridacello slid behind a tooth-shaped rock, a few paces from Bowlure, and fumbled for his zip-rope whip and small dagger.

WHOOSH, ZLLLLLLCRACK.

Tridacello's whip licked the air and then struck as the intruders came within forty feet of the ground. His weapon of choice was an interesting mechanism to watch. The handle resembled the hilt of a sword, from which metal line flashed out with razor sharp blades attached to three short cords at the end. In all, the whip could reach up to thirty feet, depending on how quickly Tridacello snapped it back. With the flick of his wrist, the wire shot out, and another flick made it recoil.

WHOOSH, ZLLLLLCRACK.

The whip's blades snapped directly over Dod and Bowlure, twelve feet up; wind from the massive winged-beasts swirled dust and leaves all around them, as the ferocious birds persisted in the air near the ground.

Tridacello snapped his whip again. This time it cracked so close to Dod that he dove off Bowlure's shoulders in order to avoid being hit.

"That was inches from my head," he stammered, looking up. The massive creatures glared at Dod as they rose above the ground, retreating; one faltered with each flap, indicating Tridacello had struck it.

"You're fortunate he's a great aim," said Bowlure, pointing proudly at Tridacello. "That flutter nearly took you home."

The two menacing demons disappeared above the trees.

"Those were flutters?" gasped Dod, pulling himself to his feet. He leaned against a fallen tree for support.

Bowlure's look of concern quickly reappeared. He bent down, so his head was level with Dod's, and gazed deeply into his eyes.

"I'm worried about you," he admitted. "It just doesn't make sense."

"What doesn't make sense?" asked Dod, repeatedly glancing skyward; he was distracted by thoughts of the birds coming back for him.

"You don't make sense," said Bowlure. "You rode flutters at the trials and were incredible! Don't you remember?"

Dod didn't recall it, and he was quite certain he wouldn't forget a feat like that, but he didn't say anything to Bowlure.

As soon as the flutters were gone, Dungo came grumbling out of the undergrowth, complaining. He barked about the prickly bushes, his aching feet, and Dreaderious.

Bowlure ignored Dungo and continued interrogating Dod. "How did you know the flutters were coming?" he urged. A look of hope glimmered in his eyes, as if that piece of information would make up for the cavernous holes in Dod's memory.

"I don't know," confessed Dod. "It just felt like we were under attack." Dod looked down at the ground, trying hard to recall how he had sensed it, and finally came up with the only logical explanation: "I think I heard them coming and then guessed."

"I didn't hear them coming," said Bowlure. "That was quite a guess. You must be psychic."

"Psychic?" said Dod, "I don't think so."

"What color are my socks?" snapped Bowlure suddenly, "—and don't look down at my feet, that would be cheating."

"You don't have any," said Dod, rolling his eyes. It seemed silly that Bowlure would even ask.

"Wow, you're right again!"

"Bowlure!" whined Dod.

"I could have been wearing socks," insisted Bowlure. "I've worn them before."

Tridacello broke the standoff with his commanding voice. "We don't have time for this right now!" he barked. "Flutters are usually sent as eyes and ears only, so they retreated; but they'll be back with riders that fight to the death. We have to get out of here."

Dungo glared at Dod and Bowlure, as if it were all their fault, and grunted irritably, "Well dank you! Now Dreaderious knows exacly where we're headed. We're nod followin' da coasd nord doward Harbin nor going da easy roude easd drough da fladlands doward Candeen, so dad only leaves soud do Janice Pass and den on do High Gade."

"HURRY!" yelled Tridacello; he was mad that Bowlure hadn't fallen in line yet. "Carry the lad and let's make tracks! I don't like to side with anyone, but Dungo's right about Dreaderious knowing where we're headed. It will be disastrous if he beats us to the pass. Let's pick up our shoulders and run. Once we're over the top, there are plenty of places for us to hide."

Without any further words, Tridacello turned and began bolting up the hill, even faster than before. Dungo hastily fell in line behind him, hunching as usual, and the two almost disappeared out of sight before Bowlure had even secured Dod on his shoulders.

"I can't believe how fit he is," remarked Bowlure, enviously watching Tridacello run. "At his age, most tredders are knocking on death's door; but look at him! It's not fair! He makes a twenty-seven-year-old driadon like me feel insecure. I'd be lucky to hit a hundred and fifty years, let alone be racing up a hill at two hundred and thirty-eight."

Bowlure made a few more comparisons, before his panting took over; however, Dod hardly heard what he said, since he was busy trying to hang on for dear life!

Up the hill, the slope became so treacherous that it wasn't possible to climb without all fours. Roots and branches were used as though they were makeshift rungs in a giant, disorderly ladder, requiring, from time to time, some planning to scale. It slowed the pace enough to make conversation possible, which led Bowlure into talking again.

"Are you sure you don't remember riding flutters?" he asked, still huffing from the exercise. He waited for Dungo, who was losing speed in front of him.

"Nope," said Dod flatly. "That was my first time seeing them. Which reminds me, how would flutters be eyes and ears for Dreaderious? They can't talk, can they?"

"Flutters? No," said Bowlure.

"Then who was riding them—to report back to Dreaderious? I didn't see anyone—" Dod wiped his face frantically, completely grossed out, when Bowlure pushed upward too quickly and sent Dod's cheek colliding into the sweaty end of Dungo's tail.

"Probably holoos," answered Bowlure, chuckling when he

realized what had happened. "They're small—fit right behind the head of a flutter to give commands—quite respected for their bravery in training them. At thirty inches, you'd think your human cousins would be scared—"

A loud creaking sound interrupted Bowlure's reply. Dod and Bowlure both looked up, nervous that Dungo was breaking a limb with his massive weight and, shortly, would be sitting on top of Dod's head.

"Uh-oh," moaned Dungo, not sounding well. He leaned heavily on a trunk-like branch, half folding over it, with his arms momentarily dangling. A waft of noxiousness, that easily beat all other nasty odors, filled the air like the heavy, wet fog from a crop-dusting plane.

"Move back down, Bowlure!" gasped Dod. "Give Dungo some room. I can't breathe."

SSSSQUEAK.

"PLEASE!" yelled Dod, his voice choked with tears. He really couldn't breathe, and the smell made his eyes water like the vapors of a strong onion.

"I can'd help id," complained Dungo. "Dad sandwich—Oh!—I dink I have gas."

"I don't *THINK* you have gas," puffed Bowlure, between chortles. "I *KNOW* you have gas!" He wasn't as bothered by the smell as Dod was, and he clearly enjoyed the commotion it created; therefore, his attempts to retreat were halfhearted, leaving Dod's cowering head completely exposed to a series of direct hits. One toxic blast thundered out with such force that it nearly parted Dod's hair down the center, and it wasn't completely dry.

In desperation, Dod finally resorted to shimmying down

Bowlure's back and onto a branch of his own, deciding that he was more likely to die from lack of oxygen, or possibly black lung, than from falling the hundreds of open feet that loomed below him.

Dizzy and in pain, Dod once more attempted to focus his mind on changing the surroundings; and when that failed, he tried magic, too. "Hocus-pocus," he muttered desperately, along with a string of other spells that he remembered from a book series he'd read—words that had done wonders for a certain scarred-wizard boy—but none of them worked for him: no transporting, no alterations of the environment, no invisible shields, and no disarmaments.

Dod's only consolation was that Bowlure, shortly after Dod's exodus from his shoulders, became more sympathetic and ready to descend a distance when he, too, was victimized by a hair-parting gust, being foolishly caught without his 'Dod-hat' for protection.

"He's got real problems!" muttered Bowlure, his eyes watering like a baby. He paused at Dod's level of the tree and wiped at his own leg with a clump of leaves, all the while glaring disapprovingly at the splatter he wore. "Why, oh why, did we follow behind him? I just bathed!"

When more sounds rumbled above them, like thunder before a torrential rain, Bowlure's eyes widened, concluding he was still way too close to the source. Without further warnings, he dropped his leaves, plucked Dod up like a father hoisting his child from a burning building, and moved with purpose. He descended far enough to choose an alternate route before attempting to climb upward again.

"Sorry about that," said Bowlure to Dod as they passed

Dungo, a safe distance on his right. Bowlure's voice was sincere. He knew that Dod wasn't pleased with how slowly he had reacted; and after experiencing the full brunt of the foul wind for himself, complete with a smattering of debris, he recognized that Dod's forgiveness would likely be slow coming.

"Flutters would make short work of this part, eh," said Bowlure awkwardly, trying to soften Dod. "I bet they tracked us with their keen sense of hearing. Hunting instincts still linger in them, after all these centuries of domestication. We could ask Tridacello about that since he's been around so long—"

"You're overrating the advantages of a long life," interrupted Dod, frazzled and cross; his hair was crustified in some places. "My grandpa died when he was relatively young, and even at that, the last few years seemed to test his patience. Of course he was still nice to us. We all miss him."

Bowlure began to say something when Dod snipped him off. "You may envy Tridacello, but at his age, it's all about everyone else."

Dod thought about Pap when he spoke of Tridacello. Pap had spent his time serving others and hadn't seemed to care about what he got in return. *What would Pap think if he could see me now?* wondered Dod. It made him feel a little bit guilty about getting riled-up over Dungo's misfortunate circumstance; nevertheless, he was immensely grateful he hadn't eaten the sandwich himself. Dod glanced down and hoped Dungo would be okay.

"Tell me," insisted Bowlure, leading back into his fixation on age. "How old was he when he died?"

"Sixty-nine," said Dod, searching above him for Tridacello. Their leader was out of sight, unaware of Dungo's condition.

"One hundred and sixty-nine," responded Bowlure. "That's

really good for a human. Did he have any ancestors from those Mauj living in Soosh? I've heard some of them lived over five hundred years. 'Course, that was before the Hickopsy killed them all off. You humans sure have frail societies. Whether it's sickness or war, you just seem to be more prone to die."

"And driadons aren't?" blurted Dod, finding Bowlure's assessment to be foolish, considering he was one of the last of his kind. Dod glanced down again and was glad to see Dungo climbing, albeit sluggishly.

"What? What did you say?" asked Bowlure. The wind had blown stridently for a few seconds, carrying Dod's voice away. The higher they climbed, the harder the breeze blew.

Bowlure didn't wait long before mumbling to himself a little song about a tredder named Ponck. It was mostly unintelligible, except when he got to the chorus:

"Oh let the sun set here,
Or let the sun set there.
I'm a Tredder through and through,
So, not a moment left to spare.
I'll be hiking up a hill
Or even chasing down a bear,
'Til the day I'm laid to rest without a care...
'Til the day they lay me down without a care."

Bowlure's singing continued for quite some duration, getting louder each time he grunted the chorus, until it came to an end. It didn't sound like much of an end; verses had been repeated a few times, making the song longer than its authentic form, and when he finally sang the last words, his voice shrilled like a young musician testing the range of a broken trombone.

"I should live to be...two hundred and sixty-three," announced Bowlure heartily. He liked the way his statement rhymed. It would have been the beginning of another song if Dod hadn't responded to it.

"Get over it! You're a driadon and he's a tredder," said Dod loudly, defying the howling wind. "That makes a big difference. I don't know of a tredder yet that married any earlier than sixty. Their life cycles are slower and longer. Tridacello may have another twenty years in him—he may actually see two hundred and sixty-three, if he's lucky."

"It's just not fair," lamented Bowlure, shifting his weight off a cracking limb. "Most driadons die off well before one hundred and fifty."

"Try seventy or eighty," retorted Dod unsympathetically. "That's the average life expectancy of humans where I come from, though I admit they live a little longer here."

Bowlure paused, searching for a good route to take. "Considering how similar humans are to tredders," he continued, somewhat haltingly, "I would think you would live a lot longer. After all, when their bands are covered, you could easily mistake a tredder for a tall human."

The limbs and roots of the trees growing out of the cliff-like hillside were increasingly smaller and sparser. Bushes and other forms of vegetation littered the wall of earth more than down below, which only added to the difficulty of scaling it.

"Too bad we're not swappers," joked Bowlure, realizing the precarious nature of their circumstance. "I've heard that they don't die—they live for thousands of years, helping people, and then retire to some distant sphere in a final form."

"Is that what your goat-herding friend told you?" chided Dod.

"Cows, not goats," said Bowlure. He held his breath and lunged for a distant branch that was a real stretch; he almost didn't make it. One arm was all that caught the limb, leaving them momentarily dangling.

"Warn me next time!" complained Dod hysterically, clinging tightly to Bowlure's head. His voice quivered as he tried to swallow his heart; it seemed to be lodged in his throat.

Bowlure swung up, sat near the trunk, and helped Dod off his shoulders.

"That was a close one, huh?" gloated Bowlure, taking pride in his feat. He wasn't afraid. He turned his brown eyes on Dod and asked, "Weren't you talking about your swapper with Dungo this morning?"

"No," said Dod, breathing heavily. He couldn't believe how near they had come to dying.

"I've got big ears," said Bowlure. He meant it figuratively and looked at Dod as though he were a principal, attempting to goad a confession out of the school troublemaker.

"Did you overhear it before the cliff experience?" asked Dod, trying not to look down.

"Yup."

"Well then, you can't blame me," stated Dod confidently. "I don't remember anything that happened before the cliffs."

"Do you remember zipping down?" asked Bowlure. He tried to jog Dod's memory of the morning's events. "You went first, setting the lines with grips and posts for us to follow."

"No," said Dod, shaking his head.

"Do you remember walking to the cliffs with Tridacello and

Dungo? We met up by the shallow pond. You were poking at frogs with a stick when I arrived."

"Nope."

"Certainly you haven't forgotten what I said about your shoes?" Bowlure began to laugh. "I thought for sure we had started off on the wrong foot."

"No." answered Dod. "I can't recall any of it."

Had Cole been at home, he would have been horribly concerned about forgetting his morning, along with much of his earlier life; however, since he *could* remember his morning just fine, including his mother's scolding, he wasn't distressed.

Bowlure looked more dumbfounded than concerned.

"What did you say about my shoes?" asked Dod.

"I can't believe it!" said Bowlure. "You don't remember?"

"No," assured Dod, leaning as close to the trunk as he could. The wind was picking back up.

"Well, I'm bad at introductions," admitted Bowlure matter-of-factly. "Anyway, when I saw you, I got nervous and said something dumb."

"What?" prodded Dod. "What did you say?"

"Well—I thought it looked like you had put your shoes on the wrong feet, so I cracked a joke about you getting up too early to put them on straight. I didn't mean any harm by it—I hope you know that, now."

Dod laughed as he glanced down and noticed that the tips of his shoes bent outward.

"See," insisted Bowlure. "It gets better each time I tell it. This morning I was just trying to get you to laugh like that."

"And did it work?" asked Dod.

Bowlure raised his eyebrows suspiciously. "No, it didn't,"

he said. "You looked at me with a blank stare, like I was the dumbest thing you'd ever seen, and then followed Tridacello."

"Oh Bowlure!" Dod began awkwardly. "I'm sorry about however I acted earlier." He felt crazy suggesting it, but finally confessed, "Honestly, Bowlure, it wasn't me! I'm not sure who it was, but I know it wasn't me."

"It's okay," said Bowlure, wearing a martyr's grin. "We're friends now, right?" He helped Dod back onto his shoulders and began climbing vigorously; he had noticed that Dungo was approaching and knew that he would likely try to pass them if he could.

Dod wished there were a way to make Bowlure believe him, but there wasn't.

At the crest, Tridacello was waiting impatiently, scoping the horizon with his noculars. His foot tapped at the ground as though it would speed things up; and he wasted no time in scolding the climbers as they neared him.

"Hurry up, Bowlure!" he said anxiously. "They could be coming any minute."

Dod glanced nervously around the open skies for flutters. He partially wished to be back in the trees, where branches and leaves had hid him.

"We're ready," said Bowlure bravely. "It's Dungo you have to worry about."

From atop Bowlure's shoulders, Dod surveyed the view. He could see for miles. To the northwest, rays of the late-afternoon sun made the distant sea look as though it were on fire, with bright colors of yellow and red, and it turned the maze-like channels of the bog purple. The face they had just scaled was more than twice the height of the sheer, rock cliffs they had climbed earlier; and they had gained another triple that in elevation from galloping up the string of steep hills that filled most of the horizontal gap between them and the sparkling water.

"Thanks, Bowlure," whispered Dod in awe. He had known that they were moving quickly, but he hadn't fully realized the immensity of the distance they were covering. Now, perched at six thousand feet above sea level, he could gaze out across the trailless wilderness and mentally plot the general course they had come. It was easily over twenty miles as the crow flies.

To the east, running northeastward, Dod noticed mountains that soared thousands of feet higher than the bluff they were on. Pine trees and bushes dotted the rocky landscape, with patches of snow cradled in the uppermost valleys. Directly southeast, across a grassy meadow, there was a narrow mountain pass, with towering cliffs and ledges on both sides. It was Janice Pass, the only traveled route through the Hook Mountains to High Gate and its neighboring cities. It was the perfect ambush location, just as Tridacello had said.

Dod stared at the tiny crack in the otherwise impassible wall of stone and wondered whether some of Dreaderious's men were waiting for them.

When Dungo finally emerged, Tridacello was more than ready to run. Fortunately, Dungo's stomach had settled and his regular hardiness had returned to him.

"Danks for waiding for me," he sneered at Bowlure and Dod, while pushing them out of his way; he didn't like being in the rear.

Tridacello led the team at a fast trot toward Janice Pass. Before they reached the entrance, they merged with a wide road; it ran north and south, obtaining the bluff by winding.

No sooner had they stepped foot on the thoroughfare than Dungo halted. "Id's a drap," he grunted, pointing upward. He tried to show Tridacello the people he could see, insisting over a dozen of Dreaderious's men were waiting near the canyon's mouth, about fifty feet up, on a shadowed ledge.

"I don't see them," said Tridacello, apprehensively, drawing his zip-rope whip and dagger. He stood motionless in the middle of the road, trying to decide what to do.

"Id's a drap!" insisted Dungo angrily, backing up. "I don' wand do be fludder food. Led's hide and waid for nighdfall."

Tridacello's ambivalence pursed his lips and furrowed his brow; he wanted to get the job done, but didn't relish the thoughts of stumbling into an ambush, especially one he'd been plainly shown.

"I guess we could wait 'til it gets dark—" confessed Tridacello hesitantly, when Dod broke in."

"Not at night!" he said, feeling uneasy. "Let's go now!"

Dungo glowered at Dod spitefully.

"I'm fine either way," chirped Bowlure; he tugged at Dod's foot to get his attention. "Is this one of your psychic things?"

"I'm not psychic," muttered Dod wearily. He was exhausted and sore, and he wanted the whole world to stop moving. "I just think we should go now. It feels like the right thing to do."

"Then I've changed my vote," declared Bowlure, turning back toward Tridacello. "Let's skedaddle. If Dungo wants to *hide* like a *coward*, he can." Thoughts of the morning's fiasco swayed Bowlure's opinion, stiffening his backbone more than usual. "Not even a spare rope," he mumbled under his breath, shaking his head.

Tridacello didn't say anything, but he nodded.

"We'll all die," protested Dungo, begrudgingly falling in line; he was annoyed, and he definitely disagreed with the decision, however, he wasn't going to lose his place to Bowlure and Dod.

In the end, the canyon pass proved to be quiet and harmless. Nothing happened as they bolted down the road. And on the other side, the gently sloping highway was dotted with carriages and horses, all heading in the same direction, to Lower Janice. The presence of others changed the atmosphere considerably.

Tridacello kept a steady, swift pace, causing Bowlure and Dungo to pant as they passed travelers. Nevertheless, his timing was perfect; they arrived near the outskirts of Lower Janice at dusk, right as the sky was turning a deep purple and a few stars were beginning to peek out.

Tridacello didn't waste any time in locating a smaller road that parted ways with the bustling thoroughfare. He trotted up and down rolling hills, passing hundreds of crude brick homes that sprinkled the landscape, fitly nestled between fields of grazing cattle. Chickens and dogs frequented the yards, chased by small boys and girls.

The farther they went, the more wagons were replaced by pedestrians. Lower Janice had a substantial, evening foot-crowd, and they responded differently to Dungo and Bowlure than the people in carriages had; young kids pointed their fingers and ran away, and adults stopped to stare. Dungo and Bowlure stood out like two sore thumbs.

The city was filled with a healthy mixture of bobwits, drats, humans, and tredders. Bobwits were short, well-proportioned humans, standing no more than four feet. Drats, on the other hand, were two feet taller, and looked similar to their human cousins, but with unusual noses that stuck upward; they also had little white beards on their chins — even the women and children. Tredders and humans looked the same, except for the bands that circled the necks of the tredders.

As Tridacello led the way, Dungo hung his head down, attempting to avoid all eye contact. Bowlure did the opposite: He warmly greeted passersby and gently teased the cowering youths, all while wearing a contagious grin.

"I'll catch you next time," he chuckled, calling out to one lady who dashed into her home when she saw them coming.

"Where's the fire?" he asked of another woman, who darted off the road like a lamb, fleeing wolves.

Bowlure laughed and enjoyed himself. He hid any signs of hurt over being considered a freak.

As the evening passed, darkness replaced twilight, and empty streets replaced the bustling ones. Homes of various shapes and sizes cast light out of their windows and out of open holes that lacked glass panes. Happy voices were heard singing and talking.

Bowlure began commenting on each smell that he recognized; the hours of toiling to reach their destination had consumed his heaping lunch and his snack from Dreaderious, leaving him hungry.

Finally they came to a bend in the road where a small forest of giant trees grew clumped together. Surrounding the grove were nearly fifty homes and buildings on three sides, with an open, cobblestone courtyard on the fourth.

"This is it," declared Tridacello with confidence. "It's been a good while, but I still recognize it."

Without hesitation, Dungo and Bowlure followed Tridacello

into the woods until they reached a gigantic stone that was wedged in between three ancient trees.

"Ah, yes," said Tridacello, approaching the rock. "Let's see, I think it was four." He picked up a stick and hit the rock squarely four times. Nothing happened.

Dod shifted around on Bowlure's shoulders and then slid down. He staggered and would have fallen if it weren't for Bowlure steadying him with a quick arm.

"I was getting worried," said someone from within the tree.

A slit of light poured out from around the edges of a hidden entrance that had been tightly sealed before.

"I've been expecting you," said the voice. "You're late."

The unusual door swung outward and an old man, about five feet, six inches, stood with the aid of a cane in the entryway. His hair was bright white and he had a pleasant, grandfatherly smile.

"Come in, come in. I've got plenty of goose liver," the man said.

"Bonboo," responded Tridacello cordially. He bent down and hugged the man with one arm. "Sorry we're behind schedule. You know Dungo and Bowlure—"

"Yes, I remember both of them," said Bonboo, squinting to look past them at Dod, who was shadowed by Bowlure. "And is this the lad you've been writing so much about?" He poked his cane at Dod and stepped aside to let them enter.

"Yes. His name's Dod," announced Tridacello.

Inside the tree house, the ceilings were remarkably high, with dozens of unusual looking, smokeless candles, tied together in tight clusters called stacks. They lit the entry like magnificent chandeliers. To the left, a spacious kitchen was hidden in the rock they had observed from outside. An overpowering smell of freshly-prepared food drew the eager eyes of Dungo and Bowlure to the table, where platters were heaped with goose liver and greens.

"Do you mind if we eat first and talk later?" asked Bowlure. His stomach growled so loudly that Dungo glanced at him and shook his head in disapproval.

"No, by all means," said Bonboo. "Come in and take a seat."

Bowlure didn't need a second invitation. He shot toward the table with more energy than he'd had in hours.

Without Bowlure to steady him, Dod swayed. He reached for a fancy, waist-high cabinet, hoping to catch himself, but instead, knocked over an old pot of dried flowers on his way to the floor; and when he struggled to get up, the world darkened around him and he passed out.

THE SHADOW

All eyes immediately turned to look at Dod when the pot broke. Sharp shards scattered across the front hall with a few smooth stones clumped around a pile of dried flowers. It wasn't until the mess filled the floor that it was apparent how small the flowers were compared to the massive pot.

"I'm sorry," said Tridacello, beginning to apologize. "We must have—"

"Are you okay, son?" interrupted Bonboo, turning his full concern to Dod's health. His cane shifted from one hand to the other before being placed against the wall. A crackling of debris on the stone floor echoed when Bonboo took two feeble steps. He knelt down next to Dod.

"Oh, he's been acdin' weird all day," grunted Dungo, making his way to the table. "Pracdically killed me dwice in roude. Why I'd radder—" Dungo searched for the words to say, but when he noticed nobody was listening, he stopped trying.

Bowlure's hunger took a back seat. "Is he all right?" he asked earnestly.

"I don't know," responded Bonboo. "I think he's injured."

Tridacello joined Bonboo on the ground. His strong arms carefully rolled Dod over on his back and positioned him so his body was upon Tridacello's knees instead of the clutter. "It might be his stomach," he said, inspecting him. "He wasn't feeling well today—ate sweets for breakfast and then complained when he got dizzy playing around on the wires after racing Dungo up the cliff. I gave him some cottlejuice at lunch to settle things. You'd think it would have worked by now."

"At least he's breathing," announced Bowlure, pointing at Dod's chest. He looked troubled, while he watched Dod's almost lifeless body being hefted from the floor by Tridacello. Dod was carried across the room and placed in a woven double-chair in the dining area.

Bonboo hobbled behind Tridacello with his cane thumping the floor.

"Let's take a better look at him over here," he said, pointing straight at Dungo with his cane. "It's lighter underneath the kitchen table. Maybe we can slide it to the side and make room for the dripchair."

Bowlure didn't waste any time in responding, despite Dungo's grumbling about barely getting situated. Meanwhile, Tridacello carefully laid Dod in the chair and pushed it right under the brightest set of hanging candle stacks.

"That's better," said Bonboo, moving to inspect him.

Tridacello nodded in agreement.

A sheepish grin crossed Bowlure's face. He was thinking something funny and having a hard time holding it back. It wasn't his usual smile, because an obvious overtone of concern filled the room. Still, something had to be said or Bowlure would burst.

CHAPTER FOUR

"It's not much to look at, but he's all we've got for dinner."

Bowlure thought it was humorous to have replaced the table of food with Dod. A few grunts came from the corner where Dungo was busily stacking mounds of goose liver and cottage bread on his plate. His face cheered up with every spoonful he took.

"Ahh," moaned Dod. He shifted around and reached for his back with one arm. "What happened?"

"You jusd broke Bonboo's ancien Hudas pod. Dad's whad happened," grumbled Dungo with his mouth full of food.

Dod blinked his eyes and searched the room.

"You're still here," he mumbled sleepily. "—or I'm still here. I thought I was waking up. My back is killing me! It must be the position I'm in. I've got to move or I'll have such a kink that I'm sure to make a fool of myself at baseball practice. They'll probably kick me off the team this time."

Dod continued rambling, while Bowlure, Tridacello, and Bonboo all listened. Much of what Dod said didn't make sense to them. Baseball practice was something they had never heard of before. And when Dod spouted out that it was about time to wake up, because he needed to leave in order to walk with Josh to his piano teacher's house, Tridacello joined the monologue.

"Are you okay, Dod?" he asked, gently placing his hand on Dod's brow. "Where are you hurting?"

Dod looked up at the three and rubbed his eyes in disbelief.

"It's probably pointless for any of you to help me," he said wearily. "As long as I'm in this dream, my back is going to keep hurting. It's the position I'm in, resting against the windowsill."

Thoughts of a prior nap flooded Dod's mind. He had fallen asleep on a couch next to Aunt Hilda, which seemed safe enough; however, after having a nightmare about being trapped in piles of seaweed, Cole had awakened to find her abundant hair flowing freely in his face.

The threesome all looked confused. None of them spoke until Dungo managed to clear his throat of food in time to say the obvious.

"You're nowhere near a window! Dis place is more like a cave, so perhaps you're really dreamin' if you're dinkin' dere's a window around—'course I jusd dink you losd your freshy-mind. Maybe da swapper and da Dod in you can'd ged along."

Dod stared in amazement.

"If I can't control this dream," Dod muttered to himself—though everyone could hear him perfectly well—"I'll go along with it. Aunt Hilda will be noticing the time any minute. She'll come looking for me. She wouldn't want Josh to be late for piano lessons. It's about the only thing he does that Mom can be proud of—"

Dod's babbling faded as he looked at Bonboo. "It's right here," he said, pointing at his middle back. "I'm hurting like crazy right here. Can you see anything?"

From the top layer, his deep-maroon jacket appeared normal, but since Dod insisted that his back was sore, they proceeded to help him take the cloak off. Underneath, reddish-brown stains covered his shirt and wrap. A hole, roughly the size of a golf ball, was torn all the way through, revealing a nasty wound that was clogged with leather and cloth.

"Dod! You were hit during the attack!" exclaimed Bowlure. "No wonder! That's why you jiggled around and had such a hard time securing the trilang for us. Why didn't you say anything?"

"That looks like a mortal wound to me," gasped Tridacello,

shaking his head. "It seems to go really deep—why, and all that blood—it's amazing you're still alive, Dod."

Bonboo poked with his pointer finger at the wound. Most of his finger disappeared inside the hole.

"Ouch!" cried Dod. "Leave it alone!"

"I'm just trying to assess the extent of the damage," insisted Bonboo.

"Then try harder to assess with your eyes," wailed Dod. "It really, really—"

Dod's words trailed off when the arm he had been leaning on collapsed out from under him and he fell flat in the chair. Still conscious, but seeing stars, his words slurred as he spoke. "Pleassse help me. Pleassse."

"We'll do our best. Don't worry," reassured Bonboo. "We're right here. You're safe now—and I know of a person that can help you. She's the best in Green."

Dod lay in pain for a long time with the world spinning. Bonboo's prodding had hurt intensely, yet knowing how bad the wound was seemed to make things even worse. Eventually, fatigued and confused, Dod dozed off to the sound of someone chewing cottage bread at his side.

Bowlure sat on the floor, determined to keep close watch over Dod, only leaving him momentarily to refill his plate until all of the food on the table was gone.

Not a lot was said after Bonboo left the bungalow in search of medical help. Everyone was exhausted. The day's journey had taken a toll on their bodies, and Dod's injury had dealt a heavy blow to their spirits.

Tridacello ate a small supper and then proceeded to take the remaining dripchair in the corner as a bed. He was tall enough that his feet hung off the end. Under his head he placed his small bag which held the triblot. It looked like an uncomfortable pillow; nevertheless, with his hands tightly clasping it, nobody could take it without awakening him.

Dungo managed to find a few hand-woven blankets in the closet. He placed them on top of a large, grizzly bear rug near the grand fireplace. It made a great cushion to sleep on. Within moments, the grunting of Dungo's snores could be heard throughout the house.

The bare floor wasn't very comfortable. Bowlure shifted back and forth, but refused to leave Dod in search of a better place to rest. He could see an old-fashioned plump-bed on the other side of the entryway, tucked in the back of what appeared to be a guest room. The bed's size was considerable. Four or five grown tredders could easily fit in it, or possibly a dozen kids. It looked soft and inviting. Bowlure almost gave in, however, Dod stirred in his sleep, which stiffened Bowlure's commitment to endure a night of discomfort.

All of the main candles had been trimmed down for the evening, leaving only a few smaller candles at the sides of the room and by the front door. Shadows danced on the walls when a slight draft made the lonely flames flicker. Things were seemingly at peace for the night, yet all was not as it seemed.

Before dawn, Dod was awakened by a strange feeling. His back still hurt bad enough that he lay motionless. Everything was quiet. His heart began to pound faster. It was as if an enemy was on the prowl. He felt certain of it.

One shadow moved across the wall slowly, methodically. Dod peered at it through his mostly closed eyes. His vision of the room around him was distorted; still, he didn't dare open his eyes all the way, for doing so would reveal he was conscious.

A quick story flashed through his mind; every detail played out in a matter of seconds. The scene was more vivid than he had ever imagined it before. It was an account his grandfather had told him. In the past, Cole had wondered whether or not it was true. But now, as he lay in suspense, his grandpa's words came to life.

Pap was on an adventure. The night was extra cold. The wind blew continually through the walls of the tiny log hut he was attempting to rest in. A handful of journeymen surrounded him on the floor. They were on their way back from accomplishing an important mission—top secret stuff. Earlier in the night, moonlight had leaked through a few holes in a corner of the roof, letting moonbeams dance on the walls, but not anymore; the world around them had become dreadfully dark. A feeling came pouring over Pap. His heart raced and the little rough hairs on the back of his neck pressed straight out against the sack he was laying on.

The purpose of the journey had been to retrieve a priceless gizmo, or at least that's what Pap had called it; and since Pap was in charge of the mission, the gizmo was stowed in his sack. Suddenly, through the darkness, a black wind blew. It chilled his men to the bone. From the first to the last, each journeyman arose and fell quickly at the hands of a silent enemy.

Pap rolled across the floor with his precious cargo tucked tightly against his chest until he reached the back wall of the hut. He knew a cowhide bag, containing hundreds of pounds of water, was hung straight above him. It had been used to quench many men's thirst over the years and was currently stored indoors to aid traveling soldiers, who frequently had their tents pitched near the cabin.

A taut rope rubbed against Pap's neck. It was the bottom part of a line which ran up to the ceiling, through a pulley, and then down to the water bag. As the dark enemy approached, Pap thought quickly and yanked on the knot which kept the container suspended.

CRASH! CRACK! PLOP, PLOP, PLOP.

The enormous sack fell to the floor, completely engulfing Pap. It was made from multiple, thick hides, so the impact didn't cause it to pop, though it did knock the wind out of Pap and produce a cracking sound from underneath him.

Immediately, he was attacked. He could feel the water sloshing as some beast bounced and clawed above him. The smell of rotting wood filled Pap's nostrils. Not all of the soldiers had been careful when getting water, so a portion had dripped and kept the wooden floor wet enough to decay. Pap dug with his hands, searching below him, and felt a break in the timbers. The impact of such a heavy weight hitting the rotten floor had broken three boards. Frantically Pap worked the hole, making it larger, until damp, musky air wafted up. It was the smell of freedom.

Pap's escape was not a moment too soon. As he crawled through spider webs and rat nests under the cabin, a flood of water came crashing down. The assailant had successfully torn the hide bag.

Pap slithered like a snake into the bushes surrounding the hut and then ran with the wind downhill. In the end, he was the only one of his party that survived.

As Dod lay injured in a strange cottage, he felt what Pap must have felt. Fear ran down his spine and made him shiver. *What would Pap do right now?* he thought. It was then that

Dod determined to take action. He decided that if he were to die at the hands of a dreadful monster, he wanted to at least see his attacker.

He opened both eyes and strained to distinguish what was making the shadow.

Dod didn't see anything at first. As a matter of fact, the shadow had stopped moving, or had completely disappeared. Dod continued to lay motionless, searching each stationary silhouette on the wall. He knew one of them had moved in such a manner that it had to have been made by someone or something. Besides, the feeling of threat didn't go away. It just got stronger. The tension was almost unbearable. It was like knowing that a horrible beast was ready to pounce and that it would pounce soon; the only remaining questions were when and from where.

Based on the location of the wall where he had first spotted the shadow, Dod tried to calculate where the creature was hiding. It wasn't easy. The few lit candles were spread out so that an object in one place could cast shade on the same wall as an object in another place, using the dim light of a different candle. The only sure way would be to see the silhouette again and then track the shadow's tail to its owner.

Dod's eyes searched the room. He even moved his head slightly to view the fireplace. In horror, he noticed his friends were gone!

Where's Dungo? he thought. *Where's Tridacello? Where's Bowlure?* His eyes raced around to find them.

Though Dod had faded off to sleep in pain, he hadn't slept well, and so he had noticed with comfort, over the course of the night, the location of each of his friends. Now they were gone!

Suddenly, Dod saw the giant shadow reappear on the wall.

It was enormous—and worst of all—the tail tracked straight to Dod! Whatever it was, it had to be moving directly behind him.

"I know you're there," said Dod in a loud voice, as he rolled toward the attacker. It took all of his courage and energy to face his assailant.

Darkness cloaked the wall, hiding whoever or whatever had once cast such a horrendous silhouette.

SWOOSH!

A giant gust of air announced the opening of the front door. Dod glanced to see who was escaping; however, the gust of wind blew so hard that it extinguished all of the candles in the house, rendering the surroundings pitch-black.

I'm as good as dead, he thought, wishing to disappear.

"Bowlure, could you come give me a hand?" grunted Dungo from the darkness in the entryway. "Id seems we have a liddle problem."

For a split second, Dod almost cried out to Dungo for help, yet something held him back. Was Dungo just coming, or had he faked an arrival? Did he really know where Bowlure was? And if a problem loomed, why didn't Tridacello ask for Bowlure's aid? Tridacello was always in charge.

The feeling of fear continued. Dod could hear his own heart beating in his ears. *Please, Bowlure, answer*! he thought; but the house remained silent.

"Hey, wake up. I need your help now," insisted Dungo. "You have do come and show me dose muscles you keep braggin' aboud."

Still, no response. Tension filled the darkness like a suffocating fog. A strong wind was blowing outside, sending large gusts of air into the cottage.

FOOM, FOOM — FOOM, FOOM, FOOM — SWACK —
THUNK!

Something darted back and forth, right over Dod's face.

"I got it!" declared Bowlure excitedly. His voice was almost
soothing enough to stop the pounding in Dod's chest. "There, and
you probably didn't see it coming. When I told you I'd stay at your
side, I meant protect you, not literally stay right at your side. Sorry
if I scared you by not answering. A venoos is terribly poisonous
and quite dangerous, you know. It attacks what it hears."

Bowlure made a fumbling noise in the blackness, and then
there was light. The big stack hanging above Dod glowed brightly,
filling the room and beyond. It was now clear that Dungo was
standing just outside the front door, propping it open with one
foot, while holding something massive over his head with all
four arms.

"Here, Dungo, let me help you with that," said Bowlure,
traversing the spacious kitchen. His long legs cut the distance
to a few strides. "Wow! What happened? I leave you for a few
moments, and now look, you've got your hands full; not to
mention, it appears you've bitten off more than you can chew."

Bowlure laughed at his own joke. Dungo struggled to hold
up a large branch that had blown down from the wind. He was
losing his grip with one hand and had resorted to biting a smaller
limb of the branch in an effort to reposition his slipping hand. It
did look like Dungo intended on eating a gigantic side dish of tree.

"Ha ha," grunted Dungo sarcastically. His faltering hand
caught hold of the branch again and freed up his mouth for
complaining. "We'll see how funny you dink id is nexd dime I
leave da job for you do do alone."

"Oh, it wouldn't be so bad," responded Bowlure happily.

"Besides, I probably should be the one doing it, since that task looks like it's a man's job—not one for a little girl."

"Yeah, I'm sure you would have done a gread job," answered Dungo crossly. "You'd have been da liddle crying girl drying do negodiade geddin' oud of da cave wid dis branch firmly blockin' da door closed. I'd have lefd id in place if id weren'd for da naggin' of Dridacello."

As Bowlure helped Dungo move the limb out into the forest, he could hear Tridacello greeting someone in the distance. Voices were distorted by the wind, but he could still clearly recognize Tridacello was in the group.

"They're coming," announced Bowlure through the open doorway. He quickly turned and focused on the images that were gradually becoming visible. A taller figure was bending down to aid a staggering one, with a few other dots behind them.

Dod's mind, however, was too preoccupied by what he saw inside to care much about what was going on outside. As soon as Bowlure had lit the lights, Dod's eyes had found the venoos. It was a twelve-legged, black spider, with a body the size of a dog. Its fangs extended like two giant hypodermic needles. Dod couldn't take his eyes off of it because of the close encounter he had just endured; and once Bowlure was gone helping Dungo, Dod was paralyzed stiff, watching the beast: One leg kept twitching—and it didn't stop!

"Bowlure," Dod shouted. "I'm glad you're done helping Dungo. Can you come in here? The venoos is still moving around." Dod glanced nervously at the doorway and noticed, to his great horror, that Bowlure had stepped out.

"Bowlure!" Dod hollered, getting annoyed. He couldn't believe Bowlure had left him alone with a dying venoos.

Dod shifted his weight and strained to sit up. With the change in position, he hoped to yell louder.

"BOWLURE!" Dod shouted. This time he yelled until his throat hurt. He felt like a baby, crying to be noticed. It wasn't just the venoos, he was nearly delirious from pain.

For a few moments, Dod had concentrated wholly on getting Bowlure's attention, but that was a big mistake! When his eyes drifted back toward the venoos, it was gone! A feeling of fear came flooding back.

Instantly, more vivid than any childhood memory, Dod recalled bits and pieces of an encounter with a venoos. It took no more than a second to completely fill his mind with a menagerie of pictures and feelings. The story was hazy, yet the information seemed to both frighten and comfort Dod.

A bobwit family had settled down for the night. All five kids lay nestled in one plump-bed. Suddenly, moonlight no longer seeped through the windows. Darkness filled the halls, kitchen, and other rooms. A child cried. With candles blazing, Mamma and Papa came running. Other children began to cry. Then they were all crying. Fear was in Mamma's eyes.

CRACK!

Two venomous fangs penetrated the bedroom windowpane. Everyone was running—but not Papa. He stood, equipped with the strangest thing—something Dod would never have imagined!

Webbing was everywhere—Papa was darting, jumping—the venoos attacking—and then it was over.

The memory wasn't much, just enough to bolster his courage. Dod started to wonder how he had seen such a clear, inside perspective on the incident, however, a noise from the corner of the room brought him back.

Dod spotted a leg! It was rising from behind a stack of wood by the fireplace. Its movements were cold and calculated, like the robotical approach of a humongous black widow. The venoos hadn't gone far. It brought comfort to know where it was, but that comfort soon faded.

"IT'S COMING!" cried Dod desperately. He hoped Bowlure would reappear with a stick to finish the job.

The venoos climbed to the top of the woodpile. Ten of its twelve legs seemed to work just fine. One fang dripped a sticky liquid that hung in a glistening line. Now Dod could see its eyes. Clearly, these weren't the eyes of a spider; they glowed red like two hot embers and were staring angrily at him.

Dod managed to reach down and untie one of his funny-looking shoes without ever taking his eyes off the venoos. It was almost instinctive. The laces were so long that they wrapped five times around his lower calf.

Suddenly, the venoos made a leap upward. It was then that Dod noticed how an intricate web filled the top of Bonboo's vaulted ceiling, up above the lit stacks. Webbing shot from the venoos and secured a line.

Dod's heart began to pound quickly. His pain momentarily dimmed from the bright light of imminent danger. He struggled to pull his shoe off. The force from tugging knocked him out of the dripchair and onto the stone floor. He looked up and saw the venoos positioning directly above him. Dod glanced around, but there wasn't anything to hide behind. His legs felt like Jell-O. One hand held his shoe, the other tried to steady him into a sitting position.

He slipped on a pile of things that had fallen out of Bowlure's bag. Dod peered down and noticed that they were rocks of various shapes and colors. Without thinking, he packed the shoe, while his eyes kept a steady watch on the venoos. Finally, as Dod wrapped the laces around his hand twice, he felt as ready as the bobwit father had been. With a makeshift weapon, it was time to break for the door.

If only I can get outside, he thought, *someone else can worry about the venoos.*

But it was hopeless. No sooner did he rise to his feet than he found himself face down, seeing stars. He was dizzy and his legs had no strength. The shoe full of rocks thumped recklessly across the floor, extending Dod's arm while cinching the laces tighter around his hand, blocking the circulation to his fingers.

Dod's nose ached, filling his eyes with water, enough that for a brief moment, he lost sight of the venoos.

Just then, a cold chill hit the back of his neck. It was the kiss of death. The venoos was upon him and Dod's futile efforts to evade the master predator were too little and way too late to save his life from the poisonous venom.

If I'm to die, Dod thought, *I'll at least do it fighting*!

"Die you wretched thing!" Dod cried, as he rolled over and swung his weapon into the air. "Die you putrid thing! DIE!"

He felt it solidly connect! For a moment in time, everything froze. His eyes were too blurry to see; however, that didn't change what he knew. It was a hit! The feeling was unbelievable. It was a euphoric high like none he had ever encountered. He imagined that sinking his first homerun, in the last inning of a tie-breaker game for a championship, couldn't possibly feel any better; and that's saying a lot for someone whose past best was making it to first base instead of striking out.

"I did it!" shouted Dod enthusiastically. "I really did it." He felt a surge of adrenaline despite his dying condition.

Dod wiped the tears from his eyes and felt the back of his neck, expecting to find blood, but it wasn't red. The venoos hadn't descended far enough to sink its fangs into Dod's neck. It was just a string of poisonous slime.

The venoos was once more at the base of the wall where Bowlure had left it.

"Are you all right?" called Bowlure from the front door. "I thought I heard you say something."

Dod looked up at Bowlure with excitement and exhaustion in his eyes.

"Would you please be kind enough to remove that *thing* from this room?" complained Dod, pointing at the venoos. His voice sounded like a mother, who was asking her son for the hundredth time to do his chores.

"Well, okay," said Bowlure. "You don't have to worry—it's dead." Bowlure entered the room and shook his head as he looked down at Dod. "What happened to you? If you wanted to get up, you should have asked for help. Bonboo says your wound is bad enough that you shouldn't be doing anything right now."

Dod rolled his eyes. It seemed pointless to explain his triumph since Bowlure was convinced he had killed the venoos earlier.

"Uh—Dod," said Bowlure, smirking as he bent down to help Dod back into the chair. "I think you have a rock in your shoe."

Dod chuckled. It was mostly a charity laugh. He felt too tired to be witty, so he simply said, "That's what happens when you leave them on the floor." It made very little sense as a comeback, but Dod was overly tired—he didn't care.

Bowlure went on to discuss everything imaginable concerning his beloved collection of stones. He included a few jabs about the rocks stinking from being stowed in Dod's shoe and the obvious jealousy Dod felt toward him, as was apparent from Dod's attempt to steal them.

Regardless, it didn't matter what Bowlure said. With the danger gone, fatigue took over and Dod drifted back to sleep.

CHAPTER FIVE

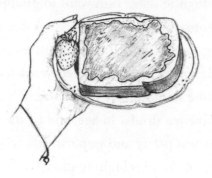

NEW FRIENDS

"I'd like strawberry jam on my toast," mumbled Cole. He heard a bit of laughter. His eyes felt like they had thick deposits from a generous sandman.

As he became more aware of the sounds around him, he realized that he had been begging for strawberry jam in response to a question his mother had asked him...in his dream! It was awkward. None of the voices was clearly recognizable, though one was definitely a girl. She had giggled loudly when he requested jam.

In embarrassment, Cole kept his eyes closed for a while and pretended to still be asleep. Part of him wanted to sneak a quick look, to see the gathering at his side before formally waking up, however, the sand made peeking altogether impossible.

Hearing the voice of a girl jolted Cole's heart into pounding nervously in anticipation. He wasn't exactly slick when it came to introductions and greetings.

"Do you think he's waking up?" asked a male voice. It sounded like Jon, the star baseball player on Cole's team. Just the thought of Jon being anywhere near him, especially with a girl around, was enough to make him want to disappear. Cole felt a sinking in his stomach.

"Well," responded the girl, "I'm not sure if he's with us yet, but he does appear to be hungry." There were a few more giggles.

Cole liked the sound of the girl's voice. It was undoubtedly connected to someone similar in age, and by the way she spoke, he imagined she was pretty and popular. It was a familiar voice, enough that Cole racked his brain to place her face; yet the more he tried, the more he realized how odd things were for him. After all, why was he in bed…and with visitors?

Cole strained to remember what had happened. His thoughts drifted to the flashflood, then to his mother's lecture, and then to the bizarre dream he had had. None of it placed him in bed, much less near a girl. The whole situation was weird. It led Cole to listen more intently for clues.

"How is he doing?" asked a gentle voice.

Cole couldn't believe it. He finally recognized someone, and it wasn't one of the people he would have expected—it wasn't even the realm he expected.

"Bonboo, you're back," said Jon, though it wasn't Jon; it had to be someone he didn't know. Cole actually felt relief when he realized Jon hadn't come to make fun of him.

"Gramps," chimed the girl. "Did you get the situation handled?"

"It's taken care of for now," answered Bonboo.

Dod could hear Bonboo moving closer to the bed. His cane made a familiar thumping sound on the floor, except it echoed more than Dod remembered.

"He should be waking up sometime today," said the girl to Bonboo. "They stopped giving him slerp last night. Higga mentioned he would be hungry when he awoke, and I think she must be right. Everything he's said for the past couple of hours has had something to do with food."

Dod was embarrassed by the thought that he had been talking in his sleep in front of other people. It bothered him. But worse than that, he didn't like hearing that he had been previously fed something unusual by the hand of a stranger named Higga. The suspense was unbearable.

"Ahhh," Dod yawned, stretching both arms up in the air. He moved slowly, acting like he was just becoming conscious. He even made a smacking sound with his mouth, followed by a heavy sigh; they were undeniable signs of someone who is just waking up. Finally, he rubbed the debris from his eyes and blinked.

"He's awake!" the girl announced excitedly.

The way she said it sounded as if she cared. Dod thought for a second and couldn't remember a time in his life when anyone, so attractive as he anticipated she would be, had said anything to him, or about him, with such enthusiasm.

It took a minute before Dod could see, partly because the room was so bright. Two walls of windows, twenty feet tall, lined both long sides of the room. A vaulted ceiling towered up from the windows, at least thirty feet in the middle. It was a massive hall, like the kind kings use when entertaining hundreds of guests. Candle stacks, like chandeliers, dangled on long chains. Dod wondered what it would be like to see them lit at night.

"How are you feeling?" asked Bonboo, sitting on a chair near Dod's bed.

Dod's eyes panned downward from the majesty of the barrel vaulted ceiling to Bonboo's anxious face.

"I'm feeling better," he croaked. His throat was dry and scratchy. It made his voice sound embarrassingly ugly.

Dod quickly looked to the side of Bonboo, expecting to see a young girl. A fifty-something-year-old portly woman stood by, dressed in a burgundy suit, its buttons bulging, with sharp-tipped collars that stuck straight up in the air; her hair was short and curly, a bit of a mess, and she had a smudge of something on her cheek. She wasn't terribly attractive, but she smiled sweetly, much like a grandmother would.

Dod searched around the room with his eyes. It appeared to be a hospital of sorts, with partitions sectioning off beds in clumps of four. To his dismay, he couldn't see the beautiful girl he had been imagining. The only other person, standing anywhere near him, was a large, handsome boy.

"You take a beating well—" said the boy who sounded like Jon. His deep voice trailed. It was obviously a polite thing to say.

Dod looked straight at him. The boy may have sounded like Jon, though that was the end of the comparison. Jon was short and wiry with straight blonde hair; this fellow, on the other hand, was nothing less than a ladies magnet. He stood at least six feet tall, with wavy black hair, bright-blue eyes, rippling muscles, and a gentle tan. He looked about seventeen. The white shirt he wore had a stylish, circular collar and his pants had two-tone coloring around the waist and cuffs. A handsome tredder ring circled the base of his neck.

It was disappointing to see an older woman stand where the voice had sounded so young. The only consolation Dod had was that he wouldn't have to watch the girl get goo-goo eyes when talking with the boy—or at least that's what Dod thought.

He knew what kind of boy most girls liked. While he was

awkward with girls when it meant anything, he still had plenty of female acquaintances; and since they were 'just friends,' as the girls often reminded him, they felt no shame in frequently sharing with him the names of the boys they really did like—and the boys weren't exactly Cole material. All the girls hoped to date boys like the one standing at his bedside.

"I'm Boot," said the boy, stretching his right arm out with four fingers apart and his thumb tucked under. One of his fingers displayed a handsome gold ring. Dod instinctively returned the strange greeting with his own ringless hand.

What kind of parents name their kid after a shoe? he thought.

"This is Higga," pronounced Bonboo, pointing to the lady. "She's an old friend of mine. It appears she's done a wonderful job of saving your life. It's good she studied ancient records from the Mauj or I'm certain she wouldn't have been able to see you through."

Bonboo looked nervously at Higga and then patted her shoulder, forcing a smile. His eyes returned to Dod and added, cautiously, "I don't think you understand what bad shape you were in, my boy. What's happened to you…well, it's miraculous, indeed, that you're alive….And it came with a price, too. Be careful."

Dod felt bad about the trouble and expense he had caused, but hearing the lady's name distracted his attention from whatever Bonboo was trying to say. If she were Higga, there was someone else lurking around—someone he was dying to meet—keeper of the angelic voice to which he had awakened.

"Oh, thank you," said Dod emphatically. "I appreciate you saving my life. And you did it so quickly." Dod reached his hand around and felt that the hole in his back had completely healed up. The skin even felt smooth and scar free. He looked at Higga and asked, "How long have I been out?"

"About three weeks," she responded. Her voice was noticeably that of an older lady. "I gave you slerp in your goop to make you sleep. It eased the pain, while I attended to your wound. I think you've just about made a full recovery. It's the quickest bounce, by far, that I've ever seen!"

She rubbed her hip, as though tending an ache, glanced an uneasy peek sideways at Bonboo and then added, "Dod, you must be made of something more durable than I am. It's your lucky feet, I guess."

Dod smiled as he popped his toes out from under the patchwork quilt he was cloaked in. The tips looked different than usual, tinged redder—nothing significant, though.

No sooner had Dod begun to inspect his special feet than Bonboo quickly slid bright-blue wool socks onto them, remarking that the hall was cool and he didn't want Dod to catch his death from a chill after remarkably escaping its grip at the hands of an enemy.

"Three weeks," Dod said. "Wow. I should be extremely well rested." He sat up and moved to stand.

"Here, let me help you," insisted Boot. A big arm wrapped around him, under his right arm and up onto his left shoulder.

"Thanks," said Dod. He felt bad for feeling jealous of him. Boot appeared to be really nice—not to mention, the way he looked wasn't entirely his fault.

Bonboo spoke with Dod while Boot helped him up and down the large hall. Dod's legs felt stiff, but they still appeared more steady than Bonboo's; he struggled, with the aid of a cane, to keep up.

"—so we brought you here," continued Bonboo. "I knew Higga would do a fine job of patching you up. As for your friends, they went on to High Gate. I'm sure you'll be happy to know that the triblot is safe. Commendus sends a high salute for your bravery and bids you join him, at your leisure, in his palace at High Gate, or one of his other palaces, if you please."

There was a stately manner in which Bonboo relayed the information. Dod felt like a recovering soldier with respectable rank. He liked being filled in on what had happened during his hibernation. As they strolled, questions began to swirl in Dod's mind; fortunately, it was a good time to ask.

"What exactly happened the night I arrived at your house?" said Dod, his eyes looking intently at Bonboo for answers.

"Oh, you mean my hut? I haven't had you visit my home just yet. I intend on bringing you there today. My little-stop is here in Lower Janice. It's actually more of a cave—a traveling way-station these days.

"I remember a time when it was more than that. I must have been barely sixty or so. The grip of fear was heavy. Almost everyone had to hide from the reign of Doss. Only the Mauj seemed unaffected. They always had a better way, even though people feared them; of course, going to Soosh at all, back then, was—well—like swimming to the bottom reaches of the sea. Few dared venture through Soosh's wilderness and nomadic chaos to the cities of the Mauj, so most folks knew very little of them, except, of course, what they heard in mystical legends.

"Yes, those were the days. I hid for years in that small thing, directing my men's efforts. We fought hard against Doss until he was finally defeated."

Boot was listening more eagerly than Dod, who found

himself distracted because Bonboo hadn't addressed his original question.

"Do you think we'll ever see the likes of another swapper like that?" asked Boot.

Just mentioning the word swapper suddenly piqued Dod's interest. He had heard the title used when referring to some benevolent person or thing that mentored people for good causes. Hearing the word used now, in the context of a villain, didn't seem to fit Bowlure's descriptions of a swapper.

"No, I hope not in a million years," responded Bonboo with a loud sigh. He slowed down and took a seat near the windows. It looked as if his thoughts weighed upon him heavily.

Boot followed quickly, plopping himself next to Bonboo with enough vigor to almost send Dod flying to the floor; fortunately, he swung around and steadied Dod with an equal zeal, helping him sit at his side.

"To think that such a thing could happen makes me concerned," confessed Bonboo. He looked past Boot, right at Dod, and said sadly, "I carry a heavy burden for a tredder." His eyes filled with emotion and he added, "There are some things that are better not shared, but there are other things that are even worse."

Dod wondered what Bonboo meant. It was like a riddle of great importance—something he was to understand; nevertheless, the silence only lasted a few moments before Boot wanted to know more.

"What exactly happened to the Mauj?"

Bonboo shifted in his seat, just enough to capture sunlight on his head. He had been shadowed before, but with light streaming through the window against his back, it seemed as though he took center stage.

"They were a great people," he whispered reverently. "Probably the best people we have ever seen in these realms. They lived in peace, despite the turbulent atmosphere of Soosh. It is said they invented the doors between Soosh, Raul and Green. When my parents sought their help as ambassadors, they freely shared their knowledge with us. They provided the triblots that still continue to protect a few of our cities—triblots they originally invented to stop raiding nomads who attacked them from time to time—not to save the Mauj—they could have killed the nomads without a problem. When they put up triblot barriers, they did it to spare the nomads from being destroyed by them in battle."

Bonboo spoke with emotion. He wiped a tear from the corner of his eye and then continued. "They even gave us the knowledge and ability to destroy Doss. Doubtless, that was the reason they died. I've heard people say that Mauj scientists created the Hickopsy as a weapon, which foolishly led to their own demise, but it's a lie."

Across the way, someone dropped a metal object that echoed rhythmically; everyone in the hall looked toward the commotion—that is, everyone except Dod and Boot: They persisted in listening intently to Bonboo.

"The Mauj fell prey to the Hickopsy. That part is true; however, we still don't know exactly what it is or how it happens. Apparently, despite the Mauj's medical technology and longevity, they couldn't stop it; they all became sick and died within a few weeks. That was right before we destroyed Doss. He knew they were helping us, so he spitefully killed them all—genocide—hoping to prevent our success."

Bonboo shook his head. He felt some measure of guilt about their deaths. They had died helping him fight Doss.

"Since then," he continued, "others have gone back to search their cities for treasures and knowledge. Few return; and those who do, eventually die from the sickness. It's as if the air around their cities is contaminated with the disease. Doss had a cruel hand in it—I can tell you that much!"

"Ah," said Boot. "Is it true that your parents also died of the Hickopsy—if you don't mind me asking? I've heard it told a few different ways."

Boot leaned in so close to Bonboo that he almost completely blocked Dod's view of him; and fearing that Bonboo would whisper, Dod shifted to his other side.

"Probably," came the response. "I can't say. My parents were friends with the Mauj, so when they all died, my parents went back to compile some of their writings to preserve their legacy of technology. It was the last tribute my parents could give them. Unfortunately, my parents were only able to write a meager sampling before they returned to Green and died. But Dod, you can thank them for your life. The technology used in saving you came from my parents."

"That part's true!" Higga agreed, startling Bonboo. She had come over in search of her patient. "Without Bonboo's parents, you wouldn't be pinky, would you?" Higga crinkled her face as she spoke, almost mockingly, while Bonboo looked at the floor and sighed.

"I'm sure we'd have buried you," Higga continued grumblingly. "We'd have thrown your body, grey and stiff, in the ground with the rest of Dreaderious's victims if it weren't for *his parents*!" Higga pointed at Bonboo.

"Thank you, Bonboo—and Higga," said Dod. He really appreciated how much better he was feeling than just three weeks before and regretted the trouble he had caused. He nearly felt like himself again.

"You're welcome," responded Bonboo. "And thank you, Higga. We're all indebted to you." He smiled politely until she walked away.

"Dod," Bonboo added, looking squarely at him. "I'm glad you're helping us to keep the legacy of freedom my parents gave their lives for. You're special—and tough times call for special people!" Bonboo said it with a twinkle in his eye that left Dod wondering how much Bonboo knew about everything going on. He seemed to be full of answers, the kind of answers Dod had been searching for.

"Do you think I'm being helped by a swapper-mentor?" asked Dod. It was one of the many questions swirling around in his head.

Boot laughed out loud, on the other side of Bonboo, and mumbled while shaking his head, "If you don't know, you're not."

Bonboo's response was much gentler. "I think there are a lot of things going on with you right now," he assured, "things we should discuss later." He pointed across the room to where Dod's bed was and added, "Dilly is getting impatient over there. It looks like she has our lunch ready."

Had any other line been used to keep him from getting straight answers, Dod would have been dreadfully disappointed, but seeing Dilly changed his mind completely. He quickly agreed with Bonboo that they could save the conversation for later.

Even from the distance, Dilly was beautiful. Her long brown hair had waves and curls which reminded him of a princess in a childhood, bedtime story.

Boot reached down and tried to help Dod walk.

"No thanks," he responded. "My legs are feeling a lot better now."

In truth, Dod struggled. He would have allowed Boot to help him, yet he didn't because he hoped by walking on his own he would make a better impression on Dilly. His eyes carefully watched her. He wanted to know more about her without letting her know he was noticing, so he guarded every glance cautiously.

Dilly wore an outfit that merged a traditional royal dress with pants as he had never seen before. It was truly original. A ruffled white top was interrupted nicely by pink leather lacing across her torso. From her shoulders—and what appeared to be slight padding on top—a creamy-pink cape trailed down her back, with pearl strands dangling and woven artistically.

The cape was attached loosely to a secondary feature that was connected firmly to her waist in the back only. Multiple layers of white lace and ruffle padding were added to the lower rear element which trailed to nearly the floor. In the front, shiny, pink leather pantaloons came to just below her knees, where they were met by white ruffled stockings. She also wore bluish-gray boots that came just above her ankles, topped off with gold buckles.

Usually, Cole did poorly with greeting beautiful girls. Somehow, this time he felt different, like that part of him had been left in the past. *Think like a man—be a man*, thought Dod. *I just have to believe it. After all, if this is a dream, it's my dream! And if it's not, these people don't need to know I'm hopeless.* It sounded perfect in his mind.

Bonboo introduced Dilly as his great-granddaughter and then added that she was called great for more than one reason.

Dod fumbled for the words to appropriately say hello. "How do you, do you do?" he said. It was awkward.

Close up, she was cuter than he had imagined. Never had he seen anyone with such exciting brown eyes. In an instant, she drew him in; very little of his brain was left to concentrate on speaking.

Dod blushed bright red and tried to recover by saying, "I mean, I'm glad to eat you." The words blurped out horribly wrong.

Where do fumbles like that come from anyway? he thought, shaking his head in embarrassment.

Fortunately, Dod was hungry from three weeks of being force-fed goop, while unconscious, and Dilly knew it.

"Well, don't eat me," she chuckled. "Try this instead."

She presented him with a slice of toast smothered in strawberry jam.

"I hear it's your favorite," she continued gleefully. Dod looked in her eyes and knew that she was being sincere.

"Thank you," he squeaked. It was two simple words, and spoken poorly at that, yet it seemed to be all he was capable of saying at the moment.

So much for Suave Dod!

Boot was amused watching Dod fumble around. When Dilly left to get more juice, he gave Dod some feedback: his elbow and a big smile.

"She's really something, isn't she?" he said teasingly.

Dod nodded his head in unison with Bonboo.

"I think fifty-one years has been kind to her," remarked Bonboo. "You can see she is on her way to becoming a woman; and as a Coosing, she's following right in her mother's footsteps."

It was amazing. Dilly didn't look a day older than fifteen—maybe a mature fifteen. Dod stared in silence. Memories flashed of the tredder people. They grew in spurts;

one at about twelve and another in their fifties or early sixties. That's why most didn't marry until sometime well after sixty.

"How old are you?" asked Dod, looking at Boot.

"A lot older than you," he responded with a grin. "I'm fifty-seven. And you're a human, so I take it you can't be any older than thirty-five."

Dod liked the thought of Boot calling him thirty-five. He couldn't tell whether Boot was serious or not. Regardless, he went along with it anyway.

"You're good, Boot. That's pretty close."

Dod found himself quickly becoming friends with Boot. It didn't take much effort. It was as if they had been tight for a long time. The age gap seemed insignificant. Dod saw Boot as a peer, and Boot played the part well.

It was common for tredders in their twenties through fifties to have human friends in their teens. They looked and acted alike. Tredders and humans were basically the same, with tredders having an extended youth and middle age. Though older, tredders had a juvenile spirit that matched their younger human counterparts. It could be difficult to tell fifteen-year-old humans from fifty-something-year-old tredders, so long as they were in social settings and wearing clothes that concealed their lower necks. Of course, in working situations, tredders had abilities which revealed their age.

Bonboo led the group at a leisurely pace out of the hospital. His cane thumped a rhythm which mirrored their steps. It would have taken forever if they had walked to Bonboo's house, but fortunately, transportation was waiting. The ride was a horse-drawn carriage of sorts—a plush twelve-seater.

"Please, everyone, make yourself comfortable," proclaimed

Bonboo, pointing at the open door with his cane. "There's plenty of room today. It takes about three hours from here to get to my home, so find a soft spot and enjoy the ride."

Dod and Boot quickly climbed inside, followed by Bonboo, who first stopped to say something to the driver. The only way it could have been nicer was if Dilly would have decided to join them; nevertheless, since she insisted on riding her black horse, Song, it wasn't an option. Bonboo tried to convince her otherwise, suggesting that Song could trot behind the carriage, to which Dilly laughed and replied that her horse was born to run, not trot!

With just three in the carriage, they rattled around with ample space to lie down if they chose. Bonboo took a nap, so Dod spent his afternoon mostly listening to Boot tell of adventures. He spoke frequently about the Coosings, of which he was a member. It was one of those things that Dod was expected to know plenty about, but didn't. The name sounded familiar, like memories of the bunch were trying to step forward from the back recesses of his mind, just temporarily detained.

Occasionally, Boot included a question or two. Dod didn't want to look dumb in front of Boot, so he usually nodded and played like he understood.

Dod enjoyed listening to Boot's ramblings, which made the ride easily better than the best of moments he had had while traveling with Bowlure, Tridacello and Dungo. Though, in all fairness, sitting comfortably and pain free, while smelling freshly bathed and wearing clean clothes didn't hurt the ambiance, either; not to mention, it was more than advantageous that he didn't need to worry about Dungo's flatulence and its tremendous capacity to befoul any circumstance, which certainly had rendered the other traveling episode a 'worst ever' incident.

Suddenly, right in the middle of Boot's stories, mysterious images—somewhat convoluted—flashed into Dod's mind. They were of a hand with a jagged scar on the back, working a metal tool against leather riggings.

The scene was unusual, considering Boot's current tale had nothing to do with leather riggings or scarred hands. As a matter of fact, Dod would have preferred that it had, for he found Boot's description of his pursuits after young ladies bordering on scandalous, which bothered him with Dilly on his mind.

Another string of images burst forward. This time, the scarred hand twisted back and forth, struggling to loosen a bolt or adjust a metal clip. The glimpses made Dod shiver. Somewhere, sometime, this wicked hand meant to harm him—he knew it! Dod would have dismissed the thoughts as mere figments of his imagination if it hadn't been for the other unusual experiences he had already encountered while in Green.

Just then, the carriage stopped abruptly. Dod looked through his open window and saw no sign of a dwelling nearby. Panic struck his heart. It showed on his face, causing Boot to laugh at him and say, "Haven't you ever taken a walk with a girl?" Dod nodded to the question without hearing it; his mind was busy, thinking about what neither of them could see.

Zerny, who was a hired drat for Bonboo and his family, insisted that Dod get out and walk near the tip of a lookout to peek at the view. Dod wasn't sure if he dared. After the things he'd just seen in his mind, he was ready to run. Everyone looked suspicious, especially Zerny; he had an uppity nose, pointed beard, and beady dark eyes. His wispy, snow-white hair blew in the wind, revealing he was balding on top. His mannerisms suggested he was impatient.

Cautiously, Dod made his way to the edge, staying behind Zerny all the way; however, he only dared do it after Boot teased him relentlessly, insisting that if he hadn't seen the view before, he had to see it now.

It was impressive. Zerny knew how to pick scenic spots. He even bragged a bit that he knew every good angle in Green, having traveled the world over at Bonboo's side.

The outcome made Dod feel embarrassed about the way he had acted. He especially regretted having given Zerny such condemning looks when Zerny had only been trying to be a good host.

On the way back to the carriage, Dod tried to make a better second impression since he had clearly ruined the first.

"Do you enjoy working for Bonboo?" he asked sheepishly. The man surprised him with his response.

"Oh h-he's a l-lot more than j-just a job," sputtered Zerny. His speech was choppy. "W-we've been friends all of my life. Our f-families are practically blood."

Zerny went on to stutter through an explanation of how he and his family were shorter than most drats, but since Bonboo was small for a tredder, they were made for each other.

Zerny stood about five feet; he was barrel-chested and strong. His white beard and unusual nose showed a clean line of drat blood, despite being nearly a foot shorter than the average, six-foot man among drats. Yet he did have a point about Bonboo: Five-and-a-half feet was below the norm for a grown tredder with noble blood.

Zerny continued, "W-we joke that being sh-short makes us

live longer. Bonboo is the o-oldest tredder by a l-long shot — three hundred and thirty-three." Zerny smiled. His face beamed with loyalty and friendship.

"Do you mind if I join you up front?" asked Dod, when they arrived back at the wagon.

"B-be my guest," responded Zerny.

Boot grinned a 'have fun' kind of look through the window of the carriage and quickly joined Bonboo in napping.

It wasn't long before Zerny pointed out the *house*. It was hardly a house. Calling it an estate still seemed to underplay its grandeur.

In the distance, a few miles down a steep hill, past fields and forests, there was a city of buildings and gardens surrounding a massive structure in the center. The complex was positioned on the borders of an enormous lake, extending across most of the horizon.

"The-there it is," stuttered Zerny; his finger pointed at the cluster of buildings.

"Which one is Bonboo's?" asked Dod.

Zerny laughed. "The-they're all his. E-everything you can see from here to L-Lake Mauj is his, and the l-lake is his, too."

"And these fields of grain?" marveled Dod.

"A-all his."

"Then who are those people down there, the ones by the homes near that forest — who are they?"

"S-some family, but mostly f-friends — guests at T-Twistyard."

Zerny, noting Dod's ignorance, went on to explain that Bonboo's parents had been the wealthiest and highest ranking nobles among the tredder people. Their kingdom had been massive, accounting for a majority of the lands in many civilized communities. Out of kindness, they had set up a government where the people ruled, patterning it after the systems they had studied while visiting the Mauj.

Despite opposition from other ruling tredder lines, Bonboo's parents had given up most of their wealth, endowing the working class with opportunities. And consequently, had 'persuaded' the nobles to do likewise—Bonboo's parents had started a revolution. Humans, tredders, drats, bobwits, and the like, had all joined in seeking a unified freedom.

Zerny continued, adding that things were very different because of them and that the stable government and lack of oppression was largely due to their efforts.

"W-what Bonboo now has," concluded Zerny, "is l-less than a speck compared to w-what he could have had as their o-only child. He c-continues their legacy of k-k-kindness by doing good things with his stewardship."

Dod turned around and looked through a small window into the carriage where Bonboo slept. *What a heritage*, he thought.

The calm moment of respect didn't last long, though. As the carriage lunged down the steepest part of the journey, something went BUMP!

A SECRET WORD

Zerny yelled to the horses as he pulled back on the reins, attempting to slow the carriage. "Whoa Dodger! Hold them! We're sliding! You've got to steady the bunch! Come on boy, whoa!"

Something had made a loud bump. It wasn't the kind of bump you hear from regular travel. It was more like the kind of bump you hear when your wagon is having complications; and obviously Zerny knew this was the case, for he wrinkled his brow.

Dod watched in disbelief. Zerny commanded the animals with unusual eloquence. It was amazing. He had stuttered through a lengthy tale, but now that he bellowed at the horses, his speech flowed clearly.

"Can I help?" shouted Dod. He began to fear the worst and wanted to do something; however, as he spoke, the wagon veered toward the edge of the road and made such a loud moaning sound that Dod's voice was lost beneath the noise.

"What?" barked Zerny, turning to look at Dod with a flash of confidence in his eyes.

"I said," Dod began, yet he couldn't finish the sentence before fear took his tongue and tied it up. He noticed the front wheel on his side was beginning to slide off the road and a steep slope waited to swallow the wagon.

Dod leaned away from the cliff, as if his shift in weight would make a difference. His eyes darted from Zerny to the seven-horse team and then down to the riggings—that's where the problem was. They had completely broken on one side, damaging their ability to steer.

It was dreadful. Dod had seen the attack in his mind. The man with the scar on his hand had sabotaged their wagon! And just when Dod thought it couldn't possibly get worse, Zerny gave him a smile as he jumped from the ride. Still clasping both reins, he landed squarely on one of the chargers.

Before Dod had time to question his motive, Zerny calmly unlatched a metal hitch, which connected the remaining riggings, and rode off with the team. He made a tight left into the gently, upward sloping hillside, all the while appearing perfectly in control of the beasts.

"How could he desert us to save the horses?" Dod muttered loudly to himself; and then the answer came. His mind replayed the last eight seconds nearly a dozen times in a tenth of one. Zerny had unlatched the hitch while wearing white gloves! His hands weren't visible. A horrid scar could easily be concealed by the gloves—and if he were the enemy, of course he would flee!

It was only then that Dod remembered Zerny had said Bonboo trusted him enough to entitle him as Head Keeper of The Lands. If Bonboo were gone, what role would he play? What agreements had they made?

Questions flooded Dod's mind, but were quickly cut short

when the wagon took a plunge for the worse. Two wheels now rolled precariously off the road at the edge of an abrupt decline—and because it was the steepest part of the journey, there was little likelihood that the wagon would naturally slow down. Something had to be done in a hurry or they all faced certain destruction.

"What in the blazing gooseberries are the two of you doing up there," hollered Boot, who still lounged across four seats, yet couldn't nap any longer.

Bonboo continued to sleep. He stirred and then went back to snoring quietly. His body would have jolted more if it weren't for a pile of old blankets that steadied him. He had brought a gift of new blankets to the hospital, and in return, the nursing staff had insisted he take the old rags home to aid in washing horses.

"There aren't two of us," Dod anxiously yelled back to Boot. "Zerny just rode off with the horses. We're doomed!"

Boot rolled his eyes. From his vantage point, Dod blocked the only window to the front, so it seemed likely that Dod was only pulling his leg.

"No, I'm serious," Dod insisted, his white knuckles clinging to a handrail. "We're heading off a cliff!"

The ride continued to get rougher as the carriage picked up speed, particularly on the side where both wheels had long since left the road for rockier fringes.

"Sure," said Boot playfully, "and I'm the Chief Noble Tredder of Green."

"Just look out your window!" Dod begged.

"What, and have you get the better of me? I love adventure as much as the next guy. If you can handle the ride, trust me, Dod, I'm just fine with it. Besides, if you race much more, you may fall off the front and crack your skull. My worst in here would be a mouthful of pillow stuffing. These seats really do make a great place to nap. You should have stuck around."

"You think I'm kidding?" shouted Dod desperately. He was completely exasperated. It seemed impossible to get Boot's serious attention. Fortunately, he didn't have to.

"What's going on?" mumbled Bonboo. One of Boot's large bounces had dislodged Bonboo's pile of ragged blankets, affecting his stability; Boot was having such fun, shaking around, that he actually punctuated each jolt with his own special hop.

"Oh, it's nothing," said Boot calmly. "Dod and Zerny are just having a little fun with us."

"Fun!" exclaimed Dod; his eyes were as big as dinner plates with fear. "Look out your window!"

Bonboo steadied himself on his right arm and rose up high enough to peek out the side porthole.

"Watch out for the cliff!" ordered Bonboo, instantly recognizing how dire their circumstance was.

"I know!" yelled Dod, beyond frazzled. "That's what I've been telling Boot! What should we do now? Zerny's run off with the horses and this carriage is hopelessly out of control. The road only gets steeper from here."

Dod slid over, providing Boot and Bonboo with a better view out the front; a teamless void, where the steeds had been, validated his claims.

"We need to jump!" urged Bonboo, crawling his way to the back of the carriage. "There's no time to waste!"

Suddenly, Boot didn't look so manly and confident. As a matter of fact, for a split second, Dod was amused and refreshed to see Boot's girlish look of distress. It wasn't that Dod didn't like

Boot; he thought Boot was a fine friend, and he admired him and enjoyed his company; but somehow, watching Boot cringe under the heat of worry made Dod feel unusually satisfied—like he was vindicated for all of the times he had been passed up to play ball by Boot-looking pals, or for all of the times a girl had swooned over Boot's type, while staying *casual friends* with Cole.

"Okay then," agreed Dod, taking a deep breath for courage. He glanced at the rocky terrain and hoped for a miraculous landing.

"What?" winced Boot, his face curled up in fear. The wagon was going fast enough that they would all be seriously injured from jumping. It was ironic that their journey from the hospital looked like it would soon become a one way ticket back—or even worse!

"Let's see you jump first," Boot suggested to Bonboo. He grabbed at the carriage door handle and gave it a firm twist. "It's locked! The door's locked! We're stuck in here!" Boot's eyes filled with terror.

The twelve-seater had been refurbished from an old jail carriage, used to transport criminals. It was as safe as they come, unless you wanted to break out. The windows were purposely small. There was no way Bonboo would fit out of them—even if the thick panes could be shattered—let alone Boot's massive body. And though the front window had no pane, it was even smaller, less than half the size of the others.

Boot gave the door a few firm kicks and found that it was solid. Tricking their way out didn't seem likely, considering the door was made with a metal casing, a thick oak center, and a cast-iron loop lock on the outside. Without a key, it wouldn't budge.

Bonboo attempted the door for a moment and then came to the same conclusion.

"You're right. It's hopeless."

BUMP!

A large rock shook the wagon hard enough to lift both rear wheels off the ground. It was obvious the ride would soon come to an end. Only a short distance separated them from a sheer cliff; it was a two hundred-foot drop lined with jagged rocks at the base. And worse still, just up the road was a sharp turn to the left. There was no way to steer the wagon from launching off the edge once it reached the bend.

"Save yourself!" called Bonboo to Dod in an unusually stern sort of voice. "You can't do anything to help us now. JUMP! Live to tell what happened. Stop whoever did this. Ask Dilly and Higga for 'the map.' Tell them HOPPAS. Promise me you'll search it out, Dod! Promise me!"

Bonboo's words caught Dod off guard. He was asking for a final favor in anticipation of his passing. Dod didn't know how to respond and wasn't ready to give up on the possibility that the two captives could be delivered.

"We'll figure something out, Bonboo, don't worry," said Dod, racking his mind. But nothing came.

"PROMISE ME, DOD! HOPPAS!" insisted Bonboo urgently. He spoke with such conviction that the only course of action was to agree.

"I promise," stammered Dod uncomfortably. "I'll do it."

Boot stared in horror. The situation was past what he could believe. His face revealed fear, and hidden somewhere in the fear was a lot of regret.

Bonboo, on the other hand, beamed with peace and satisfaction, knowing his life had been spent doing good.

Immediately, memories burst into Dod's mind, pointing toward hope. It was like a two-hour movie had been condensed into two seconds, and the conclusion of the film was just the inspiration he needed.

In his mind he recalled an exodus of sorts. Numbers of loaded wagons took their place in line. One family joined the throng with a carriage full of gear. Five of their six kids walked to the side, while one lay painfully stuffed in the far rear with a broken leg.

Eventually, a giant hill sprawled downward. All of the wagons followed like train cars, systematically increasing their speed to fit perfectly in line on the road. Walkers were left behind as the procession sped up, heeding gravity which hastened their descent. Suddenly, one cart jammed, causing the following travelers to collide. From the middle to the end, horses were injured as they trotted into other carts and two wagons had the misfortune of rolling. It was a mess, and one twelve-year-old boy was to blame!

"That's it," declared Dod with confidence. "Quick, hand me the old rags!"

Boot stared from the back corner of the wagon and yelled, "Have you lost your freshy-mind?" His hands once again began yanking fruitlessly on the locked door.

Bonboo, however, didn't waste any precious time. He complied with the strange request by moving all of the old blankets with remarkable speed.

Dod took two long rags and fed them simultaneously into the spokes on the front wheels. The wagon jolted wildly, knocking Dod forward. His feet left the buckboard and he took flight, until a quick hand grabbed him by the pants and pulled him back.

"I've got you, son," said Bonboo. "Whatever you're doing is working! Do it again!"

Friction from the blankets rubbing against the axle and the sides of the wagon formed a weak braking mechanism.

Frantically Dod lowered all of the rags into the spokes. The cart slowed down with every rotation of the wheels, but sadly, it wasn't enough: The weight of the wagon would keep it running, albeit sluggishly, right off the cliff at the bend.

Dod stomped his foot in frustration. He had come too close to just let his friends die.

The bottom of the buckboard jiggled. One of the thick, oak slats was completely free, having been dislodged by the bumpy ride.

With not a moment to spare, Dod took his board and jumped ship. He knew the consequences of jamming something in the spokes of a moving wheel thanks to Greg Sye, who in third grade had knocked out three of Cole's teeth by ambushing his bike with a broomstick.

"Brace yourself!" yelled Dod. He plunged the board into the left front wheel. It wasn't as easy as he had thought. The blankets were entirely shrouding the spokes, making it less like accosting a bicycle with a broomstick and more like stabbing an elephant with a blunt spear. He tried again and again as he jogged to the side of the wagon. It wasn't working—it seemed impossible. But finally, one jab went all the way through!

With a loud groaning noise, the wagon's back wheels took to flight and the cart made a half flip, landing on its roof. It

continued to skid until it came to a complete stop with the rear
five feet of the twelve-seater hanging off the cliff's edge.

"That was a close one," gasped Dod breathlessly. He hurried
to the front window slit and peered in. Bonboo and Boot were
heaped against the back wall of the cart.

"Oh," moaned Boot loudly. "Am I dead?"

"I don't think so," winced Bonboo, "or you would be lighter,
wouldn't you?"

Boot had come to rest on top of Bonboo when the wagon
stopped moving. Both were bruised and sore, yet thankfully,
neither had broken any bones.

"How did you think of that?" asked Boot as soon as he
revived.

Dod smiled triumphantly and began to explain. He told
about the wagon train and the young boy and finally concluded by
saying, "If a bored twelve-year-old can accidentally stop a caravan
by dipping the end of a rope into spokes, I figured the blankets
could stop this cart."

For a few moments, the tables had turned and Boot was
listening to Dod's adventurous tale; and it wasn't long before
Boot wasn't the only one listening.

Within a matter of minutes, a dozen strong boys gathered
around the wagon. They had seen Bonboo's outfit coming home
and had watched the whole ordeal from fields below and from
the road as they raced to his aid.

Dod felt comforted knowing that despite having an enemy
with a scarred hand who wished them dead, many people did
in fact like them. It was also nice to have other people show up
quickly—a group that didn't include Zerny.

"Can you help us get out?" asked Boot of his friends.

"Well sure," responded one tredder, who stepped from the crowd and bent down to peek into the front window. He appeared to be the same age as Boot, or maybe slightly younger. The resemblance between the two showed they were likely brothers.

"I'd love to help you. Just give me the key and I'll have you out in a flippy."

"Buck!" Boot exclaimed. "If I had the key, wouldn't I be out right now? Dod managed to stop this carriage at full press with no horses; don't you think he could have negotiated a simple lock?"

Buck laughed and laughed. "It's good to see you haven't cracked your head wide open, brother. Mom would have blamed me for your death—and worse still—she'd have pulled me straight out of the Coosings."

Dod heard the word Coosings, and this time he remembered. They were a group of the most elite, young, talented potentials, mostly tredders, who were practicing at Twistyard—much like a training camp. A group of the best youth from Green, Raul, and Soosh all stayed with Bonboo, first as Pots, and then if they were good enough, they were given a chance to represent their realms as Greenlings, Raulings or Sooshlings. The top fifteen individuals from each realm were then selected to join the Coosings.

The goal of everyone training at Twistyard was to support the peace and uphold the democracy Bonboo's parents had started, focusing on diplomacy and defense. The name Coosing had been given by Bonboo when he established Twistyard, shortly after the defeat of Doss. He had named them Coosings, because of the root word "coos," which literally meant "true friend;" and the Coosings were just that: a group of true friends—sort of!

Buck surveyed the mess and asked who had the key. When Dod wasn't sure, Buck paced back and forth to the side of the cart.

"Whose crazy idea was it, anyway?" he said, peering at Boot through a side window. "Locking this thing up is a death trap!" His voice clearly indicated he was done being funny and wanted to know who had almost caused the death of his brother.

Bonboo gently shifted the conversation and said that Zerny must have gotten injured while trying to redirect the horses. Dod wasn't the only one who had noticed Zerny's convenient absence; he hadn't come down the road to see the treacherous outcome. Yet Bonboo's conclusion about Zerny was different than Dod's.

A handful of boys quickly agreed to ride up in search of Zerny and the key. Dod thought about Bonboo's concern for Zerny. It irritated him to think that Bonboo didn't see the signs. It made things awkward. Dod wanted to speak openly with Bonboo about his suspicions, but circumstances were too tricky to start accusing a long-time friend of being a traitor.

At that moment, Dod resolved to keep a close eye on Zerny while holding back his thoughts, at least until he had real proof!

In the end, it took nearly an hour to obtain the key from Zerny, and even then, Zerny didn't bring it himself; he was busy 'taking the long way home to try to calm the horses down.'

Time waiting was spent telling and retelling the event that had just occurred. All of them seemed to have different angles of the tale, though they only shared their accounts after forcing Dod to retell his a dozen times. He, however, preferred Boot's version over any of the others.

Boot openly divulged his own doubts and weaknesses, while recounting a wonderful rendition of the truth about Dod's accomplishments. It was ennobling of Boot. Dod saw that there was more to him than the guy that had bragged the afternoon away in the cart. He wasn't unbearably cocky after all; or even if he was, it was nice to see that he was capable of celebrating other people's achievements as well.

Once the lock was opened, it was a matter of only a few short minutes by horseback to the house. Bonboo took off first, riding double with Dilly, who had come inquiring after his whereabouts. She arrived at the click of the key and was gone in a flash, spouting something about a party.

Bonboo's absence from the group changed the conversation quickly. The boys had spoken carefully in his presence, to show respect, yet in a moment, they turned to teasing and jabbing as they worked together to tip the wagon over and hitch it to a new team. There was, evidently, some division in the group of 'true friends'—and they were mostly Coosings.

When their task was completed, Dod gratefully accepted to ride double with a younger tredder named Jim.

Everyone ribbed Jim about a myriad of things; he had blonde hair that looked almost white, while most male tredders, younger than two hundred, had dark brown or black hair; and he was short, only five-foot-six, nevertheless, that was likely due to his young age of twenty-eight, though he looked like a twelve-year-old human; and he was an overall nice guy, perfect to pick on; but above all else, they especially teased him about his name.

One tredder, Sawb, wouldn't stop torturing him. He stood out in the group as a real tormentor, towering above the other boys at six-foot-four. He looked eighteen. His slick-black hair was well groomed and his clothes indicated that he had money. Dod knew well Sawb's type from his own experiences at school. Every group has at least one or two of them, the kind of people that can't seem to say anything nice about others; and surprisingly, they often have a following.

"Jim?" Sawb called out. "How can a dog like you ride with Dod? Go fetch it, Jimmy-dog. Run and play. Go on, boy, be a nice doggie. Run along, before I beat you with a stick. I'll be the one to give Dod a ride home."

Many of the guys laughed while Jim hung his head down in embarrassment. Dod didn't think it was funny, even if the name Jim had been regularly used in their society to mean a bad pet.

"I'm just fine riding with Jim," snapped Dod confidently. He held back his anger, as usual. For a split second he thought of his brother Josh. Dod knew Josh would deck Sawb hard if he were present.

"Jim. Jim. Jim. Jim." Sawb said, shaking his head back and forth. "Don't make Dod choose between me and you. He doesn't know your history, that you're from Soosh—some tribal lot. It's no wonder you lost so many Sooshlings to stupidity. Bad leadership! Now run along, dog. Even your mother called you a dog with your name, Jim."

"My mom thought it was a perfectly fine name—" Jim started to explain, however, before he could finish, he was rudely interrupted by more taunting from Sawb.

"My mommy calls me Jimmy. I'm her—"

"Knock it off!" barked Dod, unusually defiant. "I knew a Jim once, and he was perfectly decent. Besides, in one language I speak, Sawb is what little babies do when they cry. Is that what you do—cry like a baby?"

Dod knew they were fighting words, but who was going to pick a fight with him after he had just saved the wagon moments before? He felt like a hero, if only for a day, and considered it his duty to stick up for the downtrodden while on top.

"You may think you're funny," snarled Sawb, "but I don't think—"

"That's your problem," blurted Dod, snipping in. "You can't think! It takes a brain to think!"

It wasn't in Dod's nature to be rude, yet this was a refreshing chance to say a few things he had held back for years, and he wanted to help Jim.

Sawb gave him a crusty look and rode off on his horse, followed by seven other formidable looking tredders.

"I imagine you've made a friend," said Buck, smiling gloatingly.

"Sawb's a drip of sweat," reassured Boot warmly. "Don't worry about him. He's way too booshy for his own good. He thinks he's king here in Green; and it won't be long before we'll ship him and his kind back to Raul where they came from. Evidently, all the training in the world can't encourage courtesy among the likes of *them*—no offense to Bonboo and his hopes for the spread of tredder ideals. They're noble, but impossible."

Dod felt bad about offending someone, however, it did make him Jim's instant, lifelong pal.

"Race you back," yelled Buck to Dod and Jim. He had just helped his brother up, making it a fair two-per-horse challenge.

Jim and Dod rode at a gallop. They didn't stand a chance of beating Buck and Boot, who seemed to practically fly. Yet it mattered little; at least it wasn't another carriage ride! Dod had already set his mind to walk the distance if he had to rather than put himself into another possible death trap—at least for the day.

"So—what inspired your mother to name you Jim?" asked

Dod, tasting dust in his mouth. "It's actually a popular name in my hometown."

Jim gave Dod a very surprised look. Nobody came from a place where Jim was a common name for people.

"My mom named me after a great man that lived among the Mauj. I've heard legends about him, how he was good and smart—the real hero type."

Dod continued to listen, half-interested, as they rode to Twistyard. It was hard for him to think of anything but the near-fatal event that had just transpired.

At the 'house' there were plenty of distractions. Over one thousand tredders were gathering to feast in a large banquet hall, celebrating Bonboo's safe return. Most of them appeared to be teenagers, twelve to eighteen—or so they looked—and a few were adults. Dod hadn't realized that Bonboo had been gone for months doing important business and that his arrival was expected.

Boot approached Dod with a smirk on his face and asked, "Do you have a minute?" The crowd was loud enough that he had to yell in order to communicate across a short distance of ten feet.

"Sure," responded Dod with a nod.

The two hurried out of the Great Hall, leaving Jim and the others with the crowd. Boot led Dod to a side room where they could talk.

"I just wanted to say thank you again for saving my life," said Boot, tipping his head to one side and looking down at the floor. He continued, haltingly, "I mean…if I would have been in your shoes, with Bonboo telling me to jump and save myself…I probably would have jumped."

Boot looked squarely at Dod and added quickly, "That's not to say I'm a wippling, or anything; it's just what anyone would have done…anyone but you. You're a real friend."

Dod was speechless. The look in Boot's eyes made everything he said twice as nice. It was the kind of look Josh or Alex might have given him when saying thank you, not the kind a cool guy at school would ever give.

Before going back to rejoin the party, Boot patted Dod on the shoulder and said, "Welcome to the Coosings. I've searched for about three years now, since I was commissioned by Bonboo to choose another member, and I choose you."

Boot reached in the side pocket of his pants and pulled out a ring. It matched the one he wore on his own hand.

"Be it known to all, by this ring, that you are officially a member of the Coosings, and I am your friend—your true friend!"

Just hearing the words caused goosebumps all over Dod's arms. He couldn't think of what to say that would adequately express his gratitude; so instead he choked out, "Thank you."

It was overwhelming. As Dod slipped the ring onto his finger, he could tell from that moment it was the beginning of his first experience with something he had never had before: a best friend.

LEARNING THE ROPES

"There he is."

"Which one?"

"He's right there, next to Boot, coming up the hall."

Dod heard a crowd of mostly boys, talking by the entrance to the kitchen. Few of them looked older than fourteen, and all of them wore matching uniforms that indicated they would be serving at the feast. They kept pointing their fingers and making quite a fuss over something.

"Did you really flip the twelve-seater?" asked one boy, his eyes sizing Dod up as he approached.

"Well I—" Dod started to reply before being interrupted.

"How did you do it without horses? That thing's as massive as the hull of a forty-man jeck ship. You can't stop it without powers or something."

Dod couldn't keep track of the questions, for they poured in at him from the bustling crowd like rain.

"Are you Zippod in disguise?" inquired a persistent boy, who tugged at Dod's shirt until he was noticed. He had unusually large ears, and his military-short haircut made them look even bigger.

"That's make-believe kid stuff, Juck!" jabbed a heavier-set lad, whose face was speckled with freckles. "Everybody knows there's no such person as Zippod in real life. Dod must've done some tricky moves, like using a high tech weapon, right?" He turned and looked for a nod, adding, "Is that how you did it?"

Before Dod could say 'no,' a girl, who appeared to be the youngest in the group, raised her voice and shoved two boys aside. "Are you hurt, Dod?" she asked. Her bright-blue eyes and curly hair reminded Dod of early pictures of his mother, when she was eleven or twelve.

"Awe, c'mon guys, give Dod some space," insisted a boy, who seemed to be the leader of the younger bunch. He cleared the way with his arms, pushing people back like a rescuing bodyguard. His name was Toos. He looked about fourteen, with ruddy cheeks, light-brown eyes, and auburn hair that was parted down the center and slicked to his head.

"No offense, Donshi," he continued, glancing at the young girl before centering back on Dod. "We all hope you're not hurt; but what *I* want to know is what Sawb's face looked like—you know, when you set him straight. Tell us about that."

The little mob stirred like reporters, asking Dod more and more questions. It was obvious they had already heard second or third-hand accounts of the day's adventures and had come up with a few conclusions of their own.

"Even you wouldn't stand up straight to Sawb, would you Boot?" asked Toos, grinning ear to ear as he turned toward Boot, who was towering behind Dod. Toos's comment was less of a question and more of a tease.

"You know I would in the twitch of a cow's tail," protested Boot, grabbing the boy around the neck and playfully rubbing one knuckle up and down his spine. "You better watch what you're saying around me, Toos, or you won't be staying in my bunks anymore. And that goes for the lot of you."

Boot started to chuckle as he added a few words in his best stern voice.

"—and you know Buck's been begging to unload you for some time—asked Bonboo to swap you for a whole new group of Greenlings from the Pots—four hundred from Green alone to choose from, and I'm sure we could dip into the other six hundred from Raul and Soosh. I keep telling Buck we've gotta work with you, but he's ready to trade you in, even if it means a swap with Sawb's lot of fellow Raulings."

The mention of Sawb drew boos from the group, causing enough commotion to summon four women and two men from the kitchen to see what the ruckus was about.

"Why are you all standing about?" asked one lady. "The party is nearly ready to start and I haven't seen you so much as darken the door to get moving on drinks. We have courses to serve; and trust me, kids, the juice won't pour itself."

"Miss Mercy, that's what I was just telling these Greenlings," fibbed Boot with a smile.

"You can talk later when the food's gone," ordered Boot authoritatively to his younger cohorts, furrowing his brow for emphasis. "Get on with it. Don't slack when Mercy has a banquet to serve. I promised her the finest help, and that's exactly what I expect you to give her. If I hear you've done half-a-toe from your best, you'll be scrubbing the benjis for a week—and not just ours!"

Dod noticed Boot slid in a wink at Donshi, who at first looked concerned about the situation, yet smiled calmly when she saw the sign.

"Now Boot," interjected Mercy, "don't count on me believing you've gone tough overnight. I know you're as soft as fresh butter in the sun. You can't fool me."

"I wouldn't dream of it, Mercy."

The crowd of youth dispersed into the kitchen and returned quickly, rolling large round barrels of juice, labeled up the side: apple juice, peach juice, pear juice, plum juice, drudberry juice, grape juice, sweet-potato juice, orange juice, kwam juice and dorisil juice.

Mercy gave a few quick commands to the girls, and then yelled at the boys, before they all disappeared through a large doorway into the banquet hall.

"That's more like it," she said. "And who might this be?"

"His name's Dod," Boot quickly answered. "He was injured while raiding a ship to recover High Gate's stolen triblot from Dreaderious. We just picked him up from Lower Janice this afternoon. Your friend Higga was helping him recover."

"Oh, yes, is he the one that rode with Bonboo?"

"Well, actually, we both rode with Bonboo, but he—"

"Yes, he saved the carriage!" exclaimed Mercy, squeezing in front of Boot to get a better view of Dod. She looked him up and down, approvingly, and continued, "You're quite a hero, son. I'm looking forward to you sticking around. I hope you will stay with us for a while, won't you?"

Dod nodded his head. He wasn't sure what to say to Mercy. She looked and acted very similar to a fifth-grade teacher Dod remembered.

Mercy's hair faded from brown curls on top to peppered gray on the lower sides and back, showing signs of her age—one hundred and fifty-three. As a tredder, she didn't look any older than a fifty-something-year-old human. She wore a white apron that stretched tight in the middle of her stomach, right where a homemade oval pocket hid the majority of a browning grease stain.

"My pies, Boot! Dilly didn't tell me he was a Coosing," she said, grabbing at Dod's hand. "How come I'm the last to hear about these kinds of things? I see he's sporting the ring. That's fantastic! We need another quick mind around here these days—tough times with the likes of Dreaderious and his kind lurking about. Seems he's got some soapy friends—looking clean, but slippery as the mess hall floor during a good scrub. It makes you wish for the days when Twistyard was protected by a triblot field. Of course, that's not saying I want to run up and join Commendus in High Gate, especially after what recently happened there; it's just too bad we don't have our own protection anymore."

"There you are!" said Dilly as she came bursting through the doorway from the Great Hall. Her eyes were fixed on Dod. "We can't get started 'til you come and take a bow for the crowd. Bonboo just asked for you. He'd like you on the platform. They're all chanting your name."

"Dod, Dod, Dod, Dod, Dod." The sound of the throng was spilling over into the hall, though the name wasn't easily recognizable until Dilly explained what the commotion was about.

"Well then, my boy," announced Mercy, grinning. "You had better be off. Don't keep them waiting. I'm expecting to get a full story of your heroic deeds, one twig at a time, and first-hand, mind you, before you'll see supper tomorrow. Now be off. Hurry."

Dilly grabbed Dod by the arm and hastily pulled him away from Boot and into the crowd.

"Step aside," she said. "We're coming through. Please move. Thank you. Here's Dod. Please step aside."

Dilly didn't realize she was practically dragging Dod until he tripped over someone's leg and landed face down. It was Sawb's.

"Consider yourself welcomed," grumbled Sawb, turning to a few chuckling associates standing close at his side. The look on his face exuded great pleasure.

"I SAID, STEP ASIDE!" shouted Dilly in Sawb's face, stomping one foot in defiance. "You obviously can hear about as well as you look. You should go back to Raul, Sawb. It takes more than a ring to be a real Coosing; it takes a lot of class—the kind you just don't have."

"Oh, like wobbly, here?"

Sawb's pals had a good laugh, and not just at what he had said; Dod's awkward movements to get up were enhanced by a swift poke in the rear. A younger Rauling had jabbed Dod with a stick, while hiding behind a wall of large Coosings from Sawb's group—they were intimidating, to say the least.

"Come on, Dod," said Dilly in a perfectly civil voice. "Let's leave these rats before something contagious rubs off or crawls out of their hair!"

One Raul Coosing broke rank momentarily to offer a quick apology to Dilly. He looked handsome, but younger than the others, lanky, and self-conscious. When he pushed his way through and stuck out his arm to help Dod up, Sawb shoved him to the floor and gave him a harsh reprimand.

"Tonnis! Your father is helpless to make much out of you, despite his own greatness. I'm sure it won't be long before he'll stop trying." Sawb's eyes gloated arrogantly. He glanced at his friends, who all seemed to applaud him.

"It must be horribly embarrassing for your family," he continued condescendingly, brushing one sleeve of his expensive, white silk shirt. He grinned wickedly as he picked flecks of lint off and rudely dropped them on Tonnis, signifying his disdain. "Either learn your place or we'll send you home like this loser." Sawb pointed at Dod and laughed.

Dod continued to struggle until Dilly helped him up. His legs hadn't fully recovered from three weeks of sleeping and the fall made them ache; but despite the humiliation, Dod smiled. His ridicule didn't seem nearly as bad when he noticed Toos depositing something nasty all over the mean boys' chairs, while their attention was preoccupied with teasing Dod. It felt like a team effort, and for once he was on a team that cared about him.

Dilly aided Dod up a few stairs and across the platform. Bonboo's voice echoed throughout the hall, "—And here he is." His frail arm gestured toward Dod as Dilly pushed him to the center.

"Thank you," said Dod as he faced Bonboo and bowed. He whispered it for Bonboo, not really sure what to say to the throng; however, to his surprise, the center position of the platform was rigged to carry the sound, so it boomed, "THANK YOU," to the whole room.

The crowd went wild. Screams and cheers roared from every corner of the Great Hall, as though Elvis had just entered the building. Dod was embarrassed. He stayed in the bowing position for a few moments. Finally, he snuck a peek sideways at the audience. Hundreds of tredders, and a sprinkling of humans, drats, and bobwits all stood, many of them waving their arms, in appreciation or acknowledgment. He wondered what exactly Bonboo had told them before he entered the room.

"You can stand up straight now," whispered Dilly from behind him. Her voice, fortunately, didn't carry as his had.

Dod and Dilly made their way back down into the gathering and were glad to be greeted by a mob of Green Coosings, led by Boot.

"You're the top, Dod," said Boot with a shiny-faced look.

Bonboo raised his cane and signaled for everyone to be quiet. The hall went silent.

"I wish I only had good news to tell," said Bonboo. His voice revealed serious concern. "Dreaderious has more followers than we had hoped. Many battles have been fought in Green, over the years, to stop Dreaderious and his father; nevertheless, despite decimating his army of poorlings, it appears he has obtained a hidden hold on others. Proper diplomacy at a time like this will do more good than many armies of soldiers—"

Buck leaned over and whispered in Dod's ear, "He looks pretty serious, doesn't he?"

Dod nodded in agreement.

"But I must admit," Buck whispered again, "he sure looks better up there than he would have looked at the bottom of Drop's Cliff. You brought him home—"

"Shhh!"

Dilly put her finger to her lips and let Buck and Dod know she intended to help enforce the silence Bonboo had asked for.

"—we've suspected for some time that people with money were secretly aiding Dreaderious," Bonboo continued. "They perpetuate hunger in distant lands and then hire the starving humans and drats and bobwits and tredders—all poorlings in his forces—yet with the most recent poisoning at High Gate, and other troubles including my wagon mishap today, there is added fear that dark men lurk close by, even—"

"That sounds like the works of The Dread," muttered Boot to Dod and Buck.

"Shhh!"

"—we have reason to believe," said Bonboo in a very ominous voice, "The Dread has returned!"

"I knew it!" proclaimed Boot, celebrating. He shouldered Dod and Buck and then gave Dilly an 'I told you so' kind of look with his daring eyes, taunting her.

"We've all been suspecting him since the poisoning," retorted Dilly, playfully annoyed. She wouldn't give Boot much credit for stating the obvious.

"Pappileehonogoso was clearly the key target of the High Gate disaster," she added, pushing her curls over her shoulder. "And who would want him dead more than The Dread? He's the only one who has ever wounded The Dread and lived to tell the tale."

"But I thought The Dread died from his injuries six years ago?" whispered Dilly's little sister Sawny. She looked similar to Dilly; however, she had light-brown hair, with natural highlights, sea-blue eyes, and a slightly younger, naive look to her face. The clothes she wore revealed she was one of the Greenlings given a charge for the night to help serve dinner. She had crept up behind the group and was standing close at Dilly's side.

"What?" said Dilly, turning to her sister. It was hard to hear anything with all of the chatter around the room. When Bonboo had mentioned The Dread, it provoked gasps and a chorus of small conversations.

The Dread was a villain of evil proportions; so many stories had been told of him, over the past sixty years, that it was difficult to believe they were all about one man—one evil follower of Doss—one who sought revenge against Bonboo's family and all levels of democracy.

The Dread had deeds which were shrouded by cloaks of blackness; and nobody ever lived to tell his true identity—even Pappileehonogoso never saw behind his mask—though others lived to speak of a mysterious man: sometimes hooded, sometimes hidden by the dark, sometimes disguised in daylight. He was a master of deception!

"Be aware that these are dangerous times," emphasized Bonboo cautiously. "If The Dread is really behind Dreaderious and his forces, we have worse troubles than the occasional battles that Pious is capable of fighting with his seasoned soldiers. Truly, there are worse troubles from money and policy problems, generated by a few critical acts, the sort The Dread is capable of, than all of the damage that could be inflicted by an open assailant like Dreaderious and his men. And if it is The Dread, Raul and Soosh are both in danger, too!"

Jim poked his head through the crowd and joined the conversation with Dod, Dilly, Buck, and Boot. "The Dread is our top enemy in Soosh," he said eagerly.

"And Doss?" interjected Dilly.

"Well, since Doss was destroyed, The Dread took over. He got the noble tredder families in a fight with each other—Plooms, Hoths, Pealts, Sansters, Dollicks, and also my lot, the Gricks. It was hard restoring democracy after that. He wiped out half of the educated population by getting them to fight against each other for ten years; and he didn't even have to raise an army. His well placed assassinations and bribes led to a decade of chaos before Humberrone stopped him. Of course, that was twenty-two years ago. They haven't seen him in Soosh since then."

The look on Jim's face matched the sobering atmosphere in the crowd. It wasn't much of a celebration feast, at least not after the announcement about The Dread.

Bonboo went on to reassure everyone that he wasn't trying to scare people, he just expected them to increase their abilities and be willing to help out when needed. At the conclusion of his comments, he declared that he had rejected Commendus's request to move Twistyard inside the protection of High Gate. That announcement was met with universal cheers and sighs of relief. Nobody wanted to leave Bonboo's *house*.

Later that evening, Dod was shown around by Boot, Dilly, and Buck, before being escorted to his new bunking quarters. The size of the main building was larger than any castle he could have imagined. Over fifteen hundred people could easily be seated in the banquet hall, and there were adjoining kitchens and accessory rooms to aid in food preparation and entertaining.

The front of the Great Hall opened up directly to a grand courtyard of lush grass, lined with trees; and beyond the trees there were barns, cottages, and other useful buildings encircling the complex, like a giant wall in a semi-circle formation, with Lake Mauj on the remaining side.

Within the house, there were dozens of large rooms used for study and practice by Bonboo's guests at Twistyard. The library alone was a twenty-three story, terraced room that held more books than most university collections. Off the main corridors, halls led to less commonly used areas; conference rooms, temporary boarding rooms, and bunks for the long-standing members at Twistyard.

"Here we are," said Boot dramatically. "You'll want to remember the two large swords hanging from the ceiling. It's a good prompt that this is your stop. If you try the hall just before this one, you're likely to get an embarrassing welcome from the all-girl extended bunking quarters of Pots. They've got nearly two hundred of them stashed next door.

"And I'm sure you've tried missing this door a time or two?" ribbed Dilly.

"Not me," insisted Boot, flipping his thumb in his brother's direction. "It's Buck that's had a tough time."

"You're always blaming everything on me!" claimed Buck, getting lightheartedly annoyed. "I haven't seen an inch beyond those doors."

"So—they blindfolded you, too?" answered Boot mischievously.

"I knew it! You boys are all alike pathetic!" exclaimed Dilly. "My great-grandpa would be embarrassed if he knew how you trifled with his rules of conduct, like they were a game to be played."

"As I was saying," declared Boot with one hand in the air. "Keep your eyes out for these brilliant swords. They're our symbol. If you go one door down, you'll need to answer to Sawb; and from the likes of your encounters, I'm assuming you'd rather steer clear of him."

"Goodnight," spouted Dilly as she stormed through the big doors below the swords and disappeared to the left.

"Quite a spunky spirit," remarked Buck.

"Oh, I think she's bossy enough to run the place, don't you?" said Boot, jabbing Dod in the ribs.

"Uh, yup," replied Dod; however, his mind was elsewhere. He couldn't take his eyes off the two swords that hung from the ceiling; their golden sparkle entranced him.

"—all fifty Greenlings, and now, fifteen Green Coosings, are bunking here," continued Boot. "Of course, the girls are to the left, where Dilly just went in. They have lakeside view rooms. The rest of us bunk down in those rooms." Boot's hands pointed back and forth, indicating as he spoke.

"But don't set your heart on ever seeing a glimpse of Lake Mauj from the girls' quarters," added Buck. "Their hall door is always locked!"

Buck and Boot walked through the entry as Boot continued describing their surroundings. He even had plenty to say about the strange painting of a purple flower, which hung on the wall near the entrance.

"What are you waiting for?" asked Buck when he noticed Dod was still lingering in the larger hallway. Boot stopped his monologue to turn and look.

"Who hung these swords?" questioned Dod. His eyes were fixed on them. There was something familiar, something he couldn't quite put his finger on.

"Uh, let's see. I think it was Bonboo," said Boot. "Yup, now I remember. It was definitely Bonboo. He hung them about thirteen years ago to remind us that we could increase our sword skills faster from believing in ourselves than we could from sparring hopelessly with Sawb and his lot. It's ironic that he hung them above our door instead of Raul's. They use them to torment us. Raulings are naturally good at swordplay, with Raul Coosings being the best! As a group, we haven't ever won in tournaments against them."

"That's not true!" said Dilly through the girls' door.

"She's always listening," exclaimed Buck, knitting his brow.

The door opened up and Dilly emerged. "Well, we aren't that good at swordplay, but Bonboo didn't hang the swords. He lectured us and then asked Pappileehonogoso to help us out. Remember? He's the one that set the swords—to rub it in the faces of those cocky dregs from Raul."

"Oh, I remember. You're right," said Boot.

"As always," groaned Buck hopelessly.

"Thank you. Goodnight again."

Dilly was gone as fast as she had appeared. The information didn't crack the mystery of the swords, so Dod was disappointed; though, he knew if he kept thinking about it, the answer would come.

"Let's go, Dod," said Boot, yawning. "It's getting late and you've had a long day."

"Wait!" shouted Dod.

"Shhh," insisted Buck, "Dilly will be back any minute to lecture us on nighttime voices if you yell like that again."

Dod complied by lowering his volume. "Does Zerny have a scar on his hand?" he eagerly asked. Unanswered questions clamored for attention in his mind.

"I don't think so," replied Boot.

"You wouldn't know with the black gloves he's always wearing," added Buck.

"Don't you mean white?" asked Dod.

"Nope, definitely black; and I don't even need Dilly to help me respond to that one."

"Obviously you do!" chimed Dilly through the door. "He was wearing white gloves today!" She fussed with the handle for a few seconds before swinging it open. "I know he was wearing white, not black. Now can we all go to bed?"

"We're hardly stopping you," grumbled Buck, who was slightly sore about being told he was wrong for the hundredth time in a row. "He always wears black—I'm sure he was wearing black today."

"Actually," Dod admitted hesitantly, "I saw him wearing white gloves, while driving the horses home from the hospital."

Dilly beamed a bright, hardly-tired smile and walked five steps across the hall to give Dod a light hug from the side.

"The boy speaks the truth," she said frankly.

"Why white gloves?" asked Boot. "I don't get it. His work is outdoors. He would soil right through a pair a day."

"Well, this afternoon," explained Dilly, "he spoiled his black pair on the way to the hospital. He asked me if I had a spare—it was while we were waiting for Dod to wake up. I didn't, of course, but the nurses were kind enough to find some for him to use."

"Did you happen to see whether or not he had a scar on his hand?" asked Dod eagerly.

"No! It wouldn't be proper for me to have him take his gloves off in my presence; and if he did, certainly I wouldn't look! His family works the land for mine. It would be a dishonor to both of us."

"Oh," said Dod, glancing down and noticing some dirt under one of his fingernails. "Is it wrong that I openly display my hands?"

Dilly, Boot, and Buck all laughed.

"You're funny, Dod," said Dilly. "I think I'm going to like having you around—so long as you support my side against *them*!" She pointed a condemning finger at Boot and Buck, yet it was obviously a playful gesture.

Boot and Buck showed Dod down a hall that was lined with rooms on both sides. Snores and quiet chatter filled the air. At the end of the hall, Buck unlocked their private quarters. Inside was a large, uncluttered room, about thirty feet by fifty feet, and it only had three beds!

"You'll be bunking in here with me and Buck," said Boot. "Some of the other guys may complain about you jumping rungs up the ladder to this, but I'll happily explain it to them with sticks on the court. Just let me know."

Boot quickly got ready for sleeping and made his way to bed. The room was larger than Dod would have expected, considering Twistyard had over one thousand short term guests as Pots and a combined two hundred resident guests as Raulings, Sooshlings, Greenlings, and Coosings; and that's without counting any of the instructors, aides, dignitaries or temporary guests.

"So, how did you get this nice pad?" asked Dod curiously.

"Seniority," said Buck. "Boot's been here longer than any of the other Coosings—even longer than Dilly—a full twenty-one years as a Coosing, nine as a Greenling, and two as a Pot."

"Wow, that's a long time. What about you, Buck?"

"I've been a Coosing for twelve, 'course Boot's my brother. He can set anyone straight in a fair match with sticks, and he's about the best at everything else, too—"

"See why I keep him around?" remarked Boot with a smile.

"Except, not when it comes to swordplay and Raulings—"

"Buck! You didn't need to throw that in."

"And flying on stuff, 'cause he doesn't prefer heights—"

"That's about enough, Buck!"

"And then there's Bollirse—"

"Buck!"

"He hasn't ever been on a winning team, and Twistyard has had twelve since he's been here—six straight, from Soosh, until they banned instructors from playing—and the last six, all in a row, from Raul. They've become unbeatable, though I guess it makes Twistyard look good."

Boot hit Buck with a pillow and that was the end of the conversation.

Dod's bed was against one wall with Boot and Buck's lining the opposite. At the front of the room, a large window climbed to fifteen feet in the middle from ten feet on the sides. It gave a perfect view of some grassy playing fields below.

By the light of an unusually large moon, Dod could see the white cliffs in the distance that had almost taken his life.

"Not today," he mumbled to himself, climbing into bed with his clothes and shoes on.

"Aren't you going to at least remove your shoes?" asked Buck with a chuckle.

Dod didn't even respond. He lay down and closed his eyes.

"He's awfully tired," remarked Boot to Buck as he got up and walked across the room to open up one of the sliding panes at the bottom of the large window.

A slight gust of air blew through the room, cooling things down. Everyone got comfortable and headed off to sleep; however, it was only for a few moments.

"That's it," said Dod, sitting up. The smell of the air reminded him of sleeping by the river's edge. "I know that knot back there." He pointed excitedly toward the door where the hall led to the location of the two hanging swords, above Green Hall's entrance. "That's Pap's triple-cinch-double-loop-knot! Nobody ties a knot like that but Pap."

"You're not kidding," grunted Boot, who was startled into partially waking up. "Pap's a hero."

"You know Pap?"

"Who doesn't? Around here, a lot of the training we've received over the past fifteen years has come from that old man. He's a legend."

"Yup," added Buck sleepily. "One of Bonboo's best friends."

"We'll, why didn't anyone tell me about Pap?"

"What do you mean?" said Boot. "We've mentioned him all night. Remember at the banquet, we said he's the only one who's ever bested The Dread? And then just barely we decided he's the one who hung the swords."

"I thought Dilly said some Pappilee-guy hung them at Bonboo's request."

"Yes, it would be Dilly that can actually pronounce his full name. The rest of us always called him Pap."

"Where is he?" asked Dod. Sleep had fled from his eyes completely, snubbed out by the excitement over Pap.

"Dod, can we talk about this tomorrow?" begged Boot.

"No! Please tell me where Pap is."

There was a long silence. Dod looked out the window at the landscape and couldn't believe Pap was out there, or had at least been there.

"Come on, Boot, tell me about Pap."

"I really think Dilly should be the one—because pickles are—you know how drats look that way—"

Boot was too far gone to ask, and Buck was making obnoxious snoring noises, so it was pointless addressing him; Dod had to wait.

"I guess I'll try in the morning," he said to himself. "Besides, maybe I'll wake up someplace else, like my own bed; and if not, I'll figure this whole thing out once and for all."

Dod continued to mumble to himself long into the night, long enough to still be tired when roosters started crowing. Regardless, sleep didn't hold him captive for long, or at least, not after he opened his eyes enough to see what was right in front of him!

THE TRUTH ABOUT PAP

"Wake up. I've got it."

Dod hardly heard what was said, but out of habit he responded, "Just give me a couple more minutes."

"No, wake up! I want to show you this. You were the one asking questions last night. Don't you want answers? Besides, it's not respectable to lie around all day like a lazy, house-fed cat. At least tell me if you know the person in this painting."

Dod suddenly recognized the voice. It wasn't his mother's or Aunt Hilda's as he had originally thought in his slumbering state: It was Dilly's! He was mortified. His cheeks flushed hot red.

"Oh, I was just pretending to be asleep—resting my eyes," said Dod awkwardly, trying his best to see what she was holding.

"Well obviously you got up earlier," agreed Dilly with a smile as she tapped one of his shoes. "Nobody sleeps with their shoes on. Boot told me about your questions and said I could find you here."

Dilly misread Dod's face of embarrassment and added, "You know I wouldn't come in unannounced without you first—uh, prepping up for the day."

"Sure...of course...right," responded Dod with a morning

voice. He blinked as casually as he could, attempting to get a goober out of one eye, while trying not to draw attention to the fact that he was still squinting. Eventually, the figure in front of him came into full focus. It was shocking!

"That's Pap," he exclaimed excitedly. "How did you get a recent painting of him? It even has his fishing scar—right there, above his eye—the one he got last year."

"I didn't," said Dilly, biting her lip playfully. "Pilfering isn't my thing. You can thank your two mostly-misguided roommates. I, personally, would have waited for you to admire it on the wall in the Great Hall."

"So—you know Pap, too?" asked Dod.

"Of course. We all know Pap. The real question is how could you have thought that we didn't?"

"Well he's my grandpa—"

"Your grandpa?"

Dod would have begun a decent explanation if it weren't for what happened next. A jolt of pictures and feelings entered his mind. They were strange and complicated—everything was dark and murky—and there were voices declaring bold death threats that could be heard echoing off stone flooring and walls—and then thick beams crashed down, spewing a heavy, suffocating dust—blackness, silence, and fear followed—and there was someone struggling, trying to dig out.

"If he was your grandpa," said Dilly, "then why are you asking where he is? Bonboo said his family came and got him—picked him up—you know, after High Gate."

Dod had a hard time paying attention to Dilly because of the terrifying images. They made his heart beat quickly, like he was encountering a sudden shock in the night, the surprise of an unknown hand reaching for his throat out of the darkness. He gasped and coughed momentarily, feeling as though dust was actually in the room, not just in his mind. The man with the scar on his hand had done something awful, or was going to, shortly.

"Are you all right?" asked Dilly, looking at him with a healthy measure of confusion. When he didn't respond, she gave him a knowing look and added, "Oh—I'm sorry. It must be hard to talk about."

"What?" sputtered Dod, clearing his throat.

"You know—the poisoning at High Gate. None of us has fully recovered after that tragedy. Especially Soosh Hall! I'm terribly sorry about what happened to Pap."

For once, Dod decided to start asking questions and stop pretending to know what everyone meant.

"No. I don't know. What took place at High Gate?"

The mention of something bad happening to Pap momentarily pushed the disaster from Dod's mind and helped him to regain composure.

"The poisoning," said Dilly carefully. "About three months ago—Pap was leading a party of ambassadors on a trip to Soosh—ten Coosings from Soosh, accompanied by twenty Sooshlings, and Miz, The Great Mayler."

"The great what?" asked Dod. He was trying to follow the story, making sure he understood everything.

"Miz was a wonderful mayler; he knew how to utilize every animal, and trust me, he knew them all. I enjoyed learning from him—well, most of the time; I suppose I could have done just fine without studying snakes and spiders."

"Okay," said Dod tentatively, "Miz was a teacher?"

"No," responded Dilly with a grin, shaking her head like

Dod wasn't getting it. "He was the type of tredder that would have fed you to a swarm of gizzlers for calling him a book man. Recently, he trained flutters and horses for Pious and the troops. Some of his accomplishments are legendary—he once used a venoos in saving tredder flocks in Raul. Who would have guessed that it would prefer eating wolves, dippets, and canses over sheep?"

Thoughts of a venoos made Dod shudder. Every detail about his near-fatal encounter with the poisonous spider was still very fresh, and Dilly's mention of the creature being used as a tool sounded too familiar.

"Are you sure Miz is dead?"

"Unfortunately, yes. The group was going to help resolve a dispute between tredders and drats. Pap had a great idea. He said he was confident it would lead to peace. I wish he would have explained it to us before leaving."

Dilly shook her head in frustration. "Bonboo just returned from Soosh. Unfortunately, things are still tense there. Maybe The Dread is behind that mess, too. After all, he is, most likely, the person who poisoned Pap and Miz on their way to fixing it."

"But Pap wasn't murdered," stammered Dod hesitantly, beginning to feel less confident.

"This Pap was," insisted Dilly, pointing at the painting. "All of them were—thirty two deaths from poisoning. It's still a mystery how The Dread got them to drink toxic grape juice—and right before going to sleep in a guarded castle. With High Gate's triblot barrier, the enemy couldn't have entered or escaped without being recognized, so he must be a master of disguise."

Dod looked earnestly at Dilly and said, "Pap died in his sleep at home."

"Is that what they told you?"

"Who?"

"Well, whoever misinformed you, because this Pap died with the rest of them, while spending the night at Commendus's palace. Bonboo personally helped escort the dead Coosings and Sooshlings through the door at High Gate to Raul and then on to Soosh, where they were taken and buried by their families."

"But what about Pap and Miz? Who took them?"

"My grandpa said Pap was taken by his family, directly from High Gate, and Zerny escorted Miz to his kids in Lower Janice."

"Let's see," said Dod, trying to put the puzzle together. "Did Bonboo ask Zerny to accompany him to High Gate, after he got word of the poisoning, or did Zerny volunteer?"

"Neither. Zerny was already there—well, he wasn't in the palace; however, he was staying at High Gate with some friends. He and his son had transported the group that day and hadn't yet returned home."

"I could have guessed!" blurted Dod angrily. He jumped out of bed and began pacing the floor. "I think Zerny is the man with the scar!"

"What?"

"Zerny is The Dread, the man with the scar, the man who sabotaged Bonboo's wagon, the man who poisoned the group. He's the one, I'm sure of it!"

"Don't be ridiculous," said Dilly. "He helped bury Miz because they were the best of friends. Miz taught Zerny most of what he knows about animals; and have you seen how well Zerny can work a horse? He's remarkable. You can thank Miz for that."

"I've seen enough," snorted Dod, thinking about how calm

Zerny was when he rode off leaving the wagon in trouble. "He's guilty!"

"I'll admit, Zerny's been acting strange lately," said Dilly squarely. "But I think it's because he's in shock. He can't believe that Miz and Pap are no longer alive. As a matter of fact, Zerny's son, Jibb, hasn't even returned from Lower Janice. The deaths really shook him up, too. He's been staying with Miz's sons, keeping an eye on them."

"Zerny's son is in Lower Janice?"

"Yes—why?"

"It all fits. They're working together. I almost died by the fangs of a venoos in Lower Janice, where Jibb was conveniently lodging with the family of an expert mayler. Coincidence? I think not! And if Zerny and Jibb are so innocent, then why did they spend the night at High Gate? They could have easily made it back here."

"Dod, you're way too tense," said Dilly. "Have you ever tried to get a triblot barrier shut down at an unscheduled time? You're talking about imposing upon hundreds of soldiers to man their stations and guard the paths while lowering the protective field. Anyone less than Bonboo or Commendus couldn't do it."

Dilly shifted her weight and looked down at the floor. "Besides, Zerny has been friends with my family for nearly forever, and his son, Jibb, was a head Greenling, doing well before his injury. He's gone through a lot to prove his loyalty. If it were up to me, I would have made him a Coosing, regardless of the fact that he's an ornery drat. I don't blame him for being bitter. He fought The Dread's men with Pap six years ago and was injured the same night that Pap bested The Dread. Since then, Pone, Voo and Sham have all passed him up to become

Green Coosings—and now, you too. Poor Jibb; he's left to care for the land and horses with his dad."

"Oh," said Dod somberly. He thought for a few seconds and then started on another angle. "Well, what if Miz is really still alive. Possibly he poisoned the others and faked his own death—"

"Not a chance, Dod. The Dread is someone out there. He's devious and evil and a genius at deceiving, but he's *NOT* one of us. Don't you think Bonboo, or Pap, or Miz, or Sirlonk, or Strat, or Youk, or any of the other Greats—*or any of the Coosings*—would have figured it out by now if he were among us? And if it were Zerny, Sawb and his lot of Raulings would have accused him a long time ago. And that's saying nothing of Sawb's uncle Sirlonk. He routinely takes heartless jabs at Zerny and Jibb, so he definitely would have insisted on a full-scale investigation if there were the slightest grounds for suspecting them; of course, I guess Sirlonk jabs at everyone. He's a typical, booshy tredder from Raul."

"Maybe."

Dod still wasn't convinced, and the look on his face showed his doubts.

"I'll give you credit for thinking," said Dilly. She smiled at Dod sympathetically. "I'm sorry about Pap. I can only imagine what he must have meant to you as your grandfather. We'll eventually catch whoever did this…I promise."

Before Dod could ask any more questions, Boot came storming through the door.

"Let it go, Buck," hollered Boot as he whizzed behind Dod and used him as a human shield.

Buck followed close behind Boot with brown goo all over his hands, shirt, and face.

"Let it go? I think you'd be disappointed if I didn't share some with you."

Buck did his best to reach around Dod; his arms waved back and forth in an attempt to wipe the goo on Boot. The smell was disgusting.

"I guess you shouldn't have done it," taunted Boot.

"Me? I didn't do it. You did it! I was only watching—of course you can smell I observed from a poor angle. I knew a giant Zelda Goat wouldn't change colors, even if you fed it warsing powder and pulled its tail. Remember? I was the one that told you it wouldn't work."

Boot laughed and laughed until tears ran down his face. Dod had watery eyes, too, but they were caused by his close proximity to the nasty fumes from the goat waste. Buck had been tricked into standing in a bad location, while Boot drugged the goat into diabolical indigestion.

"I'll get you!" Buck snapped, vigorously trying to dart around Dod; unfortunately for Buck, Boot's good luck stayed strong: Buck slipped on a pile of clothes and proceeded to join them on the floor.

"Now look what you've done," declared Boot sarcastically, pointing with a condemning finger. "You've soiled our clean clothes."

"You keep your clean ones on the floor?" questioned Dilly with disgust. She didn't wait for anyone to respond. "I shouldn't need to ask by now. Come along, Dod, let's go get some breakfast before this smell chases my appetite away. Mercy will be closing things up soon."

She held the painting in one hand and grabbed Dod's shirt with the other.

"Can't we keep it in here?" asked Boot, not wanting to see the picture of Pap leave the room. "There's a perfect spot, right there on the wall."

Dilly looked shocked that Boot would even ask. She almost spouted a list of reasons why it had to go back where it came from, though before she could say anything, she noticed Dod's hopeful look.

"I guess," she said with reservation. "He is Dod's grandpa. Besides, it's not like *I* had anything to do with *you* taking it." Dilly set the painting on Dod's bed and then led him toward the Great Hall for breakfast.

Dod followed, partly listening to Dilly's commentary on the history of Twistyard, while also thinking about the strange images he had dismissed. The only portion of the tour that drew his full attention was the mammoth sized display of ribbons and medals and awards that littered the walls around Raul Hall. It was impressive.

Dilly paused for a brief moment in front of the spectacle and let Dod glance around; however, when she saw Dod's look of admiration, she quickly explained that Raul Coosings and Raulings were not as good as they thought and shamefully superficial, flaunting their 'trinkets' to compensate for their lack of real ability.

Regardless of what Dilly said and the quick arm she used to hurry Dod down the hall to more meaningful locations, it couldn't hide the truth: Bonboo's guests from Raul were very talented, even if they were snobbish.

Dilly enjoyed pointing out all sorts of things as they traveled a series of corridors, and she took great pride in sharing details that seemed unimportant to Dod. It was particularly the case when she spotted a row of ornately carved columns and went straight into ten minutes about the grandeur and majesty of the hall when it had been decorated for the Spring Ball.

It was the girly talk that sent Dod right back into trying to figure out when The Dread was going to attack. His recent images were too real to mean nothing. Besides, he didn't see much need in listening closely to how Sawny had hoped this boy or that would have asked her to dance and how Donshi had spilled orange punch on the white something or other that Dilly had lent to her.

After winding around the castle, until Dod's stomach began to growl, Dilly had Dod close his eyes and walk the last bend. It seemed strange. He couldn't understand why she would have him enter the Great Hall blind; unless she had planned a surprise party for him. It made Dod hope that eating was their first order of business at his party.

"Here we are—open your eyes." She finally announced. "Just as I promised."

Dod was puzzled more than surprised. It wasn't a party, and he wasn't in the kitchen or the Great Hall. The air didn't even smell like breakfast. She had led him to an open courtyard where five passageways merged together. Somewhere in route, between Dilly's explanation of how dashing the boys had looked in their suits at the dance and what color of pink the streamers had been in the hall, she had slipped in a word about where they were going, and it wasn't straight to breakfast as he had thought—of course, he had already been wondering why it was taking an eternity to find the Great Hall when it had been so close the night before.

"I was under the impression that we were going to eat breakfast," said Dod, disappointed.

"We will. We will. But as I was *just saying*, we took the scenic route so you could see for yourself all the trainers and scholars and nobles that we commonly have here at Twistyard. Look up there." Dilly smiled with respect as she pointed her finger toward sixty paintings. "Those are most of The Greats, though I think they could certainly add a few more if they were trying to be complete."

Dod quickly discovered that many of the faces were familiar, while a few didn't seem to stir any memories. It was fascinating; simply glancing about the wall flooded his mind with information concerning lots of the individuals to the extent that it was as though he had known them for years.

"Oh yes, there's Pap, and there's one of Bonboo—I thought Boot and Buck stole Pap's painting."

"They did—the one from the Great Hall. There are quite a few paintings of Pap in this place. He was one of the best."

"There's Commendus," remarked Dod. "It's fitting to see him with the *Know It All Book of Commerce* in his hands."

"And doesn't Sirlonk look smug holding two swords," added Dilly enviously. "If I ever learn that double-sword move, I think I could give Raul a good run. That's probably why Sirlonk saves his best teaching for Raulings and Raul Coosings—'course he helps Sawb the most—scrubbing up to Sawb's father, no doubt."

"There's Miz," said Dod. "I guess, now that I think about it, he doesn't seem to be the traitor type. He looks good on a stallion."

"Do you recognize the horse?" asked Dilly.

"Uh, I'm drawing a blank."

"That's Song, my horse. He trained him and then gave him to me for my forty-fifth birthday."

Dod scanned the collection and marveled at the diversity: Pious stood in full military attire with soldiers in the backdrop; Strat bent in an action pose, swinging a wooden club with one hand and deflecting an object with a shield on his opposite arm; Ascertainy held five books and was positioned in the library; Tridacello posed awkwardly in a three-piece suit with a triblot in one hand; Youk pointed with a narrow stick to a strategic play on a map, while wearing an unusually large, white hat with a feather out the back, and bright white gloves on his hands; Higga sat comfortably in an over-stuffed chair with a tray of medical equipment on her lap.

Dilly jabbered on and on about many of the people, but her thoughts usually circled back to Sirlonk, The Great Sword Instructor. She seemed to have an unlimited supply of stories, each testifying of his outstanding accomplishments. Regrettably, however, as she spoke, the air got thicker and thicker with envy. Had she continued much more, she may have greened like a spinach clump and lost her appetite entirely for the regulars of real life.

Fortunately, Dod appeared to need help, and as Dilly focused on her job of teaching, she melted back into a girl.

"Come on," she said. "This is the last and most important one."

"I can tell," said Dod. "They've put him at the top and made his portrait twice as big. He must be really special."

In truth, Dod couldn't have cared less who it was. He was starving and sick of guessing.

The bearded mystery man had a cowboy-like hat, unique to him alone, that hung low enough to cast a painted shadow over his eyes and nose. He could have been a rough-tough outlaw from the old west, who had just robbed a bank, or at least that's how he looked from where Dod was. His questionable appearance made him stick out from the rest.

"Is it Jesse James?" joked Dod apathetically.

"No," said Dilly, giving Dod a strange look. She had no clue who Mr. James was or anything about the trains he'd robbed.

"I can't believe you don't recognize him," she continued, poking Dod in the arm. "Maybe it's the beard. He didn't grow it out until the last year or so."

"That must be it," responded Dod, happy to have an out.

"And he is up awfully high on the wall," admitted Dilly. "I have the advantage of remembering when it was down lower, where the shadows didn't hide it."

"So, who is it?" begged Dod, wondering whether breakfast was over. The face of the ruffian was intriguing. There was a hint of superiority in his eyes, regardless of his unkempt appearance.

"He's the one and only—legendary—Humberrone!" said Dilly. "That's why the painting's bigger than the rest. He lived larger than life, so it didn't do him justice until they hung an extra-sized one to remember him by."

The name Humberrone sounded right, however, it jarred few memories.

"Was that his nickname?" asked Dod.

"It depends," answered Dilly. "I once heard from Bonboo that he was also called Fransilly, but Humberrone didn't want that getting out since the name implied—uh, well at least he felt like it implied a foolish girl. I think Fransilly is perfectly respectable for a man. Don't you?"

Dod chuckled. "Fransilly? No wonder he grew a beard!"

"Hey, you have to admit," said Dilly, as they left the wall of paintings in search of food, "he was the best of the best. In the short time of fifty years, nobody did more than he did. There are enough stories circulating to fill the library with books about his accomplishments, and Bonboo said most of the greatest things he did were in secret. That's actually why his painting is the biggest on the wall. Bonboo knows plenty of those secrets."

"Okay—then if you had a match between Pap and Humberrone," joked Dod, "who would you put your money on?"

"Put my money on?" questioned Dilly with a confused look on her face. "You say the strangest things, Dod."

"Well, who do you think would win in a battle of skill, Pap against Humberrone?"

"That's ridiculous—they were fighting for the same causes."

"I know, but who was better?"

"Oh, that's what you're getting at. Why didn't you just ask that in the first place? Humberrone! And they wouldn't even need to have a match; Humberrone would win before they started."

Dod gave Dilly a cross look that clearly stated, 'I can't believe you would down on my grandpa like that.'

"It's the truth," said Dilly without apology. "He would win just as fast against Bonboo—and in his prime, too. Humberrone was unbeatable."

"Then why isn't he still around?" said Dod smugly. "He was beaten eventually, wasn't he?"

"Nope," said Dilly. "Humberrone wasn't beaten. He chose to—well he uh—well—"

"Do you know what happened to him?"

"Not completely," confessed Dilly. She quieted her voice to a sigh, not wanting to be overheard. They were entering the

Great Hall where hundreds of tredders were still eating, a very comforting thing for Dod to see.

"Bonboo wouldn't tell me exactly what they were doing," whispered Dilly. "He was with him when Humberrone sacrificed himself. Gramps says he could have escaped just fine, but it may have ended our democracy; so he chose to die instead. I admit I don't know how, though you know Bonboo wouldn't lie to me. It's been fifteen years since Humberrone left, but just talking about it makes me feel like it was yesterday. He was a one-of-a-kind supernova."

Dilly and Dod joined a group of Greenlings, who were already eating, or at least trying to. Toos kept making people laugh. Apparently he had witnessed Boot's prank on Buck.

"I can't believe how those two are always teasing each other," said Sawny, sliding over to make room for Dilly and Dod.

"It's a sibling thing—they can't help it," answered Toos with a chuckle, his hair seemed to be glued to his head, parted down the center. "I'm just glad they mostly keep it to each other. I definitely didn't want to be on the *wrong end* of the joke this morning."

Donshi was disgusted, or so she played. She shook her light-brown hair, 'til her ringlets bounced up and down, and mumbled to the boy next to her that it wasn't nice, but she did giggle when Toos said *wrong end*. It conjured a vivid picture in her head of what Toos had just described three times in a row. Fortunately, by the third telling of the story, Toos had recognized the material wasn't all table worthy and had toned down the details of the conclusion, simply calling it 'the moment of explosion.'

"Dilly's my sister and we don't torment each other," Sawny interjected matter-of-factly, challenging Toos's theory on sibling rivalries.

"Yeah, because you're so different," said a boy who arrived at the table and squished in next to Dod. He looked enough like Boot and Buck to be a cousin. His wavy black hair, six-foot frame, and contagious smile drew pleasant glances from some of the Greenling girls, sitting close by, despite the piggish pile of food on his tray.

"That's not true!" insisted Sawny, her searing blue eyes connected with his. "We're so much alike that you're jealous of us because you don't have any siblings."

"I do too," said the boy. He reached over and put his arm on Dod's shoulder. "Here's my brother."

Dod looked at the boy and decided he liked him, while Sawny sighed, disinterested in their foolish games.

"I'm Pone," whispered the boy to Dod.

"Yup, Pone's my brother all right," announced Dod in a loud voice. He tried to go along with the gag as well as he could.

It was then that the secret side of Dod, the side that he had only shown to himself in the shower, the side that wanted to be a ham, came pouring out. He told a tale of two twin brothers, who were separated at birth and had only recently found out about their true kinship from an old hag on her deathbed.

"I doubt it," stated Sawny frankly. She smiled at Dod and added, "but you did tell it well."

DONG-KA-DONG…DONG-KA-DONG.

A large bell announced that breakfast time was almost over.

"Ten more minutes before practice," said Dilly anxiously. "We'll have to eat quickly."

Dod nodded his head and searched for the salt to go with the pile of hash browns and eggs on his plate. While looking, he noticed that Sawny was much taller than the others at the table, at least while sitting. She was perched on something that elevated her.

"Man, you've grown," said Dod, teasing Sawny.

"The increase is up here," she responded, pointing to her head.

Dilly nudged Dod and read aloud the titles to all six books Sawny sat upon: *Dark Deeds of The Dread, Deception and Destruction, Dangerous Creatures, Dueling Strategies for Winning, Delirium and Poisoning, Destruction of the Mauj.* Each book was at least two inches thick.

"Have you read all of them?" asked Dod.

"No," answered Sawny honestly. "I still haven't finished the notes at the back of *Delirium and Poisoning*. Last night I calculated I would have enough time after breakfast to finish it off before returning the books to the library, though it appears I am slightly squeezed."

She stood up and scooped the pile of books into her arms, quite a physical feat, and then turned to a boy that seemed to hover as close to her as he could, and asked, "Could you clean my tray for me, Juck?" She gave him an angelic smile he couldn't refuse.

"I—I—well sure, Sawny," he said, blushing, his big ears even tingeing red.

"Thanks. I need to hurry if I am to stay on schedule and finish the interesting Ds this week. You can understand how disappointed Ascertainy would be if I missed my goal."

Sawny started to walk away when she spun her head around, curls flying, and added, "Oh, and Dilly, have fun with your games or whatever."

"It's practice," said Dilly.

"Right. Well, have fun and be safe. You know how dreadfully

lonely it was for me when you got injured and took leave of this place."

"Don't worry," responded Dilly, "Sirlonk has promised me that he will personally check the blades before each match to make sure nobody has accidentally slid in a sharp battle-striker, like last time."

After Sawny buzzed away, Dilly broke into laughter.

"I think my sister is cute and irreplaceable," she said to Dod. "Having her around is like having a portable library—and mother! But we make a great team: She learns the facts and I get to use them!"

"See, that's just what I was talking about," blurted Pone with a mouth full of food. He put his hand up, covering the gaping hole-of-consumption as though nobody could hear the food sloshing around, and continued on: "Didn't I say they were different? If Boot and Buck weren't so much alike, they probably would stop torturing each other."

"Who's torturing whom?" called a voice from two tables away. Boot had managed to make it to the hall in time for breakfast and was interested to know what people were saying about him.

"You, of course," Pone yelled back. He swallowed hard, forcing the food down, and added with a clearer voice, "You're the top, Boot. I think you're great."

Dilly rolled her eyes. "Pone, do you realize Dod is bunking in the big room with Boot and Buck?"

"What?" gasped Pone, choking on a mouth full of ham he had just shoveled in. "And after all the grub-eating I've done," he continued, not bothering to lift his hand anymore. "I was getting really close."

"Not as close as you thought," said Dilly with a satisfied look. "At least you can stop with the Boot compliments. The last thing *he* needs is another ego propper." She looked over her shoulder at Boot who was wide-eyed in the middle of a story he was selling to a dozen Greenlings that seemed to hang on his every word.

Dod raised one hand in apology to Pone. He started to say he was sorry when Pone cut him off.

"Hey, I'm glad you got the room," he said sincerely, as though the disappointment was over. "Besides, after what you did yesterday, you deserve it. It feels good to have fifteen of us again. I was starting to wonder if Boot would ever be able to fill the spot—you know—I don't blame him for moving slowly."

Dod looked confused, so Pone continued, this time with bread and jam in his mouth, though he politely reinstated his hand to hide it.

"—After his little brother had to leave three years ago, choosing another Coosing must feel like he's replacing him; and nobody can replace Bowy. I can honestly say that Bowy was the nicest out of the whole lot of us and, by far, the best at swordplay."

"I'm getting better," exploded Dilly.

DONG-KA-DONG…DONG-KA-DONG…DONG-KA-DONG.

"That's it," said Dilly, rising to her feet. "We've got to go—wouldn't want to be late on your first day. Sirlonk can be brutal."

Dod and Dilly hurried with the cleaning of their trays and headed for the open, grassy field, out in front of the castle.

Boot shouted to them across the noisy room, but Dilly was so bent on being prompt to practice that the only thing they heard was, "—so Bonboo said I should give it to you."

Dod wondered what Bonboo wanted to give him; and had he known that Boot wasn't headed in the same direction, he unquestionably would have waited for Boot and abandoned going to practice altogether, which could have averted a lot of trouble.

THREE KEYS

"See, isn't it nice over here in the shade of these trees?" remarked Dilly. "It sure beats meeting indoors. I wish we practiced out here all the time."

"Why are we so lucky today?" asked Dod.

"Sirlonk promised to show us some clever moves with trees and grass and rocks as terrain. After all, you won't always be indoors when dueling with an enemy."

"I guess," admitted Dod hesitantly. He thought about swordplay, and though it sounded very exciting, he didn't like the idea of ever dueling in a real battle.

A crowd of nearly fifty tredders, mostly Coosings, Greenlings, and Raulings all gathered under gigantic trees, which lined the outer perimeter of the open field. Across the grass, Bonboo's house stood a massive mountain of stone and glass. Trees and gardens in the outer patios and courtyards, at different elevations, gave the great castle a look that resembled a city on a hillside rather than one building. Its layers towered skyward, reaching heights of nearly thirty stories in the middle, yet it was well-proportioned and comely.

"That's a big house," said Dod to Dilly. He couldn't help being amazed at the sheer size, not to mention the unusual architecture.

"Yes, it's the biggest I know of. I'm sure plenty of people are jealous of Bonboo, but he has always used it for good purposes; and that's more than anyone could say of Terro."

Dod thought for a moment and then remembered bits and pieces about Terro. He currently reigned as the Chief Noble Tredder of Raul; however, despite the fact that they technically had a democracy like Green, Terro's leadership leaned increasingly in the direction of a dictatorship.

"Terro's house," Dilly added, "is the second largest—and by far the largest one in Raul—unfortunately, most of it sits empty unless he's entertaining dignitaries and nobles or rewarding senior officers in his army; that's about it for the Chantolli Estate. I wish Sawb would take his lot from Raul and go home to live with his dad in their castle. They have plenty of space. A few years back Bonboo suggested they create an extension of Twistyard there, but Terro insisted he wouldn't have young people pointlessly frolicking about his manor in support of a dying purpose. I find it nervy of him to send his son Sawb and his brother Sirlonk, along with so many others from Raul, while separating his wealth from the cause."

Dod started to speak in agreement when Buck suddenly came up and put his hand over Dod's mouth.

"Sirlonk's here. You had better both show him some respect." Buck then lowered his voice to a whisper. "I agree they're all arrogant, especially Terro and Sirlonk; nobody from Green would dispute that—"

"Do you have something to share with us?" bellowed Sirlonk in a condescending manner. Everyone jumped to attention and stared at Buck.

"No sir," answered Buck apologetically, standing respectfully stiff.

"Good, then I shan't have you tittering with your friends. Pots meet elsewhere, along with the ill-mannered sorts like your brother Boot! You're welcome to join *them*."

Buck cringed when Sirlonk mentioned Boot. Dod looked around and noticed that he was missing from the crowd.

"Now then," continued Sirlonk in a proud voice. "When you've fought as many battles as I have, you take swordplay very seriously. I don't waste my time on beginning levels of engagement. Others can trifle with that. You are the best at Twistyard—pathetic as you are—so as a favor to society, I'll continue to bear with you."

Sirlonk was unusually good looking. He had the face and figure of a muscular movie star, with jet-black hair, dark piercing eyes, and olive skin. As he paced back and forth in front of the youth, Dod noticed the precision of every step; he walked and talked as a noble tredder and was indeed the embodiment of royalty. Even the rude comments he made seemed justified when spoken from his lips.

All six-foot-three of Sirlonk was adorned in the most costly apparel; a white three-piece suit, white shirt, white gloves, and white leather boots. The tips of his sleeves were closed by shiny, gold buttons that matched the golden clasps on his boots, and each of the buttons had a fancy family insignia.

"—if you listen closely," Sirlonk arrogantly insisted, "you will obtain three keys from me today. They are keys that will unlock the door to your escape."

Toos nudged up behind Dod and courageously whispered in his ear when Sirlonk was almost at the farthest point of his pacing route.

"Take a look at those medals; with all of the white he wears, you'd think he wants to make sure everyone notices them."

As Sirlonk made his way back, Dod quietly counted the twelve golden and ruby awards pinned across the front lapels of his outer coat. He waited for Sirlonk to continue his prance back to the other side before whispering over his shoulder to Toos.

"What are the medals for?"

Dilly poked Dod in the ribs with her elbow and gave him a cross look.

"He's decorated for bravery," said Toos quietly. "He's completed hoards of successful missions. On some of them, he was the only survivor. Sirlonk's a regular hero to High Gate, recovering bunches of triblots and stuff."

Dod nodded his head, remembering Dilly's torrent of stories about Sirlonk and in acknowledgment of hearing Toos. Unfortunately, the motion caught Sirlonk's attention and happened to coincide with the wrong segment of his lecture. Sirlonk had just asked a rhetorical question: "Would you have dared to face twenty of Dredarious's men by yourself?"

By nodding, Dod appeared to be dismissing Sirlonk's heroic experience as commonplace.

"You!" blurted Sirlonk in a harsh voice. He pointed at Dod. "I don't believe you were ever invited to join us. You're nameless to me, and I can see you're a human, so that quickly rules you out as being anyone important. It's criminal to waste my time with your games. Leave now before you find yourself at the tip of my cold blade."

The group was speechless, and many of them had a look of fear for Dod, except Sawb and his group of Coosings and Raulings; they appeared perfectly happy.

Buck and Toos both sympathized with Dod, but didn't dare say anything. The silence was smothering. Dod could feel his face getting hot. He was terrified and furious at the same time.

"I invited him, sir," said Dilly in a respectful voice. "After the tales I was told by your friends Tridacello, Dungo, and Bowlure, I assumed you knew of Dod or I would have requested permission to make a formal presentation of him."

"Dod?" said Sirlonk. "Hmmm, I don't recall ever hearing of Dod. How old are you, boy?"

Dod was flustered by the confrontation. It was difficult to get his mouth open enough to answer him. Dilly nudged again with her elbow and prodded Dod to speak.

"I'm fourteen," he squeaked.

Everyone started laughing.

"Fourteen?" said Sirlonk with a chuckle. "You're hardly weaned. Where's your mother? I should expect she is worried stiff that you've escaped your crib. I suppose someone has loaned you as a youngling to keep Jim company, eh? Perhaps you've lost your way and are looking to help Zerny and Jibb in the stalls?"

Sirlonk walked up close to Dod and breathed down on him. His glare was bone-chilling.

"Bonboo has developed a terrible, weak side to him," snorted Sirlonk bitterly. "Inviting a fourteen-year-old to play in this dangerous place—well, that's just laughable. Accidents happen, you know. He's too old to know what's proper anymore."

"Come on Dod," said Dilly loudly, clenching one fist until her knuckles went white. "I guess I introduced you incorrectly.

We'll wait 'til the banquet at High Gate and have Commendus do a better job when awarding *you* for the recovery of their recently stolen *triblot*! Besides, if Sirlonk is too busy to aid in the training of *Pap's* grandson, he must be *really* busy."

It was unbelievable that Dilly dared say her part. She had attempted to be polite at first, yet she passed her limit when Sirlonk made fun of Bonboo.

Dilly grabbed Dod by his shirt at the shoulder and whisked him away from the group. She pulled hard enough that Dod actually smacked right into Sirlonk on the way out. Sirlonk's torso felt like a brick wall.

"See you at the tournaments, losers!" yelled Sawb; he had held his tongue up to that point. His buddies all seemed delighted that Dilly and Dod were on their way out.

Sirlonk didn't ask Dilly to return, but he focused his attention on scolding Sawb and the others for not informing him that Dod was Pap's grandson and a recipient of attention from High Gate.

Dilly vented her mind while they crossed the field and walked the halls of the castle. Astonishingly, she appeared to be mad at Dod, not Sirlonk. It was perplexing to Dod until Dilly finally cooled off enough to explain.

"You haven't said much this whole time, which leads me to believe you think I'm wrong for being mad at you."

Dod gradually nodded his head in agreement, quietly listening.

"What you need to understand is that I plan on winning—and not just at the tournaments. If I can learn from a snake like Sirlonk to be better with a sword, I'm going to bite my tongue and leech his skills. He's a horse's tail, I know it! Don't you think I would love to have Bonboo draw him out and send him on his way? Of course! Though that's too easy; then he wins! He'd take his sword skills and his stories of glory and leave me a worse pupil."

Dilly came to a stop in front of two large doors and turned to look at Dod.

"I've had my share of problems. It's hard to learn from him. However, he's still the best! And until someone else, some Humberrone comes along with better skills I'm going to keep trying to glean from his swordplay."

Dilly pushed one of the doors open and led Dod up some stairs and into the back of a packed conference room. It was an amphitheater, so even the rear had a decent view. Most of the four hundred people appeared to be Pots, with a few Coosings, Greenlings, Raulings, and Sooshlings in the mix. They all stared in anticipation at the front of the room. You could have heard a pin drop.

Youk stood quietly, facing the audience with a long, slender stick in his hand.

SMACK!

It happened in the blink of an eye. Youk's rod hit the podium and he disappeared behind it. Only his white hat with a large feather on top remained visible. Everyone gasped with delight. Apparently he was demonstrating something he had just discussed.

Dilly poked a young Pot and asked her what he was doing.

"He's talking about trickery—" she responded, craning her head to see over the spiky hair of a taller boy. "He said our best tool to mislead an enemy is the art of surprise, using their expectations against them."

Just then, an obnoxiously boisterous lad at the front yelled, "I think we get the point, Youk! Come on out. You're not hiding very well. We can still see the top of your hat."

"Then you've only got my hat!" rumbled someone from the back of the room, right behind Dod. Everyone turned in amazement.

Dod was startled nearly out of his seat. The man's voice was powerful—more so than his appearance would have suggested. He had successfully sneaked up on Dod unawares and used masterful deception to do it!

"Never assume what you see," he continued as he made his way to the stairs. "Always question the unusual, but be particularly skeptical of the apparent. Your opponent, if he or she is witty, will capitalize on the obvious to ensnare you. Don't fall for it."

The rest of the discussion entailed maps and stories of strategies he had employed to beat armies and others he had utilized to entirely avoid war altogether. It was fascinating. Youk was friendly and inviting. His accounts were told well enough that the whole group was patient to the end; and many of them begged for more when the session was over.

Dilly insisted on introducing Dod to Youk, so they waited for people to leave the room and then made their way down. He was busily compiling his maps and securing his papers in a case.

"That was great, as usual," said Dilly. "Thank you."

"Oh, you're kind, my dear. You should be thanking your grandfather, not me. He's the one who taught me most of what I know. I was once a Coosing, for a while, when I was your age. Those days are still some of my best memories. I'm just glad Bonboo has let me come back to this place…despite everything, you know. He's a generous man."

"This is my friend, Dod," announced Dilly.

"Nice to meet you," said Youk with a tip of his hat. He drew his hand down and noticed his white glove. It had a black smudge across the back.

"I hate it when I soil my slips," he said irritably. "It seems like I can't keep a pair clean anymore. I'm ready to give up on fancy dressing."

Youk wore nice clothes. He was built like a six-foot bean pole, though the formal, silk shirt and ruffled pants helped him look more natural. His attire portrayed a refined, yet creative individual.

"Don't stop," answered Dilly. "We would all be disappointed if you shed your suave style and dress. Besides, tell me Saluci would allow it and I wouldn't believe you! How is she these days?"

"She's fine—pushes me to do more and then insists I'm spending too much time going about. If she could make up her mind, I'd be able to keep her perfectly happy."

"You must have known that would be the case," added Dilly. "Marrying into her family would have to be like signing up for a lifetime of impossible goals. Nothing seems to be enough for the Zoots."

"How right you are. If I didn't love her so much, my aspirations would be a lot simpler. As it is, I'm constantly reminded at every family gathering of the nobility in their blood, all the way back to Dossontrous. Some in the lot are crazy enough to wish the world would revert to the way it was. The last thing I would ever fancy is to erase the technology and civility we've gained over the past three thousand years and trade it in for ruling all of Green.

Who in their right mind would honestly want to be a dictator, anyway?"

"Just about anyone from Raul," snapped Dilly. She was still worked up from her encounter with Sirlonk, and it showed on her face.

"I don't even think your pals from Raul would have liked it. Back then, ruling was another way of saying that you spent your life with the soldiers, killing and being killed. It was a real bloody mess. Besides, trying to preside over part of Green today would be a nightmare, let alone the whole thing. I'm doing well to manage my own life and occasionally give advice to my kids. It's a good thing we have democracy; and even then, I feel for political leaders like Bonboo and Commendus."

"Bah! I think you're being humble," insisted Dilly. She nudged him on the shoulder with her fist. "You'd make a great Chief Noble Tredder of Green. After all, you have come up with a lot of grand strategies to help keep the peace. You're right in line to be chosen when Gramps is gone—and make sure you tell Saluci I said so."

"Oh, I will," said Youk, hurrying out the door. "Sorry I've got to run."

Dilly and Dod followed behind and both reached for the handle, yet neither got a chance to use it. Before they could, Youk returned, swinging the door wide open. He looked right at Dilly.

"Have you heard from Doochi? Any word from Raul?" Youk searched Dilly's face for an answer.

"I sure liked that boy," he continued. "He had some great ideas to bring home. I would have enjoyed working with him a little longer. They were just the kind of strategies Raul needs right now."

"No," responded Dilly. "I assume he's still too embarrassed from quitting the Coosings to drop a line. You know Sawb and the others from Raul; they tease mercilessly! Even without him around, I've heard Sawb make all kinds of jokes about him. I guess leaving a note in the middle of the night was a poor way to quit. He should have at least explained his case in person."

Dod stared at the door handle, prickling with goosebumps. There was something about Youk's voice or the conversation that triggered the morning images to return. He could hear people scheming, shrouded by darkness—someone was listening, eavesdropping—the voices grew louder and louder—they discovered they weren't alone—they attacked—beams collapsed.

This time Dod saw more detail than he had before; two hands used a saw to cut through support beams, which caused the collapse. The hands were gloveless, and the right hand had a familiar, jagged scar. It was the same scar he had seen on the hand that had doomed Bonboo's wagon!

Dod froze as he watched Youk walk confidently down the hall. Dilly started rambling on about Youk's wife, Saluci, and how impossible she was to please, though Dod didn't hear a word she said. This time the scene in his mind was too real to dismiss. He felt like the man with the scar was about to attack, and it appeared he was The Dread.

Dod determined something had to be done, but before he could say so much as a word to Dilly, Boot jogged up to them and broke in.

"There you are!" he said, exhausted. He was out of breath. He leaned on Dilly and Dod, sandwiching himself between them. "I've been looking all over for you. I thought you were planning on attending Sirlonk's practice."

"We had a change of plans," said Dilly frankly, "which is fortunate for you. I know you'd rather speak with us here than be anywhere near Sirlonk after last week."

"Well, if I had known you were coming *here,* it might have been more fortunate. Sirlonk sends an apology for the misunderstanding this morning. He said he's perfectly all right with accepting Dod into the group if his skills with a sword are similar to the others; and by the way, that was a more pleasant message than the one he told me to bring to myself."

"You went to practice?" choked Dilly with a laugh. "Sirlonk expressly stated that he didn't want to see your face anywhere near his precious matches or he'd teach you a lesson you'd never forget. Not to mention, you obviously showed up late. You have a horribly short memory or a thick skull, don't you?"

"No, I just have an urgent delivery from Bonboo. He left for High Gate this morning and asked me to give this to Dod before my regular routines. I tried to pass it along in the Great Hall, but *someone* played deaf."

Boot handed Dod a small wooden box.

"So—what's inside?" asked Dod.

"I wouldn't know. Bonboo said it was for you and nobody else."

"Didn't you peek?"

"Maybe quickly," he admitted. "It was hardly long enough to consider it peeking. I closed it right up.

Dilly looked at Boot suspiciously, while Dod examined the intricate designs on the outside of the container.

"He's giving you three keys," confessed Boot.

Dod opened the box and found that Boot was right; a miniature scroll was tucked neatly underneath them.

"I didn't know there was a message," said Boot. He struck like a snake and snatched the note from Dod, even before it was out from under the keys.

"Here, allow me," said Boot. He read aloud:

"These three keys belonged to your grandfather. His room is still the way he left it. I've kept it locked since the assassination. Please have Boot or Dilly show you to it. I'm sure it may be hard for you to see his things, but they're yours now, as is the room. His clothes are about your size, though, if it's hard for you to wear them, feel free to let Mercy know. She volunteered to help you acquire a wardrobe."

"Mercy?" exploded Dilly, looking appalled. "Mercy doesn't know a thing about clothes. If you need help with clothes, let me help you. I insist!"

Boot glanced at Dilly and snapped, "Do you mind? Dod wants to hear the rest of his personal letter."

"And he probably wanted to read it alone," replied Dilly.

"It's okay," said Dod. "Read on."

"Please, know that your grandfather was a dear friend to me. I miss him greatly. Also, I still plan on having that discussion I promised you. We can meet as soon as I return from High Gate. The large key is for the room. The other two were his, but I can't say what they open—I'm sure they're very important. Keep them safe. I'll see you soon.
—Your friend, Bonboo."

Dod looked around and made sure that nobody was near them in the hall. He especially checked to see that Youk had continued walking and was out of hearing range.

"I need help—from both of you," said Dod quietly in a confidential voice.

"Well, of course," responded Boot. He was loud and jovial. "You haven't the slightest idea where to find Pap's room, and this castle is monstrous enough to make a random search quite daunting. Don't worry! I've been there a hundred times and can easily find it with my eyes closed."

"Thank you, Boot, but could you keep your voice down," said Dod, getting agitated. "I have something else to discuss that's more urgent than seeing Pap's stuff."

"You're kidding, right?" gasped Boot, peering at Dod through slits; he wore a face full of wrinkles in disbelief. "Pap has the coolest things! I'm dying to look through his cabinets and cupboards."

"No, I'm serious," insisted Dod. He shushed Boot before continuing. "I don't want anyone else to hear us. I know that The Dread is going to attack, and I think it will be here—and soon!"

Dod tried to look courageous even though the blood had drained from his face in fear. He felt as though the mass murderer, who had poisoned his grandpa, was now targeting him.

"I think The Dread is already among us," announced Dod. "He's in disguise!"

Dilly rolled her eyes while Boot's widened with excitement. Dod had actually wanted to say that he thought The Dread was someone like Youk or Zerny; nevertheless, after Dilly's lecture that morning, Dod toned it down to suggesting he was near them.

"Great!" whispered Boot excitedly. "You can count me in. What do you know?"

Dilly pulled Boot's arm off her shoulder and shoved him. "Boys!" she said with disgust. "You two can't focus on reality long enough to sit through a course on swordplay. It's always something!"

"Not this time," said Boot in Dod's defense.

"Oh really?" answered Dilly, shaking her head. "What about the time you accused Strat of infiltrating Twistyard as a traitor? You said his purpose was to sabotage our game of Bollirse. What became of it?"

Boot was embarrassed that Dilly had brought it up in front of Dod. He squirmed uncomfortably and searched the air with his eyes for a good explanation.

"That was different," he finally blurted. "You can't get mad at me for being suspicious when a new Bollirse instructor had us spend our time focusing on throwing zull berries and cutting weeds—and with dull sticks at that! It appeared to be malicious."

Dilly enjoyed the moment. She clearly thought it was fun to torture Boot.

"And don't forget he was close friends with Bly!" added Boot, attempting to defend himself. "Back then, any association with Bly drew concern."

"And what happened?" asked Dilly with a smile on her face. She knew the answer already, yet wanted him to have to explain how poor his judgment had been.

"Well—he turned out all right," admitted Boot reluctantly.

"Just all right?" prodded Dilly. "Wouldn't you say he turned out more than all right? The first two years may have been spent on rigorous training, but the last six years of winning The Golden Swot have proven his training works! Besides, even if he's unconventional, nobody could dispute his greatness. And as for his relationship with Bly, it's not a bad thing anymore, is it?"

Dilly poked at Boot with her elbow and turned to look at Dod before continuing. "The charges against Bly as a war criminal in Soosh were all dismissed, and Commendus personally led that investigation. Bly is now one of the wealthiest entrepreneurs, and thanks to Strat, he shares some of his money with Twistyard in support of our cause."

"Okay, you're right," confessed Boot, raising both hands in the air. "Run me through with your sword and get it over with. I admit I was wrong. But this time we're not talking about *my* judgment, we're talking about Dod's; and if you have a problem with his, you'll need to explain it to more than just me: Dod saved Bonboo's wagon with his quick thinking."

Dilly wasn't entirely convinced; however, Dod and Boot were her friends, so she patched things up using a half-apology mixed with heavy skepticism.

"As I was saying," Dod finally continued, "I feel The Dread is near. It's like I can see glimpses of what he's about to do or what he's recently done."

"You're psychic!" blurted Boot gleefully. "I knew it! The way you handled yourself on the wagon—I mean, it wasn't typical."

Boot stopped Dilly in her tracks and spun her toward Dod, using his powerful arms, and said, "Take a look at him! We've got an extrasensory genius! This is the best thing that's happened to us—to the Coosings—to Green Hall. Do you know what this means?"

Dilly began to laugh. When Boot had taken his sweaty arm off Dod's shoulder, he had jumbled Dod's hair on one side of his head, coaxing it to stand on end, while the other side looked normal. It made Dod appear less like any kind of a genius and more like a confused, bed-head kid.

Boot jumped in and smoothed Dod's hair, apologizing for his contribution of sweat, and hopped back once more. He wiggled his fingers in Dod's direction and tried to recapture the moment he had attempted to present to Dilly, but it was pointless. Dilly continued to laugh.

"He's psychic, Dilly! He's psychic!" Boot repeated the phrase, getting more and more excited each time he said it.

"Could you tap in on Sawb's game plan?" asked Boot, rubbing his hands together.

"What?" said Dod.

"Or Sirlonk—Dilly, we could use him for you, too!" said Boot, his eyes growing bigger by the second. "Dod could do his thing and come up with the right way to impress Sirlonk, maybe pull a few memories he hasn't shared with very many people—Oh!—better yet, he could see the next time something unlucky was going to happen to Sirlonk and you could *magically* be the one to warn him. Think of it Dilly! This is great."

Dod stared at Boot, not wanting to be the one to pop his bubble, but suddenly realizing he had to.

"Boot," said Dod hesitantly. "I wouldn't really call it being psychic."

"You wouldn't?" said Boot; he studied Dod's face with hopeful eyes. "Then what would you call it?"

Dilly went quiet momentarily, controlling her laughter enough to hear Dod's own description of his 'super power.'

"It's more like—well—being lucky."

Dilly roared. She laughed so hard that tears streamed down her face.

"You've got," Dilly said haltingly, trying to speak in between her explosions of laughter, "—a scary...weapon...for a friend."

"So—it's luck?" said Boot, disappointed.

"Kinda," muttered Dod, feeling embarrassed. Boot hopped in quickly and tried to make him feel better.

"I know," said Boot, faking a chuckle. "We really had Dilly going, didn't we?" He slid up next to Dod and together they began to walk down the hall again, with Dilly attempting to regain her composure, trailing behind.

"Okay," said Boot, "before we pulled that one on Dilly, you were saying something…"

"Yeah," said Dod. "It's hard to explain. I've had a few weird dreamlike things where I've seen—well—I think it's The Dread—and he's hurting people here at Twistyard.…Maybe they're nothing."

"No," said Boot. "They could be right. Do you have any idea of where?"

"I don't," admitted Dod. "This place is huge and I've only glimpsed a tiny bit of it. I guess you could help me try to figure out the location based on details I remember."

"Sure," said Boot. "Go ahead."

"The floor was made of stone, just like this one."

"That's the whole castle and half of the surrounding buildings!" said Dilly, exasperated. She rejoined the boys to taunt them.

"And the walls were made of the same stone," added Dod. "I don't remember any fancy wooden trim or decorations, except a little on the support beams—maybe at an entrance. It also seems like the halls were more narrow than these, probably half the size, and the smell was really musty or something."

"You smell in your dreams?" teased Dilly, mocking the effort.

"I'd say it's the storage chambers beneath the stables," said Boot, ignoring her.

The last word caught Dod's attention because it naturally connected the trouble to Zerny and Jibb.

"I doubt it," responded Dilly, finally entering the conversation for real. "What purpose would The Dread have under the stables? It's probably in the basement of Sword Tower."

"And how would *you* know what *that* basement looks like?" asked Boot. "Bonboo has had it quarantined and guarded for over fifteen years, since the triblot field came down."

Dilly's face showed she had incriminated herself, though she looked more proud than sorry.

"Oh, I've seen it," she said smugly. "I have a sword collection that occasionally needs new recruits. Bonboo thinks they are too dangerous to have about the castle in our care, so I keep mine under my bed—about two dozen. You never know when we might wish for a quick sword."

"Dilly!" said Dod in a surprised voice. "I thought you kept all of the rules."

"I do," pronounced Dilly with confidence. "I keep all of the rules that need keeping!"

"That would explain the occasional clanking I've heard," said Boot, connecting the dots in his mind. "I thought part of your nighttime ritual included hitting a metal bar, like the superstitious do for good luck, until Sawny assured me that it was the chatter of your squeaky bed frame. And I suppose she was at least partially right: It was your bed frame, telling the world of your contraband sword collection!"

The threesome made their way down the hall, continuing to assess the possible locations, all the while being cautious when around other people. In time, they discovered that there were twenty-two conceivable spots, spread out around the complex—mostly the basements of various out-buildings.

Dod wanted to quickly walk through each of them. Boot

was willing and even began to figure a logical order. Dilly, on the other hand, pretended to be disinterested. She said a lot about how pointless the effort was—that is, until after Dod shared some of his other experiences—the ones that included flutters, a venoos, and the sabotaged riggings of Bonboo's wagon—then she believed enough in his kind of 'luck' to want to be an active part. As a matter of fact, she insisted that she should take the lead, considering a few of the halls were off limits and would be impossible to enter, except at night with her expert abilities.

In the end, Dilly calculated it would take at least a week to check the locations in their spare time. Dod tried to convince her that the matter was urgent enough to warrant missing regular activities; however, Dilly concluded with an irrefutable response which tingled Dod's ears with fright.

"If The Dread is among us," she said, "then we must act normal. Any suspicious behavior would certainly lead to a swift and fatal meeting with him!"

NIGHTTIME MISCHIEF

The rest of the day was spent trying to find time to nonchalantly check some of the twenty-two targeted locations. It was difficult. Once Dilly believed Dod's insights, she insisted on caution, reminding Dod and Boot that the less people who knew, the better; though they agreed that they could let Buck and Sawny in on their secret. Other people, especially the guest trainers and experts, had to know nothing of their covert investigation.

When their daytime attempts to search failed, Dod, Dilly, Sawny, Boot, and Buck unanimously decided to sneak down to the basement of the castle late at night. It was their only chance to check it unnoticed, and of all the possibilities, the castle's lowest corridors seemed to fit Dod's descriptions the best.

"Are you sure this is a good idea?" asked Sawny in a nervous voice as she and Dilly left the girls' rooms to meet the boys under Green Hall's twin swords. Sawny lagged sluggishly, and when she did move, it was with heavy feet.

"It's the only way," insisted Dilly, prodding her sister along. "You know we tried at least half-a-dozen times earlier, but every occasion was spoiled by something or other. We can't trust anyone."

Sawny had willingly agreed during daylight hours, however, now that the world was quiet and the halls around her were black, it seemed different. Even the clothes she and her sister wore were foreboding. They skulked around in dark outfits with trailing cloaks, in hopes to better hide from possible danger.

"You know we'd wait 'til later if we could," said Dilly, nodding sympathetically. She did her best to convince her sister to stop grumbling. But it was useless. Sawny had changed her mind and didn't want to go.

"Even if he does identify the spot," said Sawny, groaning loudly, "will it do any good? How is it going to help?"

"It'll work," said Dilly, cracking a smile before concealing it. "If we find where The Dread plans to strike, we can determine what he wants and devise a plan to run him through."

Dilly was excited about the possibility of real action, and though she tried to hide it from her sister, it showed on her face.

"Oh," sighed Sawny miserably, reading her sister's delight. She could see Dilly was getting wound-up like a pack of hounds that had just discovered the scent of a fleeing fox. She moved closer to Dilly, made eye contact, and added, hopelessly, "Wouldn't it make more sense to go looking for a person with a scar on his hand?" She knew what she said wouldn't change Dilly's mind.

"We will. We will. Don't worry, Sawny," said Dilly. "In order to stop The Dread, we'll follow every lead we can—even the search for a scarred hand, yet Dod admitted that the man with the scar wasn't working alone—and who knows which one is The Dread?"

"Could you please stop saying, *The Dread*," pleaded Sawny,

pushing hair out of her face. "These glowing rocks don't cast light like candles do. I feel all—Aaaah!"

She broke off abruptly with a shriek.

"Did I scare you?" choked Boot. He had a hard time saying anything through his laughter. He had hidden his glowing rock under his shirt and then had approached the girls quietly.

"You're just lucky I didn't draw my blade," declared Dilly smugly, pulling back her cloak to show off her weapon; it was sheathed and slung at her side.

"You brought a sword?" gasped Boot, admiring it. The shiny metal of its casing looked magical in the dim light. It was plastered with intricate designs around a beautiful family insignia, and the name Bonboo Tillius was etched prominently down the side.

"Well," said Dilly gleefully, "you don't think I'm crazy enough to go searching for trouble in the dead of night without equipping myself, do you? Protective gear is a must. Who knows, we might get lucky and find The Dread."

"Oh—I guess so," said Boot, slightly jealous. "Good for you."

Dod and Buck came trotting up. Their glowing rocks bounced on the chains around their necks.

"We've got about an hour," announced Dilly, who had assumed the lead position. "Strat said these things may glow longer, for two or more, but to be safe, we should plan on only one—and that's if you've fully filled them properly."

"How fully?" squeaked Buck, whose rock seemed to glow dimmer than the others.

"I told you Bly's specific routine before use," scolded Dilly. "Four hours of direct sunlight and then keep it in a lit room."

It was obvious Buck hadn't followed her directions very well. "How can Bly get wealthy on gadgets like this?" he moaned, swinging his dimming rock necklace. "They're way too hard to use—too many instructions. I thought four hours of candlelight would be good enough."

"Apparently not," jabbed Sawny. She took part with Dilly in teasing the boys; however, in truth, their arrival bolstered her confidence. They made it seem more like a fun outing, not a search for some bloodthirsty villain.

Boot patted a leather pouch at his side. "Don't worry, Buck, if these things don't work, I've got good old-fashioned buster candles—they'd light the whole hall for as far as you can see."

"No!" insisted Dilly, shaking her head. "Don't bring them. It's too dangerous. We can't have that much light. Leave them here or I'm not going."

"Are you serious?" asked Boot, who couldn't believe her audacity.

"Totally!" responded Dilly, putting her foot down. "We have to think before we act. If The Dread's at work, he mustn't see us sneaking around. Don't forget who he's already killed."

"All right, you win," said Boot, giving in quickly. He wasn't afraid of the dark or The Dread; he had only brought the candles because they seemed logical. Sawny, on the other hand, turned pale, aghast, when Dilly bluntly mentioned the 'K' word. She didn't like the thoughts of running into The Dread, much less, what he could do to them.

"Are you sure we don't want the candles?" asked Sawny nervously, watching Boot comply with Dilly's request; Boot took his leather pouch off and slid it into the corner of the entry to Green Hall.

"Trust me," said Dilly confidently. She fidgeted around and then, WHOOSH, disappeared.

"See! We can become virtually invisible in the dark if we need to," she said as she pulled her rock out from under her cloak and reappeared on the other side of Dod. "The light is dim enough to stay close to us, yet bright enough to get the job done. Now stop fretting and let's get on our way. We have a basement to check."

The group walked the halls quietly. At first it seemed like everyone else was asleep; nevertheless, as they neared the Great Hall, it became apparent that that was not the case. Dilly signaled for the stones to be covered, and then they proceeded in darkness, holding hands to stay together.

"I'd b-be most p-pleased if y-you could — " a voice stuttered before being cut off. The dissonant sounds bounced clumsily around the empty corridors and were easily heard.

"That's why I agreed to help you," said an impatient voice. "Now let's grab a snack from the kitchen. I can't ride like this, in the middle of the night, without having something to eat along the way. I'm dreadful at late hours. You're one lucky little creature — waking me up like that!"

"In y-your c-clothes? I thought m-maybe you—?"

"I drifted to sleep in my easy chair with some reading and hadn't shifted to bed yet, so yes, I was dressed and ready. Juny's back in Raul visiting family, you know, or she would have certainly prompted me to pajamas hours ago."

Dilly gasped. She recognized the two men to be Sirlonk and Zerny — an unusual duo.

"Quick," whispered Boot. "Let's hide over here." He was the center link in the chain of hands, but still managed to pull the group behind a row of chairs, right in front of the kitchen doors.

"I never noticed these before," whispered Dilly in amazement.

Buck responded in an even quieter voice, "That's because you don't spend half of your day thinking about the next meal, like Boot here."

Soon the hall lit up with candlelight as Zerny led Sirlonk to the kitchen. They rummaged around for a few minutes and then swiftly departed the way they came.

"He's wearing Jilser!" exclaimed Dilly after muffled sounds from the nighttime visitors had completely faded.

"What?" asked Dod.

"Jilser—his fighting sword. Whatever they're up to right now includes trouble. I think we should follow them."

"Are you crazy?" winced Buck, attempting to climb out from behind the chairs. "They're heading off on horseback in the middle of the night!" Buck's courage dimmed like his quickly fading light.

"Besides," he continued, "I'm tired and my stone isn't working very well. Maybe tomorrow we can make sure to take naps, while giving our rocks their proper soak in the sun, and then go searching the basement halls better prepared."

Sawny's light also began to dim, though not nearly as much as Buck's. "Let's go back," she said quietly.

Dilly stood up and started walking toward the Great Hall, as if she hadn't heard them. Dod and Boot followed close behind.

"Why don't you guys turn in," said Dilly over her shoulder to Sawny and Buck. "Go and get some sleep. If something happens to us, you'll need to carry on."

It didn't take much convincing. Buck and Sawny offered a 'good luck' and then disappeared rapidly toward their rooms.

Dilly, Boot, and Dod picked up their pace too—in the opposite direction. When they stepped out into the courtyard, moonlight made visibility better.

Dod stared at the unusually large moon. It was much bigger than the one he remembered seeing from Earth. The sky was strange and different. During the day it was less noticeable because the sun and clouds looked identical to the ones he knew, but seeing a different set of stars made him feel impossibly far away from home.

Gazing upward, Dod started to think about his outings with Pap, when they had studied the constellations together; however, Dilly quickly pulled him back.

"Hide your light," she ordered curtly, reaching past Boot to poke Dod. "I don't want them to see us. It looks like they're heading toward the master barn—over there." Dilly stretched her arm and pointed at two figures, jogging in the direction of a large building. She started to move out into the grassy field when Boot grabbed her.

"Wait," he said. "Let's stick to the shadows and we'll hide better." He pointed at two rows of trees which followed a road that jutted almost straight from the castle front to the tree-lined, half-circle of buildings. It was farther to walk, but the shade would conceal them completely.

By the time the threesome made it to the barn, Zerny and Sirlonk had saddled up and were heading out the other side, with a third rider. Zerny remarked as they left the barn, "Th-thank you S-Strat for coming so qu-quickly."

Dilly ran to the stalls, and in a matter of a few short seconds, she emerged riding Song bareback. Boot was still searching for his horse, Grubber.

"No time, boys," called Dilly, "I'm riding after them. You catch up."

"But I can't ride Grubber bareback," complained a muffled voice from the darkest part of the barn. "I can't even seem to find where they've put him. He's not in his regular stall. And when I do, it'll take me a few clicks to rig him."

Dilly slowed her horse momentarily at Dod's side. "Do you want to ride with me or wait for Boot to find his sorry horse?"

Dod extended his hand, indicating he would ride with Dilly. He hadn't ridden horses very much, so Dilly's accompaniment was welcomed. His experience at home was limited to a two-day camping trip in the Uintas with his Boy Scout Troop, and even then, they had taken turns riding an old horse named Buttercup.

"Great. Let's be off," Dilly cried. She was in her element—riding bareback on her stallion, in the middle of the night, wearing a sword and following trouble.

The ride ended up being longer than either of them would have thought, and Boot never caught up. To avoid being detected, Dilly left the highway completely and rode from one lookout point to another, hiding in the shadows, watching for Sirlonk—he was the only one of the three that carried a torch and, therefore, was easy to spot in full moonlight or shade.

From one small hill, Dilly and Dod were close enough to see all three travelers clearly—Zerny leading in the front, Sirlonk and his torch trailing in the middle, and Strat straggling in the back.

Dilly was remarkable on a horse. She kept up with the men without having so much as a cow trail to chase. She stuck to a line of trees near the top of a ridge that followed the general curve of the road below. The shadows from the trees hid them.

Eventually, Zerny left the road and began to meander through a field toward three small tents. Dilly and Dod watched from a safe distance. Sirlonk had been right behind Zerny, but stopped on the road near the camp and waited for Strat, who had fallen much farther behind the others.

"Poor Strat," said Dilly in a soft voice. "He's never cared for riding horses. I bet this is his first night ride. Zerny must have really begged to get him out like this. Who do you suppose is in that camp?"

Dod had a strange feeling. "It's not who is in the camp that worries me," he said. "The camp is the bait."

"The bait?" said Dilly, raising her eyebrows.

"Yes, the camp is the white hat."

Dod made reference to Youk's masterful display of deception, and Dilly remembered quickly.

"If the camp's the bait, then where's the enemy?"

Dod didn't have an answer; however, the feeling of danger got stronger. He searched the valleys and hills with his eyes.

Nothing happened. Song grew impatient as Dilly and Dod watched intently. Zerny entered the camp and six men joined him in lighting a large fire. Strat finally caught up to Sirlonk and together they rode the last leg.

"Strange," remarked Dilly. "Why are Sirlonk and Strat staying on their horses? I wonder what they're saying. It's all driving me crazy. I think we need to ride down there."

Just as Dilly moved her leg to nudge Song into action, Dod whispered, "Wait!" He pointed at a hillside, up the same ridge they were currently on.

A small outcropping of rocks, fifty feet high, crowned the top of the bluff, directly above the little camp.

"Look, right there!" Dod pointed below the crown.

Dilly surveyed the spot, yet didn't see anything special.

"I thought I saw something move," said Dod. "Why don't we ride up the ridge farther—at least as far as we can in the shade of these trees."

Suddenly, an image flashed in Dod's mind, like a glimpse of a photograph. It was brief. He saw the faces of a group of drats, concealed in bushes, holding bows and arrows.

"They're hiding at the base of that cliff—down in the rough. Quick Dilly, cross to the back side of this ridge, then ride as fast as you can. We've got to get above them, before they attack."

Dilly didn't wait or ask questions, she just rode, convinced by the energy in Dod's voice. It was only a matter of moments before they reached the rear of the rocky outcropping.

"We'd better leave Song here," whispered Dilly cautiously. "His hooves would clank and give us away."

Dod and Dilly hustled to the top on foot. From there, they could clearly see that Sirlonk and Strat had dismounted and that Sirlonk was heading for a tent. He went inside and seemed to be investigating something; his torch made the fabric flicker as he moved around.

"What do you think he's doing?" said Dilly impatiently.

Before Dod could give an answer, arrows began to fly. They launched from the bushes on the hillside below. Sirlonk hurried out of the tent and fell over, hit with an arrow. He attempted to crawl away from the attackers with his torch still in hand. Everyone scattered—except Strat.

"There they are," said Dod, pointing at some shrubs that were now walking. The enemy had disguised themselves as bushes and were moving swiftly toward the camp—about a hundred of them.

"Oh no!" groaned Dilly, overcome with sorrow. "Our friends haven't got a chance!" She pointed out that their horses had been frightened before the attack and were some distance down the road, running away. "Even Sirlonk's sword is no good against an army of men with bows!"

Strat stood by the fire, fearlessly waiting. He was the only one that didn't run. He held a paddle in one hand and a shield in the other. As arrows flew at him, he swung the paddle, effectively deflecting them, and occasionally he used his shield to block them.

"What's Strat doing?" cried Dilly. She was becoming overwhelmed with the view of her friends' last stand. "It's not Bollirse, Strat, this is war!" she sobbed to herself. One of her hands clasped her sword handle, but she didn't draw it. The scene was too hopeless. She almost couldn't bear to watch.

Dod was silent, and when Dilly finally looked toward him, she realized he was gone!

"Dod?" she said frantically. "Dod? Dod!"

He had vanished from her eyes. She nervously walked a few steps, down from the top, to check on her horse—her escape. Song was standing where she had left him, calmly chewing a mouthful of grass.

Suddenly, the ground began to shake. A low groaning noise filled the air. Dilly rushed to the top of the hill just in time to see a wall of rocks and dirt rumble down the other side. It quickly engulfed all of the moving bushes of arrowmen and, fortunately, stopped short of the camp. A moment of silence followed.

"So, what do you think of that?" said Dod in a proud voice as he pulled himself up from the front face of the cliff. A cloud of dust filled the backdrop behind him.

"You did all of *that*?" gasped Dilly in shock. Her joy over the rescue of her friends was quickly replacing fear.

"Well, I didn't do as much work as the fifteen-foot log I just used. The secret is leverage. Once big rocks start falling, they generally don't want to stop before they pulverize the heck out of stuff. I lost my tent at Scout Camp, last year, over that one."

"You say the strangest things, Dod; but at a time like this, I wouldn't care if you pranced about on fours, howling up a willow, and claimed to be a dwarsomliver. You did it! You saved them!"

Dilly rose up and began to wave her arms in the air. The dust was starting to settle and her friends around the camp were faintly visible.

"You can't do that," ordered Dod, tackling her to the ground. "We have to get out of here before someone sees us."

"What do you mean?" asked Dilly, confused. "We just beat the terrible ones. Who else is left but our friends?"

"Probably whoever planned this!" responded Dod adamantly. "Don't you see? It was a setup. Someone wanted them dead, and maybe that someone is still down there, watching you wave and waiting to target us as well!"

Dod and Dilly crouched on the bluff behind a little shrub. They accounted for the men, one by one. The last person to make it back into camp was Zerny—and he wasn't walking! Apparently he had managed to escape on a horse, while the other men had remained stranded for the slaughter. It was suspiciously reminiscent of another attack, when he had unhitched the whole team and ridden to safety.

"Zerny looks fine," remarked Dod in an agitated voice. Dilly knew just what he meant.

"Well, he is a horseman," she said in a less than convincing manner. "He's quite a master with them. Maybe his responded to a whistle when the others bolted."

Regardless of Dilly's allegiance, when Zerny rode close to the fire and looked up at the rock outcropping—the exact spot where Dilly and Dod lay hiding—it was time to take Dod's advice and race to Twistyard before risking the outcome of getting caught.

Back at the barn, Boot was waiting to greet them. The morning sky was just starting to get light in one corner and the roosters were waking up.

"Did you see what they were doing?" asked Boot excitedly as he rolled out from under a pony blanket. He had spent the night on a pile of hay.

"We did," answered Dilly coldly. "No thanks to you." She was mad that he hadn't come along, even though he couldn't have done anything. Her real problem was lack of sleep. It made Dilly irritated at everyone.

"I would have come," defended Boot, "but my horse is gone. Look for yourself. By the time I realized Grubber was missing, I knew it was too late to follow on someone else's—you were already at least twenty minutes out."

Dilly joined Boot in walking up and down the barn, this time with a candle, searching all two hundred stalls, only to discover that Boot's horse was missing. Meanwhile, Dod occupied himself in the darkness.

"What in the slickers are you doing to Song?" asked Boot as he neared Dod with the light. He stared, dumbfounded.

"My horse!" shouted Dilly, brewing with anger. "I'll have to order him scrubbed first thing. Whatever caused you to abuse my dear Song after he walked all night for you? Some thanks!"

Dod had taken an old rag and was using it to rub manure on the stallion, especially on his legs and hooves. He also mopped sweat off the horse.

"We've got to make him look like the rest—to hide our identity," said Dod. He spoke with confidence, though he sheepishly oozed concern from his wearied face. "The clay and dust could have easily given us away—at least if someone took the time to check."

Dilly didn't seem to buy Dod's reasoning, but Boot caught on. "You're right," he said, "If we hit a few others, Song won't stand out."

The job was disgusting; nevertheless, Boot didn't want trouble to come knocking, as it often did for him, so he grabbed a rag and began to help.

Dilly sleepily watched. She had done more of the work riding than Dod and was extremely exhausted. Her glazed eyes said it all.

Boot and Dod worked frantically at the task and managed to wipe half-a-dozen horses before a noise made them freeze. A rider was coming toward the barn at a gallop.

"Quick, let's be off," whispered Boot, poking Dod to get his attention.

Both boys ran to the other end of the barn and out the door. They barely escaped meeting the visitor. It was close—too close!

"We forgot about Dilly!" said Dod.

"Didn't she already head back to her room?" asked Boot. Neither of them knew for sure. They sat outside, hidden behind the weed-infested wheels of an old wagon, listening carefully.

"Dilly," said a gruff voice. "Why are you sleeping out here?"

"Oh—sleeping?" said Dilly tiredly, following a long yawn.

"I was just about to head back in. I came to check on my horse—had a bad dream last night and couldn't rest 'til I saw him. It looks like the poor beast spent half the night lying down. I hope he's not sick. Will you attend to him for me, Jibb?"

"When I get some time," he muttered in a cantankerous way. "I've got a few things I need to first straighten out."

"Well—it's good to have you back," said Dilly cheerfully. "I'd better be going. I'll see you around."

Dilly skipped out of the barn and headed for the castle. Boot and Dod caught up.

"Wow! You sure perk up after a short nap," said Dod, who was feeling completely drained.

"It's an act!" said Dilly in her previous, grumpy voice. "We must make people think that everything is normal—*especially...*"

Dilly trailed off for a moment. Dod looked at her and knew what she was about to say; however, he didn't rub it in.

"All right, I'm beginning to think Zerny and Jibb are suspicious," she confessed. "There, I said it. It's probably just the circumstance, and I'm confident they have a logical explanation for everything. Still, we can't risk asking them—not at a time like this."

Boot, Buck, and Sawny were all dying to know what had happened during the night, but Dod and Dilly went straight to bed, claiming near insanity from lack of sleep and overexertion; and they didn't reenter life until after supper that night. Fortunately, the day's routines were disrupted by a dozen different things, so nobody noticed they were missing.

FINALLY WAKING UP

"Do you want some dinner?" asked Buck, gently shaking Dod.

"Ah, I think so—" he responded, opening his eyes and giving a big sigh. "Are you headed down soon?"

"It's long over, but I brought some back for you—a pile of roasted ham, two freshly baked rolls, cooked peas and carrots, and cream cake. I figured you'd be hungry after sleeping all day, and without eating breakfast—though this morning's meal wasn't exactly worth staying awake for. A lot of people got sick in a hurry. Some did, some didn't. Today was quite a day!"

Dod dove into his food the moment Buck handed it over. It was heavenly; having skipped breakfast and lunch made every bite taste like Christmas Dinner at Aunt Hilda's.

"I see you've revived," called Boot from down the hall. He was banging around, bouncing a leather ball back and forth on the wall. "That's it guys," he said to the boys that were with him, "I won again."

The young boys begged for a rematch, claiming he had

cheated somehow; nevertheless, typical of Boot, he left while he was on top.

"Is Dilly all right?" asked Dod as Boot strolled into the bedroom, his thumb tucked under the checkered vest that stretched tight across his chest. Boot closed the door firmly behind him, did a clever spin, and plopped himself regally on his bed. A pleased look spread across his face. To read it, you'd think he had just finished the Boston Marathon in first place.

"I'm sure she's fine," he said, gloating over something he was flauntingly keeping a secret. "And don't worry about having been missed today, either; I took care of that for you. Enough other people were disrupted that nobody would have been able to tell you were sleeping off last night's escapades."

Boot resituated to an upright position and added, "—anyway, what happened with your tracking?"

Before Dod could respond, Buck jumped in and pointed a finger of condemnation at Boot, saying, "It was you! I knew it!"

"What are you talking about?" said Boot, grinning.

Buck groaned with disgust, "You made people sick at breakfast!"

"No!" gasped Boot, acting horrified.

"—and set that herd of cows loose in the front courtyard, too..."

Boot shrugged.

"And I know you're the one that hid Ascertainy's key after locking all the library doors—the library's never been locked in all the years I've been here. They want people in, not out."

Boot tapped his foot against the floor, nearly ready to burst from concealing his story; however, he didn't bend under pressure.

"Do you really think I would do all of that?" Boot finally asked. His eyes twinkled with glee.

"Yes!" said Buck, flopping down next to Dod. "Especially since half of Raul's Coosings were trapped for hours—missed lunch and had to spend the afternoon reading in the library—and without Sawb's help; he spent his time wandering around with 'Tainy, like a leashed pet. She was sure he'd done it to teach them a lesson for choosing to skim books instead of wagging after him when the cows came calling."

"Thank you, Buck," said Boot, smirking. "You're too kind, giving me the credit. But I'll never admit it."

"You already did—said you'd taken care of everything for Dod," grumbled Buck, knitting his brows. He was more irritated than mad.

"Oh," sighed Boot, beaming as one who had been caught the unnamed hero. "What I meant is, Dod and Dilly are lucky to have been able to sleep on a day that was busy enough for them to go unnoticed."

Buck shook his head silently. He was ready to give up when someone knocked at the door.

"Come on in," said Boot cordially, jumping to get it. He was flying high on the adrenaline of an exciting day.

"Thank you. Is Dod in here?"

It was Bonboo. He walked past Boot and into the room, where he found Dod sitting on his bed.

"Sorry I didn't connect with you earlier," said Bonboo. "I meant to meet up this afternoon when I first returned from High Gate, but it seems we've had a terribly busy string of misfortunes." Bonboo's eyes drifted to Boot, who was now looking less pleased and more guilt-riddled.

"Perhaps we could talk," said Bonboo to Dod, approaching him gingerly. "—unless you've made up your mind to go to sleep."

Dod hid his half-eaten dinner behind his back and smiled; he had snoozed all day in his clothes, because he didn't have any pajamas or any other changes of attire, so he was more than ready to fish for answers.

"I'm awake and dressed," he said heartily, popping out of bed. "Now would be a great time. Do you suppose we could talk in Pap's room? I haven't gotten a chance to see it yet."

Bonboo smiled with a knowing look. Dod held up the three keys he had been given; he had them attached to a chain around his neck.

"Well, of course," declared Bonboo in a pleasant voice. "I was thinking that would be a good idea; it would be fitting for me to show you some of your…um…Pap's things." He pointed the way with his cane, but before he left the bedroom, he examined Boot with his eyes and added, "Please, son, try to be good tomorrow."

Boot apologized and slunk into the corner, while Buck beamed in glory, having correctly detected his brother's devious activities. Dod almost explained what had happened—he really, really, wanted to, especially with Boot getting in trouble for helping him—nevertheless, he knew it wouldn't be wise. Bonboo could be trusted with the world, but if he had knowledge of their investigation, he would likely bring it to a sudden end out of concern for their safety.

It didn't take long to get to Pap's room, which surprised Dod. The castle was large enough that he assumed it would take forever at Bonboo's snailish pace. Instead, right across the way from Green Hall's entrance, there was a single door that led to a mini conference room. In the front, on the left side of a wooden stage, there was another door, hidden behind a dark-maroon velvet curtain. It was made of solid iron and firmly locked.

"Could you use your key, Dod?" asked Bonboo.

Dod was puzzled. "Is this it?" he blurted, without thinking. "I mean, I thought only windowless meeting rooms and storage chambers were over here. Why was he living in a closet?"

Bonboo laughed when he heard it. "Just open the door and I'll show you," he said.

The big key fit perfectly, and on the other side was a small, square room, about fifteen feet across. The ceiling, however, was higher than the candle's light could reach. Ropes hung down the sides of the stone walls in a number of spots.

"This is a strange place to live," said Dod, surveying the clutter. He was mortified to think that Pap had spent his time there, among the ropes and dirty crates and chests. It was disappointing to say the least, despite the array of fascinating gadgets and tools that spilled out of the various containers.

Bonboo grinned, knowing Dod hadn't figured out where they were headed. He pointed at a thick cord that trailed upward into the darkness and said, "Come on, Dod, give that a tug and you'll see where Pap really lived."

Dod was instantly relieved and hoped Bonboo hadn't noticed the frustration on his face. He yanked excitedly, waiting for the wall to open up or a trap door in the floor to click ajar. *Anything could happen*, he thought. It was brilliant.

As Dod pulled, he wondered whether it was Pap's idea or Bonboo's to have the real entrance hidden in a closet. The rope hissed and whizzed like the calling of stage curtains before a play. He knew it was doing something, though he didn't know what.

"Good thing Pap improved this place, geared it twenty-to-one, or we'd be here all night," said Bonboo, his eyes glistening with memories of Pap. "Your grandfather loved inventions. This one is a favorite of mine."

A wooden box, framed neatly with oak planks and brass pegs, eventually lowered in front of Dod and Bonboo. It was large enough to sit four people on little benches that lined the inner sides, with a hinged seat in front of the door.

"Climb in," said Bonboo, his voice drenched with anticipation. "Since giving up on riding flutters, this is as close to flying as I get these days. You'll want to hold on tight, son!"

Bonboo entered the box, clasping a short rope that attached to a lever on the wall. After shutting the door and making sure Dod was secure, Bonboo pulled the rope and let go. It released the lever and away the two flew—up, up, up—at least twenty-five stories up.

It wasn't anything like an elevator. Short of a rollercoaster ride at Disneyland or Six Flags, it had few comparables. The air blew Dod's hair violently around and the surge was strong enough to completely rearrange Dod's inners, making breathing nearly impossible. He almost lost the dinner Buck had so kindly brought to him—especially when the box bounced up and down at the end, settling into position. Bonboo's candle didn't help the ambiance, either. It would have blown out if it hadn't been resilient, like a flare; instead, it hissed and sputtered, flickering as a strobe light.

When the ride finally stopped, Dod paused, panting, waiting for his head to come back to him. The world swirled around.

Bonboo, on the other hand, seemed unaffected, other than to display great pleasure in having flown. "We get out on this side," he said cheerfully, pointing nonchalantly to a hallway that led to another door. "If you try the opposite, you'll find the step is quite large." He chuckled at his joke until his cheeks pinked, though they were already on their way from the thrill of the ride.

Dod peeked over the edge, as he staggered to his feet. It was a complete free-fall to the bottom.

Bonboo led the way and Dod followed, using his key, when they arrived at the door, in order to get into Pap's 'room.' It was much nicer than Dod had expected. It was a house full of rooms! Cabinets and cupboards were everywhere, containing all sorts of gadgets and things Dod had never seen before. He understood why Boot desperately wanted to accompany him. It was like entering a shop of wonders—and they were all Dod's, or at least the note had said they were.

"It's no surprise to me that Boot likes this place," said Dod excitedly.

"Boot hasn't seen this one," insisted Bonboo, shaking his head. "He's only seen Pap's decoy on the main level, just down from the kitchen—uses the same big key. Pap said it was convenient to nap in, and for storing a few outfits, but I know why he kept it—in case someone felt the urge to root through his stuff. They could take those things and leave satisfied without getting anything truly important. I'm one of the few people who still know about this spot."

Bonboo paused to think; his eyes varnished with memories of the past. It took a minute before he returned to the conversation.

"The shaft was a quick-rappel from the roof, long ago, back when we…um…did a few things up here. Anyway, it's a lot different now. Pap and I rearranged it about six years ago—for

Pap's safety. He has enough food and beverage in his kitchen, right over there, to last for months—just in case."

Dod looked over and noticed a large room with vaulted ceilings and a wall of windows where Bonboo's hand had indicated was the kitchen.

"Your grandfather liked technology and told me I'd be surprised if I knew what I was missing here in Green; but I always reminded him that I had heard plenty from my parents who spent time with the Mauj—not to mention, much of what you'll find in here originally came from them—bit by bit. It's quite a collection; you won't see one better anywhere else."

"So—you let Pap use your stuff?" said Dod hesitantly, assuming the things in the decoy room were what Bonboo had planned on giving to Dod, not the museum of supplies he was now looking at.

"Yes," stammered Bonboo. "—well, sort of..." He disappeared, once more, into deep thought, furrowed his brow, and shook his head. It was like he was having great difficulty in finding the right words or discerning what he dared share.

"In any event," he finally said, unabashedly "it's all rightfully yours now, Dod—this whole place and everything in it. I'm just glad you've chosen to come here and use it."

Bonboo sat down and made himself comfortable in an easy chair that resembled a recliner Pap had enjoyed in the duplex. It had been his favorite place to sit.

Dod stared, mostly in shock that Bonboo had just said the place was his; it was substantially larger than both sides of the duplex at home—possibly double or more—and it was elegant and brimming with expensive-looking things.

"Pap had this chair custom-made," said Bonboo, breaking

into Dod's trancelike stupor. "I fell in love with it enough to have a replica fashioned for me, too—sits in my bedroom. I sure love your family....Your grandpa was incredible. We had many good times together. He fought with the strength of a lion and still lived as gently as a man."

Dod took a seat close to Bonboo, to listen well, though his eyes busily drifted around the unusual surroundings. He couldn't help himself. It was like Christmas morning, only a much grander pile of presents—a mansion filled with presents! There were so many things to investigate, and the light from two lit stacks in the entry room made it possible to glimpse parts of three more rooms and a short distance down a wide hall.

"You're not being aided by a swapper," said Bonboo frankly.

It was all Dod needed to hear in order to refocus his full attention on the conversation.

"I was there when your grandfather first came to Green," Bonboo continued, his honest eyes revealing he had a wealth of hidden knowledge.

Dod was shocked. His heart pounded loudly in his chest and his eyes grew intense. It was the first time anyone had addressed his strange circumstance as though there was a logical explanation.

"It was in a cottage, down by the seashore, in a city called Dossip. Pappileehonogoso was a long-time friend of mine. He had been aided by a swapper, though under strange conditions, the mentor had been released prematurely; and amazingly, my friend still clung to life. I went to visit him in his home—brought Higga to see if there was anything left to try."

Dod was all ears. This was the discussion he had been waiting for.

"Higga assessed him and indicated that it was far too late to do anything," said Bonboo somberly. "Pappileehonogoso was already a casualty of the wars with Dreaderious's father, Dreadluceous. Higga left to see another friend in Dossip, but I stayed. That's when it happened. In an instant, Pappileehonogoso rose out of bed, looking bewildered, yet excited. I asked if he felt all right, and he answered…let's see, in his words…'I haven't felt this good since yesterday.' I thought it was a strange thing to say."

Dod chuckled as he remembered Pap saying the phrase. He had used it often, even while battling through surgeries and illnesses. It was a reminder of how optimistic Pap had been.

"So it was Pap?" said Dod inquisitively.

"Yes, Pap was standing there, fully clothed in Pappileehonogoso's pajamas. I, of course, thought it was my friend at first, until I noticed his face; and when I looked down at the bed, you can imagine how surprised I was to find Pappileehonogoso was lying there, dead, right where he had been before. It was strange and frightening. Upon making that discovery, I inspected Pap and found that he looked similar to my friend, but was clearly a different person."

Bonboo fidgeted with a bag until he produced a small painting of a man that resembled Pap. He handed it to Dod, who looked at it closely and then couldn't help wondering how anyone could think Pappileehonogoso was enough like Pap to believe they were actually the same person.

"What did you do?" asked Dod.

"Pap helped me bury Pappileehonogoso. Afterward he accompanied me here, to Twistyard. I would have felt obligated to tell others of this extraordinary event if Pappileehonogoso had had living relatives; however, since his wife had already passed away and his three sons had died childless, while fighting Dreadluceous, not to mention Pappileehonogoso was himself an only child, I decided not to say anything."

"Wow," said Dod with excitement. "Pap was really transported here somehow—and I guess, that would mean I'm—"

Dod's words trailed as he pulled up the right leg of his pants; a rough scar ran two inches down his shin from falling out of a giant cottonwood tree when he was nine.

"You're a hundred percent you," responded Bonboo, enjoying the wonder on Dod's face. "After the unusual things Bowlure told me at my hut in Lower Janice, I sent two young friends to go and search for a dead 'fisher boy' of your general description on the Carsalean Seashore, below the cliffs you scaled. They found him, and we buried him. I'm still a little surprised that Tridacello didn't notice the differences between you and the other Dod, but with his busy situation, not to mention your remarkable entry, I can understand how he overlooked it. Perhaps we can keep your arrival story a secret. We don't want people thinking you're crazy."

"And what of Dod's family and friends?" said Dod, feeling guilty about having stolen someone's identity.

"Dod was an orphan who roamed the streets penniless. Tridacello found him a short time ago—took him in as a helper of sorts until the boy began to be mentored by a swapper. At that point, Tridacello felt like Dod had a purpose to perform for the greater good of society. He hired a few men to spend time training him and then brought him on his first mission to recover a stolen triblot for High Gate. That's when you showed up. It appears the swapper died along with the other Dod, much the same way the swapper died before your grandfather's entry."

Bonboo continued to talk while Dod shifted in his chair and waited for the right moment to break in.

"I thought swappers live a long time and aren't susceptible to death, like we are," said Dod, confused by what Bonboo was suggesting. It went contrary to Bowlure's lengthy explanations.

"Traditionally that's been the case. A few people, tads, have the capacity to be aided by swappers throughout their lives and to be chosen at their deaths as swappers. They then are capable of discerning experiences from many relatives, connected in family chains—"

"Called golden chains?" interrupted Dod.

"Yes, and they can pass that information, with advice, to the right people at the right times, assuming the people are tads. Many great victories have been won thanks to them. It's a system that has helped good prevail over evil for tens of thousands of years. Though recently, swappers have been targeted and destroyed by a technology that most people couldn't possibly know exists. I'm still not sure who has it and how they got it. It's disturbing and perplexing."

Dod put his hand on Bonboo's shoulder. The old man was getting tears in his eyes and was obviously distressed by what he knew.

"I haven't told anyone, and the Mauj are the only people I know of that had such a powerful technology. Regardless, dark forces are triumphing in the destruction of the whole system. There used to be many golden chains. Now there are only a few. And the swappers are young—younger than me; the oldest one I've heard of in years is only two hundred and eighty. I remember the days when they were all over a thousand years old. It seems today that the experiences they can draw from are so recent, they are limited and shallow. It's devastating."

Dod wasn't sure how to respond. Bonboo was crying, and he held in his eyes so much more than he was saying.

"Promise me you'll seek out the full truth and the secrets after I'm dead. Since Hoppas was overheard by Boot, the new code word is Dossum. Remember to follow through and ask. Also, get Higga's half of the map first and then ask Dilly for hers. Neither of them knows who will come, so don't be surprised if Dilly gives you a hard time about it. I'm sure she'll be expecting someone more like Commendus."

"Can't you tell me the secrets now?" pleaded Dod eagerly. "That would save me searching—not to mention, I'm sure I'll have plenty of questions. If you trust me with the information, I'll help you figure out what to do. Besides, I'm dying to know what they're about."

Bonboo shook his head. "I have promises to keep, and among them, I promised to restrict the secrets in this way… despite everything that is happening now." Bonboo looked straight into Dod's eyes and added, "If anything should happen to me, obtain them quickly…if you know what I mean." It was as if he were telling him something he couldn't exactly say.

"Of course," said Dod. He really had no idea, but he knew the look in Bonboo's eyes would stay on his mind for a long time.

"I'm sure you must have many questions about how your circumstance works," said Bonboo, wiping away the tears and straining to smile at Dod. "It would probably be best to let Pap answer them."

"He's alive?" gasped Dod, his eyes full of hope.

"I'm sorry, no," said Bonboo, flushing with embarrassment. "He was poisoned at High Gate. I arrived when he was already unconscious, on death's door. He faded soon after, and with his passing, his body disappeared. Only his clothes and those three keys remained. After that, I told everyone his family had picked him up from High Gate."

Bonboo patted Dod on the knee and added, sadly, "I assume he made it back home to Earth for a traditional burial."

"Yes," said Dod somberly, remembering Pap's funeral.

"I meant his books when I suggested he could explain the situation to you. Your grandpa took great care in recording his thoughts and discoveries, not to mention he inherited a fabulous collection of diaries from…"

Bonboo hesitated momentarily before continuing, with a glint in his eye, "The diaries are from someone very special—someone you and Pap have got a lot in common with; but I'll let you read about him for yourself. Pap kept them in his office, down that hall, up above his desk."

Bonboo pointed his finger toward a darkened corridor.

"Oh, and I have Pap's first volume in my care," added Bobnoo. "I was trying to think of what I needed to tell you, and I figured his writings would jog my memory."

Bonboo grabbed his cane and struggled to stand. Dod quickly hopped up and helped him to his feet.

"Anything else?" asked Dod, wishing Bonboo would stick around and share more.

"Yes," said Bonboo. "Now I remember something else your grandfather touched upon. Your time here and at home is a lot like licking two lollipops, one in each hand. When you leave home, it waits for you. When you leave Green, it also waits, so long as you continue to wear your medallion."

"The medallion—Pap's good luck charm—of course! That's how I'm here!" said Dod excitedly. It was like a light bulb had been turned on in his mind. "Now I know why my grandpa had such a fit with an old lady at the library. She told him that time waits for no man. I guess she was wrong because it did wait for him."

"And it waits for you," said Bonboo. He patted Dod on the head. "While you're here, you won't age much, but be careful; you could be injured or killed and it would stay with you. Your grandfather did gain quite a few scars while he was here; especially when he was seriously wounded six years ago in a fight with The Dread. Pap bested him with his sword before quickly retreating home to get fixed at a '*real hospital*,' and when he came back, he was two days too late to finish the job. I guess someone had taken his medallion off or something."

Dod stared in amazement. It all fit together perfectly. He remembered sitting with his mother at his grandfather's side while Pap lay recovering. Pap had been injured in the torso with lacerations, reportedly from a driving lawn mower, but Cole hadn't believed it.

In the end, when Pap had regained consciousness, he had been very disturbed that someone had taken off his 'good luck charm.' Apparently, the nurse had followed hospital policy that required all jewelry be removed before surgery.

"It's starting to make sense," said Dod. He followed Bonboo in the direction of the entrance after helping him trim the lights off.

"You'll have to come back tomorrow," said Bonboo. "Take a look around in the bright light of day; and don't forget to flip through those books. However, Dod, please keep the information secret. I'm certain Pap wrote down enough about his adventures to overly enlighten darker minds—let alone the other collection! Too much truth in the hands of a liar is more dangerous than a world of lies told to the truthful. When people like The Dread are mostly honest, they're more deadly."

"Is that what made Doss dangerous—he knew so much as a swapper?" asked Dod innocently.

"Doss wasn't a swapper, and he wasn't aided by one, either, regardless of what people say. A swapper couldn't do what he did. The role of a swapper is to give advice, not take control. Ultimately, the destiny of each individual lies within his own agency; and Doss was no exception. He was powerful and evil, and yes, he was very unique, but more like you than a swapper. Besides, we don't need to worry about him anymore, or hopefully, the likes of him, forever!"

Bonboo slammed the door, making sure it was tight. Dod reached down to secure it with his key and was greeted by Bonboo's hand. "The door always locks automatically," he said. "You need the key to get in, not out." Bonboo led the way down the hall toward the narrow shaft.

"Here comes the fun part," said Dod naïvely.

"Oh, I prefer the ride up," replied Bonboo. He was trying to prepare Dod for what was coming.

"Why don't you like the ride down?" asked Dod, becoming nervous.

"Probably because I'm too old to do it with a candle in one hand, like Pap used to." Bonboo walked past the wooden box, to a ledge. He took a harness from the wall and started fidgeting with a rope and metal contraption.

"Aren't we riding down?" asked Dod apprehensively.

"No, son. I'm sure your grandfather could have rigged it that way, but he always liked the feeling of a quicker drop, so he didn't."

Bonboo noticed Dod's concerned look and added, "If you're afraid, you can wait in the box and I'll pull you down once I reach the bottom."

It was a tempting offer, yet there was more than physical health to think of—like Pap's reputation. After all, Dod was his grandson.

"I'm coming. It looks fun," responded Dod hesitantly, following a few moments of contemplation. He rigged up and they both prepared to drop.

"Are you ready to go?" asked Bonboo.

"Looking forward to it!" said Dod in a faked-happy voice. He was still trying to convince himself that it wasn't so bad.

"Good!"

Bonboo dropped his sure-light candle. It fell the full distance and remained burning once it hit the stone floor. Dod was terrified. The task had seemed more manageable when darkness had hidden the bottom. Now, the little spec of light appeared to be the size of an ant, or smaller, revealing how high up he was. It made Dod tremble and wonder how he had been able to draw the box down in the first place.

Side by side, Dod and Bonboo descended. It wasn't as hard as Dod had thought; and despite the fact that he had to do it in complete blackness, the rope was secure and close enough to Bonboo's that he jostled into him occasionally, making the venture less horrifying, and the gloves Pap had left at the top did a good job of minimizing the burn.

"I once tried this with white slips," said Bonboo in passing.

"It shredded them and left me with a nasty rope burn. These gloves are much nicer. They're perfect for gliding along, aren't they?"

Dod agreed in mumbled tones.

Once they reached the floor, Bonboo picked up his light and made his way to the door as if nothing had happened. Dod, on the other hand, wanted to do a celebration dance. He had never scaled down a massive cliff, or at least he couldn't remember doing so, though it quickly brought a question to his mind that he knew he needed to ask.

"If I'm all me and not the other Dod, then when was I injured? I don't remember getting hurt while climbing; and Tridacello was right behind me."

"You phase in slowly the first time, or at least that's how it was with Pap. He hobbled around like he was sleepwalking, muttering all kinds of strange things for about ten minutes, before becoming fully aware of the situation—of course, later he was proficient enough to zip back and forth without any confusion. If I had a guess, I would say that the same person who killed the orphan Dod must have wounded you before you were conscious enough to know. It's surprising you survived."

"I was shot while sleepclimbing," muttered Dod.

"I suppose. After all, you don't seem to remember getting hit or stabbed; and it did sound like you were disoriented on the cliff—at least that's the version Dungo rudely insisted. He doesn't have any manners, does he?"

"In his defense," said Dod, "if I was sleepclimbing, I'm sure I didn't help the ones below me much. It probably was my fault poor Bowlure landed in a Glantor-Worm pit."

Bonboo reached down and turned the door handle.

"This one doesn't need locking, either; just remember to shut it firmly. We wouldn't want anyone wandering in." Bonboo gave Dod a look. It was as though he had also said, 'Don't be inviting Boot and Buck to join you in playing around in there. Someone will get hurt.'

Dod nodded in agreement and they made their way toward Green Hall. Dod felt like he was finally waking up. The pieces of the puzzle fit together perfectly. Many things Pap had said in the past were now logical; and the cuts and scrapes Pap had always displayed fit, having come from battles rather than the stories he had told of fishing precariously or mowing recklessly. It was empowering to at last know the truth.

Below the swords, Bonboo patted Dod on the head and reassured him that he was glad to have him around. As he turned to walk away, Dod had one last question:

"How, exactly, do I get home—not that I want to go right now, or anything like that—just in case I want to visit?"

Dod sounded embarrassed; he felt like an ungrateful child asking to leave a special party early because it wasn't good enough.

Bonboo put one hand in the air and said, "I really don't know for sure. It seems Pap would concentrate on something and then zip, but you should read his writings. He wrote all about it."

Dod said 'thank you' and 'goodnight,' while heading into Green Hall, however, his mind was already halfway back to Pap's house. He couldn't stand the thought of waiting until morning. And to make matters worse, everyone was getting ready to sleep, a thing he had already done plenty of that day. A few rooms along the hall had trimmed their lights off and snoring noises could be heard.

Dod looked back at the open doors and noticed Boot's bag, lying in the corner near the entrance. It contained buster candles.

In a flash, before anyone had a chance to detect his return, Dod grabbed the bag and ran. In the distance down the hall, he could see Bonboo walking slowly to his quarters. Dod crossed the corridor and slipped into the conference room. The space felt more than just vacant. Chills ran down his spine until his knees bumped against each other. He broke out a buster candle and struck the wall, the way he had seen others ignite them. It filled the room with plenty of smokeless light, more than the candle Bonboo had used, but still, the uneasiness didn't go away.

"Perhaps I should wait until morning to return to Pap's bunk," said Dod to himself. His voice echoed a little in the room. "Then again, if I go now, I could read books half the night, catch a quick nap, and be ready to meet the day head-on tomorrow. Not to mention, I need to think of what others might conclude; spending my time alone would draw suspicion."

Dod mumbled as he inched his way toward the curtain. "I'll do it!" he said forcefully. "After all, it was Pap's house—and now it's mine!"

The door creaked when Dod opened it with his key. Inside the small space, Dod hastily searched for the right rope.

SWOOSH, SWOOSH, SWOOSH.

The cord squeaked and whistled as he drew the basket. This time Dod noticed that a giant counterweight rose as the box came down.

"That's how he does it," said Dod. He spoke to himself to calm his nerves, though it wasn't working. Something was off.

Once in the basket, Dod felt like a magician; he pulled the string and—Presto—he shot upward. It was exhilarating. Having already done it before prepared him so that the ride was more enjoyable and less nauseating.

At the top, he noticed one rigging hung alone. "Next time I'll bring up the rest from the bottom," said Dod, remembering that he had seen a pile of seven or eight. He stopped to make a mental note. It would be dreadfully difficult climbing down without one, unless Pap had a spare in his house.

At Pap's front door, something in Dod's head made him pause. He put the key to the lock six times before he conjured enough courage to turn it. When he finally pushed the door open, blackness was instantly replaced by light. He had intended on putting fire to the big stacks, yet there was enough light from his one buster candle that he momentarily forgot.

"Let's see," he quietly spoke to himself. "I wonder what that is."

Dod walked over and worked at a jammed drawer until it opened, releasing the object that had been partially visible before. The drawer held all sorts of miscellaneous gadgets. He took the remaining buster candles out of Boot's bag and began to refill it with the most interesting things.

"Wow, that looks neat," whispered Dod, climbing on the back of a chair to reach something that was sequestered at the rear of a cluttered shelf. The contraption appeared to be made of five red golf balls that were directly attached to separate thin black cords, which joined together into the head of a twenty-five-foot rope.

"Maybe it's a strange lasso," said Dod. He put it in the bag and went on muttering as he looked at everything.

It didn't take long before Boot's bag began to droop from its heavy load. Dod was still contemplating spending the night at Pap's place, but he hadn't gotten comfortable with the feeling in the house, so he filled the bag just in case he chickened out—at least he would be able to examine the stuff in the dormitory, while Boot and Buck slept close by.

Dod had only searched half the devices stowed in the entry room, yet he had already overfilled Boot's bag; the weight caused his right shoulder to sag, and consequently, when he walked, he rocked back and forth. His distorted reflection in the glass on the outside wall of the parlor, over by the hall entrance, took his breath away—it was scary!

"It's only me," sighed Dod, attempting to regain his composure. The blurred image of what appeared to be a hunching beast with a bag was enough to incite Dod's already tense senses, though little did he know, he was in for real trouble!

THE ESCAPE

"Let's see," whispered Dod to himself, feeling very alone. "Bonboo said the books were down the hall, in Pap's office, directly above his desk. I should at least take a quick look. Maybe he left me a decent record of how to zip home. It could come in handy the next time I get in a bind with a venoos, or something worse; I could zip out of here and let time pass with my luck charm on a chair, not around my neck—someone else could deal with the venoos—that would definitely be lucky."

Dod continued to talk as he made his way to the hall. It wasn't what he had expected. One side of the twelve-foot-wide passage was filled with unique objects: a gigantic stone pot, filled with weapons that spilled over the top; a fake tree, adorned with hats, gloves, boots tied at the laces and hung in pairs, and other weird apparel; a rock waterfall that had stains, revealing it had worked at times; an empty, multi-level cage of sorts, fashioned out of sticks and lashings, which almost touched the fifteen-foot ceiling; an enormous bowl, held eye level by two Roman columns; and many other eccentric items of curious origins and constructions.

On the other side of the hall was a battalion of statuary: a man wearing a fancy uniform, complete with hat, gloves, sword, and multiple awards across the lapel; four men displaying various types of armor, shields with small spikes and others with smooth plating, thick bronze and silver breastplates, one to three-piece helmet gear, leg and arm attachments, chain meshing, and steel-plated boots; two men exhibiting leather wear—jackets, hats, shirts, pants, boots, belts; and other statues holding mysterious objects.

During the day, the hall would have been light due to windows that lined the vaulted ceiling; however, at night, darkness and shadows shrouded everything. Dod's frightful encounter with his own hunching reflection made him hesitate. He didn't want to venture down the hall. The statues on one side and objects on the other merged and crossed in the middle so that a person would have to wind back and forth in order to traverse it.

"Perhaps tomorrow," said Dod curtly. He turned to walk away when the thought of Sirlonk making fun of him entered his mind. He could see him laughing, calling him a child. It made the blood flow hot in his face.

"Or today!" proclaimed Dod triumphantly, spinning around. "It doesn't matter. Now is as good a time as any to look at Pap's books."

Dod did his best to convince himself that he was indeed brave enough.

The hall was a mess. Dod nearly fell flat on his face as he darted around a spear, jutting out from one statue, only to have his right leg caught by a web of twigs, jutting up from the floor, which stuck out of a fallen, reed container. The debris under Dod's feet made a crackling noise that set his nerves on edge.

A few steps—a shuffle to the right—duck under another spear

—shuffle, shuffle—quick left around the stone waterfall—shuffle, clank, a sword and sheath under foot—jump over a fallen statue wearing armor made of a shiny golden metal—shuffle, shuffle—a large doorway opened on his right with the hall continuing directly in front of him.

"Here it is," said Dod confidently. "I've found the office." He entered and immediately saw that the books were gone! The cabinet above Pap's desk was completely empty; and the rest of the room was turned upside-down. Someone had been there in search of the books and had taken them!

Goose flesh covered Dod's arms. Images rushed his mind of a dark figure, hiding in the shadows of Pap's cluttered hall. *Danger! Fight! Run!* echoed in his mind. His eyes quickly combed the disheveled office to detect if anyone remained among the scattered items. Nothing moved.

"It's all in my head," whispered Dod. "Whoever did this is long gone. Don't panic. You're going to be just fine—"

Dod's voice trailed off when he heard something.

CREAK, CREAK, BANG—CREAK, CREAK, BANG.

The noise came from farther down the hall, where Dod hadn't been. It seemed to be getting louder. Someone or something was hurrying toward the room. Dod searched for a place to hide, but immediately realized that whoever or whatever had successfully mastered the entry of Pap's secret house would easily find him in the office rubble; and he or it would have seen the light from the candle.

A sword collection lay strewn across the floor in one corner. Dod reached for a battle sword and found that it was heavy enough to throw his balance off and he tumbled over. The gear in his bag clanked against the web of swords on the ground. One protruding blade slit his pants across the knee and drew blood.

CREAK, CREAK, BANG—CREAK, CREAK, BANG.

Dod's heart was pounding like the beating of tribal drums at the end of a war council. His hand seized upon the handle of a lightweight, thin sword, and as he drew it from its scabbard, he knew exactly what he had to do.

Dod took the candle and smothered the flame out. The room went completely black. Crouching in a defensive position, Dod waited for his attacker.

CREAK, CREAK, BANG—CREAK, CREAK, BANG.

A slight draft swirled around. The enemy had entered through a different door or had broken a window, causing the smell of the night air to encompass the darkness. Tension continued to mount. The clamor of shuffling and crackling occasionally joined the creaking sounds.

Instantly, without any hesitation, Dod leaped for the open doorway. His eyes had adjusted as much as they could, which was hardly useful in the blackness, but it did make large objects slightly visible. Light from the night sky leaked in through the ceiling's thick glass windows as a murky glow.

Dod looked only briefly down the hallway toward the source of the sounds. A giant enemy was barely visible, skulking in the darkness. One peek was plenty. His legs froze in shock and fear.

Suddenly, to his rescue, he could see in reverse the labyrinth he had struggled down to get to Pap's office. It was all in his mind; nevertheless, the clarity of the map enlightened him just enough to dare run.

Dod bolted like a rabbit escaping from a mountain lion; he scurried back to the entry room and staggered in search of the front door handle.

But it wasn't over yet!

CREAK, CREAK, BANG—CREAK, CREAK, BANG.

The haunting sounds got louder as they echoed rhythmically off the vaulted ceilings and were increasingly joined by the clatter of objects being displaced and broken. An undeterred enemy was on the approach!

Dod rushed out the door and headed for the drop, all the while remembering the story of Pap's escape from the monster in the dark cabin; the creature hadn't used a light while destroying Pap's men. It made Dod wonder whether he was being pursued by the same demonic beast.

Feeling the wall, Dod desperately searched for the last pair of gloves and harness—over here—over there—up a little—down low—he couldn't find them fast enough! Every second felt like minutes. The enemy would soon catch up, and the gear was gone!

The shaft was pitch-black. No light entered the room. Dod momentarily wished he still had one last candle to use, if only to find the exact location of the drop and the ropes. With a sword still in one hand, he crouched on the floor and began to scurry toward the edge—or at least what he thought was the edge!

WHOOSH.

Directly in front of Dod a slight draft accompanied an almost imperceptible crack of dim light; someone was opening the door, and Dod was crawling in the wrong direction! Instinctively, he leapt to his feet and dashed across the floor to the drop. By the faint light, emanating from the crack, a rope was barely visible—or was Dod imagining he could see it? He couldn't tell.

Glimpses of an old pirate movie flooded his mind. He took the sword and bit the thin blade, holding it with his mouth, and then used both hands to reach for the rope. It was real. He pulled it close and wrapped Boot's leather bag straps around it twice.

WHOOOOOOOOSH.

The crack of light became a full stream as the door opened. Someone had lit a candle and was pursuing after him. Without delay, Dod grabbed the two ends of the straps and jumped, positioning the heavy bag between himself and the rope. It hissed as the rope burned the bag.

Dod flew downward, occasionally using his feet against the rock wall to moderate the drop, but also trying hard not to slow down.

Eventually, and it did seem like a long time, Dod hit the stone floor. He hadn't known when it was coming, because of the blackness, so it caught him off guard.

For a few moments, Dod lay on his back in pain looking heavenward, holding the sword in his hand. He noticed a slight glow, twenty-five stories up. The door was still open. And worse still, someone was working a rope, quietly coming down to get him—he could hear the hissing line! There was no time to waste. He staggered to his feet and untied the pouch as he rose.

Unexpectedly, something grabbed his neck! It began to choke him ferociously. He struggled to run, but couldn't budge. The more he pressed, the harder he was choked. He swung his sword back and forth, left and right. It was all awkward. Dod had never used a weapon before, yet somehow, as the blade sliced through the air, he felt powerful.

Finally, one lucky strike set him free.

Flailing, and dragging Boot's bag, Dod fell forward and hit the door. It was just the break he needed. He dashed out into the conference room and instinctively stumbled to the entrance.

In the larger hall, two dim lights interrupted the darkness. They confused him; he knew one of them was the opening to Green Hall; but which one?

Before Dod could make up his mind, the corridor lit up. It was Jibb. He was waiting on a bench, a short distance away.

"Well, look what I've caught," said Jibb in an ornery voice, pulling methodically at his pointed beard. "I expected to find at least one of you sneaking about."

"I'm not sneaking!" said Dod defiantly.

"Then why are you walking in the dark, without so much as a glowing stone? If that's not sneaking, I'm purple and pink," snarled Jibb, jumping to his feet.

Dod remembered to hide Pap's sword behind his back when he noticed Jibb was wearing one at his waist.

"What about you, Jibb?" asked Dod, slowly shuffling sideways toward Green Hall. "Why are you lurking out here?"

"It doesn't concern you," snapped Jibb. "Besides, I have permission to *lurk* at night." He pointed at a golden badge below his left shoulder, while stepping in front of Dod, blocking him from Green Hall's entrance. Jibb reached for the hilt of his sword.

Images flooded Dod's mind. He saw what looked like the same badge, reflecting candlelight, as a man labored with a saw to cut through a support beam—it was the man with the scar on his hand—he was the one who wore the same badge as Jibb, only his was partly concealed beneath a black outer cloak. "...So, I'll ask you one more time, what were you doing?" demanded Jibb; the more angry he got, the more he snorted through his uppity nose.

Dod was shaking, his knee stung, and he could taste blood in his mouth. He cried out in his mind, wishing someone would help, wishing Bonboo would come back and resolve things or Dilly would bubble-up, spilling over with her usual stories, and distract Jibb.

Dod had almost died at the hands of an enemy in Pap's place and, now, was fighting off images of another, pending doom—a doom that looked fatal—which haunted him; and all the while, Jibb stood in front of him, glaring, clutching the handle of his blade.

"I—I—uh—was—"

"There you are," said Boot in a loud voice, dashing into the conversation. He was a rescuing angel. "I told you to put it in the supply closet across the hall, meaning inside Green Hall, not out here."

Boot stood at the doorway, below the twin swords, and held a candle like Jibb; however, Boot's light was much brighter than Jibb's.

"You really think I'm dumb enough to believe that's *yours*," said Jibb condescendingly as he pointed at the bag and gave Boot a cross look.

Four more men, dressed in black and with swords at their waists, approached from down the hall. They all wore identical golden badges.

"Are the Green Coosings still giving you trouble?" boomed one large man, who towered above the others. "What's this all about?"

As the newcomers drew near, it was apparent by their characteristic white beards that they were also drats, only larger than Jibb. All of them spoke in authoritative voices, so it was difficult to tell who was in charge, or if they were equals.

"I just caught this boy out roaming the castle, doing who

knows what sorts of mischief and treachery," said Jibb with disdain. "After last night's events and the trouble here at Twistyard today, we should be very cautious. We'd better bring him down and lock him up....And you," Jibb pointed to the largest drat, "—stay here until I get back. Don't let anyone in or out!"

Jibb held seniority and gave commands; the other men quickly moved to carry out his orders.

"Wait everyone, hold on!" interjected Boot, throwing himself between the drat security officers and Dod. "There's been a little mix-up. It's actually kind of funny. My new friend, Dod, simply misunderstood where I wanted him to stow my things. I'm having him clean my room—you know, making him earn his right to bunk with me." Boot nodded his head, flailed his arms, and made good eye contact as he spoke, selling his story as well as he could.

"I told him," Boot continued energetically, "to put the bag in the supply closet in the hall. He thought *this* hall instead of the one inside there." Boot pointed to Green Hall and smiled. "That's why he doesn't have a light; it's not dark down by our room."

"At this time of night?" asked Jibb contemptuously. It was obvious that he didn't believe Boot; Jibb's eyes glared coldly.

"Yeah, that's part of the initiation," responded Boot, forcing a chuckle. "I'm planning on having him scrub the floors and everything. He won't be sleeping much. And trust me, I'll have him about the regulars tomorrow, too. You know me, Jibb; I have a cruel streak, three cow hides thick."

"That's true," growled Jibb, enviously noticing the sign of a Coosing on Dod's hand. "Funny...I'm the one wearing a badge. And guess what, boys? It trumps a little ring!"

Jibb waved his hand and the men moved toward Dod,

disinterested in Boot's explanation, until one pointed at the sack and read out loud: "*Boot Bellious Dolsur III.*"

The guards paused to look at Jibb as one asked, "Who's that?"

Jibb fidgeted and squirmed, annoyed, and then consented begrudgingly, "You're *lucky*, Boot, that I'm in a forgiving mood. Don't let your games spill onto the rest of us. I'll be watching you. Stay in your halls, as Bonboo ordered! We have important things to attend to—safety issues. I'm sure you can learn all about them from Youk. Who knows, one day you might grow up and be commissioned *like me.*"

Boot hardly heard the spiteful dribble that poured from Jibb's mouth. He knew it stemmed from jealousy. Instead, Boot focused his attention on finding a way to distract the guards from noticing that Dod was trying to conceal something behind his back.

"What's that over there?" said Boot. "Is he one of yours?"

Boot pointed into the darkness, pretending to see someone loitering by Raul Hall. All drat eyes followed his finger, while his other hand reached down and nudged Dod behind him. Together they backed up until they were safely within the large double doors of Green Hall.

CLANK, SHLANK.

Boot closed and locked the doors, first with a key, then with a thick plank of wood, bracing them against assault. He then patted the bulwark gently and sighed, "I never thought I would want to lock these things. This is a first. But strange stuff is happening tonight. Even I'm turning psychic; it was like I knew you were out there in the hall, needing my help."

Boot started to walk away when he swung around abruptly. His eyes said it all, before he spoke. Dod pulled the sword out from behind his back and held it up to the light. The blade glistened, showing an emblem at the base and fancy designs all the way up to the pointed tip.

"Wow!" blurted Boot. "That's a beauty. I see it was Pap's—has his insignia right there."

Dod nodded as he dragged the bag with his other hand, clanking it along the floor. He was exhausted from everything, and now, in locked quarters, safely among many friends, his body was willing to give up.

"Here, let me carry that," said Boot, beginning to crack a look on his face that revealed he was gloating over having bested Jibb and the other drats. "After all, it is *my* pack."

Boot picked up the bag and carried it into their room.

"Did you bring me any surprises?" he asked, smirking at Dod. "—Hey, and why were you walking around in the dark? Didn't Bonboo send you back with a candle? Not to mention, I thought I had a whole pile of them right in—"

Boot's eyes glanced down at the things that were beginning to spill out of the sack, and he realized they weren't clothes and other basics, as he had expected.

"Whoa, Twistyard Baby!" said Boot in an excited voice, his eyes widening with glee. He bellowed loud enough to awaken Buck from slumber.

"I can't believe this is all ours," exclaimed Boot, shutting the bedroom door with one hand and putting the other on Dod's weary shoulder. "I don't remember Pap ever showing me any of this stuff....Now you came by it honestly from Pap, right?"

Dod nodded and collapsed on his bed. His mind was still trying to process every detail of his encounter with the enemy in

Pap's place, his 'chance' meeting with Jibb and the other drats, and his flurry of reoccurring images. How did they connect, or did they? It was all a mystery that begged to be solved.

"Wow! Look at this, Buck; he's got a palsarflex! I've only heard of them—never actually had anyone confirm for sure that they were real."

Boot held up the five ball contraption on a rope. Dod smiled; it made him happy to see that Boot thought the items he had chosen were important.

"What, exactly, does it do?" asked Dod, reviving enough to sit up.

"Oh, this is a great tool," said Boot. "These look like normal balls, but they're not. Watch." He held the balls over the stone floor and let them drop. They didn't bounce; instead, they flattened out on one side and stuck to the floor. Boot tossed the white rope over to Dod and said, "Here, try to pull them off."

Dod tugged and pulled, to no avail.

"That's amazing! How do you retrieve them?"

"Like this," responded Boot. He loosened the rope and then wiggled it back and forth gently; the balls released their grip and came up from the floor, reforming instantly once they were in the air.

"It's a tool for climbing walls and cliffs. The globes only stick to stone, so when you use it, make sure the surface you're throwing them at is pure rock—dirt, plants, and wood can break the connection.

Boot went back to the bag and started to dig for another item when there came a quiet knock at the door.

"Are you awake in there?" whispered Dilly.

Buck climbed out of bed and fumbled for his robe as he mumbled, "The moment we get our hands on good stuff, we have to count on her coming around. Quick, hide it!"

Boot shook his head. "What's the point? She'll detect it anyway; then we'll have to explain why we were concealing it from her. She'll think we stole it." His eyes drifted back to Dod. "Bonboo really did help you get this stuff from Pap's room, right?"

Dod nodded his head again. He knew there was a lot more to the story than Boot had been told; however, none of it changed his ownership of the gadgets.

Dilly rushed in the moment the door was opened, dressed in daytime clothes. She was wide awake from hours of napping and had plenty to say.

"Have you seen how many soldiers they've brought?" she rumbled, waving her arms in the air. "A new batch of them are positioning their camp right below my window. You've got to come and take a look. I bet there are at least five hundred of them. Agreeing to host a few swordsmen is one thing; but this is ridiculous! Bonboo didn't consent to *this*!"

"You're inviting us into your bedroom quarters?" gasped Boot. It was the first time ever. Both Boot and Buck stared in amazement.

"Well, you can't see them from your window," said Dilly matter-of-factly, glancing at their wall of glass. She turned back to Boot, popping with energy, and began again. "I noticed we've locked our hall doors—which was a good move—no telling what the real motive is for this unusual nighttime invasion. Our safety? My little finger! I think there's a lot they're not saying."

"Youk announced it at dinner," said Boot politely, trying to act mature, while attempting to rub it in her face that he, for once, knew more than she. "Commendus ordered an emergency meeting today. He counseled with Bonboo and some of The Greats, and they concluded a few men would be a good thing for our own protection."

"I heard it all," responded Dilly, surprising Boot. "You didn't think I slept through dinner, did you?"

Dod grinned as he found his half-eaten plate and began to finish it. Dilly saw him and rolled her eyes.

"I went up and spoke with Youk privately after he made his formal proclamation. He told me there are accusations from Lower Janice, and a few cities along the coast of the Carsalean Sea, that Twistyard is home to some troubled sorts. Apparently, damage was done to a few buildings in Lower Janice and flocks were stolen from the coastal cities—the claims reportedly had proof of a Twistyard connection. *That's* why the troops are here. They want to find out who's involved—"

"But that's a good thing, isn't it?" interjected Buck, stopping Dilly momentarily. He rubbed his sleepy eyes.

"Good?" exploded Dilly. She looked as much shocked that he would say it as she was mad that he didn't understand her concern. "They're searching for anyone they can blame—anyone who stands out as possessing the skills necessary to have committed the assaults. That could be any one of hundreds of us. I'm sure they'd take Bonboo if he appeared to be what the people wanted."

"Now that's an over-exaggeration," said Boot, trying to calm her down. His swagger and tone implied he had been around long enough to be a voice of sound reason. "You don't have to worry about Bonboo. He's safe. They wouldn't take Green's Chief Noble Tredder!"

"You wouldn't think so; but that's because you didn't hear

what I overheard Sirlonk telling Youk and Strat. The drats in Lower Janice are incited by a dozen ambassadors from Soosh who are trying to build legitimacy for their case against tredders in their own conflict back in Soosh—the conflict Pap and Miz never got a chance to resolve. You know drats outnumber tredders five to one here in Green, and how many major political leaders can you think of that are drats?"

Boot tried to refute Dilly's argument using statistics on the number of educated drats versus educated tredders; nevertheless, try as he did, he couldn't dispute away what it looked like—bold faced discrimination! Dilly spoke the hard truth. Even Dod had quick recollections of the very few drat leaders. Dilly's statement built a case that seemed worthy of concern.

"Don't you think Commendus would sell any friendship to keep the peace and maintain his position?" asked Dilly. She no longer seemed angry, just worried. "Wouldn't he later justify it as a cost of *democracy*?"

They were rhetorical questions. Regardless of the fact that Commendus was kind and generous, everyone knew he loved the current democracy in Green enough to do anything to uphold it; and as the head political leader, he had an extraordinary amount of power over the other ruling representatives and dignitaries.

"Perhaps Sirlonk knows more than he's telling," said Boot, his eyes revealing he was now getting agitated. "When he returned this evening, I noticed he was wearing a sling on his arm. It appears he's been involved in some sort of scuffle; and with the condescending comments I've heard him make about drats and humans, it wouldn't surprise me if he knew who was behind the harassments."

"I know all about his injury," said Dilly frankly. "Besides, if Sirlonk really had such true disdain for drats, he would have ignored Zerny's request last night, and that would have prevented his misfortune. I admit he's egotistical and loves to put everyone else down, but in his heart he must be good, otherwise he wouldn't have taken an arrow in company with drats.

"Taken an arrow?" choked Boot, eager to hear the rest of the tale. "How do you know he was shot?"

"Dod and I watched it happen. Poor Sirlonk was hit with an arrow during the ambush. He didn't even have time to draw his sword before he fell wounded."

"AMBUSH?" said Boot and Buck in unison.

"Didn't Dod tell you?" asked Dilly. She smiled with delight upon hearing that Boot and Buck were completely oblivious to the prior night's excitement.

"Nobody told us anything," said Buck glumly, sitting back down on his bed.

"Well, if he hasn't told you, then allow me—Dod probably didn't want to sound like he was bragging."

Dilly shut the bedroom door and moved farther into the room. She sat down on Dod's bed, next to him, while he finished his cold supper. Boot sprawled out on his own bed and put the bag of gadgets on the floor.

All eyes were glued in anticipation as Dilly unfolded the adventure. She made sure to emphasize the part where Dod stopped the attackers by himself, at least a hundred of them.

"—and doesn't that sound like something Pap would have done?" she concluded. "He's definitely Pap's grandson!"

Everyone pondered in silence for a few minutes, trying to think of how the incidents fit together. Dilly had learned from Strat that the secret night ride was in acceptance of an invitation to a private meeting with some influential drats from Lower Janice. Evidently, they were concerned about the recent harassments and their implications on Twistyard, and therefore, as Zerny's friends, they were willing to open up a channel of unofficial communication—in the form of a clandestine, middle-of-the-night meeting—for the purpose of swaying both sides to a peaceful resolution.

It was a while before anyone spoke. Dod stared at the wall and tried to include other pieces of the puzzle that his friends didn't know about—Pap's books, and the enemy that was in his secret house, and also the things that Bonboo had said to him. Dilly looked around the room, though it was obvious her focus was elsewhere. Boot and Buck lay quietly with their eyes closed, pondering.

"Who would attack representatives from Twistyard and Lower Janice, tredders and drats?" mumbled Boot. He was starting to think out loud, but Dilly took it as a real question and started spouting more information.

"They're claiming it was a mob of tredders, disguised as bushes; unfortunately, nobody will ever know the truth: The rock slide is deep enough to completely bury them for good."

"Tredders?" said Dod quickly. "They weren't tredders, they were drats!"

"How do you know?" responded Dilly. "We couldn't see them very well. All we saw was a wave of shrubish camouflaged soldiers—if that."

"I just know. In my head they were drats," said Dod.

"But they couldn't have been drats," said Dilly insistently. "The representatives from Lower Janice are certain that tredders attacked them. That's one of the reasons the troops surrounding this investigation—*invasion!*—are all drats. It was part of the agreement from today's meeting. Commendus felt it was only fair after hearing the six testimonies. The men asserted all sorts of things in common—but there was a discrepancy as to who asked for the rendezvous in the first place. What a death-trap!"

"At least we have some representation," interjected Boot in a hopeful sort of voice. "They made Zerny and Jibb head coordinators with the troops, and Youk is the investigation advisor—reports directly to Bonboo and Commendus. It seems to me that everyone sincerely wants to get to the bottom of this. Maybe having soldiers stationed here will help us find The Dread. After Bonboo's comments the other night, I'm assuming plenty of people, including Zerny's friends from Lower Janice, are really looking for The Dread. Besides, drat troops cost a lot less than tredder forces. Commendus probably made his decision based on money; he's a businessman before a bureaucrat."

Dilly shook her head in disgust, but it was apparent from her composure that she considered his arguments plausible and reassuring. Dod, on the other hand, didn't like the thought of Jibb and Zerny, or even Youk, being critically in charge. He began to say something when Dilly snapped in.

"Regardless of who is controlling the troops, I'd feel much better if the Coosings, Greenlings, Sooshlings, and Raulings were able to carry swords. These are troubled times. Our best protection would come from our friends, not hired unknowns."

"Then you'll be happy to hear what Dod acquired," chimed Boot enthusiastically. "He's got Pap's sword."

Dod held up the shiny blade for Dilly to see.

"It Looks like Bonboo is starting to make exceptions on his rulings," said Boot, partially teasing Dilly, rubbing it in that Bonboo had not yet allowed her to legitimately carry one.

"Does Bonboo know you have it?" asked Dilly. She was surprised, and the look in her eyes revealed agitation.

"Actually, he doesn't know," confessed Dod. "I went back to Pap's place after Bonboo was gone. But he said I could have all of Pap's stuff, and that would include this sword as well."

"He kept a sword in his room?" said Dilly doubtfully. "I thought his swords were kept with everyone else's in Sword Tower—Twistyard rules, to keep accidents from happening."

"Pap wasn't accident prone," snapped Dod defensively.

"Not accidents by The Greats. If a disgruntled Pot swiped a sword from Pap's bedding quarters, they could cause problems."

"Oh," said Dod, nodding his head. "Then I guess that's why Bonboo allowed Pap to keep weapons in his house—no chance of others—uh—wandering in without being invited."

"Hardly," insisted Dilly. "His bunk is close enough to the kitchen to be a prime target for dipping."

Dod smiled with satisfaction. Apparently, Bonboo was right about the secrecy of Pap's living quarters.

"Look what else Dod brought back," said Boot proudly, changing the subject by hefting his bag from the floor. "It's full of all kinds of neat stuff. I didn't realize Pap had these things. He's even got a palsarflex!"

"Palsarflex?" choked Dilly in disbelief. "A *real* palsarflex? And it works?"

"Yup, I was skeptical, too."

Boot pulled the palsarflex from the bag and gave Dilly a show.

"Wow!" she proclaimed in amazement. "What else did you bring back?"

"A few things that caught my eye," responded Dod. He

was dying to tell his friends about Pap's remarkable place, and it showed on his face.

"Like what?" asked Dilly. "Are you teasing us? Why are you smiling?"

"That's just the tip of the iceberg," he said, pointing to Boot's bag of gadgets. "There are rooms filled with neat gear, and weapons, and books, and all kinds of stuff. It's incredible!"

"Pap's stuff?" said Dilly, drenched with misgivings.

"Yes. Bonboo showed me his real living quarters. I was stunned, too. But you have to promise me that you won't tell anyone—except maybe Sawny. He has a house, hidden on top of the castle, with a secret entrance, and these rope things, and everything."

"Really?" said Dilly, not wanting to be duped. She knew the boys were prone to that sort of thing. "I think you're leading me on, and it's hardly the time. With troops patrolling, we'll need to come up with new plans for accessing our twenty-two spots—and there's the—"

Dilly was cut off abruptly by a vigorous knocking at the door.

"You guys up?" asked Sawny urgently. "Open up. You won't believe what I just saw."

Buck made his way to the door and unlatched it. "So, what did you see?" he asked calmly, leaning toward her.

Sawny pushed past him, barging into the room, flustered in the face, and looked nervously around.

"Perhaps you should dim your candles first," she said. "With your large windows, everyone out there, down below and up above, can see in—or at least can see you're awake."

"Let them know," said Boot boldly. "I'm not afraid of a few drats noticing I'm a late night kind of guy."

CHAPTER TWELVE

"What about night riders?" asked Sawny, deathly stern.

"Who?"

"Mysterious men on giant flutters—two of them. I saw them against the backdrop of the dark sky. They weren't carrying lights and probably would have gone unnoticed by most people. I happened to be using my noculars, trying to get a closer look at some movement I thought I saw in the rooftop gardens. I wondered who would have access, especially at night, so I increased my peek and thereby happened upon two flutters. They were being ridden by people or things cloaked in black. One of them must have been twice the size of you, Boot."

"Or the flutter was smaller than you think, making the man look bigger," argued Boot, puffing his chest and standing muscled. His six-foot-plus frame was handsome and formidable at the same time.

"No, I doubt that," said Sawny honestly, recounting exactly as she remembered it. "I admit there's a chance more than one person may have been riding on the second—really close together—though I doubt it; but I know for sure they were on giant flutters. I saw them launch from the crest of the castle, above the top garden, heading toward Lake Mauj. They went right past the huge fish statue, and one of the flutters was at least as big as it, and the other, just a little less. The Fog's so thick tonight that they disappeared almost as soon as they left the roof. What would they be doing up there?"

"And who could they be?" added Dilly eagerly, her eyes flashing with excitement. She couldn't have been happier in front of a pile of birthday presents with her name on them. "We don't have any flutters here at Twistyard right now; Miz and Zerny loaned our five to Pious for the war effort, and nobody else around here keeps them. They're hard to come by these days, even with money...let alone giant flutters! They're nearly extinct."

Boot struck out the candles and everyone waited for their eyes to adjust. Dod sighed uncomfortably. The darkness quickly brought back ominous feelings he had felt in Pap's house; and hearing Sawny mention two mysterious riders on the rooftop reminded him of his first assumptions: The Dread was near and not alone!

DILLY'S SPECIAL BOOK

"I have something to say," whispered Dod to his friends as they sat in the dark. "But you can't tell anyone. Can you keep a secret?"

In the murky dimness, Dod could see well enough to notice four nodding blobs.

"Like I was saying before, Pap's house is built on the roof. You have to climb up through an old quick-rappel to get to it. Pap's been living there for his safety, ever since his encounter with The Dread. Bonboo told me practically no one knows of it."

"Whoa, that sounds neat," muttered Buck excitedly.

"And you're being serious?" asked Dilly.

"I'm totally serious. I'll take you there when it's safe. I went back to it alone, after Bonboo showed it to me. I wanted to skim through some things my grandpa wrote, but they were all stolen; and someone was still there, in the darkness. He chased after me—I barely escaped with my life."

"So the men on flutters were raiding Pap's house?" said Sawny.

"I think so," answered Dod. "It would be a pretty logical

way to get in since I have the only key to the front entrance. Even Bonboo doesn't have one."

Dod patted his lower neck and felt his heart begin to pound in panic.

"My keys! Where are my keys? I had them right here!"

"All three of your keys from Pap?" asked Dilly apprehensively.

"Yes, I kept them on a chain, and now they're missing."

Dilly searched her pockets and produced two brightly glowing stones. "We need to find those keys. Are you sure you don't still have them?"

Dod felt his neck and searched his clothing. When he came up empty, Dilly moved in. She appeared more concerned about the keys than Buck and Boot.

"I must have lost them during my escape," groaned Dod painfully, feeling the tug of a sinking pit in his stomach. He couldn't believe that he had already failed to keep them safe.

"Oh, great!" grumbled Dilly sarcastically as she leaned over, inspecting him. "It appears they were torn from you." She ran her finger across a fresh, thin scab.

Dod felt the ring of dried blood. It circled halfway around his neck, ending near his ears.

"You must have known when they were taking your keys," insisted Dilly, perturbed. "Someone pulled your chain until it broke. Couldn't you have protected them? You had Pap's sword!"

"I was in a hurry, trying to escape with my life," complained Dod miserably. "It was pitch-black. Everything happened so fast."

Dod was surprised that Dilly seemed even more bothered by the loss than he was, and she didn't appear the slightest bit troubled by him having been assaulted. He retraced his steps in his mind, mumbling audibly, "I ran down the hall and out the door, searched for a harness, rappelled the wall, and then was attacked—"

Dod's voice trailed off. The choking had taken place as he arose from the floor of the shaft. In retrospect, it was hard to remember what had strangled him—possibly it was just his chain, stuck to something; and furthermore, the enemy hadn't fought back when he wielded his sword.

"I think I know where the keys are," admitted Dod, feeling stupid. "At least I hope I do, unless The Dread followed me down and found that I left them."

"You ran from The Dread?" squeaked Sawny; the soft light illuminated the distressed look on her pale face.

"Yes, I'm pretty sure it was The Dread. Who else would have been smart enough to figure out where Pap's hideout was and capable enough to get inside? He was determined to steal Pap's records, along with another collection Bonboo spoke of."

"All that intrigue over a couple of notes," said Buck, giving a doubtful look. "Even Sawny doesn't like books that much."

"They were more than a couple of notes," insisted Dod. He leaned in, closer to Dilly's rocks, until his face was clearly visible, and explained vigorously, "Bonboo said they were volumes which contained details from top secret missions. If The Dread stole them, he will be able to gain key information—the kind of facts he could use to destroy kingdoms. Think about it; that's how he works, right? The Dread plays everyone, like a game, for his own purposes. Those diaries could be worse in his hands than nuclear weapons."

"What kind of weapons?" asked Boot, chuckling. He wasn't very worried.

"It doesn't matter," rumbled Dilly, taking charge. "Dod—you said you think they are at the bottom of a quick-rappel—so where is it? Let's go."

Dilly grabbed Dod's shoulder and rose to her feet, determined to get the keys back.

"Whoa, Twisty!" said Boot, hopping up beside her. "We can't be going anywhere tonight. Jibb's sitting outside, polishing his shiny, little security badge, waiting to haul us off if we so much as crack the doors open."

"Anyway," Boot continued awkwardly, searching for the words to dissuade Dilly, "What's the big deal? If we can't find the keys, or even if they have been stolen, we can ask Bonboo for assistance. I'm sure it wouldn't take long to replace the locks."

"You're missing the point!" wailed Dilly, growing unusually anxious. "The issue is trust! We don't want to go to Bonboo and tell him we've lost the keys and need help getting into Pap's place. Besides, you don't know what the two small keys go to, so how could you replace them?"

"Well, Twisty," said Boot playfully, grabbing her by the arm. "If we don't know what they go to, how would we be able to use them anyway? And if we find we're locked out of something, I can always bust it open for you."

Boot posed in a manly way, flashing his fun-loving eyes.

"Aaagh. Boys!" spouted Dilly in agony. "You always think you're so smart. Trust me! We need to get Dod's keys back—and fast! They may be more important than you think, *Booty*! And stop calling me Twisty. You know even my mom hasn't called me that for years; my hair is now more of an elegant, curly-wavy."

Dilly reached into the lowest pocket of her pants and produced a red leather-bound notebook and a small black stick.

She flipped past many pages until she came to one that was near the middle, and then she wrote, *obtain keys from hidden shaft.* Dod looked over her shoulder and began to read the list that accompanied the most recent entry.

"Do you really expect to do all of that?" he asked, shocked by her aggressive to-do list. "How do you propose personally counting the number of soldiers? Wouldn't it be easier to ask someone like Jibb?"

"You said it yourself—he can't be trusted," said Dilly curtly.

Boot and Buck quickly joined Dod in glancing down her agenda. They knew Dilly took her slates very seriously; if it was written, it had to be done.

"I can do that one and that one," said Boot, pointing at two of Dilly's entries: *casually interrogate Strat concerning Bly's recent whereabouts* and *coerce Sawb into an unofficial, full-out round of Bollirse, triple team, Green against Raul, while Dilly and Sawny search Raul Hall unnoticed.*

"—and I think Buck and Dod can help me do that one," said Boot. Below his finger was written, *break into Zerny's quarters while he's out.* "But there is no way—and I mean absolutely no way—you are going to get me to do that one!"

Boot pointed firmly where Dilly had scribbled, *have Boot apologize to Jibb for not choosing him as a Coosing.*

"It's not what you think," remarked Dilly.

"Doesn't matter—no chance there."

"I just wrote that down to remind me of the whole task—you jolt Jibb as a friend for some facts on the current situation. He once looked to you for orders. Maybe he'll bend and say something."

"I doubt it. What do you think, Dod?"

Boot looked at Dod, who was more than fully aware of the

not-so-warm feelings between the two, having just seen Jibb and Boot squabble in the hall. Dod shook his head. "That one's hopeless."

"Besides," added Boot, looking back at Dilly, "after what Jibb said to Bowy, I don't care what I could get from him. It's not worth it."

"Think of it as you will," said Dilly, changing gears. She got a glint in her eye that sparkled with glee at the challenge of convincing Boot into doing her bidding. "Just pretend to be his dearest friend," she continued. "Forget what he said. You know he said it because he was mad."

"I know what you're doing, and it's not working."

"What?"

"You still think he should have become a Coosing instead of Pone or Voo or Sham, and you want me to smooth things over."

"Don't you feel sorry for him?" asked Dilly.

"No. Not after what he said to Bowy. It was the last pebble."

Dilly rose to her feet and moved toward the door, closely followed by Sawny. "Sleep well," she said in a pleasant voice.

"Don't you want us to check out the troops from your window?" asked Buck.

"No, you can see them tomorrow from the field."

The girls took their lights and disappeared into the hall, closing the door behind them. It was only a matter of a few silent moments before the door reopened and Dilly added her last thoughts.

"I'll be back early in the morning to discuss the schedule of things. We've got seven pages of tasks to do, and that's not counting the spots we've got to check to prepare for The Dread's future attack, so hurry and get to sleep."

Dilly was gone in a flash, leaving the room dark again. Buck and Boot climbed into their beds, while Dod took a seat by the window.

"I can't believe The Dread has Pap's books," lamented Dod, gazing out at the hazy night sky.

"I can't believe you lost the key to Pap's place," groaned Boot. "I'd wager he's got a boatload of gear up there—the kind of stuff I've never seen before."

"Well I can't believe Dilly uninvited us to look out her window," whined Buck. "And here we came so close—the mystery is still a mystery."

"Get used to it," responded Boot. "Girls are a mystery!"

"That's true," added Dod. "I don't have any sisters, but my aunt is always saying that a woman's first right is to change her mind as many times as she wants, and a man's first duty is to accept it."

The conversation died down and the threesome drifted off, with Dod falling asleep last, sagging pathetically against the windowpane.

In the morning, everyone was busy. Dod went begging throughout Green Hall for an hour and gathered a small wardrobe to wear, tiding him over until Pap's clothes could be reached. Buck coordinated with Sawny to produce a copy of the 'all-encompassing list,' prioritizing and organizing as they went along. Dilly slipped out early, fraternizing with drat forces, using her social skills to assess numbers and obtain tidbits of information. Boot went to work on establishing the exact location of Pap's place and determining an alternate entry.

The next few days were similar, fast paced and list oriented. A lot of the tasks weren't hard, just time consuming. Other

Green Coosings and Greenlings were enlisted by Boot or Dilly, privately as favors to them, to get some of the things done. They were utilized on less difficult jobs—searching for Boot's missing horse, Grubber; obtaining a current list of important guests at Twistyard; examining the Pots for characters of unusual behavior; visiting surrounding villages, all the way from Janice Pass to High Gate, in order to collect rumors; befriending the more than six hundred drat soldiers camped at Twistyard and recounting any interesting conversations. Oddities were all reported to Dilly and added to her Book of Everything.

In order to find The Dread, or at least determine his connection to Twistyard, Dilly insisted on investigating every plausible lead. Fortunately, with the commotion created by the arrival of the soldiers, things at Twistyard were interrupted from their regular schedules. Many of The Greats were commissioned by Bonboo or Commendus to attend to other responsibilities, usually undisclosed to the public, and were thus unable to hold planned training sessions. Consequently, less structured events and peer practice groups became the temporary norm. It was a perfect climate for accomplishing Dilly's agenda without appearing too suspicious.

After a week, Dilly asked to hold an early morning meeting in Boot's room, despite Buck's protests that he needed his sleep in order to be competent enough to help her find trouble. As usual, Buck's complaining was useless. Dilly convinced Boot, through the door, to 'ready things' so she and Sawny could enter, and then she proceeded to have Sawny read 'the most essential notes,' taken from her Book of Everything.

Her indispensables were beyond lengthy. They went on and on, listing all sorts of facts and conjectures that had been compiled from the week's efforts. And Dilly felt the urge to interrupt and explain much of what she had written; so, by the time Sawny got to the end, someone had to reawaken Buck. A long arm over his eyes was Dilly's first clue that he wasn't paying close attention; and near the conclusion of Sawny's reading, he had begun snoring.

"Buck!" snapped Dilly, shaking him back to consciousness. "You need to concentrate. If we don't figure this out, who will?"

"Ah…you're right," said Buck sleepily. He hadn't fully heard her question.

"Wake up and listen," said Dilly. "We don't have time to go over all of this again."

"Yeah," agreed Boot with a sigh. He had participated respectfully, but couldn't help noticing that it had already taken nearly two hours. His stomach was aching to eat breakfast. And that wasn't all; despite having helped to accomplish so many tasks during the week, Dilly's list of things for him to do had actually grown larger than the one she had started with because jobs were being added faster than he could complete them. It was too tiring to think about on an empty stomach.

After Boot's pleading, Dilly agreed to reread only a greatly abbreviated update of the highlights. They were the ones she personally thought were critical enough to go over twice.

- *Pap's house is unreachable from any normal passage—shaft door is unusually secure and unbreakable—only logical entrance is from Youk's private quarters, off the balcony, up a twenty to thirty-foot wall to roof gardens and up another undetermined wall to Pap's hidden patio.*
- *Zerny and Jibb had nothing unusual in living quarters—seem committed to soldiers—disinterested in Boot's friendship—won't*

divulge any information on the matter of current affairs—Miz's two sons now staying with them.

- Sawb accepted Boot's invitation to play Bollirse, triple team—pending opportunity and Strat's schedule.
- Rumors at High Gate claim drats and bobwits are mounting an alliance to change the mode of government—rumors around Lower Janice claim tredders want to change the mode of government—neither location can substantiate source of rumors, both groups are agitated—never got a chance to meet with twelve ambassadors from Soosh—people say they were headed up the coastal cities.
- Grubber reportedly seen near Lower Janice—never found.
- Sirlonk introductions—Dilly met thirteen dignitaries, none of them appeared overly suspicious—one of them was related to Youk's wife, Saluci, was wacky in the head, but not deemed dangerous—two were ordinary at swordplay—one was overly fascinated with the Mauj and acquainted with Bly and his inventions—eight were stuffy in the hat, typical royalty—one was quiet and sickly, seemed a pest to Sirlonk, who was attempting to entertain them at Bonboo's request.
- Seventeen locations checked for Dod's 'suspicious vibes' of a future attack from The Dread—none appeared correct—remaining five spots are all heavily guarded—need a plan to enter them—Sword Tower, Tonnis Barracks, Histo Relics Building, Sonto Museum Basement, Grand Hall Diplomacy Council Basement.
- Dod read first volume of Pap's record from Bonboo—very detailed about each event, though no specific information about The Dread, probably written too early—one important observation at the end of the book, The Dread seems to fit in well with royalty—should check the thirteen dignitaries' assistants

and travel associates for anyone of interest (reportedly thirty-six people).

- *Sent letter to Doochi in Raul but no response yet—seeking more detailed reason for leaving suddenly when he quit Raul Coosings—perhaps see if anyone heading to Raul could check in on him and hear his story in person.*
- *Had conversations with many of The Greats to pry clues:*
- *Tridacello—an unsuccessful attempt was made to steal triblots from High Gate—he said it had to be an insider—wouldn't say why—he stayed at Twistyard briefly, spent time with Ascertainy in the library and Sirlonk in Sword Tower, and then headed toward Lower Janice.*
- *Strat—both sides of the nighttime, clandestine meeting had received invitations, supposedly from the other party, hand delivered by an unknown drat messenger—they were confusing and suspicious—that's why Sirlonk and Strat were slow to dismount their horses—in the end, Sirlonk was sent into the tent to read the drat's invitation letter, allegedly signed, 'your close friends at Twistyard.'*
- *Youk—Twistyard-centered search might be a lure to keep eyes focused away from the real points of concern—he was more worried about possible corruption at High Gate, based on them possessing the only operating portal left in Green (to Raul, and from Raul to Soosh).*
- *Tinja—Hatu expert (martial arts) and Treep (food and poison specialist) were assigned by Bonboo to live in Soosh Hall with Jim and the remaining others from Soosh, to protect them after a death threat was received by Bonboo, claiming The Dread would finish his work.*

"And that's about it," said Dilly, finishing up. Boot wondered why she couldn't have given them that version the first time, though he didn't dare say anything for fear she would drag things out and delay his breakfast. Dod did his best to appear alert, which was a mountainous task considering how late they had been out the night before and the frequent insomnia that plagued him personally, driven by his fears about confronting The Dread.

"Everything else is small stuff," said Dilly, sounding and looking like a teacher as she finished flipping through her pages. "We need to focus our efforts on the most important things and move faster."

"Most important to whom?" whined Buck, barely entering the world of the living. He was still wiping sleep from his eyes, having napped perilously through much of Sawny's reading and having nearly dipped off again during Dilly's synopsis.

"We've been chasing around here, nonstop, for a week," Buck continued, following a big yawn. "We've been working all day and sneaking about the halls 'til the middle of the night—nearly getting caught by *Your Buddy*, Jibb, and his security pals."

Buck looked at Dilly and Sawny and groaned loudly, like a little third-grade nag, who didn't want to practice his times tables any more. "Can't we take a break?" he said, moaning as though in horrendous pain. He rolled onto his back, flung his hands out in both directions, and begged for freedom.

It was quite a show, especially coming from Buck, who typically kept himself appropriate and complained sensibly.

Dilly and Sawny stared, vaguely amused. Boot and Dod crossed their fingers behind their backs, hoping that Buck's actions weren't summoning another lengthy lecture.

"We could go fishing on Lake Mauj," said Buck, dribbling on, since he appeared to have the stage. He misread Dilly's silence as a sign that he was actually making headway.

"And look! It's a perfect blue sky," he added, rolling sideways to point at the window. "After all, the troops have settled down enough that they're playing games half the time. If there was an imminent threat against Twistyard, or a real danger to the democracy, don't you think other people would be concerned, too?"

"They are," responded Dilly sharply. "Didn't you hear what we just barely read? Everyone is concerned, especially Bonboo."

"Yes, I heard," said Buck glumly. "But if things are relaxed sufficient for Sirlonk to take a vacation, I'm sure we could take a few moments—"

Buck swung into a sitting position, his eyebrows raised, and added, "Well? We really should ponder over and discuss the facts we've obtained—"

"While fishing?" blurted Sawny.

"Okay, so you see where I'm going," said Buck in a subdued, excited way. He was partially hopeful, but mostly cognizant of the reality that Dilly would kibosh his efforts in the end.

"Out on the lake we could talk about this kind of stuff all day and nobody would hear us," said Buck, plugging in his most logical point. "That's the real reason I want to go fishing."

He looked at Dilly and Sawny with his best angelic face, his big, wounded-puppy blue eyes pleading, and waited for a reply.

"How do you know Sirlonk's taking a vacation?" snapped Dilly, redirecting the conversation to her priorities. She completely ignored Buck's request for a day off and didn't even address it with an answer. Sawny stayed silent, but squirmed, feeling guilty, when Buck's critter eyes did their best begging and were still rejected by her sister.

"Oh, I bumped into Juny last night in the hall," said Buck defeatedly, lying back down, his arm once more across his eyes. "She said they were heading off to a family gathering in Raul. I got her to promise me that she would bring back some chouyummy from Dirsitch. She might even be successful if Sirlonk doesn't eat it all in route. He's not big on sharing, you know."

Dod's mouth started to water at the thought of chouyummy. It had a flavor that tasted like the creamiest milk chocolate ever invented; and Dirsitch, Raul was the holy city of sweet treats, known for making the best desserts in the three worlds.

"Can we continue this rendezvous after breakfast?" begged Boot. Apparently the mention of chouyummy was too much for his growling stomach to take.

"Please, hold onto your chins for a minute," insisted Dilly, positioning herself firmly between the boys and the door. "If Sirlonk and Juny are headed to Raul, they might be able to check in on Doochi. Did they say at what time they were planning on leaving?"

"I don't remember them being specific about that," answered Buck, "but I'm sure they've got to be heading out soon or they'll miss the lowering of the triblot barrier at noon. You know how slowly Juny rides."

"Quick, Dilly, let's go!" said Boot with a smile on his face. "Why don't you and Sawny run ahead to the stalls, while we go and search the Great Hall?"

"All right," responded Dilly happily. "You take the long corridor, by the wall of pictures—we'll go straight. Hopefully we'll catch them in time."

Dilly stowed her Book of Everything and, tugging at Sawny's arm, hurried toward the door. Buck and Dod nodded at Boot, acknowledging his cunning manipulation of Dilly's morning energy; however, as though Dilly had eyes on the back of her head, she added a last request as she slipped out of the room.

"Don't take too long eating your breakfast, Boot. I shall be expecting you to bring us food in a flippy. We have plenty to do today and you know how cross I get when I miss a meal."

The girls disappeared with a flash of bouncing curls. Buck walked to the door and waited until they were out of hearing range to begin complaining. He muttered a few statements about 'Miss Princess Twisty' returning to her old throne and found his canker spurred Boot to tell a gamut of jokes at their expense. But Boot wasn't genuinely huffed like Buck, who sincerely wished to spend the day fishing; on the contrary, he was caught up in the moment, having fun until the humor snowballed into a carnival-like atmosphere.

Dod, on the other hand, hardly noticed what Boot said or did as they prepared to leave for breakfast, which was really something considering Boot's repertoire included material that made Buck laugh so hard tears streamed down his cheeks, rendering him unable to tie his shoes or button his shirt.

Instead, a catastrophe flooded Dod's mind, consuming his attention with eerie images. It was an instant replay of a horrible nightmare he had already endured three times that week, a dream that wouldn't go away and had caused him to lose sleep. This time he could see a mountain of rubble, a heap of stones and support beams, and Boot's leather bag on the top. Moans and cries for help seeped through the cracks from countless voices; it was a dreary chorus of hauntingly familiar voices. To Dod, the message was distinctly a reminder of The Dread's pending attack, and the stone pattern on the floor was definitely Twistyard.

"Hey guys," whispered Dod ominously, breaking into their jovial fun; his eyes panned across the room and rested on Boot's bag, making the pictures in his mind all the more real. Buck and

Boot noticed his apprehensive face and recognized he had serious things to say.

"We need to check those other five buildings—and soon!" said Dod bracingly, knowing he was sounding like the Lovely Twosome who had earlier set themselves up for Boot's buoyant ridicule. "The Dread is coming. I keep seeing glimpses of the destruction he plans. And it's horrible. He wants us dead—as many as he can get here at Twistyard!"

"Could we do it after fishing?" asked Buck, jokingly, trying to hold back his laughter. He couldn't help it; the impersonation Boot had just done of Dilly, refusing to let them go out on the lake, was enough brotherly medicine to fix Buck's spirits for a week.

"Maybe," said Dod hesitantly, missing Buck's humor. "We will need to plan well if we are going to break into Sword Tower tonight."

"Sword Tower?" said Buck, sobering a little. "Do we have to begin with the most heavily guarded building?"

"Probably," agreed Boot, having fully regained his composure. It was the first thing he had said in five minutes using his own voice instead of imitating Dilly's. "From the start," he began, but he had to stop and clear his throat before continuing.

"Dilly's been saying, from the start, that Sword Tower was the spot. And she's usually right, but don't tell her I said it. Besides," said Boot, his tone becoming more serious, "I'm sure if The Dread wanted to damage our ability to defend ourselves, he would logically seek to destroy the sword-filled basement vaults—reportedly bigger than the field out front. Most of them haven't been touched since the destruction of Doss. I've heard there are enough swords to instantly raise a mighty tredder army if the time ever arises. We should sneak in for sure—tonight if possible. I'd say—"

The conversation ended abruptly when it was disturbed by someone knocking on the open door. Buck and Dod threw nervous glances.

Toos rapped his knuckles and cocked his head awkwardly, sensing he had interrupted something important. He had a puzzled look on his face, while standing proper, like a tin soldier.

"I have a message to deliver," he started to say when Boot seized him with a warm welcome.

"Come on in, Toos," said Boot jauntily, sounding his usual happy self. He quickly hid any indication of the more serious conversation he had just begun with Dod and Buck. It was amazing. Boot was a masterful people person, capable of figuratively throwing a blanket over a chest of pirates' gold, right under the nose of the captain, and get away with concealing it for himself. One moment he was creatively directing Dilly, the next, lifting his brother from depression to gleeful contentment, then discussing serious, life-saving matters, and finally, cleverly hiding trouble with an outer cloak of boisterous lightheartedness. His voice and mannerisms didn't miss a beat.

"It's a great day to jilt the boockards out of Raul," said Boot, instantly snaring Toos's full attention with the mention of sports. Anything Toos had accidentally heard about Sword Tower seemed to float away, leaving him wistful-eyed. "Have you come with news from Strat on the Bollirse time? We haven't played a full-out round of Bollirse, triple team, for years. I'm ready to show them who's going to win this fall—not to mention, I've still got to determine those three empty spots. We'll be the ones to represent Twistyard this year—and you can rest assured, we'll bring back The Golden Swot!"

"I did speak with Strat this morning," responded Toos

eagerly, glad to be impressing Boot. "He said he had a few important things he needed to attend to over the next three days; however, after that he'd be willing to call a fair match and hold the unofficial Bollirse battle."

Toos walked into the room and made himself comfortable on Dod's bed. His head had left him for somewhere else at the mention of Bollirse.

"Do you really think we'll beat Raul this fall?" asked Toos, somewhat dazed. He blearily looked at Boot and said, "I'd love to be on a team that wins The Golden Swot for Twistyard. If you pick me to help out, I promise I won't let you down. My great-grandpa was a real pro back in his day. I'm sure if I played on a winning team, my dad wouldn't stop bragging for years; the whole town back home would have sore ears before he'd be done."

Dod pointed to the door and said somberly, "We should probably go."

Every time anyone brought up the subject of Bollirse, it made Dod sick to his stomach. Hearing Toos go on and on about it chased away his desire for breakfast.

He wanted to have fun with the other guys, but he was terrified of making a complete fool of himself, of destroying the respectable image he had worked so hard to create. Regular practices were about to begin in a few short days, and Dod knew Boot and Buck would soon come to realize that he wasn't very good at sports.

According to the official rules for creating teams to compete for the position that would represent Twistyard, all fifteen Coosings from Green had to play on the same team, only dipping into the Greenlings and Pots for replacing vacancies or injured persons, and of course for filling the remaining three spots to round off the team at eighteen players. Raul Coosings and Soosh Coosings formed their teams the same way. After that, Lings and Pots had their chance to create teams of eighteen players to compete for the same position, giving the Coosing teams practice. Yet never in the history of the game had a non-Coosing team been victorious enough to represent Twistyard in the real matches for The Golden Swot.

It seemed horribly unfair; the last thing Dod wanted was to dash Boot's dream of winning by hexing the team with his presence, and the first thing Toos wanted was to fill a spot. Dod kept telling himself that it might be different, that his abilities would be better, and that his skills at sports would rise to the occasion somehow; but it didn't work very well. He still felt sick.

"Oh wait, before you go," chimed Toos, his ruddy cheeks reddening with embarrassment, "I forgot to tell you—I have an important message from Dilly. She said the three of you need to hurry yourselves to the stalls. You're leaving for High Gate right now."

"What?" said Buck. "She's gone for a couple of minutes and already she's decided to order the rest of our day without asking our opinions. I think Dilly is getting bossier than a full-grown bull, stalled up with calves."

"Actually," added Toos, "Bonboo recommended you accompany Dod to High Gate in response to a letter he received this morning from Commendus. I heard him telling Dilly, right out there in the hall. She sent me here to fetch you, while she and Sawny went on to get the horses saddled up."

"See Buck," chuckled Boot, "her whole family has voted to ruin your day of fishing. Let's start moving. If we hurry, we'll have time to grab something to eat. I bet Mercy would even pack us lunches."

Toos begged to come along until Boot whispered in his ear. Right away, he settled down and grinned wide enough to fit three popsicles.

"I'll do it," he responded happily, gliding his hand across the top of his slick hair as though it would make it flatter than it already was. His part down the center was immaculate, and he looked like a banker who had just closed a substantial deal.

Down the hall, Buck and Dod pestered Boot, wondering what he had asked of Toos that so quickly replaced his usual persistence with compliance.

"I simply gave him orders to stay home and play pranks on our friends from Raul, especially Sawb," said Boot, cracking his mischievous smile. "I figure we need to get them ready. We want to have a Bollirse showdown like none other; and we all know we play better when they're mad at us."

Dod looked up at Boot and knew there was more to his whisper than that, but Buck didn't catch on.

"Really?" said Buck. "I'm amazed that Toos responded so promptly. You're becoming a great leader, Boot. I don't know how you do it."

Buck's sincere compliment made Boot feel guilty enough to confess the rest of the deal.

"I may have also promised Toos a spot on the Bollirse team with us."

"I see," muttered Buck. "It's just as well that you stop torturing poor Toos. He's the best Greenling at Bollirse and yet you've had him guessing, all this time, whether or not you would let him hit with us on the field this year? I can't believe it! Or actually," said Buck, pausing to size Boot up, "since I'm your brother, it's sad to say, but…I can."

When the boys arrived at the kitchen, Mercy was waiting, holding an overflowing satchel of food. She appeared annoyed and excited at the same time; her head shook back and forth, working on a good scold, before Boot ever got close enough to reach for the fare.

"You're way too slow," she chided, poking at the boys in a grandmotherly way. She was strangely stern and kind. "You'll miss the noon drop at High Gate if you don't quicken your little steps. Dilly said you'd be coming at an expeditious pace, but if that's what you're doing, don't be entering any races. I've seen newborn pups move faster with their eyes still shut."

"We have plenty of time to ride and make it long before the shield comes down," responded Boot, giving Mercy a sideways squeeze with one arm, while reaching for the food with the other.

Mercy held onto the bag. "I don't know, boys," she said.

"Of course you don't—you wouldn't," suggested Boot hastily. He waited for Mercy to look up at him, horrified by his statement, before he continued on, smirking, "You wouldn't know because you haven't been on a horse in company with Dilly lately; Song never walks or trots. That horse has one speed: Fast! We'll be lucky if we don't eat our horses tonight, after their misfortunate retirement, given the quick pace of Dilly's stallion—though Grubber could keep up if only he'd first show up."

"Yes, that's awful about your horse," said Mercy, changing the subject. She spoke quickly as though it made up for continuing to keep the boys captive with her jabbering, all the while maintaining a relentless grip on the food. "You've had him for many years, haven't you, Boot? Higga said people spotted him in Lower Janice earlier this week, tethered in a field on the outskirts. He'll probably turn up soon. They usually do. Grubber's got a look that stands out. Whoever stole him will likely not appreciate the attention he attracts. They'll have to leave him behind or get caught.

"And speaking of nice-looking," continued Mercy, grabbing Dod's arm. "You're sure shined-up today. Have you got enough clothes and such? If you need anything, I'd love to help. Bonboo requested I attend to it. He trusts my taste, you know. Why there was the time that—"

Mercy babbled on and on, talking rapidly, ever clinging to the bag of provisions. It was ironic that she had tormented the boys with how they were destined to be late, yet wouldn't release them from her verbal grip. It was typical of Mercy.

Finally, after five minutes of nodding and agreeing, and fearing Dilly's wrath, Boot carefully grabbed for the satchel, right in the middle of a sentence.

"Manners, boy!" snapped Mercy firmly. "Always remember your manners." But the rebuke was quickly followed by warm wishes, and hugs, and another admonition to be off in a rush.

The boys made tracks, down the corridor, through the Great Hall, and out into the front field. On the way, Dod asked how long they would be staying at High Gate. He had noticed that nobody seemed interested in bringing any personal belongings or changes of clothing, despite the fact that the triblot barrier was only lifted once a day.

"I would imagine just a couple of nights," responded Boot. "We have to be back before Strat holds the Bollirse challenge. I wouldn't miss it for anything, including being pampered by Commendus."

"And we don't need any luggage?" asked Dod carefully. He had a hard time openly saying that he preferred having pajamas to sleep in and a fresh outfit each morning. After all, he had spent the first few days wearing the same thing, so it would sound hypocritical to start getting picky. Not to mention, he had even worn his shoes to bed in front of them; but that was a safety measure while adjusting to the new world filled with surprises, like venoos attacks in the middle of the night.

"When you're personally invited by Commendus, there's no need to pack," assured Boot. "He takes pride in giving his guests the best of everything, down to the clothing he provides. You can't say no to him, either. If you were to show up with a suitcase, it would likely offend him."

At the barn entrance, Dilly and Sawny were waiting with horses, saddled and ready to ride. Youk had loaned Dilly his two horses for Boot and Dod to use; he had even helped get them ready, saying that Juny and Sirlonk had left an hour before, so if Dilly hoped to catch up, she would need to hurry.

Dilly gave orders, as always, and insisted they follow Youk's advice. They would race until they reached Juny and Sirlonk, and then they would slow down and enjoy the remaining stint to High Gate. She even added, as a motivating tool, that no one could eat the food Mercy had packed until they joined their friends; and to better enforce her rule, she snatched the satchel from Boot and tied it to the back of Dod's horse.

Having stated her plan, she took Commendus's invitation from her front pocket and tucked it away, safely inside her Book of Everything, telling Dod he was lucky to have been invited to a private meeting with Commendus.

However, Dod didn't feel so lucky. He hadn't been given a

chance to see the fancy note addressed to him that Dilly brooded over. And when the others mounted their horses to ride, Dod didn't want to make a fuss, but his seemed ornery the moment he sat down. And worse still, once Dilly nudged Song into a quick trot, Dod struggled to keep up.

At first, he thought it was just his poor riding skills — but he was wrong — and by the time everyone discovered the truth, it was already a complete disaster!

ROAD TO HIGH GATE

The main thoroughfare between Twistyard and High Gate was compacted flat, like pavement, and wound back and forth through fields and forests, gradually gaining elevation. Because it was built for all sorts of wagons and heavy loads, it wasn't the fastest route.

Dilly wanted speed in order to catch up with Sirlonk, so she insisted they leave the well-paved lane for Coyote Trail, which didn't even slightly resemble a road; it was like a dried-out, avalanche chute. It went nearly straight up a steep, rocky hill before reaching a more manageable path on the other side.

The shortcut would reduce the first third of their journey significantly; and from the top of the rise, before dropping down to where the trail bisected the road, Deer Leg Lookout Point would offer a perfect place to scope for Sirlonk and his wife.

Unfortunately, the moment Dod left the thoroughfare, the horse he was riding, Brown Sugar, began to fuss. The mare had already trotted awkwardly, and now, despite Dod's attempts to straighten her out, she wasn't responding. And with rocks jutting out of the ground on both sides, it was dangerous to wander even an inch from the path.

"I don't think my horse likes the terrain," yelled Dod to the others, who were quite a few paces ahead.

Boot called back casually over his shoulder, "Give her a gentle kick and she'll follow the rest of us."

Dod proceeded to nudge Brown Sugar, and it worked, she did move faster, though something wasn't right about the way she trotted. Each step jolted excessively or jiggled unsteadily. It was like riding a ticking time bomb. And with the dodgy landscape surrounding the cantankerous mare and the distance that Dod still had to go, he felt disaster was certain. Not to mention, Boot's horse in front of him didn't seem to sway at all. It wasn't fair.

As Dod pressed forward, each minute was filled with terror. The path continued to get steeper, and his friends, who clearly had spent a lot of time riding horses, were breaking away from him, eager to be done with Dilly's shortcut.

"My horse is acting weird!" Dod finally called out desperately, his voice quivering. He hoped at least Boot would be able to still hear him and help. "I'm not sure what's wrong. Can we please stop for a minute to take a look?"

"At the top," responded Boot loudly, grunting as he pulled arduously on the reins of his horse. "The hill's too steep right here. We'd better wait until we're on the level bluff. Besides, I'm starving—aren't you?"

Dod tried to press on with courage, but a prevailing feeling of concern washed over him. Something was definitely wrong. He looked down at his horse's legs as she clanked up the rocky slope. They appeared fine; however, when a bothersome stone in the path neared the mare's front steps, the horse bucked and swayed. It was then that Dod realized giant thorns were concealed beneath Brown Sugar's long dark hair that hung just above her hooves like black socks; a few spiny quills protruded far enough to be visible, and even then, Dod only noticed them because he saw how the mare reacted when she gingerly bumped against the taller rocks.

"I have a problem!" yelled Dod in panic. He was petrified. "I need help!"

Boot and Buck turned in curiosity and found Dod was no longer behind them on the trail; he was passing them, white-knuckled and bulging-eyed, heading hazardously through jagged rocks on the steep hillside. And with each painful step, the distressed horse was spurred to heightened levels of spastic movements. She had become a bucking bronco, with Dod riding like a gold-buckled cowboy, his life depending on it.

To make matters worse, Dod's riggings were falling off. He clung to the reins for all he was worth, attempting to dismount the faltering saddle and plant himself on the horse's bare back.

Perhaps if the ground were level it would have been possible, but with so many opposing variables, it wasn't. Dod flew through the air, arms and legs flailing.

"Boooooot!" he cried.

The horse had launched Dod sideways, right over the top of many knife-like stones, smack-dab into Boot. It was unbelievably lucky. He flopped across the front of Boot's lap, with his pants catching on the saddle, causing them to tear.

"If you wanted to ride with me," Boot said playfully, "you should have asked—no need for these crazy games." He was joking, though his trembling voice and gaping-mouthed look relayed heavy concern over what had just happened.

Dod struggled to readjust, while everyone else watched the frenzied mare. It bucked and kicked on the slope, clanking and clattering against the rocks, and completely fell down twice. It finally staggered toward the base of the hill, miraculously still alive.

Once on flatter ground, Brown Sugar leaped into a clumsy run, zigzagging, and disappeared into the distance.

"Wow!" said Buck, shocked by the spectacle. "You would have been worm meat if you had stayed on that crazy thing. I wonder what got into her. She's been Youk's favorite horse for over ten years, his first choice by far. I hope she finds her way back to Twistyard."

"She better!" growled Dilly, incensed, her eyes narrowing as she glared at Dod. "Youk trusted me with that horse."

"It's not my fault," responded Dod, feeling guilty. He went on to explain about the thorns and loose saddle, but they weren't good enough excuses; Dilly offered no words of sympathy. Nevertheless, after the group had made it safely to the flats, Dilly admitted it was possible that foul play was involved. "We will at least need to be careful," she concluded as she pulled out her Book of Everything. She scribbled vigorously a page of notes, while Boot dismounted his stallion and searched for thorns.

Sawny prodded her horse over to an outcropping where she used her noculars to scan for Sirlonk and Juny. "It looks like we're right on track to merge with the others," she said, quickly locating them. "At the pace they're going, I'd judge we'll easily hit the big bend in the road before they do—and Dilly, did Youk mention who was accompanying them? I thought they were going alone—just a family gathering—but someone else is riding along."

Dilly didn't know anything about the mystery person, so it fueled the journey into a faster-than-needed descent through the meadows.

Dod enjoyed doubling with Boot on Youk's larger horse. It was a beautiful chestnut with reddish streaks, and its legs were longer than Song's, making it effortless to keep up with Dilly. They rode smoothly across the grassy fields toward the road, almost as if they were floating. It was remarkably more comfortable than the best of moments Dod had experienced on the mare, and that was despite being positioned on the horse's bare back, behind Boot's saddle.

As they flew, Dod listened. Boot told two fascinating tales about the stallion they were riding. He had a gift for telling stories.

"Pious gave Youk this war horse to thank him," said Boot, setting the stage. "This horse was the last colt of Rossiana—you know, the mare Donis rode to victory at the Battle of Rocky Ridge. After successfully taking the pole tower, Donis let Rossiana run free in the meadows below, symbolically representing the freedom of the people."

Dod nodded his head, as though he remembered; however, tales of Rossiana were blurred from the unusual set of memories he did have of Donis and Bollath at Rocky Ridge. It didn't matter to the conversation: Dod was sitting behind Boot, and Boot couldn't hear a nod.

"Ironically," said Boot, in a melodramatic voice, "Big Red, the horse Drake was riding when he led the opposition against Donis, was left to himself in the fields after the battle, the same fields Rossiana roamed. It wasn't long before this horse came along, streaked with blood red like his father. Shortly thereafter,

Rossiana died protecting her colt from none other than Big Red. The villagers of Rocky Ridge were outraged, and they shot Big Red for his offense. That's where this horse got his woeful name, Shooter."

"Oh, that's how he got his name," piped Dod to keep the conversation flowing. He really hadn't known the horse's name in the first place.

"Yup, that's how he got it," said Boot, nodding in rhythm with the horse's gallop. "After that, some people saw this horse as a symbol of hope and freedom, because of Rossiana—she bore him as a free mare in the fields and then died protecting him. Others, of course, noticed the bloody streaks and quickly remembered the tyrannical offenses of Drake and the cruelty of Big Red murdering Rossiana. That's why Pious got the horse in the first place. I suppose if this stallion were only brown, he'd still be lazily chewing grass in the fields below the pole tower at Rocky Ridge, and let me tell you, *that* would be a tragedy!"

"Really?" said Dod. He didn't mean to actually say anything. It just slipped out. In his mind, it didn't sound so bad for the horse to have remained roaming free, representing something Rossiana had started. Besides, if Boot wanted to use the word tragedy, he could have used it next to the horrible deeds of Big Red or the orphaning of poor Shooter.

"Definitely," insisted Boot. "I think you could call it a tragedy if something as great as this horse never got its chance to shine—to truly be special. Don't you think so?"

"I guess," said Dod in a reserved voice.

"It would be like Humberrone never getting his chance to save the day, or even like Pap—you know—what if Pap had spent his life sitting around getting old, never doing what he was made to do, never drawing a sword, never saving people, and never teaching us to follow. Why Pap alone left a giant legacy of good, not to mention Humberrone. It would have been a tragedy if they were content to be anything less than they were made to be."

Dod realized he didn't know very much about the accomplishments of the horse he was riding, so he quickly consented to Boot that he was right. He also found Boot's comments fascinating, especially for his unique circumstance.

Dod felt his heart pound with pride as he thought about Pap, who had taken the opportunities afforded him by the charm and had flourished with them.

"You know, Boot," said Dod, "the more I think about it, the more right you are."

"And it's taken you all of this time to figure it out?" joked Boot. "I should have warned you when we first met that I would always be right. I could have saved you the mental effort."

"No," responded Dod. "I mean about becoming. We mostly think about tragedy in terms of what has happened, not what could have happened."

"All right, you're getting close to losing me," said Boot. "That was almost a Sawny phrase, quoted straight from *Driggin's Truths about Life*."

"It was your idea!" said Dod, jabbing Boot in the side with his fist. "I just restated it."

"Really, Sawny? Is that what I said?" mocked Boot in his precious Dilly voice.

"Yes, Dilly!" said Dod, playing along. "And it makes a lot of sense." Dod smiled as he thought about becoming like Pap. He felt destined to greatness, bound by his genetics and unique circumstance, and determined to give his best effort to do it. After all, time did indeed stand still for him, too—or at least he hoped it did.

"So, tell me your favorite story about this horse. When was his best moment?" asked Dod. He enjoyed Boot telling him stories.

"That's easy. Pious was outnumbered, twelve to one, fighting against Dreaderious and his poorlings on the shores of Lake Zulritter. He had taken a firm stand by having his men camp in the thick trees on the top of six plateaus. Every night, they set fires along all of the cliff edges, creating the appearance that their army was equal in number. Men on flutters couldn't count heads from above the tight tree cover, and any that ventured below were easily shot down. The guise worked for months. Meanwhile, Commendus raised a formidable force. It was Youk's brilliant idea."

"I remember a little bit about the battle," said Dod honestly, recalling parts of it. "But how does Shooter enter in?"

"Keep listening and you'll see. He's a real hero," said Boot, turning momentarily to smile at Dod.

"Pious received word from Commendus that he had gathered together an impressive number of troops and that they were currently camping in Soonick Valley, about five hours march from the plateaus. It was wonderful news; unfortunately, Dreaderious had his spies and knew of their approach. He decided to ambush them that night. By the cloak of darkness, thousands of poorlings marched quietly past the plateaus, far enough away to avoid being struck by stones or arrows. They headed straight for the sleeping men in Soonick Valley.

"At first, Pious ordered his soldiers to descend, in an effort to stop them; but they were met with such heavy opposition, they quickly retreated back to the safety of the plateaus. Only one road led down from each, so it was easy for Dreaderious to set troops at the bases, assuring nobody escaped to tell. He also hadn't seen any flutters used during the prior weeks, which led him to correctly assume that they didn't have any. Pious and his men were helpless, unable to get word to their unsuspecting friends."

"Oh, yes, I remember now. Was Shooter the horse?"

"Yup, he's the one," said Boot, patting Shooter on his neck. "Pious knew he couldn't let his friends in Soonick Valley be ambushed during the night, and he had already tried the blocked road down the plateau, so that only left one option: Test the legend of the wild horse!"

Dod felt a wave of excitement when Boot mentioned the legend. Everyone had heard it. Hundreds of years before, men had rounded up nearly all of the stray horses in the Lake Zulritter area to break in as stock horses. However, one strong stallion kept eluding them.

In an attempt to catch the magnificent animal, two hundred men chased him up the only passable trail to the wooded flats of Dorran Plateau. They thought they had him, but for his freedom, he jumped The Seven Steps—seven plateaus that each decreased in size and were each separated by twenty to thirty-foot-wide gullies, the shallowest of which dropped hundreds of feet. After that, nobody tried to touch the stallion; he had earned his freedom!

"Oh, it was at The Seven Steps!" said Dod. "That's how Pious did it."

Boot paused for a minute and began shaking his head side to side. It looked like he was saying no, until Dod realized Boot was trying to shake loose a few bees out of his hair. They had ridden through a small swarm, and since Dod was sitting lower down, without a saddle, and was directly behind Boot as a shield, he hadn't been hit by any of them.

"I hate bees," whined Boot, brushing the last one from his right ear. "Anyway, as I was saying, Pious was a firm believer that Shooter represented liberty; and as Rossiana's colt, surely he could take The Seven Steps to freedom. In a bold move, Pious left the command of his armies to his son Bravous, and took the ride of his life: He jumped all seven gullies and rode across the steps. He's the only one I know of who's tried it and lived to tell.

"On the flats, Shooter continued to trot all night. Pious quietly rode past the poorlings and lit fires in the trees and brush, all along the front line. At first, he did it to awaken his friends in Soonick Valley; however, the prevailing winds blew the flames toward the poorlings in great swirling torrents and created such a barrier that they turned and fled back to the sandy shores of Lake Zulritter. More than half of the poorlings deserted Dreaderious that night, out of superstition, citing that the pay wasn't high enough to fight against the monsters of fire. Dreaderious lost so many men to false notions that he had to retreat and completely abandon his designs for two years.

"In the morning, as soon as Pious dismounted, Shooter lay down and couldn't get up without help. It turned out, he had fractured one of his legs while jumping The Seven Steps, but despite his injury, he hadn't stopped moving until the battle had been prevented. Now doesn't that sound like a true hero?"

Dod nodded his head and patted Shooter with one hand, still clinging tightly to Boot with the other. He couldn't help feeling envious of Youk for owning such a wonderful horse.

CHAPTER FOURTEEN

When the group met up with Sirlonk and Juny, they were happily surprised to find out that Strat was the mystery man. He was heading to Raul for a meeting with his good friend, Bly, who was currently spending time away from High Gate, improving a few new technologies. Dilly popped the question about Doochi and found Sirlonk and Strat both willing to check in on him, but when Strat mentioned that it would increase his stay an extra day or two, Boot quickly intervened.

"Sirlonk," he said in a most respectful voice, "I think it would be fitting if you stopped in on Doochi—why, after all these years of him idolizing you. Maybe he would decide to come back, as a demoted Rauling of course, if you gave him a word of encouragement."

"Yes, I suppose I should be the one to see his face," responded Sirlonk arrogantly, looking down his nose at Strat. "I'm certain he'd prefer a chitt with me over *him*—no offense, Strat, but a legendary swordsman from Raul commands a certain level of admiration. It beats a mere Bollirse enthusiast, ten-to-one, rain or shine, and in your home stadium, too. Silly sports can't compare to real skills."

Dilly's eyes rolled to Boot, disgusted by Sirlonk's attitude and in acknowledgment that she understood Boot's motive for speaking up was to make sure his beloved Bollirse game against Raul Hall was not postponed, though she didn't say anything. It still served her purpose of dismissing another duty on her lengthy list of things to do.

Dod glanced momentarily at Strat, right in the middle of Sirlonk's slam on him, wondering how he would respond. But he didn't. He spoke to Dod instead.

"Chirrumpi, Dod. You don't like horses, either?" asked

Strat, noting that Dod rode double with Boot. Strat looked motion sick, slumping on the back of a beautiful black mare. Not only did he ignore Sirlonk's degrading jab, he didn't even seem bothered by it. He could have been if he wanted to; Strat had earned the right to get annoyed by statements like that, for he was the instigator of a six-year winning streak at Bollirse, claiming The Golden Swot for Twistyard—and with Raul Coosings, no less! It was akin to being the head coach of a team that repeatedly triumphed at the Super Bowl.

"No," responded Dod. "It's not that I don't like them, I just don't seem to be very lucky with them. My horse had problems coming up Coyote Trail, so when she ran off, I ended up on the back of Shooter, here." Dod gave the horse a pat.

"What kind of trouble?" asked Strat. He tried to straighten-up, and his eyes flashed with excitement, breaking through the nausea momentarily.

Dod wanted to be frank and discuss the suspicious thorns, yet caution held him to a conservative response.

"My horse didn't like the steep hill with rocks. Maybe there was a burr in her saddle or something. Anyway, she bucked me off and ran back to Twistyard."

"Really?" said Strat. "How strange. Just this morning, poor Sirlonk nearly took a spill when his horse had problems with the riggings—didn't you, Sirlonk?"

Juny, Dilly, Sirlonk and Buck were so busy talking that Sirlonk didn't even hear Strat. Boot gave Shooter an extra nudge and jolted forward, sliding between Dilly and Sirlonk, which abruptly cut their conversation.

"Strat just told us your saddle didn't like you this morning," said Boot in a sedated, teasing voice.

"Yes, I could have died," said Sirlonk dramatically. "Some dosippitous corranus handled my riggings today. It's the last time I'll let that happen! Zerny, or one of his grubby barn handlers, no doubt, must have neglected their sleep and accidentally missed a hitch. Of course, if I knew it was purposeful, I'd invite the knave to meet the end of Jilser."

"Dod had issues with his horse, too," added Dilly, trying to worm her way back into the conversation. "His circumstance, however, was more precarious, I must confess. We didn't discover the problem until nearly halfway up Coyote Trail, at which time he had to abandon the mare or die on the rocks."

"My goodness!" gasped Juny. Her proud face showed some concern, though more theatrical than genuine.

Juny was dressed in elegant layers of clothing; her color choices were white, pink, and maroon, with a rose tinted cape adorned by gold rings and beading that nearly covered the back of her prancing horse—it was in danger of being soiled if the horse listened to nature's call. Her face was long and slender, matching her tall, skinny body; and straight midnight-black hair flowed down her back, nearly to her waist. She looked and played the part of a queen.

"I'm sure necessity would have forced me to react similarly if we had scaled Coyote Trail," grumbled Sirlonk, exuding disdain for any remark that placed his horse experience as being inferior. "I simply chose a better path from the start."

"Certainly, my sovereign," said Juny patronizingly. "We are all glad you were wise enough to escape harms way; unfortunately, if Dod had troubles, as you did, how many trees need to fall before it's not just the wind?"

"That's true. I fear you are right," responded Sirlonk

solemnly. "And what a coward the perpetrator must be not to face us man to man." Sirlonk glanced at Dod and smiled coolly.

"My Dearest Juny, when we return I shall inquire of Youk whom he constrained to prepare our horses. Even with an impaired arm, I would gladly face the rascal—what a chicken-hearted play indeed, troubling us like that....So, Dod, do you know who set your horse for you?"

"I—I'm not exactly sure," stuttered Dod, not wanting to give out key information. He looked at the ground and avoided Sirlonk's eyes.

The news that Sirlonk's ride had been blighted was a definite sign that someone purposefully intended harm; nevertheless, providing the truth openly to an angered pair of aristocrats didn't seem wise. If Sirlonk reacted hastily with his sword, the real trouble maker, who was probably The Dread, would slither away like a startled snake in the bushes.

"If I had a guess," raged Sirlonk conceitedly, "it was that frazzle-bearded, tippity-nosed Zerny, or one of his similarly pathetic drat helpers. Ever since he led me into that bloody trap with his friends, he's acted standoffish. I can't logically understand why Bonboo tolerates such incompetence—except that he himself is too old to see it!"

"He's a kind man," said Strat, trailing behind the others, but spurring his horse to speed up enough to enter the conversation. It was fortunate Strat spoke up or Dilly would have burst: Nobody spoke ill of Bonboo in front of her without incurring an outpouring of wrath.

Dod tilted his head and took a second peek at the celebrated Bollirse instructor. Strat wasn't much to look at; his pants and shirt were typical small-village, homespun; his right boot was visible, with a hole in the toe; his height and body build was a short-average for a grown tredder; his mud-brown hair was messy, spiking in clumps recklessly on his head; and his face was sunburned and peeling with sparse stubble on his lip and chin only.

The one exception to Strat's otherwise ordinary appearance was his daring eyes. Clearly, he was mellow enough not to challenge Sirlonk over a rude comment made about him, and he was unquestionably ill from riding a horse, but Strat was not afraid of Sirlonk—and his eyes seemed to say that he wasn't afraid of anything.

"Come now, my Chantolli friends," said Strat as he guided his horse and stole Boot's position. "I won't hear disparagement about Bonboo. He's equal to your brother Terro in class, and he's more than surpassed him in wisdom from age, so let's tread carefully, dear companions."

Strat spoke with a smile on his face, yet not a word of it was facetious: He meant them all!

Sirlonk became enflamed with controlled anger; his ears turned red and his nostrils twitched slightly. If fire could have come from his eyes, Strat would have become a pile of ashes in an instant.

"I don't recall ever inviting you to use my family name," chided Sirlonk coldly. "I would appreciate more respect in the future. *GOOD DAY!*"

Juny and Sirlonk took the lead and quickly upped their pace until they parted from the others, far enough to be out of hearing range. Song tried to join them until Dilly restrained him. The Chantollis needed their space.

At the outskirts of High Gate, the group met up with

Sirlonk and Juny again, however, this time there was a crowd of hundreds of other people, so direct conversation with them wasn't necessary. Dod and Boot stayed on Shooter, while the others dismounted their horses and mingled with the people. Dilly was in her element, socializing with acquaintances she hadn't seen in a long time.

Everyone was waiting in and around a large, open pavilion. The road widened out directly in front of the structure and continued without any bends for about a mile, where another pavilion full of people stood. Beyond the second edifice, High Gate towered majestically above the fields, crowning multiple hilltops with buildings, houses, roads, castles and gardens.

An old, fifteen-foot, stone wall surrounded High Gate, with lookout towers interrupting the battlement every couple of miles. In front of the wall, light-green fields of well-grazed grass extended for a few hundred yards, completely void of trees and bushes; cows meticulously searched, cropping anything higher than an inch.

In contrast, lush grass, bushes, and tall trees grew directly next to the depleted fields. It was as if someone had drawn an imaginary, impassable line which the cows all respected.

As noon approached, the crowd grew impatient, waiting for something to happen. One bobwit man, with all four feet of him dressed in a stately suit, stood near the front, holding the reins to a horse that was laden with goods. Next to him, a large wagon, pulled by a team of horses, was filled with nicely dressed tredders. A little girl sat toward the front and held a shaggy brown dog in her lap. Situated in the wagon was also a boy, about the same age as the girl, who kept poking the dog with a stick, every time the girl looked away.

One large poke was too much for the crabby dog to take; it leaped from the girls lap, flying out of the wagon, and landed on the ground, barking obnoxiously at the base of the wheels. The neighboring horse, loaded with bobwit tradeables, broke free of its master and bolted forward down the road, heading straight for High Gate. It only went about two hundred feet before bucking uncontrollably. It reeled back and forth, spilling most of its load to the ground; and then it made its way in the opposite direction, running right past the pavilion at a racing speed.

"Poor horse," said Boot, cringing sympathetically; he shook his head as he spoke to Dod. "I once tried walking into the barrier. It was a stupid dare. The noise inside my head was extremely loud, even though I covered my ears, and my insides felt like they were going to explode. It looks like nothing, but there's something very real surrounding the city. I think the Mauj were brilliant, inventing the invisible triblot barrier. It's pathetic we haven't the slightest clue of how to replicate it or how to create new triblots."

DOOOOOONG.

A large bell, hung in the distant pavilion, declared the beginning of the process of dropping the barrier.

DONG, DONG. Another bell, from the first watch tower, responded.

DONG, DONG, DONG. The next watch tower continued the musical chain.

Bells pealed, from one tower to another, becoming quieter until they could no longer be heard. Dod assumed it was the official announcement to enter safely.

"Shall we get going?" he asked naively.

"In a minute," said Boot. "We don't want to enter until the lead guard tower indicates the barrier is down. You can't see the triblot field, so you have to trust the bells. Besides, I always let someone else go first, just in case."

After a while of waiting, a quiet sound of ringing bells chimed from the other side of High Gate.

"See, here it comes," said Boot.

DONG, DONG, DONG...

"Thirty-two," counted Boot. "That means they have only three more towers to go."

"What are they doing?" asked Dod.

"Getting ready—there are thirty-five towers around High Gate, and each one must initiate a triblot drop-down sequence. When the tower peals its number, it means their portion of the shield is ready to come down and that the guards are on watch, prepared for an attack."

"Wow, that's quite a system," said Dod. He was impressed by the continued alertness of the troops, armed with swords for defense and equipped with unusually loud bells for communication.

When the thirty-fifth tower indicated its number, it then began a quick one-dong chain from tower to tower. Within less than two minutes, the chain had made its way entirely around the city, reconnecting with the beginning, whereupon an extra large DONG sounded. That was the final signal that the shield was officially down.

All of the waiting people made a rush for the wide lane, with Dod and Boot lingering back, pausing until Dilly and Sawny had remounted their horses.

Those exiting had freedom to go as they pleased; however, all of the individuals entering High Gate were met by a battalion of soldiers. Proper papers, indicating approval to enter, were needed in order to pass the guards. Dilly showed a fearsome tredder Dod's note from Commendus and then pointed at Sawny, Buck, Boot and Dod. The guard looked the group over and nodded his head.

Most of the people entering showed papers or badges and were admitted relatively quickly. Two carts were detained for a time, while soldiers searched their contents, but shortly thereafter, were sent on their way. The only apparent exemptions to the rule for entrance were Sirlonk and Juny; they proceeded forward into the crowd of soldiers and continued on without showing any paperwork or even saying so much as hello.

A GIFT FROM COMMENDUS

High Gate was filled with beauty and elegance. The smallest homes and apartments were built with such wonderful craftsmanship that it was clear everyone in town had plenty to eat and could safely be considered a city-slicker. The roads were all paved flat or cobble stone, and the gardens were beautiful and orderly. The metropolis was picture-perfect. Even the garbage collectors, out working the streets, appeared well groomed and happy.

At the top of the first knoll, which appeared to be the highest point of the city, Boot forced the others to stop by a charming monument so Dod could take in the stunning view. High Gate was huge. It spanned tens of miles, covering hills and valleys in a circular bowl shape, with thousands of towering buildings and structures poking above the tree-filled landscape. It was mind bogglingly large, considering it was entirely protected by an impenetrable triblot field.

"Wow, this is High Gate?" sighed Dod, astonished. It was much bigger than Salt Lake or Las Vegas.

"You've been here before, haven't you?" asked Dilly.

Dod didn't say yes, but he nodded. It wasn't exactly a lie.

He couldn't personally recall having visited the city, yet he did have memories of High Gate. He recognized the view he was looking at, almost like it had already been shown to him in a photograph; and he knew where certain shops were, and he even remembered who lived in some of the houses. Many of the roads were so familiar to him that he could foretell what was behind each bend.

Buck poked Dilly for asking such a ridiculous question. "Of course he's been here before," he chided. "Dod worked for Commendus, remember? He helped Tridacello, Dungo, and Bowlure to rescue the stolen triblot from Dreaderious. This spot just makes you feel awestruck, doesn't it? And to think Bonboo's parents gave this place up. It could have been yours, Dilly."

Dod glanced down at the statue in front of him, which was surrounded by pigeons. It was a bronze of two people, holding hands, looking out over the valleys, and below them, the words *Tillius—Freedom For All.*

"I'm perfectly satisfied visiting, thank you," answered Dilly with a grin. She was obviously pleased at the thought of being an ex-heiress to the magnificent city. "In truth, it wouldn't be so magical if we still ruled over High Gate. Democracy breathed life into it that the finest of monarchs couldn't have achieved. And educated, wealthy, wonderful people came from everywhere to be a part of what we see today. It's the best in all of us, the grand dream, the lingering hope of what my family trusts can one day become everyone's inheritance."

Dilly's eyes filled with tears as she said "May this spread. Long live democracy!"

It was a patriotic moment. Dod thought of Pap, standing proudly, saluting the American Flag as the anthem was sung before a Bees game in Salt Lake City. He had never spent time considering what exactly Pap had so solemnly saluted until that moment. Pap had paid respect to the flag because of what Dilly had just described—the beauty and power and glory of democracy—a cause worth fighting for and, if need be, worth dying for.

Buck's horse pranced between Shooter and Song long enough to change the conversation.

"Shouldn't we hurry to the palace?" said Buck, looking at Dod. "I bet Commendus has lunch ready for us, which would be nice since *somebody* smashed the provisions Mercy gave us."

"It's not my fault," argued Dod helplessly, peering at Buck from behind Boot. Everyone had missed breakfast, due to Dod's regrettable horse experience, so the mention of food was a sore topic.

Fortunately, it didn't take long before Dod recognized they were getting close. They had only ridden for about fifteen minutes when they came to a crowded complex of gigantic buildings. A wide courtyard, sprawling like The Mall in Washington D.C., was paved with red stones and was lined on each side with twenty glorious buildings. They were identical and made of the most beautiful white marble and adorned with magnificent carvings and golden trim. In front of the entrances, decorated poles rose fifty feet out of the ground, giving the buildings a way to tell them apart. The fancy posts were like flags to the people in Green and were decorated intricately—a white one with red dots; a blue one with yellow and black steaks; a red one with white squares and green triangles; a purple and green swirled one with yellow capping at the top; and so forth—forty in all.

Thousands of people, a vast majority of whom were tredders,

moved about the strip with purpose—either as tourists or professionals. Most of them were on foot, though a few carefully made their way, as Dod and his friends did, on horseback. However, there were no wagons or other conveyances allowed in the courtyard.

As Dod thought about it, wondering how such a vast number of people came and went, he found that recollections flooded his mind, answering his questions. Behind the buildings, back roads webbed efficiently, allowing all sorts of chartered transit to flow in an orderly fashion. And also, more amazingly, an underground waterway transported people in mini-submarines, whizzing them up and down the hills of High Gate inside a pipe-like stone system. It was pollution-free and ran on pressurized water that ingeniously utilized a series of lakes. The network was made possible because of a mighty underground river that poured into High Gate from the towering Hook Mountains to the north and west.

In the end, a majority of the water eventually made its way past the southernmost point of the city and into a small body of water called Lake Charms. There, a port harbored ships from all over the world of Green. With the proper paperwork, vessels were allowed to come north up the Blue River, a six hundred mile journey from Port Glantor on the Carsalean Sea. It was baffling to think that most of the people visiting High Gate crossed oceans to eventually disembark at the doorstep of the grand capital that was cradled in the foothills of the mountains—only a few locals came by horse.

Dod looked around gawkingly. There were millions of inhabitants in High Gate, yet the feeling was warm and inviting. He was so mesmerized by what he saw that it took

Dilly three attempts before Dod realized she was talking to him.

"Now, Dod! Where are you from?" she asked, glancing at the poles respectfully.

"I'm a—from all over," said Dod. He didn't know how to respond. Dilly clearly wanted to know which post he hailed to, for the beautiful displays were actually representing the forty areas in Green, and the buildings they were in front of, were filled with dignitaries and ambassadors who represented hundreds of millions of people. It was the political nexus for the whole world of Green.

Dod stumbled on his answer because an honest one would be none of the posts—or rather, the American Flag. Fortunately, before Dilly noticed Dod's distressful blush, Sawny began blurting a string of things about their beautiful pole that was completely pine green with one white circle at the top; it symbolically portrayed the world in harmony with nature and ruled wisely by truth and knowledge. The pole was right in the middle of the strip, and as they approached it, Sawny drew her arm to the square, honoring all it represented.

Dod felt dumb recognizing he had walked past an identical one, dozens of times at Twistyard, and had thought that it was sloppy to put such a bizarre thing in the open field.

"I think Yorkum has got to be the greatest province in Green," said Sawny patriotically, beginning on a lecture about the factual realities that made her homeland the best. "From Terraboom in the north, with its world class industry, to the fertile grain fields surrounding Crosswinds, to the ambiance and culture of Carsigo, to Port Glantor in the south, with its unsurpassed prowess at global trade—we've easily got five times as many educated people in our cities as the best of the others; and just look—High Gate!—our crowning jewel. It's the only place—anywhere!—that you can see the splendor and wealth of buildings like this meet up with the functionality of an underground public transit; and it's all well protected by a triblot field."

Dod wondered what she would say if she could see Chicago or New York, with their skyscrapers, airports, and subways, but he didn't say anything.

"I wouldn't be talking, Missy," chided Buck, getting annoyed that Sawny was overly complimentary of her own province, which contained both her childhood home in Terraboom and her great-grandfather's estate at Twistyard. "Have you ever been to Stallboosh?" he asked, challenging her.

"She wouldn't need to," answered Dilly, getting ruffled into the dispute. "What's in Stallboosh? Nothing but an ocean of hills and sheep. It's barely got enough people to call it a province at all."

"Hardly," said Boot, quickly defending his homeland. "It has twice as much dirt as Yorkum; and Ridgeland alone has nearly half-a-million people—and it's got as many scholars as Lower Janice, per capita. Not to mention, since you're from Terraboom, only a couple-hundred-miles to the south, what's your excuse for never having scampered your way up to see it when you were young."

"I suppose," said Dilly smugly, "because you were living there! Besides, Ridgeland isn't the average city in Stallboosh—it's nearly the only one! I'm more than confident Terraboom alone has more people than your whole province—and the two above yours as well."

"It's because so much of the ground is wasteland," added Sawny wryly. "You can't blame people for wanting to live here instead of there. Yorkum is beautiful."

"Like you don't have your share of garbage?" said Boot, chuckling.

"How can you call *that* garbage?" asked Dilly, pointing northward at the Hook Mountains that towered above the buildings, gracing High Gate with a beautiful backdrop.

"Think east," said Boot, raising an eyebrow. He looked at Dilly and waited for her to get it. When she didn't respond, he helped jog her memory by pointing at his foot.

"Oh yeah," said Dilly, looking embarrassed. "I guess some of our province is—well—not as nice."

Buck traded smiles with Boot.

To the east of High Gate, the Ankle Weed Desert covered hundreds of square miles. It was indisputably the most barren land in Green. Its sand was poisonous to roughly all plants, rendering it void of vegetation, regardless of rainfall.

"Here's to the two of you, then," said Sawny, looking self-satisfied as she pointed at the last post on their right, as they passed by; it was brown with black and white goats up the side. "From your pole, I'd say Stallboosh is trying hard to make sure everyone knows how educated and advanced your people are up north."

Dilly smiled while Boot and Buck winced.

Just around the corner from the busy hustle of the plaza, Commendus had his monstrous estate. It sat on a hillside, looking out over the beautiful city; and its substantial acreage was all fenced with a stone wall and guarded by soldiers at the entrance.

Once inside, Discommo Manor and the surrounding grounds were breathtaking. There were hundreds of well-manicured acres of grass and foliage, a lake, a castle, and a few other ornate buildings; the property was surprisingly open and pastoral, like a hundred-million-dollar estate in the English countryside, and hardly fit the crowded neighborhood, where the expensive real estate was thoughtfully organized with business and political buildings for miles in every direction. A wall of metropolis jutted upward along the outside perimeter of Commendus's grounds, like the stone city surrounding Central Park in the middle of New York, except the adjoining structures here weren't as big and the commotion from the area was less raucous.

Commendus was the beneficiary of his family's land, which had originally been passed down as an inherited stewardship. Later, when Bonboo's parents possessed it, they gave Commendus's family full ownership; though it was modest back then. It wasn't until Commendus took claim that the grand palace and surrounding luxuries were built, along with the burgeoning metropolis around it.

Before him, Commendus's progenitors had been legendary farmers and cattlemen, giving him a perfect platform to launch his first successful business: a chain of stores selling meat and vegetable products with a uniform standard. The Discommo Stores were an instant sensation, combining the family's reputation with Commendus's business-savvy. After that, everything Commendus did seemed to flourish, including politics.

At the entrance to the grounds, two dozen stones, shaped like real cows, dotted a flower garden. On each rock was engraved the full names of past stewards and owners of the land—Joshionnock Dilliono Discommo, Dossontrian Dillionus Discommo, Joshionnelli Commendo Discommo, and twenty-one other names. The garden resembled a herd of cattle, mischievously grazing on forbidden flowers and bushes.

"Okay, Dilly," said Boot, "tell me how that one is going to fit in the family garden." He smiled and pointed at an eighty-foot granite rock, carved in the shape of a hand that reached upward from the ground. It had Commendus Joshionnelli Discommo carved across the palm.

"It's not supposed to," answered Dilly plainly. "He's not a farmer, he's a civilized thinker. I like it. He's probably symbolizing democracy rising out of the ground, and his proportions are perfect—we are only a twitching hand with most of us still buried in uncertainty."

"Well, if that's to represent democracy, then it's funny he wrote his name across it," said Boot proudly.

"He's the big hand that's helping democracy," responded Dilly.

"Or he's the big hand that's ruling out democracy," contended Boot.

Dilly didn't answer with words, yet the expression on her face said plenty—'GROW UP!'

Beyond the immediate gardens at the front, grassy fields lined with gigantic trees surrounded a fifty-acre pond. On the other side of the water, a massive bright-white palace towered upward. Dod almost expected to see Cinderella running down the front steps with a handsome prince close on her heels. It was that kind of castle.

Sawny took the lead, leaving her sister farther back, still

crossing eyes with Boot. The group rode beside the lake, trotting along on a beautifully-designed drive strip. Suddenly, three gardeners and a well-dressed man came bounding out of some shrubs, calling words of caution regarding something of interest.

"Commendus," shouted Dilly. "I wouldn't have expected to see you out gardening."

"You should expect the unexpected with me, My Duckling," said Commendus in a loud voice. "I was just about to be shown our most fascinating visitor. The gardeners found her a few minutes ago and insisted I see for myself."

"My Duckling?" whispered Dod to Boot.

"She swam a few times with the ducks in his pond," responded Boot in an equally quiet voice. "He gave her a fitting nickname, though you probably shouldn't try it. I know she's cold on the idea unless he's the one using it—goes over even worse than Twisty."

"I'm curious. Who's your visitor?" asked Dilly.

"Watch out," called one of the gardeners to Commendus. "You'd better move while you talk. Here she comes."

Commendus jogged until he was next to the other gardeners and then turned to see his guest. What he saw was clearly a surprise to him, and it made him quiver!

A fifty-foot long snake came slithering out of the bushes. It was silky black and covered in mud. The girth of the snake, at its widest point, was similar to Shooter's neck, and its eyes were a glazed white, as if it were dead. Commendus and the others dodged frantically to get out of the serpent's path as it made its way across the grass and road. Within a matter of a few seconds, the entire snake disappeared into the depths of the murky lake.

"That's your guest?" gasped Dilly in horror. "And to think I used to enjoy a nice dip in that water. Never again!"

"That looked like a diasserpentous," remarked Sawny in amazement. "I thought we didn't have any of those here in Green."

"We didn't," said a man who was dressed as a gardener, yet appeared older and more refined than the other two rougher-looking men. He stood up straighter, unlike the others who slouched, and his hair was well combed and graying. He also had a notebook protruding from his front pocket instead of shovels and gloves.

"Let me introduce Doctor Shelderhig Grick," interrupted a slightly cowering Commendus. "He has joined us here at the palace doing research, and I suppose he knows as much as anyone about that creature we just saw. Miz gave her to me years ago to keep in my exotic fountains on the back patio, but apparently, when she disappeared, she wasn't eaten by a bird as Miz suggested. And to think he promised me she wouldn't grow an inch longer than four feet!"

"Living on guppies in your fountain, Miz would have been right," said Doctor Shelderhig. "Unfortunately, the fish and waterfowl in that pond will likely keep her nice and healthy, growing up to a hundred feet if you don't poke her out. Of course, there's no need to take drastic measures too quickly—she won't be out of the water much, since she has gills like a fish, so if you refrain from swimming, you'll be all right for now."

"But she was just up in the hedge—nearly had me for breakfast," sobbed the anxious gardener who had had the misfortune of originally discovering her. "If you don't get her, someone's gonna be filling her gut. And it won't be me! I can assure you of that! I'm not going anywhere near that pond until she's gone!"

"Don't worry," Shelderhig reassured, as he disappeared into the thicket of shrubs. When he came back he held up a clear sack of golf-ball-sized eggs. They actually looked like little golf balls, without the dimples.

"She was putting these in the ground," he said. "Their young start out breathing air—opposite of frogs, you know."

"They're not fertile, are they?" asked Commendus, with a look of concern crossing his already flustered face.

"Actually, yes they are," said Shelderhig factually. "They're like worms—can multiply pretty quickly…all alone, too."

"I have a lake full of *those*?" moaned Commendus, grabbing at his face torturously. "I'd kill Miz if he weren't already dead!"

"Don't get overly excited," said Shelderhig kindly. "I'm sure her past hatchlings slipped into your pond and mama ate them for breakfast. There's not enough room for two in that pool when one is over fifty feet."

"That's reassuring," said Commendus semi-sarcastically. He gazed irritably at the lake and shook his head in disapproval.

"For what it's worth," added Shelderhig, "that's the best fed diasserpentous I've ever seen, and I've seen quite a few of them over the course of my nearly two hundred years in Soosh. When you keep a pet, you really go all out."

"Well," confessed an exasperated Commendus, "Now I know why my guests haven't been lucky anymore at fishing for my famed thirty-pound chublings. That *thing* has eaten them all!"

"Then dispose of her," said Shelderhig bluntly.

Commendus shuddered. "I don't care for excitement of that

kind. Adventure in the wild has never been my forte, much less retaking my yard from the coils of a physical contender. I think you, My Dear Doctor, are just the man to do something about my unusually healthy *pet*. Perhaps you could put your knowledge of diasserpentouses toward contriving a plan to exterminate it. I'd deeply appreciate your efforts. If you succeed—why, I'll—I'll buy you the whole list of things you indicated you hoped to eventually study; and I mean it!—that red-blooming, pricey whatever-you-called-it included—I give you my word!"

"Consider it done," responded Shelderhig. He drew himself into a soldier pose and strangely saluted Commendus with a tight fist over his forehead—Green's military style—even though Shelderhig was his senior. It was mostly a show of excitement from hearing his research agenda could be quickly funded if the feat were accomplished.

"I admire your enthusiasm," said Buck, who had quietly listened to the conversation, wondering whether or not all the pampering in the world, which was likely to be provided by Commendus, was worth dwelling in a structure so close to the home of the beast he had just seen.

"Oh, it shouldn't be that hard," stated Shelderhig confidently. "There's always something for getting something else." He made his way to the lakeside, taking big strides with every step, and began measuring the width of the muddy skid marks where the diasserpentous had just entered the water. It was obvious he was a scientist. He instantly became more concerned with the facts surrounding the creature than he was of the danger it presented.

Commendus took a ride, doubling with Dilly, to the thickly wooded side of the castle where the stables were located. He mostly spoke about the regrettable escape of the rare Dilcon

Diasserpentous, originally given as a *special* gift from Miz; and how based on its current size, he no longer felt so *special* owning one. He also mentioned in passing that Dr. Shelderhig was Jim's uncle, and that despite being from the backwoods of Soosh, a member of the Grick clan no less, he was rather well informed of the various plants and animals.

Sawny, like the others, mostly listened while Commendus spoke, except mentioning she had read eight books Dr. Shelderhig had authored. Dod was hidden enough behind Boot's frame that he never entered the conversation, not even to be welcomed by The Great Head of Democracy, notwithstanding he was the one that had been personally invited.

Commendus was a man of interesting and somewhat dichotomous characteristics; he was much bigger and more muscular than most tredders, a solid six-foot-eight, yet proclaimed having little interest in adventure or physical challenges; and was sweet and generous to everyone, yet also condescending; and commanded a worldwide nation and ran many successful businesses, yet distressed at the sight of a large pest.

His one consistent theme was money. He wore expensive clothes, lived in an elegant castle, insisted on the best for himself and others, and quickly resorted to using money to resolve problems—as he had when offering to generously fund all of Dr. Shelderhig's research in return for catching the snake.

In the palace, however, Commendus perfectly fit the role of chief boss. No sooner did they enter through a side door than he was ordering preparations for his guests—rooms to stay in, food to eat, and new clothes to wear. He also apologized to Dod for not introducing himself properly before; and he promised to sit down with him privately that evening, after returning from other pressing business, to discuss his appreciation to Dod for helping to retrieve the stolen triblot. His manners and style were befitting of a noble leader.

Many people stayed at the castle as guests, most of whom had political or business affiliations. From the back patio, a number of other smaller buildings were visible, dotting the colossal two-thousand-acre estate. One building looked particularly significant. It was apparent, from the double wall around it and the battalion of soldiers standing near the structure, that it housed something of great importance. And Dod knew exactly what it was: the only working portal from Green to Raul.

Sirlonk, Juny, and Strat had preceded Dod and his friends to the palace and had continued their journey through the gateway. This they learned from one of the waiters at lunch, who like most people it seemed was dear friends with Dilly.

After eating, Dilly charted an itinerary, mentioning that it was needful to take the opportunity, while in High Gate, to go and speak with her long-time family friend, Gollium, an old and retired war hero and ambassador to Soosh; she wanted more information on the twelve trouble-causing representatives from Soosh who were allegedly in Green, and she knew he would be up on the most reliable gossip. Boot and Buck tried to wiggle out, hoping for a more relaxing afternoon, but were promptly denied.

Dod, on the other hand, thought the visit sounded amusing until he heard they would need to ride their horses for an hour to get to his cottage, since he was off the beaten path of the sub routes, and another hour to return to the palace; the morning's adventures on horseback had already left Dod sore enough to dread sitting, much less riding, unless absolutely necessary, so he claimed to be terribly fascinated with botany and wouldn't back down from joining Sawny on her important meeting with Doctor Shelderhig.

At the locked gate to the enclosed gardens, situated below the farthest west patios, Sawny and Dod met up with the mad scientist. He wasn't exactly crazy, just mad. Apparently, from his calculations, the creature they had all seen wasn't a Dilcon Diasserpentous, as Commendus had suggested. Instead, he highly suspected it was a Bloon Diasserpentous.

The change in type wasn't direly important to Dod, and since Sawny knew very little from what she had read of the creatures, it didn't bother her either, until Shelderhig explained the situation. He mentioned that in the latter breed, and only in that breed, it actually took two creatures to produce eggs at all — they didn't lay non-fertile eggs — and to make matters worse, papas were more than twice the size of mamas!

How were there two creatures? And how were they a different variety than the type Miz had given to Commendus? Perhaps someone else had planted them, or Miz had misnamed the breed, or possibly the good doctor was mistaken. These were all suspicious things Sawny knew Dilly would need to add to her Book of Everything.

Inside the garden, Doctor Shelderhig became so enthralled with describing the particulars of each species of plant included in his studies that he completely changed gears and didn't mention another thing about the diasserpentous disaster.

Sawny asked enough questions to fuel the fire of Shelderhig's lecturing, and the two of them were content reveling for hours about the strangest discoveries; common grass would turn slightly orangish-yellow instead of brownish-yellow if certain fertilizers were applied before winter; and the leaves on Bollus bushes were digestible to dung beetles but not cows; and (what a treat to know) the roots of Bongus plants would grow twice their regular length if denied water to the point of near death and then revived properly.

Somewhere in the conversation, Dod's mind wandered away and noticed the beauty of the setting. The garden was filled with flowers and trees that looked unusual and smelled wonderful; and the foliage was planted close enough together to provide a mini-jungle of sorts. A stately, twelve-foot stone wall surrounded the half-acre plot, with only one entrance—a locked gate near Shelderhig's temporary lab and living quarters. It was a remarkably secluded place to sit and think, tucked away from the busy atmosphere of the palace and surrounding courtyards.

Dod mumbled to himself, because he was envious of the doctor's secret place, "I would love to sleep here tonight."

His comment wasn't meant to trigger a response from anyone, but it did.

"Then you're a bolder man than I would have thought," responded Shelderhig. "Of course you'd be perfectly safe, as long as you walked in the dark, didn't eat any of the plants, and didn't sleep directly on *these two*."

"What?" said Dod, realizing he was once again part of the group.

"The two plants right here—the Doloranus and Doloopus are notorious for claiming the lives of children back in Soosh, especially near more civilized cities; parents forget to teach their young to avoid touching them for prolonged periods."

Shelderhig lay down on the soft, cushioned leaves of the two species of ground cover.

"I can understand why people would want to nap here," he said, making himself comfortable.

When Dod and Sawny gave horrified looks, the doctor added, "—however, you're fine for an hour or so. After that, the plant releases a toxin, produced when something heavy presses upon it for a while, and the poison takes effect through the skin almost instantly, causing sudden death."

Sawny asked a few more questions and Shelderhig directed her attention to the plants surrounding where he lay. They were all relatively harmless unless digested or intentionally injected, except one: the Dilopotus Demonstrous, commonly called The Night Devil by indigenous tribesmen in Soosh.

When Shelderhig began to discuss the evil plant, Dod decided to move. He had been standing with the vines all around him, like an ape in the jungle. The plant looked harmless enough—half-inch-thick vines and eight-inch closed pods—but it was actually capable of capturing prey. At night, when anything discharging light came near the vines, they attacked. Their main course in Soosh was usually the Giant Glow Moth and the Darglow, a one pound bird that emitted small amounts of light to attract bugs.

Doctor Shelderhig went on to note that the vines had snake-like agility when striking and that within the pods, fang-thorns released venom, which temporarily incapacitated the creature and aided the blood to flow for the plant to drink.

"—and so, when you sleep here tonight," concluded Shelderhig, standing up and smiling broadly at Dod, "don't bring a light!" He took a step and fell back to the ground, blaring horribly "—aaaaaaah! Help!"

The good doctor had ensnared his two legs in the vines and

began to roll back and forth, as if he were being attacked. Dod and Sawny jumped back in terror, and Sawny even screamed a blood-curdling cry, until they noticed Shelderhig was laughing uncontrollably.

"I got you," he said playfully.

Sawny gave him a deathly cold glare, then turned away while scoffing, "Boys and their pranks—"

Dod chuckled and tried to act cool. "So, the plant isn't dangerous, is it?" he asked, implying with his body language that he hadn't really been scared, he had just gone along with the joke to make Sawny jump.

"That depends on what you are," responded Shelderhig happily, pushing back a clump of hair that was matted to his sweaty forehead from tussling with the weed. "If you're a Giant Glow Moth or Darglow, this is a deathtrap; but if you're a human, walking through the forest with a torch, the plant wouldn't cause you any harm, only startle you when it darts at your fire. The heat would repel the plant before it could pose a real threat."

"Oh," said Dod, nodding his head.

Sawny was still looking away—truly annoyed.

When Dod noticed Sawny's upset face, he felt bad, even if he hadn't been the instigator of the prank. "Which of these plants is the most deadly?" he asked, hoping an educational conversation would revive Sawny by alluring her with intellectual treats.

"It would have to be the Hissolop, over there," answered Shelderhig, pointing his index finger at a very plain-looking weed. It was only two feet tall, with small yellow leaves and a single, two-inch pod at the base.

"The Hissolop?" said Sawny in a pouting voice. "We have those all over Green. You need to practically beat the thing to death with a stick, over and over, before it strikes; and even then, you'd have to be leaning right up next to it for the thorn to make a hit."

"That's true," responded Shelderhig, "but more adults die from trying to pull the baby weeds out of their gardens than probably all of these other plants combined—the poison is extremely toxic."

"I guess they might be dangerous to a tired gardener," admitted Sawny, looking at the weed with a greater fascination.

"Would you like to see what I have in my lab?" Shelderhig asked, directing Dod and Sawny out of the garden and toward his living quarters. He locked the iron gate behind them and entered the castle through a thick, wooden door. "This is it," he said proudly. "This is where I make magic."

Doctor Shelderhig spent the next two hours droning on about mixing plants to create creams and poisons and everything in between. It wasn't very exciting to Dod, who was busy wishing his posterior hadn't forbidden him from visiting Gollium, the war hero. Sawny, on the other hand, was clearly in her element, discussing things she had read in books and trying to decipher the facts from the various scientists' speculations.

At dinner, Dod had a hard time controlling his drool. It wasn't the food, it was the souvenirs Gollium had given to Boot and Buck; each of them had been allowed to choose a fancy-looking pocket knife before leaving, to remind them of the ongoing conflict.

Dilly was pleased with the information she had received from her dear friend, so it didn't bother her that Boot and Buck walked away with better parting gifts. Gollium was an old fashioned man of war who didn't see any place for ladies in the effort and therefore never offered her anything special, just an antiquated book about ladies' kitchen tales.

Sawny and Dilly swapped notes, while the three boys ate their dinner and listened. Boot thought the idea of a hundred-foot male diasserpentous was exciting. On the other hand, Buck tried to figure out how he could convince the maids that he needed to sleep in a room on the top floor of the palace, preferably with a dozen armed guards.

Dod's ears perked up when Dilly mentioned that Gollium was confident there weren't twelve touring representatives from Soosh. In Gollium's own words, it was all pig feed. He didn't believe the rumors and assumed anyone with reasoning capabilities would quickly see through them. To the best of his knowledge, there were only a small handful of people officially representing Soosh as ambassadors at the time because of a rare, month-long convention that had pulled the others home, and the remaining few were at High Gate, having been gathered from various towns after the poisoning.

Dilly paused just long enough for Dod to slip in a question: "If the poisoning happened at High Gate, wouldn't it make more sense to have the ambassadors stay where they were?"

Dilly thought for a moment while flipping through her other notes.

"Probably not," she said confidently. "After all, High Gate is the safest place, even if one breach of security occurred here. If the ambassadors stayed spread out, whoever's aiming to kill would easily find them waiting like daisies in the garden."

Before the group had finished eating, the head waitress indicated to Dod that Commendus was ready to see him. As he followed her, she first took him to a giant walk-in-closet and introduced him to a chambermaid. Suits of every color and size lined the walls and fancy shoes and boots lined the floor.

"We need you to be presentable," said the waitress.

"Oh, thank you. That's kind, but I was already given these clothes," responded Dod, pointing at his stylish pants and ruffled silk shirt.

"Certainly, you needed something to wear when you were out. Now that you've had your supper, it's time to dress up a notch. Commendus is in his official office, so I can't have you barge in like you've just returned from a stroll through the courtyards. You need to show respect. Have Jooshi help you try some of these on."

The lady walked out of the room, leaving Dod with the chambermaid.

"How about this?" suggested the girl, directing Dod's attention toward an outfit that was organized neatly on a table; it contained a charcoal-colored formal five-piece suit, complete with shoulder attachments and gold cufflinks, a dazzling white shirt that did appear to be fancier than the one he was wearing, a pair of shiny shoes with unusual tassels, a black hat that fit perfectly, and a pair of dark wool socks.

"The suit-up's right there," said Jooshi, pointing to a small room with no windows. The door was unusually thick, and the lock was on the outside.

"Can't I change somewhere else?" asked Dod nervously. "—like…what about over there." Dod indicated in the direction of a cozy corner, where drawers of clothes blocked the view adequately to provide some privacy.

"Don't be silly, I'm not that kind of girl!"

"Oh, no—no, no, that's not what I meant," apologized

Dod, blushing three shades of red. "I just thought the lock on the outside of the suit-up was a little strange, that's all."

"Yes," said Jooshi, glancing hesitantly at Dod. "The carpenter recently had to replace the door. We suffered a mishap with the last one. Unfortunately, when you order from afar, miscommunication can happen. Don't be bothered. I'll stand right here to assure your safety—even lockless—or I suppose I could lock it if you preferred."

"No thank you, unlocked is just fine," said Dod apprehensively, stepping into the tiny room. He fidgeted with the door while taking off one shoe and sock; then, using the sock as a wedge, he finished shutting the door such that the lock wouldn't meet properly—just in case.

The room was uncomfortably small, even though it was plenty big enough to use for trying on clothes. Near the ceiling, a petite smokeless candle burned brightly, making every inch of Dod's concerned face clearly visible in the mirror on the wall. He had never felt claustrophobic before; however, given the circumstance, he had a new level of sympathy for anyone that had.

It didn't take long to complete the task. Dod finished by sliding his left foot into a shiny black shoe. He smiled at himself, noticing how good he looked in the incredible threads, and explained to his reflection that it was silly to have been worried about a chambermaid locking him in the closet.

No sooner had he let his guard down than something prickled his neck until the tiny hairs stood on end.

CLINK, CLINK. The lock made a noise.

Dod froze. He wanted to throw his weight at the door, but also feared whoever was trying to lock him in. It was like confronting a thief in the night. He couldn't decide whether to face the person and attempt to escape or remain in the closet, safe from immediate harm. Thoughts of running out of air rushed his mind.

A few moments passed in silence with Dod praying it was only his imagination; and then it happened again.

CLINK, CLINK, CLINK.

This time it was unmistakable. Someone was definitely trying to make sure Dod couldn't get out; and whoever it was, was realizing Dod's ingenuity had thwarted his plan to use the lock.

"I refuse to die in a closet," muttered Dod.

With a big kick, the door exploded open, making a thunderous boom as it swung around and pounded the adjoining wall. Dod lingered back, terrified, hunching double-fisted and prepping to run; but to his surprise, Boot was standing in front of him, smiling.

"Whoa, Zippod! Cool down," he said, rubbing his elbow that had been grazed.

"I—uh—thought you were someone else," confessed Dod sheepishly, flushing with embarrassment as his hands went limp.

"Well, it's a good thing Jooshi left. She was hugging the door like moss on a stump, guarding you. If her dress had bumped the handle…"

Boot paused and looked down at the floor while shaking his head slowly; and then he jumped unexpectedly at Dod with his hands flying in the air.

"BOOM!" he blurted obnoxiously.

Dod startled backward, his exhausted heart once more racing.

"Jooshi would have been squeezed out permanently if I hadn't come along," said Boot proudly. "You're lethal!"

"I thought someone was trying to lock me in," complained Dod, attempting to regain his composure.

"Actually, I was," admitted Boot, nodding admiringly. "Nice trick with the sock. I'll try to remember that one."

Dod squinted uncomfortably, leaning over and still gasping. "You got me," he said, forcing a pathetic chuckle.

Boot shuffled one foot as though tormented by his conscience. He looked like he sincerely felt bad. "You know me, Dod…" he confessed with a heavy sigh. "I can't seem to help it. Pranks follow my path—not intentionally—they just slip out everywhere I go."

Boot stuck out his hand and helped Dod to his feet. "Sorry if I got you worked up." The serious apology faded quickly as a grin crept across his lips. "You should have seen the look on your face, though," he added, nudging Dod with his sore elbow. "It was priceless. Who did you expect to see, anyway?"

"The Dread," said Dod flatly.

"Here in a closet?"

"I expect him everywhere," said Dod, feeling frustrated. "I know we'll meet soon, and this little episode in the walk-in just reminded me of how unprepared I am."

"You mean the suit-up?" clarified Boot, smirking. "Don't confuse it with a regular small room in front of noblemen. They get awfully particular about the wording of their things. Besides, relax and stop worrying. I've never met The Dread, Buck's never met him—Dilly hasn't even met him, and you know Dilly, she flirts with everyone."

Dod squirmed uncomfortably. "I'm sure you must think I'm crazy, Boot, but I feel he's onto us—especially me."

"That's all right," assured Boot, losing his playful tone. "Just don't get so anxious that you accidentally knock a poor maid unconscious." He then stood a little taller and added confidently, "Besides, if The Dread wants to mess with you, he'll have to face us both."

Boot reached into a leather bag that resembled a fanny pack and produced a shiny gold pocket knife; it had an ivory eagle inlayed in the middle.

"Here," he said, carefully handing it over to Dod. "I talked Gollium into letting me choose one for you, too. I would have given it to you over the dinner table, but did you see the jealous look on Dilly's face when Buck and I showed them off. She wanted a knife, not a kitchen book. Don't tell anyone, all right?"

Dod gently turned the present over and noticed the other side of the knife; it had a horse—the exact same ivory horse Boot had held up at the table, including a tiny brown scratch on one of the rear hoofs. And when Dod commented about how wonderful the craftsmanship was, Boot excitedly gave part of the same story, explaining how it was the last knife made by an expert swordsman who had died defending liberty; though when he realized Dod was catching on, he added a few different, clearly fictional details, hoping to keep his act a secret. Boot knew Dod wouldn't take the knife if he found out it was his only present from Gollium.

It was a special moment. Boot often played the part of a handsome trouble-maker, or a privileged, upper-crust brat, or an I-can-do-anything-better-than-you-can kind of jock, yet this was a glimpse of his hidden sweet side, the good boy that wanted everyone to be happy and would give you the very shirt off his back rather than see you go cold.

"Wow," responded Dod, suddenly feeling choked up. "I'll cherish this forever." He looked the knife over respectfully and slid it into his front vest pocket, under his suit coat. Regardless of the noble individual who had made the knife, Dod loved it because Boot had been generous in giving it to him.

"It'll bring you good luck," added Boot, his eyes beaming with the joy of having secretly done something nice. "Come on, I'll show you to the formal office. You don't want to keep Commendus waiting—and here, let me first help you with that tassel. You put it on backwards."

The meeting with Commendus was mostly like a stuffy, forced greeting from the CEO of a major company. Almost everything sounded canned and proper. He officially offered thanks on behalf of High Gate and issued a written invitation for Dod to return another day, with one guest, to receive a gold medal of honor. He also suggested the names of some influential people that would be attending the banquet and then asked Dod to come dressed in the new suit he was wearing, adding in passing that of course Tridacello, Dungo, and Bowlure would all be present to receive medals, too.

When the formality was over, Commendus stood and pointed toward the door.

"Did you know my grandfather?" asked Dod, feeling uncomfortable about saying anything after having received a commission to leave.

"Your grandfather? I don't think I've ever had the pleasure of meeting him, or if I have, I don't recall it off hand. I'm busy enough that I meet a lot of people casually in my travels—you understand."

"You don't remember Pap?" asked Dod boldly, finding his nerve.

"What? Your grandfather was Pap?" sputtered Commendus, looking surprised.

"Yes, and he still is Pap. I prefer to think of him as having gone on a long trip," said Dod.

"*The* Pap?" asked Commendus, unconvinced; his eyes narrowed as he reassessed Dod.

"The very one that was poisoned in your house," blurted Dod quickly, sensing a chill of hostility the moment he said it. "Though I fully understand that you couldn't have done much to prevent it—I mean—when The Dread sets his sights on something, he doesn't stop until he gets it."

"Yes, that's very true—The Dread—my goodness, I hate thinking of The Dread," said Commendus hastily, looking annoyed and flustered. "I would rather hope that the wine they were drinking was poorly brewed."

"You mean grape juice, Pap didn't drink alcohol," said Dod.

Awkward glances were exchanged during a moment of silence. Apparently, people didn't usually correct The Great Head of Democracy, especially young ones with no clout.

"Yes," said Commendus coolly, searching the air for a better answer. "I suppose they could have been drinking poorly—uh—gathered grape juice."

Commendus stumbled over his words, letting the truth sag, and was caught three times by Dod, until he finally snapped and vomited out his true feelings—selfish and calloused as they were—for he couldn't hold them back any longer with platitudes.

"It was an awful night for *me,* Dod!" he yelled bitterly. "You can't even imagine how bad it was. As a proper host, it was my duty to explain to everyone else that the strange occurrence was not likely to happen again—and all the while, I had to keep looking over my shoulder, protecting myself from the assailant—I mean, Dod—it was sad that Pap died, but what would Green do without *me*?"

Dod blinked at his arrogance and candor, more stunned than anything.

"Anyway," continued Commendus, purging himself of his hidden thoughts. "Anyone who thinks for half-a-sneeze about it can see that I was the main target of that attack! Clearly! The toast to good health would have been mine if I hadn't been so troubled by the nagging of a sudden business mess that night. I was moments from death, holding an empty cup, when chance snatched me—called me away to solve a dilemma before the juice was poured—and here I am, by the thickness of a thread, left alive."

Dod was wide-eyed and all ears, finally hearing the firsthand account of his grandfathers final hours, but feeling simultaneously uncomfortable that he was witnessing the meltdown of a great leader.

"My men are idiots not to see it," blared Commendus. "Who could be so dumb as to suppose that Pap and those kids from Soosh were the targets—what foolishness! I'm sure *I* was the one that The Dread really wanted dead. Just look at me!—look at this!" Commendus waved his arms about, pointing at his opulent office, the likes of which Dod had never seen before, nor could he imagine anyone else having.

"And even Bonboo has turned blind," exploded Commendus, raising his voice as he raged. "He's tilted his glossy eyes at the pile of droppings and missed seeing the whole team of mules pulling the cart. Nothing in Soosh—and I mean

NOTHING!—could be nearly as important as *ME* …and all the good that *I* do….And I ask of you, Dod, who cares that I nearly died? No one!"

Commendus took a deep breath, walked over to his desk, and plopped himself down in a large leather chair. Sitting appeared to help. Bit by bit, serenity and control returned to his face as he shuffled a pile of papers, repeatedly flipping them apart and then straightening them.

"I'm glad you escaped him," said Dod, trying to offer anything that would replace the deafening lack of conversation; the silence was twice as bad since it followed the thunderstorm of words that probably shouldn't have been said. Dod nearly slipped out of the room—every part of him wanted to bolt—but he couldn't until things were normal.

"They've all lost confidence in my ability to provide safety," said Commendus slowly and calmly, looking discouraged as he gazed at nothing. He was somewhere else in his mind. Eventually, and it did take an awkward amount of time, he revived enough to resume a conversation.

"Pap was a dear friend," he said sadly, glancing at Dod. "I'm terribly sorry about what happened. I don't know where my men went wrong—letting such a horrendous crime take place in my house."

There it was: a hint of remorse, a twinge of guilt, a slight indication that he somehow felt it was unfair that he had cheated death while Pap had sipped his last breath.

"Did you get a chance to speak with Pap?" asked Dod hesitantly, pretending like he hadn't heard the past ten minutes. "For me, and the rest of his family, it was almost like he faded away in his sleep. We weren't able to say goodbye or know what was on his mind. If you can remember anything he said, please share it with me."

Commendus stroked his hairless chin and furrowed his brow, recalling the night. "Yes," he said gradually, nodding. "Yes. I did speak with Pap that night. He was a wonderful person to be around." Commendus smiled and turned soft; it was as though a huge balloon of frustration and anger within him had deflated.

"Pap had been reading a book and said that I might find some fascination in reviewing a few passages before bed. As a matter of fact, here it is. I still have it."

Commendus spun around and reached for a brown leather book that was sitting on an elegantly carved table. From the exterior, it appeared to be old and well used, though as Commendus flipped through the pages, Dod could see they were in good condition.

"Your grandfather had been studying this intently," said Commendus. "He said he found wisdom in it that he needed. Perhaps you would like to have it now; after all, Pap only loaned it to me for the evening, so I'm more than overdue in returning it to—well, let's see—a rightful owner."

"Thank you," said Dod respectfully as he took the book. He eagerly opened it to see the title page. What book had Pap been studying right before he died? Perhaps it was a book about The Dread, or information surrounding his deeds; or maybe it was a book about strategy, to catch The Dread—no wonder he was poisoned; or possibly it was a book about new swashbuckling moves.

To Dod's great surprise, the important book Pap had been studying, while on a critical mission of great consequence, had a shocking title: *How To Be A Positive Influence On Your Grandsons*!

Dod was speechless. After realizing how important Pap had been to Green, Raul, and Soosh, Dod had assumed that Pap's efforts had always been dedicated to pressing concerns related to democracy and crushing evil; it had never crossed Dod's mind that Pap could have been thinking about him, and Josh, and Alex.

Commendus said a few more words of sympathy about Pap and apologized for 'blowing wild' as he put it; and as Dod moved to leave, Commendus also asked him to keep quiet about the poisoning—especially the part about Commendus nearly being a victim; however, Dod wasn't really paying attention anymore: Pap had been thinking of him!

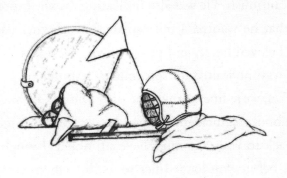

BOLLIRSE

The rest of Dod's stay at High Gate was relatively uneventful. Boot and Buck prevailed upon Dilly and successfully obtained a day-and-a-half of lounging around, being pampered, eating pleasant foods, playing games, talking, and relaxing in luxuriously padded chairs. Dilly and Sawny spent their time more prudently, studying books while overseeing the boys' activities. Dod read too, though the book he couldn't put down was of little importance to stopping The Dread: He read passages from *How To Be A Positive Influence On Your Grandsons*.

Leaving High Gate was easier than entering. When Dilly heard the first set of bells ringing, she whipped the others into order and they rode down to the passage as the triblot field was being lifted. It couldn't have been timed better.

Back at Twistyard, Youk was the first to greet the group, dressed in his usual white attire with a flowing feathered-cavalier on his head. He was riding on Brown Sugar, the mare that had caused such disastrous trouble for Dod.

"I'm surprised to see you all made it back in one piece," said

Youk cautiously. He was also indicating, by the expression on his face, that he wanted a full explanation of what had happened to his beloved horse, and possibly, why Dod was still breathing; either way, he waited for someone to respond.

"Yes, we're fine, thank you," said Dilly. "Oh, and I'm terribly sorry about the incident. It's good to see Brown Sugar found her way back to you. She must have stumbled through some nasty thorns before you loaned her to us, for when we made a press up Coyote Trail, the rocks set her off, nearly sending Dod to a stony end."

"That's curious," remarked Youk with a look of skepticism. He didn't continue to explain his thoughts, nor did he push anyone for further details. He patted Brown Sugar affectionately with his white-gloved hand and added, "I'm just glad you're all right."

The way he rolled into a completely different subject without first getting the whole tale was bizarre, especially for Youk.

"So—are you up for the big match?" he asked, glancing at Dod.

"Like a pig waiting at the trough," answered Boot, jumping in enthusiastically.

Dod didn't say anything. He stared pensively at the ground.

"It'll be a great day," continued Boot, glowing with excitement. "We haven't played a full-out round of Bollirse, triple team, for ages. This is our year to show up Raul—I can feel it—and there's no better way to start off the season than to play the first game with everyone—them against us."

"What do you think of it, Dilly?" asked Youk.

"It will be entertaining," she responded candidly. "I hope I can spare the time—I have so many things going on right now—of course I'll be playing in the regular tournaments later this year when they count."

"Right, I'm sure you'll do fine," assured Youk. "I'll be watching your matches. It would be nice to see Green back in charge of the field." He swept his eyes over the group one last time as they rode the final hundred feet to the barn. Stablemen were waiting at the doors to help them off their horses.

"We'll see you later, Youk," called Dilly cheerfully, turning to lead the group to their quarters; her arms were loaded with bags of clothing, given as gifts from Commendus.

Youk waved and then walked inside the barn, accompanied by drats who helped care for the horses. A few moments later he came jogging out and caught up with them.

"Boot, how was your ride on Shooter?" he asked.

"It couldn't have been better," said Boot, turning to heartily rap Youk's bony shoulder. "Thanks for letting us borrow him. That's a great horse you've got. I think he's fully recovered. Therapy must have worked. He didn't falter in the slightest, even following Song up that crazy Coyote Trail."

"Good, that's good—I'm glad to hear it," Youk sighed. "And to think most people would have put him down after his injury. Miz was right."

Youk waved his hat in the air, nodded at Dilly and Sawny, and parted ways; he trotted back to the barn where he joined two stablemen that were waiting for him at the entrance.

In the Great Hall, Pone approached the group and fell in line, walking between Boot and Dod. His wavy black hair bounced slightly with each step he took.

"Good to see you bro," said Pone to Dod, nodding. His smile engulfed his whole face. He turned to Boot and changed his tone. "Just a quick word," he said carefully, looking to the right and left. "Weird stuff has been happening around here while you were off getting your feet massaged."

"I didn't have time for a foot-rub," replied Boot playfully. "We were doing important business our entire stay—hardly ate or slept."

Pone rolled his eyes in disbelief.

"Yeah, Gollium instructed us and gave us orders," added Buck earnestly. "We were all over High Gate, not just lounging around Commendus's palace. We have knives of gratitude to prove it!"

When Pone continued to wear a skeptical face, Buck furiously dug through his pockets. Eventually he produced his wonderful present and held it up; the ivory bear on his knife was dirty white from years of use, yet the gold surrounding it had been polished so many times by Buck that it glistened brightly.

"Boot's is nicer," he insisted excitedly. "Go ahead, Boot—show him."

"Aw, I don't want to make Pone jealous," said Boot, glancing quickly at Dod, then back to Pone. "Besides, I want to hear what he has to say. Tell us, what happened while we were out?"

"For starters, Raul Hall had some middle-of-the-night intruders," said Pone, raising his eyebrows and counting with his fingers. He only got to one before he used his hand to smack Boot on the chest. "They caused plenty of trouble—the kind that usually gets *you* in trouble."

Boot smiled proudly. Dilly and Sawny both looked humorously disgusted by Boot's pleasure at being touted as a rabble-rouser.

"As you can imagine," continued Pone happily, "Sawb brought the complaint straight to Bonboo, insisting you were the instigator. Fortunately, your trip to High Gate squashed his accusations flat."

"Intruders?" said Dilly curiously. "What did they do?"

"What startled skunks usually do," responded Pone smugly. "They fouled the place up bad enough that Raulings will be keeping their windows open for the next hundred years—it's nasty! You have to plug your nose when you walk past. And the smell's not staying in their rooms, either. Don't sit too close to them at dinner or you'll lose your appetite in a hurry."

Pone grinned roguishly at the girls as he added, "Just ask Donshi."

When everyone showed by their eyes that they were dying to hear the rest, he finished.

"—she lost the remains of her lunch on Tonnis last night before she'd even made it far enough in line to see dinner."

"How disgusting!" gasped Sawny, looking ill.

"I know," said Pone gleefully. "And Sawb's claiming their stuff was rifled through, too. Can you imagine it? The skunks must have been digging about their belongings for hours looking for food. I bet their clothes will reek for weeks."

"Hmm," said Dilly, throwing a side glance at Boot. She obviously suspected he had influenced the occasion, due to its spiteful effects on Sawb.

"Don't look at me," retorted Boot defensively. "I was with you the whole time—miles away from the striped assailants." He turned quickly from Dilly, before her eyes had time to work on him, and prodded Pone for more info. "Okay," he said eagerly. "What else happened?"

"A small fire in the little ribble-barn. It could have been a lot worse if Jibb hadn't found it so quickly. It might have taken the whole row of barns down to the stones. We would have lost a lot of our best riding horses."

"A fire, too?" complained Dilly, appearing as if she felt bad that she had missed the excitement.

"Yup, and that's not all!" said Pone with a buoyant glint in his eye. He once more paused to let the suspense build. "Sirlonk's gonna be as mad as a hideless cow with a sunburn when he gets back. His private office and visiting quarters were invaded by someone, and his *unbreakable* door was broken. Zerny and Youk have left men to secure it until he gets back. They say it appears as though nothing was taken."

"It serves him right!" interjected Buck. "After the way he taunted everyone two weeks ago—when he had his door taken out and reinstalled with Raul parts, claiming Bonboo didn't know a thing about security—it offended me enough to want to rip it off just to let him know that Raul's doors are no better than what we have here in Green."

"Anything else?" asked Boot.

"The rest is smaller stuff," confessed Pone smoothly. "A group of Raulings were soiled by mud balls while on a morning jog; and a note, signed 'Lovingly Zippod,' was mysteriously left for Sawb, informing him of his pending loss to us at Bollirse; and a loose-leg-mishap occurred at dinner last night, causing Joak's food to end up on his lap—and nearly Sawb's as well."

"Now that sounds like pre-game fun," admitted Boot pompously; and then catching Dilly's condemning eyes, he quickly added, "At least the last few items—"

As the group approached Green Hall, they quickly noticed the doors were shut. The smell in the air answered the question why: They were too close to Raul Hall to be left open.

"Dod, are you excited for the big game?" asked Pone, helping Boot push one of the large doors open.

"I guess," said Dod hesitantly. Hearing about the match made his stomach start to churn.

Boot studied Dod's face and noticed the concern. "We should practice today after dinner," he casually suggested. "—Go over the rules and basic techniques for all of the Greenlings that haven't played much. With full-out, triple team Bollirse, we can technically include all of the Lings at the same time, and I'm sure Sawb will insist every Rauling join their Coosings on the field, so we better make sure we get as many of our Greenlings as we can. Numbers are everything."

Once the door was closed, blocking the putrid air, Greenlings and Coosings seeped out of the bedrooms, greeting Boot and Buck with inquiries about the upcoming event. Dilly and Sawny disappeared into their separate quarters, where a few female voices welcomed them.

"I did it," whispered Toos, who approached Boot quietly from the rear.

"So I heard," responded Boot cautiously, glancing over his shoulder to make sure Dilly wasn't eavesdropping. He, Buck, and Dod invited Toos into their bedroom and then closed the door tightly, but only after Boot had yelled down the hall, "Meet at the Bollirse field after dinner for some warm ups and strategy talk—WE'RE TAKING RAUL DOWN!"

Before anyone had found a comfortable spot, Boot asked Toos for the truth: "You didn't have any part in the barn fire or Sirlonk's door, did you?"

"No, I don't know anything about them. I stuck to the basics—the non-harmful kind of stuff—mud balls at joggers, mysterious notes from fictional superheroes, an extra dose of salt at dinner, and other mild annoyances like that—certainly nothing destructive."

"Good," said Boot, sighing heavily. He looked relieved to hear that he hadn't accidentally influenced anything too malicious.

"I liked the skunk one," added Buck, chuckling as he lay on his bed. "How did you manage to sneak them in? With Zerny and Jibb roaming around at night, leading the Drat Patrol, you must have really worked hard."

"Well, I uh…it was tough," claimed Toos, smiling uncomfortably.

"Just for the record," Boot interjected, "the skunk prank was pushing the limit, but funny nonetheless. Next time you use stinkers, maybe you could have Sawb and his crowd fall prey to a spraying outside of the castle—let them enjoy the smell while minimizing the interior damage."

"No kidding," said Dod, sniffing his shirt. The strong smell in the hall had attached to his clothes.

Toos stared at the ground and finally confessed, "I didn't do the skunk prank. Someone beat me to it. If I had done it, I'd probably smell like a skunk right now. You all know I'm not exactly a mayler."

"Really?" said Boot as he lay down on his bed.

Toos and Buck carried on with small talk and eventually left the room for dinner. Dod and Boot, on the other hand, withdrew from the conversation to think and then traded notes with Dilly and Sawny on their way to supper.

"It doesn't make sense," said Dilly, looking puzzled. "Who would have started the fire, skunked Raul Hall, and broken down Sirlonk's door, all while drat guards roamed the halls on duty?"

She pulled at one of her curls while she thought. "It must be the works of The Dread," she concluded, "or at least one of his helpers. But what's he doing it for?"

"And why the two attacks against people from Raul?" added Boot. "The Dread seems to favor them while punishing Green and especially Soosh; even the death threat Bonboo received was specifically aimed at people from Soosh staying at Twistyard."

"Don't forget about the incident Sirlonk had on the way to High Gate," said Dod, grabbing Boot's shoulder. "It was more than a coincidence that he experienced a rough ride on the same day I did. Maybe The Dread has decided to play us against each other, affecting people from Raul as well. What better way to stir up conflict than to lead conceited nobles like Sirlonk and Juny to believe everyone's against them. You heard the way he spoke about Zerny and the other drats. He naturally assumes they're the ones that poorly situated his saddle; and though it may have been Zerny, it also could have been Youk, or anyone else. We really don't know. After all, Youk did help with saddling our horses, didn't he?"

"Well," blurted Dilly, shaking her head. She stopped in the hall and looked at Dod. "I'm sure Youk wouldn't have hurt his own mare. So if the same person set a trap of both horses, we can rule Youk out."

"She's right," said Sawny, agreeing with Dilly. "But for the love of Saluci, that mare is foremost in Youk's heart. I remember the time he wouldn't leave the barn for a week, even to eat, when his horse was ill; and despite Shooter's full recovery, he never rides him—he's always on that mare."

"And to think Youk trusted me with his favorite horse!" moaned Dod.

"No," interjected Dilly sorely. "He trusted me, handing both horses over in the barn—you just happened to ride the mare."

"Anyway," said Dod, groaning loudly. He hadn't meant to create a fuss. "I'm just saying, I think The Dread is striking around us, prodding people to get angry at each other, even if what he's doing doesn't make much sense. Maybe he's trying to frame people—get them in trouble with the soldiers and Commendus. I'm even beginning to wonder about Zerny and Jibb; they could be innocent after all—victims of The Dread's web."

"I've told you before," insisted Dilly. "I can vouch for them."

"You didn't seem so sure the morning we returned from the night ride," contended Dod. "Remember how you acted around Jibb….I would still feel better about them if I could see their bare hands. Besides, why does Zerny stutter at times and speak clearly at other times?"

"He doesn't," said Dilly, beginning to walk toward dinner. The others followed.

"He's had difficulty from birth. If you thought you heard him speak clearly, you must be mistaking Jibb for Zerny."

Before Dod could respond to Dilly's accusations, Sawny broke into the middle of the conversation with her own question.

"Have you had any more of those impressions, Dod?"

"Not since the one I had right before we left for High Gate—which reminds me, we should break into Sword Tower tonight. If The Dread is causing the problems we've had around here, he's eventually going to do what I've seen, and it's dark—people are gonna die! We need to stop him."

"Sword Tower tonight?" moaned Dilly.

"It's on your list," argued Boot. "And you've broken in before—why not tonight?"

"OOOOH!" Dilly complained. She glanced at Boot and then looked at the floor before explaining, "—Dod hasn't gotten his keys back yet."

"What does that have to do with Sword Tower?" asked Boot, raising an eyebrow.

"One of his keys is to the Safety Vault Building, next-door to Sword Tower, and another one is to a box inside...or at least I think so. With a key to the front of the Safety Vault Building, the guards stationed there will let us enter. And once we're in, I know of a fire escape tunnel that leads to Sword Tower's inner courtyard. Soldiers don't guard it. From there we can easily pry a garden window open...and just like that, we're free to roam Sword Tower."

"That's genius, Dilly!" exclaimed Sawny admiringly. She had known her older sister was clever enough to make it past the guards to acquire swords for her *necessary* collection—just in case the Coosings needed to take arms quickly, and they were hers by right of inheritance anyway—however, this was the first time Dilly had revealed her system.

"—then, how did you get a key before?" asked Boot.

"Pap...uh...lent it to me—he actually lent me both keys. One is for the front door and the other unlocks a special box, though I've never seen it. I don't even know which one of the thousands of boxes it is. I only wanted a back entrance to Sword Tower."

"Why didn't you tell me before?" gasped Dod. He thought of how miserable it was that he had lost the keys necessary for getting into a safety box, along with the key to Pap's house.

"I wasn't sure if they were the right keys," answered Dilly. "And with Boot around, I didn't want to be wrong. I figured we would try them out when we got a chance. We just need to go look for them, and if they're gone—well, let's hope they're not."

"That means we'll need to break into Youk's quarters and climb up the wall from his balcony," said Boot eagerly.

"Shhh," whispered Sawny, reminding the group that they were entering a busier area. The closer they got to the Great Hall, the more traffic buzzed around them, drat soldiers included.

"Maybe we could arrange a meeting with Youk," said Dod, not particularly wanting to chance getting caught. "If we all went together, a few of us could slip out onto his patio, while he's fetching something from another room, and then the rest of us could make excuses for why the others had to leave."

"That's a great idea," agreed Sawny. She, too, didn't like the thought of doing anything that could be misconstrued as an evil act against The Greats, especially after someone had already broken down Sirlonk's door, leaving them to be blamed if they were seen wiggling into Youk's private rooms uninvited.

"I'll line it up," said Dilly, stepping prominently into the lead position of the conversation. "It may not be for tonight, but I'll get him to see us as soon as he can to discuss his historic strategies. Once he starts talking about the past, it'll be easy for me and Sawny to distract his attention long enough to buy you boys plenty of time on his patio."

As the group entered the Great Hall, Dod shivered disconcertingly. Jibb was walking in the opposite direction, explaining to Zerny that he had personally searched Sirlonk's quarters without finding anything noteworthy; and that guards held the entrance, awaiting a new door.

Dod felt chilled for a number of reasons. He had just seen Zerny and Jibb, sporting their white-gloved hands, their swords, and their shiny golden badges.

After they passed, Dilly remarked that she felt safer seeing soldiers walking the halls with weapons; however, it made her terribly jealous.

"Safer?" hissed Dod. "Are you crazy? Didn't you hear what Jibb said? He's the one that broke down Sirlonk's door to search the quarters. There's no stopping them from their witch hunt."

"That's not what he said," argued Dilly. "He said he personally searched Sirlonk's quarters without finding anything of concern. I'm sure he was in charge of overseeing the break-in investigation, and as part of his job, he checked for any signs of rummaging. After all, he is one of the head security officers. Besides, he just said he put soldiers there to guard the door. If he bashed it down to have a look inside, do you really think he would stick around and call the soldiers up to notice his handiwork?"

Dilly made a good point, but it didn't change Dod's uneasy feeling about the circumstance.

During dinner, the hot topic at each table was the pending Bollirse game. Everyone was either a player or an interested fan; and notwithstanding the snobbery of Raul Coosings and Raulings toward everyone else, most people at Twistyard were expecting Raul Hall to rule the field. Regardless, Boot and Buck bragged up enough confidence to almost convince a few tables that Green Hall had a fighting chance.

At the same time, Sawb and his close buddies Joak and Kwit reveled in their past wins, boasting gleefully to their peers from Raul. They even managed to lead a sizable group in a chant against Boot. The presentation was choppy at best as each tormentor strained to read the gibberish penned by Kwit.

We don't know why
Boot thinks he's hot,
His style needs class,
He's a hopeless Pot,
And all he brags to us,
We know he's really not,
So a beggar can't be a chooser,
Go home like Bowy you loser!

One girl, a Raul Coosing, shamelessly trying to impress Sawb, stood on his table during the chant and made all sorts of flirtatious hand signs that were supposed to fit the words. Upon finishing, she smirked wickedly at Boot, pushing her long black hair out of her face, revealing her shiny red lips, and said, "When you get home, tell your nutty brother I can't write him anymore."

She hopped down coyly, readjusted her skirt, and walked up behind Sawb before adding, "Long distances are one thing, but when he can't even remember my name, it's too much."

The Raulings laughed and oooed, while twitting their fingers in Boot's direction.

He took offense, yet stayed in control. Had they only made fun of him, he probably would have laughed it off; however, joking about his younger brother's serious condition was despicable. It infuriated him. He had to speak up.

"Clever," said Boot coldly to the crowd from Raul Hall. "Though I must warn you all, if you keep listening to Sawb, you're likely to continue stinking…those poor little skunks, bumping into the likes of a real stench in the night—Sawb!

"Oh, and Eluxa, if you think Bowy ever noticed you, you're the one with a horrible memory!"

Boot turned away and walked slowly across the room and out into the courtyard. He partially hoped Sawb would follow him; but, he knew the best way to show him up would be at the Bollirse game.

Dilly went nuts, chattering with the other girls about how trashy Eluxa and her clique were. It made her blood boil. She insisted that Bowy would never have paid any degree of attention to the likes of Eluxa, or her pathetic friends from Raul, and that the only truth was her heartless reference to poor Bowy's injury, which only proved all the more how classless and tasteless she was. It irritated Dilly so bad that when Pone teasingly noted how 'smoking-hot' she was, Dilly dumped her entire cup of milk down the front of his shirt.

"You should have expected that, bro," said Dod, smiling at Pone, watching him attempt to wring the milk out. "You just don't go there and expect to come back alive. Cat fights are wicked."

Dod hopped out of his seat and went to fetch another cup for Dilly.

After the commotion died down, Greenlings and Green Coosings finished their dinners and headed for the field. Dilly and Sawny kept Dod company as he nibbled. He wasn't looking forward to practicing Bollirse. To him, it was like knowing he had to perform in a piano recital without having a song to play.

Before they finally left to meet with the others, Tonnis walked passed Dilly and then tripped, clumsily dropping his tray on the floor by Dilly's feet.

"Tell Boot I'm sorry about the way they acted," whispered Tonnis nervously. "They're stupid idiots today. We all understand about Bowy."

Tonnis quickly picked up his tray and walked away, playing the part of an awkward-footed fool.

"There goes one person from Raul I can actually tolerate," said Dilly.

"He's from Raul?" gasped Dod in surprise, not recognizing him.

"Yes, he's one of the newest Raul Coosings. It's amazing how someone like that can survive living with the rest of *them*." She looked over at the other members of Raul Hall, who were still lingering at their tables. They were boisterously laughing in unison at Sawb's jokes, like the bleating of a herd of sheep, despite the fact that most of the things he said weren't very witty.

The Bollirse field was located on the outer edge of the complex, beyond the grassy courtyard, on the other side of the half-circle wall of trees and buildings. It was similar in shape to a rectangular football field, only twice as large and completely surrounded by a twenty-five-foot retaining wall, for the entire court was below ground. Entrance to the field was down one of two rope ladders, positioned at the ends. Outside the retaining wall, a stadium-like hill of grass rose up two hundred feet, with no trees, enclosing the playing field in the middle—perfect seating for spectators.

On the field there were sixty posts that resembled mini telephone poles, thirty per side, each thirteen feet tall. They were placed symmetrically, with a dense concentration of them at the two opposite ends of the court and a scattering of them in the open space between. Their purpose was to hold leather bots—hollow eighteen-inch cones with team rags protruding out of the tops. A three-foot stone wall split the playing field down the middle, and in the very center of the wall was a thirty-foot post, situated to hold the final bot.

Seeing the setup unlocked memories of the game in Dod's mind. Bollirse was a combination of dodge ball, capture the flag, mock war, and baseball. Traditionally, there were eighteen players per team—though full-out, triple team Bollirse was a Twistyard invention, allowing the Coosings and their respective Lings to play together on the same team, up to fifteen Coosings and fifty Lings, if everyone participated.

Players were allotted a shield, swot, jung, head-guard, and also eight globes. The shield was light weight and perfectly circular, about two feet in diameter. The swot resembled a mixture of a bat and a paddle. The jung was a leather bag, used to carry up to twelve globes—it attached to the waist and one leg with leather straps, bracing it tightly against the body. The head-guard was a thick-hide helmet, with metal wires crossing in front of the eyes, nose, and mouth, barely close enough to shield against a globe, and with woven padding on the inside that trailed below the helmet, draping down far enough to completely cover the neck. The globes were slightly smaller than baseballs, made of leather, wrapped and sewn around dried hous fruits after being dipped in a sticky bean-glue mixture.

Regulation play called for one head judge to stand toward the middle, outside of the field, up on top of the retaining wall. It was his job to start the match, oversee fair play, make final decisions, and ultimately declare a winner. To aid the judge, four referees roamed the field, keeping a close watch on players.

The object of Bollirse was very simple—knock all thirty of

the opposing team's bots down and then close by dislodging the neutral, winning bot, or eliminate all of the other team's players.

Dod, Dilly, and Sawny made their way down a rope ladder, entering the field just in time to catch Boot's explanation of the game.

"Remember the rules. Judges are quick to enforce them, and you can bet tomorrow will be no exception. Stay clear of the players from the other team. If you touch them, or even if you only bump them with your shield or swot, you're both out. Keep that in mind—no contact!"

"But what if it's an accident?" asked a younger Greenling named Kurt, who was seated on the grass close to the front of the mob. He looked twelve and terrified. His spiky brown hair drooped with concern while he clicked his fingernails.

"Doesn't matter, a touch is a touch. And if you do make contact, even if it's an accident, speak up quickly and exit the field before we're penalized another player for breaking the rules."

"And that goes for a globe hit, too," added Buck, who was standing next to Boot, beaming with a look of sheer excitement. "If you're hit, fess up quickly and exit the field, up our ladder. That's how you can help our team the best at that point. Trying to fudge isn't honorable, and they'll catch you for sure—the globe will leave a welt for a short while—and then it's a mandatory one man penalty when they call you off the field as a cheat. You can bet that whomever we choose to exit with you will be flastered for weeks, as will the whole team if we lose on your account."

"Do the globes hurt?" asked Donshi, fidgeting nervously with her light-brown curls. She was sitting next to Kurt. Together they formed a mini-coalition of newbies.

"How many of you haven't played before?" bellowed Boot,

making sure everyone could hear him. His eyes panned the group.

Six hands shot up, all sitting at the front with Donshi. They were the youngest Greenlings in the bunch, so it was no surprise that they hadn't played.

Dod almost raised his hand, too; however, he felt self-conscious wedged between Dilly and Sawny, two expert players. Besides, he rationalized, he did have memories of the game—they flooded his mind when he saw the field—and they were so vivid that he almost felt like a seasoned player. Where a knot had filled his gut during dinner, a bit of excitement was building. Something inside him wanted to play, and the new-found memories gave him grounds to hope he would perform acceptably.

"Would you do better without us?" asked Donshi.

"No, no—of course not. We're a team, and that's the way it's gonna be," said Boot convincingly. "Everyone is important. This game is all about sticking together. If you're good at throwing, focus on getting within range of a couple of bots before the other team gets you—and don't worry about being hit by a globe. It may sting for a few minutes if the globe is fresh off a swot, but that fades faster than the sting of defeat."

Kurt and Donshi didn't appear convinced: Pain did sound worse to them then losing; however, disappointing Boot and Buck was clearly worse than that, so they continued to listen.

Boot reviewed the rules, emphasizing key things to remember, and then grilled the newcomers on their retention. Dod listened intently and took confidence from hearing Boot explain what he already knew from memory.

The globes were considered 'live' when launched from an

opponent and continued to be live until they hit the ground. If a live globe made contact with a player anywhere on his body, including his helmet, the player would be out of the game and would need to leave immediately, and couldn't, by regulation, have further influence on the game—including vocally giving advice or commands to other teammates.

If a globe was launched from one player to another player on the same team, it would not be considered live, as one team member handing off a globe to another team member. If a live globe was deflected by a shield or swot, it instantly became live against the opposite team and no longer live for the deflecting team, as in the case when a live globe is hit with a swot back to its originator, or its originator's teammate.

Players started the game with eight globes in their jung, and could attain additional globes from the bases of the posts, where piles of ten lay at the beginning of the game. All of the globes were fair ammunition for both sides. Globes could be thrown, kicked, or hit toward opposing people in an attempt to reduce their forces. The same globes were to be used in knocking the opposing team's bots down.

In order to win, a team needed to knock down all thirty opposing bots, plus the winning bot, or eliminate all of the players on the challenging team.

In the event of an injury, a 'freeze' could be called, though the injured person would be escorted off the field by referees—even if the injury proved to be minor—while the other players remained stationary, ready to resume play as soon as the judge declared continue.

Buck repeatedly interrupted Boot, adding strategic elements to the game. "Let's assign some defenders to stay in the back on home ground and send attackers in groups to knock down opposing bots—keep less skilled players protected, so we can use them to gather globes for the seasoned players—position us on opposite sides to split the enemy's forces and to provide leadership."

As Buck and Boot planned for the following day's game, Dilly leaned over and whispered her discontent to Dod and Sawny.

"Here it comes, Boot's going to assign us to back defense and then blame us, as the final defenders, if Sawb finishes us off tomorrow."

"I thought you and Sawny were going to be rooting through Raul Hall unnoticed," responded Dod. "Wasn't that the original purpose of this match?"

"It was," said Dilly, rolling her eyes, "but did you scc how many drats are stinking up their clothes, sitting guard at the entrance to Raul Hall? It's pointless. Besides, if their quarters were targeted by The Dread with skunks, it doesn't seem likely that they are connected in a friendly relationship."

"Dilly and Sawny," shouted Boot, "we'll be depending on the two of you to cover back defense tomorrow. You'll be joining us, won't you?"

"Yes," said Sawny with a smile, starting to laugh at how predictable Boot was.

"And Dod," he continued. "What position do you usually play? Take your pick and make it stick!"

Boot spoke with the tone of a general, organizing real forces for a pending battle. It was amusing to see how serious Boot and Buck took the game. After all, it was only a game.

"I—uh—I," stuttered Dod, "—I like to see where I'm needed the most and then fill in—make sure we win."

"Well said," praised Buck, smiling uncontrollably, fueled by his contagious enthusiasm. "SEE," Buck shouted to the group, "WITH DOD ON OUR SIDE, WE'LL BREAK THEIR PRIDE...WITH DOD ON OUR SIDE, WE'LL BREAK THEIR PRIDE...WITH DOD ON OUR SIDE, WE'LL BREAK THEIR PRIDE—"

By the third time Buck chanted the rhyme, all of the others chanted with him. It was a battle cry of sorts. Dod felt slightly discomforted, for he would rather have gone unnoticed on the field unless he proved worthy of the attention.

Game day came quickly. With the afternoon return of Strat, an early evening time was set. Crowds of people took their seats surrounding the pit, eager to watch the Halls battle it out. Many of the spectators even brought their dinners with them, fearing that they wouldn't get a good spot if they first ate in the Great Hall.

With both teams suited up, tradition had them nod heads in line, face to face, before climbing down their respective ladders; it was a show and promise of fair play during the game.

As Dod crossed paths with Sawb, a foot reached out and helped Dod to the ground; and unfortunately, on his way, he knocked Dilly and Sawny over with him. They landed in a heap, awkwardly encroaching into Raul Hall's line.

Eluxa pulled her shoe out from under Sawny's chin and casually wiped it across Sawny's sprawling hair, all the while giggling obnoxiously with two beanpole-thin girls in front of her. They fully enjoyed the predicament.

"I see you're still having trouble walking," mocked Sawb, pointing a condemning finger at Dod's legs.

"For your sake, I hope you can run, *boy*," responded Dod in his manliest voice. He hadn't had time to think, so the line flowed from a movie he had watched many times with his brothers.

Sawb chuckled and walked on, completely unaffected by Dod's warning.

Despite the traditional nod, most of the Raulings and Raul Coosings suggested by the look in their eyes and their general demeanor that the nod was a formality and it meant very little with regard to integrity of play.

On the field, spirits were high. The smell of damp grass floated around the shady battlefield, carried on an evening breeze. Everyone waited anxiously for the purple cloth to indicate the start of the game, and no sooner had it waved than a barrage of globes filled the air. Within a minute, six Greenlings and two Green Coosings had been struck and were on their way up the ladder. Donshi stopped every few rungs to rub her shoulder, making it clear she had felt the blow that sent her out, and Kurt followed close on her heels, looking relieved to be done.

Boot led a right flank attack with ten mates, waving his swat in the air as he prodded them to charge. Together, they breached the center wall like a band of angry chimpanzees. It was less thought-out and more adrenaline, pushing hard to claim vengeance for their quick losses; however, in their ambition to be the first group to cross into enemy territory, they clumsily ventured too deep, lost three players from side-snipers, and were forced to retreat.

Meanwhile, Buck played a safer game. He kept a steady stream of globes flowing from his troops, who had some success. They knocked down seven Raul bots and sent five Raulings packing.

Dilly paced in the backfield. She was agitated that she

wasn't storming the front, especially after the way Eluxa had just treated her sister.

Sawny, on the other hand, was content to watch, leaning against a post.

"We'll get our chance, Dilly," she said patiently. "We need to save these globes and our energy—you know what's coming."

Dod climbed halfway up the pole Sawny was leaning against and, using a protruding knot hole, perched himself in a position to call the plays of the field for Dilly and the others on back patrol. They were all getting ready to attack or defend, depending on orders from Boot.

"It looks like Sawb is holding the middle with twelve, and Joak has our left, a third of the way back, with about fifteen. Kwit is on our right, farther back than Joak; he seems to be doing something. He's got a lot of people. Now they're moving forward…now backward. It's like he can't make up his mind—oh, I see, he misunderstood orders from Sawb."

"How is Buck doing?" asked Sawny.

"He's still knocking globes forward, but his pace has slowed down. They must be getting low. They need to restock."

"Maybe a few of us can move up and help Boot and Buck," suggested Dilly, gripping her swot white-knuckled with anticipation.

"Hold on," said Sawny, chuckling at her sister's exuberance. "Let's wait for the signal. Unless Boot's down, he's our leader; then Buck, then you."

"Aaah," groaned Dilly, wild-eyed with frustration. "By the time I get to lead the game, we're always hopelessly behind."

Dilly's lament gave Dod an idea. He hopped down from the pole and smiled at Dilly and Sawny.

"Tell me, who leads Raul when Sawb goes out?"

Both girls looked at each other and thought for a few moments. Their answers were almost in unison.

"I don't know? I don't remember ever seeing Sawb go out," said Sawny matter-of-factly.

"When we attack with a group, he always retreats and hides," added Dilly, smirking. "He's a coward."

"Yes," said Dod, his enthusiasm mounting, "but he's the coward that's leading their every move! Who knows what the game will be like when he's gone?"

Without saying anything more, Dod ran for the front line. His heart was pounding rapidly. He hadn't been very good at baseball, yet it wasn't because he couldn't run. When he neared the stone wall, he stopped for a minute behind a pole to take off his jung; it was slowing him down. He threw his jung, filled with globes, toward Buck and yelled, "Launch them in Sawb's direction. I'm going in."

The stone wall was easy to hop, though once on the other side, Dod realized how determined Raul was to defend their soil; every Rauling and Raul Coosing within throwing or hitting range of Dod proceeded to volley their globes at him. It was a hailstorm! Thoughts of retreat crept into his mind; nevertheless, a stronger image came bursting to the forefront and, like the rising of the sun in the morning, it melted away the dimly lit stars of doubt: He could see Strat, standing alone by the fire, batting and blocking arrows—and with a rush of confidence, Dod knew he could do it too!

When the globes came showering down, rather than running from them, Dod stood in the open and received them. All of the attackers were far enough away that any given globe could be detected and deflected by focusing on the nearest one first, and then the next, and then the next, and then the one after that. Every moment was intense—to the right—now left—an upward block with shield—a downward block with swot—center block—quick step to the side—lower leg block—step, hop left—quick high block left, low center block—step, hop, step.

During the course of four minutes, which felt to Dod like an eternity, over a hundred and fifty globes were hurled without any of them hitting him. It was unprecedented. The pile of globes at Dod's feet littered the ground. Cheers roared from behind him. Boot's voice distinctly chanted, "Dod, Dod, Dod," until the crowd in the stands began to follow suit, "DOD, DOD, DOD!"

Sawb shook his hands and pointed toward Dod in frustration and anger, while Kwit and Joak appeared to be leading their forces in slowing down the number of globes they were using as their supply began to run low.

Three more minutes passed and another eighty globes were added to the heaps on the ground at Dod's feet, the majority of which came from Sawb and his pals in the middle. None of them had connected. The crowd, who had become so involved that most of them had risen to their feet, continued to chant on and off, "DOD, DOD, DOD," as well as clever variations, such as, "SAWB CAN'T HIT, DOD WON'T QUIT," and, "BLOCK DOD BLOCK, SAWB'S JUST TALK."

Finally, the moment came: Sawb lost his temper and actually pushed one of his own teammates to the ground, apparently for holding back a spare globe. Within a few seconds, the middle field forces were completely out of ammunition. They began to scamper backward, retreating in search of more globes to hurl.

That was Dod's cue—the race was on! After raising his swot high in the air and yelling 'attack,' Dod ran straight for Sawb.

In the commotion, and while turning around to give orders to his troops who were retreating, Sawb didn't notice Dod's approach until he was within twenty feet; and when he did, he looked like a scared schoolboy running from the class bully, despite the obvious reality that Sawb was much bigger than Dod. It was a moment Dod would cherish for a long time; and from the sounds of the crowd, Dod wasn't the only one who was enjoying Sawb's distress.

To increase speed and prepare for his attack, Dod dropped his shield and swot, and in the true spirit of an American Boy, he gave Sawb a lesson in another sport: Football! The tackle was perfect!

Clumps of grass and dirt hung from Sawb's mangled faceguard as Dod helped him to his feet.

"I thought I told you to run, *boy*!" said Dod, grinning with his whole face. "Apparently my legs work just fine."

Sawb limped as he took a step.

"You've lost your freshy-mind, fool!" he growled bitterly; his eyes narrowed to slits in anger as he straitened up, rubbing his back. "Now we're both out of the game!"

"I know!" said Dod proudly. "It's all going as planned."

Boot and Buck quickly followed behind Dod, securing the piles of globes. They proceeded to massacre the leaderless troops of Raulings and Raul Coosings with ease, and Dilly even got her chance to peg Eluxa, right in the posterior, as she fled. It was a wonderful sight for Dod to view while climbing the rope ladder—not in defeat, but in strategic victory!

ALL ALONE

Everyone at Twistyard congratulated Green Hall for their unusual victory over Raul Hall—that is, everyone except Sawb and his team of losers. It was the only thing people were talking about for days. Dod did his best to share the glory with all of his teammates; after all, he hadn't even thrown a single globe. But overwhelmingly, fans saw Dod's deflection moves and strategic tackle as sheer genius.

The next week was relatively uneventful. Dilly did her best to line up an engagement with Youk, though the meeting kept getting bumped by urgent business relating to preparations for Bonboo's next trip. Tridacello had returned to Twistyard and was insisting Bonboo accompany him on a brief journey to Soosh.

Sawny spent a lot of her time in the library, consulting with Ascertainy and reading books. Specifically, she studied a myriad of things about The Dread and did some research on plants Dr. Shelderhig had mentioned.

Boot and Buck were so energized by their Bollirse victory that they hardly found time to talk about anything else; and in their wave of interest in the game, the brothers spent their days off at the field, holding practice matches and training. Kindly, however, they didn't insist everyone show similar attention to the sport.

Dilly and Dod spent their time differently. They puttered around, casually continuing to investigate things on Dilly's big list. During their lull time one afternoon, Dilly suggested they practice swordplay, since Sirlonk's injury and vacation had completely ended her opportunity for staying sharp. Boot's room was the perfect spot for exercising because there was plenty of space and privacy, given most of Green Hall was ensnared in the Bollirse binge led by Boot and Buck.

The offer was enticing to Dod. He really did want to learn, yet the thought of swishing swords with Dilly was concerning. He had hardly held a sword, let alone become anywhere near proficient enough to duel.

"How about I watch you practice," responded Dod, doing his best to hide his ambivalence.

"Watch?" said Dilly in surprise. She furrowed her brows for a few moments, until her face melted into a look of recognition. "Oh, I see," she said confidently. "You don't want to swing Pap's sword around. I guess I didn't make myself clear enough. You don't need to worry, I have spar swords in my collection—you know, they're dull and they retract into the hilt when you strike. There's no chance of you accidentally hurting me. They're quite nifty creations. Bly is definitely on my list of favorite inventors."

"And I assume you think I'm pretty good with a sword," stammered Dod sheepishly.

"Obviously," said Dilly. "You've battled for real! But I must warn you, I've practiced a lot. I've even originated a few moves of my own—not for competition—for last resort against a rogue like The Dread. Who knows, maybe I could teach you a thing or two."

"I'm sure you could teach me more than you think," divulged Dod, groaning dejectedly. "It's embarrassing..."

Dilly studied Dod's face and could tell he was uncomfortable; he was hiding something he didn't care to discuss. Her eyes showed concern as she treaded carefully.

"Are you still recovering from your accident?" she asked.

"Sort of," said Dod, stealing a glance at her before looking away. "Since the event—" He paused for a moment and then decided there was no need to clarify everything about his unusual circumstance. "—well, anyway, after the accident and everything, some things are clear and other things fade in and out. It's hard to explain. I'm not always able to competently do what people say I've done in the past."

"Oh," said Dilly, looking sympathetic. "You've got some memory loss."

"I guess," admitted Dod hesitantly.

"Don't be ashamed," snapped Dilly. "It's not your fault."

Dod felt guilty in describing his circumstance as partial amnesia, but that seemed more believable than suggesting he was from an entirely different realm—not to mention, Dod still didn't understand where the memories came from and why he knew so much about some things and so little about others. In truth, it did feel like he was gradually regaining his memory, one flash at a time.

"You heard what happened to Bowy, didn't you?"

"Only bits and pieces," responded Dod.

"He had a hard time remembering things, too, after his accident. He was seriously injured during a sword fight while accompanying Pap. Something happened and Bowy ended up underneath a pile of logs. He spent some time in the hospital, unconscious, and when he returned to Twistyard, his broken arm recovered faster than his memory."

"Oh," sighed Dod.

"If everyone would have been a little bit nicer to him, I'm sure he'd have stayed. Some things just take time. If you can't remember how to do something, pretend you haven't done it before; and then, with practice, you'll likely find it will come back to you."

"Do you think so?" asked Dod.

"I'm sure of it!" said Dilly, smiling. "Just look at how well you've fooled us so far. I wouldn't have guessed you had any memory loss if it weren't for a few strange comments—you know, like when we entered High Gate; you acted as though you were seeing it fresh."

"You're right," admitted Dod. "When I saw High Gate, it was like I was seeing it for the first time. It took a few minutes for the memories to follow."

Dilly swung a large bag off her shoulder and clanked it on the bedroom floor. She bent down and began to pick up the loose shirts and socks that Boot had left around his room and heaped them on Boot's bed. "Let me guess," she said. "You're nervous about dueling."

"Terrified!" confessed Dod. "Would you teach me?"

"Sure, I'll give you a refresher course; but you have to promise that you'll keep practicing with me later, even when it all comes back to you."

Dod nodded his head and agreed to the terms. The situation was perfect. It had been bothering him that despite bursts of inspiration, he lacked real battle skills, like swordplay, which would eventually matter when facing The Dread, or a venoos, or any other enemy.

With the deal struck, lessons began, and they continued every day thereafter; unfortunately, advanced swashbuckling wasn't exactly a skill that could be acquired overnight.

Dilly quickly assessed that Dod truly didn't 'remember' how to fence, so she taught him a reassuring move she had invented herself; it was called *disaster*. In the event that Dod needed to fight for his life, disaster was ideal. It was a clever trick where one fakes a backward stumble while lunging forward with a sword. When done properly, it deceived the eyes just enough to catch an enemy off guard.

Dilly calmed Dod's feelings of inadequacy by insisting that if he only mastered disaster, it alone could save his life in the event of an attack, so he didn't need to worry about how slowly he was remembering swordplay.

After a week, when Sirlonk and Juny finally returned, Dod was one of the first people to welcome them back. He had promised Boot that he would join the others in a practice game of Bollirse that afternoon, as soon as he finished his Hatu lesson from Tinja (similar to Karate). Dilly had specially arranged for Tinja to help Dod regularly in an attempt to 'bring it back,' which Dod didn't refuse. On his way to the field, Dod approached Sirlonk and Juny who were dismounting in the barn.

"How was your trip?" hollered Dod happily. He was feeling pretty good and enjoying the perfect weather.

Sirlonk looked over and raised one eyebrow, just enough to acknowledge that he had heard Dod's welcome, but went right on busily doing something. As Dod entered the barn, planning on cutting straight through to the Bollirse field, he realized

Sirlonk was verbally lashing someone who was standing on the other side of his horse.

"I should have known something like this would happen," chided Sirlonk. "You're incompetent! That's the problem, you're all incompetent!"

As Dod passed, he didn't stop or get involved, and he even avoided looking at them, due to the embarrassing nature of the conversation; however, he was curious to find out who Sirlonk was scolding.

"We did everything in our power to keep things safe, I assure you—" said a voice that clearly revealed the mystery man behind the horse to be Jibb. He was cut short when Sirlonk continued chastising him.

"There's no excuse. None! And I don't doubt you've had your grubby hands all over my things, taking advantage of your troops' careless efforts to secure Twistyard with any basic standard of safety. It's really amazing I'm foolish enough to keep returning here. We're crazy! Aren't we, Juny? Crazy!"

"I can assure you," said Jibb in a controlled, polite voice, "nobody has stepped foot in your quarters since my guards discovered the door had been breached, for we all know how dearly you cherish your privacy; but now that you're back, under your watchful eye, we would be happy to do a thorough walk-through investigation, if it would please you."

"You, investigate? That's preposterous! Why that's the most absurd thing I've heard all week; and after Juny's aunt offered me advice on swordplay, I thought I had heard it all."

"Please accept my personal apology for our momentary lapse in security and know that we are currently working on apprehending whoever is ultimately responsible for this crime.

When you have assessed the damage or loss, please inform us. I'm sure it will help our investigation."

"I'll make it known, you can count on that! Though it won't be to the likes of you, *drat*! I'm going straight to Bonboo. This incident proves what I've been saying for years now—he's out of touch and too old to see what's going on around him."

Dod continued on his way to the field, so eventually Sirlonk's angry voice faded into the distance, yet overhearing the dispute raised a question: Was Jibb lying? And if not now, what about before in the hall?

Regardless, the blurred truth didn't stop Dod's impression of Jibb from improving, based on the situation. He was surprised to see how dignified Jibb acted in handling such a precarious conversation, which would have sent a lesser leader hiding from Sirlonk in anticipation of the confrontation rather than awaiting his return in the barn.

After Bollirse practice, Dilly announced at dinner that Youk was tentatively planning on a casual chat that evening in his quarters. She beamed with satisfaction, having persisted long enough to accomplish her goal.

Sawny gave her a skeptical look.

"You really think he'll make time for us tonight?" she asked.

"He said he would, and I actually believe him," replied Dilly with confidence. "Bonboo just left with Tridacello, Zerny, and Jibb a few minutes ago, so whatever preparations Youk's been up to for Bonboo must be done."

"Is Bonboo going to High Gate tonight?" questioned Dod; he wondered how Bonboo would get past the triblot field.

"No. He's first visiting some friends that live in High Gate's border town," said Dilly. "He'll go on to Soosh tomorrow."

The conversation turned to discreetly planning the evening's efforts to recover Pap's keys, when it was suddenly shut down by the unexpected approach of Sirlonk and Juny. Both of them looked aggravated.

"Dilly!" thundered Sirlonk. "Where's your great-grandfather convalescing? Surely he's hiding in some corner of this palace, trying feebly to gain strength enough to address the regular downpour of incompetence. I have urgent business with him. Where shall I find him?"

The tips of Dilly's ears and the high of her cheeks began to tinge red-hot. Nobody spoke ill of Bonboo without facing her wrath, not even hostile aristocrats.

"You've just missed him," said Buck, jumping to his feet. "Come this way—and hurry! We might catch him if we run."

Buck led the miserable twosome from the Great Hall, while explaining that Bonboo was on his way out of town to do important business. Dod, Boot, and Sawny all watched Buck disappear into the front field, but Dilly was busy looking down at the floor and counting to a hundred million in an attempt to control her venomous outbursts.

Within a few minutes, Buck came jogging back. He looked very pleased with himself.

"I sent them down to the lake shore—said that Zerny was going with him; and since Bonboo wasn't in the barn, he might have gone to Zerny's before departing. I think the walk will do them some good."

"They'll need to walk farther than the shore to do me any good," snapped Dilly. She was still mad, yet appeared grateful Buck had helped her avoid getting sour with them.

"Oh, and I asked Sirlonk about his visit with Doochi,"

added Buck. "He said the boy is in poor health and didn't want to make an issue with everyone here, so he simply slipped out at night. Sirlonk also said that if we're lucky, and the boy fully recovers, he might be coming back in a year or two."

"That doesn't sound like Sirlonk," jabbed Boot with a smirk. "Are you sure we're talking about the same Sirlonk? After someone from Raul has fallen, I can't imagine that they would ever be received back."

Sawny noticed the time and prodded everyone to get moving. She wanted them to be punctual for their meeting with Youk and knew that the flights of stairs would be brutal. Dod, Boot, and Buck ran back to their room for gear and then met up with Sawny and Dilly in the resting hall by Youk's quarters. They were all out of breath, but just in time; within seconds of arriving, Youk came floating around the corner with his big feathered hat waving as he chuckled to himself.

"You're here," he said. "A ha, ha, ha…I'm sorry…A ha, ha, ha. I was just remembering something terribly funny; unfortunately, I think it is only funny to me. Come on in. Don't let the crazy man scare you."

There was something noticeably strange about Youk. He was erratically cheery, enough that it felt fake to Dod and the others. There was also something hidden behind his eyes. Regardless, the group entered his quarters and began small talk, acting as if everything was perfectly normal.

"I like what you've done to your front hall," fibbed Dilly, noticing Youk had taken down his wall of paintings and replaced them with bizarre antiques. "Are those tools or weapons?"

"Some of both, my dear—some of both," said Youk pleasantly. He stepped closer to the collection and smiled. "There's no telling what these relics were used for. The bloodstains seem to indicate a violent purpose, though, don't they?"

Dod felt a chill as Youk turned his way, his smile shifting to more of a grimace. "I like them," Youk continued. "My favorite is this one." He pointed at an old wooden rod with six rusted blades protruding out of the top. It was hanging at about eye level, surrounded by other objects of curious origins.

"I don't have any swords around," Youk confessed frankly. "You know, Bonboo's current policy—"

He then plucked his favorite weapon from the wall and pointed it directly at Dod, adding sternly, "—so I decided to freshen up my entry with useful art. Intruders may find my interest in historic particulars, especially the use of this zarrick, dangerously cold."

"Classy," blurted Buck, watching Youk flash the zarrick around in the air before putting it back.

Buck and Sawny sighed with relief, grateful they had decided to enter as invited guests; Dilly drooled jealously at Youk's battle skills; Boot gazed toward the patio door, obviously plotting his next step, hardly aware of the show; and Dod cringed with concern, not terribly happy to have had the demonstration aimed at him and wondering whether Youk was still sore about the Brown Sugar incident.

"Please, come in and take a seat," insisted Youk, gesturing with his arm toward an elegantly decorated greeting room. "Your company as friends is welcomed in this lonely place."

"With Saluci around, it couldn't possibly be lonely," said Dilly, bubbling with charm. "She loves entertaining, doesn't she?"

"Well—" said Youk, drawling despondently; his cheerfulness

dimmed as he looked around the room, inspecting the emptiness of his quarters. He walked over and plopped himself down brutishly into a feather-stuffed chair, uncharacteristic of his usual, refined ways, and then continued on with the conversation.

"Lately," he admitted slowly, "she's been too busy to come here…and the kids are helping her. She's gone up the coast for a while—charity work."

"Oh," said Dilly, feeling sorry for Youk, "Now that you mention it, I haven't seen her for a couple of weeks. What city are they staying in, Terraboom?"

Dilly casually sat down in a reed chair that had an obnoxiously straight back. The piece of furniture looked great for being in a museum, with its golden tassels, embroidered, purple-velvet backing, and delicately carved trim, but it didn't look comfortable like Youk's.

"I can't say," replied Youk calmly. "You know how it is with her, even if she told me where she was going, I wouldn't feel confident that she would stay there for long. Something always comes up and she's off like the startled tips of a roseweed."

After that, the room went quiet for a few horrible minutes. Sawny took the matching seat next to Dilly, while Dod, Boot, and Buck situated themselves on the floor at the girls' feet, not wanting to take either of the remaining chairs that were on the opposite side of the room, snuggled tightly against Youk's.

Mentioning Saluci had turned the atmosphere from that of a carnival spectacle, with Youk proudly at the head of ceremonies, into a deserted ghost town, lacking so much as a warm body to stir the dust. Sawny's squeaky chair was the only audible sound once the boys were situated; it made Sawny blush until she elbowed Dilly in the ribs.

"That reminds me," said Dilly, attempting to revive the deceased conversation, "I met Saluci's uncle Neadrou the other day. Sirlonk was introducing me to a few visiting dignitaries, and he was one of them. He's quite ambitious, isn't he?"

"Yes, Neadrou. Ah, ha, ha, ha. Neadrou's a one-of-a-kind chump."

Mentioning Neadrou perked Youk back up and sent him rolling forward, like he was unfolding a classroom discourse, without needing any further interjections. Neadrou had fought in various battles over the years, and Youk, as a master of strategy, knew the particulars of every one—not to mention, he had planned more than half of them.

The evening flew by with plenty of laughing and joking, never dipping back into the bucket of melancholy they had seen Youk momentarily wallow in. But despite repeated attempts to persuade Youk to do otherwise, he cautiously refused to leave his post at the side of his guests. At one point, Dilly made a comment that seemed to indicate she was hungry, hoping Youk would be a proper host and head to his kitchen for a snack; however, he happened to have a full bag of strups—similar to dried apples—and a box of chouyummy in his parlor cabinet, so while continuing another war story, he produced a perfect refreshment.

Dod sat on the floor between Boot and Buck, fidgeting occasionally to stop the tingling in his behind. One hour of stories was nice; nevertheless, by the time the sun had set, some three later, it was uncomfortable to sit any longer.

"It sounds like you've seen it all," said Dod, interrupting Youk in the middle of another delightful tale. Dod rose to his feet and rocked back and forth, endeavoring to get the blood flowing enough to stop the throbbing.

"I think part of me has already fallen asleep—" said Dod, and then noticing Youk's face, quickly sputtered, "—not because of your stories, they're wonderful. I just have—ah—a problem with my legs."

Dilly could see that something had to be done, if they hoped to accomplish their mission, so she faked a coughing attack and asked for a drink; unfortunately, like her other attempts, it didn't work. Rather than head out of the room, Youk offered a logical solution, making it difficult to persuade him otherwise without appearing suspicious.

"I'm afraid to say I don't have anything special," said Youk apologetically. "With Saluci gone, it's pointless to stock up when I can eat downstairs; three meals are plenty. Perhaps we could go to the Grand Kitchen together and find some juice. I'm sure Mercy wouldn't mind. Shall we go?"

"That sound's great," interjected Sawny, who jumped to her feet.

Dilly gave Sawny a *"What-are-you-doing?"* look the moment Youk turned his head to walk toward the door, but Sawny responded with her own *"Please-trust-me!"* look.

"Oh, Youk," said Sawny inquisitively, raising her eyebrows. "Is this the leaf of a Burris Calpos plant?" She bent down and picked up a dried, brown leaf from off the floor in the corner of the room. "I just got done reading a book written by Dr. Shelderhig, where he claims they don't do very well as house plants in Green. Do you happen to have one?"

"Yes, as a matter of fact, I do," said Youk, straightening his back. "And it's thriving very nicely, thank you."

"May I see it before we go?" asked Sawny, blinking her eyes innocently and pouring on a heavy dose of charm. "It would be wonderful to have something to dispute with Dr. Shelderhig next time I visit High Gate."

"I suppose you can have a quick look," said Youk hesitantly. Concern crossed his face, but he still led Sawny into the rear of his apartment.

The moment he disappeared, Boot, Buck, and Dod hurried out the back door onto his patio, while Dilly moved to the front door and opened it up, making a clanking and stomping sound with her feet.

"Are you all right?" asked Youk, surprising Dilly with how suddenly he reappeared; he had left Sawny still admiring his plant in the kitchen.

"I'm fine, it's just my feet—they've drifted off like Dod's—I was attempting to get them back by stomping.

"Sure, that chair slows the blood to your legs, doesn't it?" responded Youk. "Sawny, are you about done in there? It appears the boys are anxious for their juice. Shall we be at it?"

Sawny took her time and eventually came plodding down the hall, studying a sample she had taken. "You have a fascinating specimen!" she said excitedly, appearing to be very interested. "It's the best I've ever seen, inside or out. How do you get it to thrive in your kitchen?"

"I cheat!" said Youk frankly, and then he laughed manically. "Let me show you my back patio, it's the secret to my success with plants."

Youk moved toward the door through which the boys had just exited as he continued explaining his technique. "I rotate them out there and only bring them in occasionally. If you were to know the truth, Sawny, I don't actually do very well at keeping a traditional house plant. They all seem to die on me."

Sawny peered out the hall window as she passed by and noticed the boys were clearly visible, moving around in the darkness. "I'll take you up on the offer another time, if you don't mind," insisted Sawny nervously, shuffling her way to the back door before Youk. "It's too dark for me to enjoy your garden right now."

"And we need to hurry," added Dilly from the entry hall. "I think the boys have already left us." She poked her head out the front door and pretended to be surprised that she couldn't see them."

"Very well, let's go," said Youk abruptly, spinning around. He tapped his hat three times with a fancy stick that he had plucked from a large vase near his coat closet and then pointed the way for Sawny.

Meanwhile, Dod, Boot, and Buck were busy on the dark patio, assessing what part of the stone wall to climb. It was more of a challenge than they had imagined. In the blackness of the moonless night, stars glimmered from between clouds with just enough light to see the wall, but not enough to judge its height.

Boot pulled the palsarflex from his waist pouch and threw it high in the air with the very end of the rope wrapped around his left hand. The red balls did their task and clung tightly to the stone surface, twenty-five feet up. Regrettably, the full length of the rope was clearly a distance short of the top.

"If we climb up, how will we make it the rest of the way?" complained Buck. "It's a dead end."

As Dod gazed at the rope leading to the middle of the wall, an idea entered his mind. He could imagine someone scaling a cliff with a palsarflex. Each time the person got to the top of the rope, he took two short knives and jammed them in cracks, then rested his weight on the knives while repositioning the palsarflex. It was daring, but brilliant.

"I'll do it," said Dod. He volunteered before his nerves had time to convince him otherwise.

"Are you sure?" asked Boot tentatively. "It looks to me like we should abandon this plan. When Bonboo gets back, let's come clean with him about the whole problem. He could have men remove the solid door downstairs in a flippy. You'd get entrance to Pap's place, and at that point, you could search for Pap's keys without risking your life."

"No," responded Dod. "Bonboo wouldn't be able to trust me anymore. Besides, if Bonboo had men break the door down, it would create enough of a stir that I doubt it would stay a secret; and there's no telling who's a friend and who's not. I've got to do this!"

There was a basket of gardening tools that lay on the ground by Buck's feet. Dod bent down and started rummaging, assessing its contents by what he felt.

"Perfect—these are perfect," sighed Dod apprehensively. He held up two weed prodders that resembled sturdy screwdrivers, though no one could see them very well.

"Wish me luck," he said, taking a deep, drawn-out breath. His heart was racing.

"You really don't have to do this," whined Buck. "Besides, if you fall and get hurt, we'll all be in trouble—eyeball deep."

"Come on," said Dod, wishing he could muster a sterner voice, but lacking anything louder than a groveling whisper. "Help me by holding the line tight." He tucked the tools in his back pocket and began to scale the wall.

The rope jerked and swayed until Boot stepped in and anchored it pole-stiff.

"You're one crazy Coosing," muttered Boot, both excited and nervous for Dod.

"Not as crazy as the two of you," said Dod, feeling more confident as he made his way up the rope. "I just don't want to be caught in Youk's place—he'd use that zarrick thing on me."

"Oh tick-blood!" moaned Buck in agony, realizing they had to exit through Youk's quarters. He hoped the patio door wasn't locked and that Youk would take a long, long time fetching juice.

Grasping the rope with both hands brought back childhood memories for Dod. In second grade, Cole's teacher had insisted everyone in her class attempt climbing a rope that was connected to the ceiling of the gymnasium. A few boys and one girl had made it to the top. All of the kids had climbed at least a few feet off the floor, except Cole; his hands hadn't been able to grasp the rope tight enough to pull his body up. The mean boys had been ruthless about it, teasing him mercilessly.

However, that wasn't where the memory ended. For the next year, everyday, Cole had squeezed two palm-sized balls Pap had given him. They strengthened his hands and forearms until he had been able to climb a practice rope, hung in a willow by the stream near his house. In fourth grade, the next time everyone had been required to climb the gym rope, Cole had insisted he go first and had set the fastest time. It was empowering to remember.

So with years of practice behind him, Dod felt at home gliding up the palsarflex line. It was something he did well. And within a few short seconds, he reached the balls at the top. Nevertheless, that was the easy part.

Next, he searched the rock face around him with his fingers for any cracks, while his feet and knees held the rope. It was a circus-like act to perform. He prodded each tiny rift with Youk's gardening tools until two holes in the mortar were discovered; in one he placed a tool to stand on and in the other, a tool to hold. Once the instruments were inserted firmly, they were precarious, but secure.

Finally, perched on one foot, and holding the upper tool with the bend of his left arm, Dod did the unthinkable: He jiggled the palsarflex until the balls let go of the wall. Down below, Boot and Buck strained their eyes as they watched silently, hoping Dod would be all right, but powerless to do much of anything if he weren't.

"Just throw the rope and climb it," muttered Dod to himself as he coiled the line. He was terrified stiff, balancing on a painfully-small roost, mumbling to ease his nerves. "Throw it, climb it. It's just that simple!" whispered Dod. "I can do this!"

HWOOSH.

Dod gave the palsarflex an upward toss; however, it wasn't hard enough; much of the rope remained in a clump, preventing the balls from sticking to the wall.

HWOOSH.

Another failed attempt.

HWOOSH.

And another.

It was awkward for Dod to get the line in position without compromising his stability. Each unsuccessful try was followed by a methodical recoiling of the rope and stretching of his muscles.

After ten minutes of persevering, Dod's left leg began to wobble and seize up. It had already been cramping horribly and now was reaching its limit. He knew he had to hurry—possibly only one more attempt. If he couldn't get it, he dreaded the alternative of securing the balls to the wall next to him and climbing down to his buddies on the patio below.

HWOOOOOOSH!

Dod gave it everything he had, determined to succeed. Unfortunately, his prior assessments that had kept him throwing cautiously were well grounded; the force of his attempt dislodged the top tool completely and sent him flailing off the wall. For a split second, time stood still.

The thoughts that raced through Dod's mind were diverse. He thought about Buck and Boot below him and wondered whether they would try to catch him. He thought about his conversation with Bonboo in Pap's place and about the unusual circumstances in Green. He thought about Pap telling him to never give up. And finally, he thought about his mother and two little brothers.

It was his final thought that left him wishing earnestly. In his heart he solemnly promised that if he could live and return to Cedar City, he would apologize to his mother for all of the times he hadn't helped her out and for all of the times he had let her down. She had been just as lonely as he had been, only she had been left to deal with three difficult sons as well—one of whom had become substantially more troublesome since Pap's passing, as though it were her fault.

Apparently, the dimming light of death brought a brightening recollection of life. Everything seemed so much clearer.

If he could just live, he would live differently—more unselfishly, especially with his family at home. Dod didn't expect to escape harm, yet he still hoped somehow Boot and

Buck would soften his fall before he landed on the cold, stone floor.

GRRRRRRRRNNNKKK.

The rope cinched tightly around Dod's left hand and squeezed all of the blood out of his fingers. The balls on the palsarflex had landed squarely against the wall, inches from the top, and had instantly attached to the stone, leaving Dod dangling at the end of a tight line. It was miraculous.

Within moments, Dod was climbing for his life, glad to see safety within reach. His left hand and shoulder ached, but the rush of survival numbed the pain.

Once on the roof, Dod turned to look down. Boot and Buck weren't visible in the darkness.

"Did you make it?" Boot asked. His voice carried softly up the wall to Dod.

"I'm safe. I'll be fine. Meet you back at our room," responded Dod in a hushed voice. That was all he said before continuing on his journey.

The roof was covered with vines, bushes, and small trees; and because there was no direct access to it from inside the castle, it was completely overgrown, without any trails or walkways. Its purpose was to look beautiful from the distance as well as to provide protected nesting grounds for some rare varieties of birds that lived around Lake Mauj.

As Dod fought through the undergrowth, birds flew in every direction. It was as if there were more creatures than plants. Each step brought more startling movements. To calm his nerves, Dod whistled, hoping some of the birds would launch before he bumped them to flight.

Gradually, light began to cut through the thicket; it was the moon, rising across the horizon. Its dim rays appeared bright, revealing how black things had been in the grove and making everything visible.

The garden was much bigger than it looked from the ground. It spanned at least fifteen acres and wrapped completely around a windowless, twenty-foot stone structure. Dod could see part of Pap's place on top of the building, surrounded by another level of gardens.

"That's some penthouse!" said Dod to himself, making his way to a relatively vine free part of the wall.

Within a few minutes, Dod had secured his palsarflex and scaled the barrier. On top, the gardens were drastically different than the larger sprawl below. They were orderly, with walkways, and had many different varieties of bushes and flowers and trees. One path led down a stairway to a locked enclosure. It was a giant cage, filled with shrubs and grass; bars tightly crisscrossed the roof.

In the center of the highest gardens was Pap's place. It looked like an elegant home, sitting in the middle of a well-planned estate. If someone had blindfolded Dod and taken him to the spot where he stood, he would have never guessed that he was on top of a monstrous castle, unless he was allowed to walk to the edge of the lower gardens, where tapering levels below would have given him a hint of the circumstance; however, even at that, he would have presumed that the floors below were multiple dwellings, tapering down a hillside, not the levels of one unbelievably large structure. It was mind-boggling to think of anyone designing and building Bonboo's castle.

"I'm home," said Dod to himself, hurrying along a path that led to the house. He was trying to build up enough courage to enter. Thoughts of his last visit to Pap's place flooded his mind, but he pushed them out, whispering to himself, "Nobody's in there. I'm all alone."

A clanking sound stopped Dod dead in his tracks, about twenty feet out. It was familiar—he had heard it the last time he visited Pap's place. It made chills roll down his spine and across his arms. His eyes searched for an enemy while his hands reached for the knife he had secured in a large pocket on the back of his shirt. The knife was gone and so were the two buster candles he had brought. They had all fallen out when he had struggled during his climb up the first wall.

Pap's door inched open. Dod froze. Someone or something was coming out of Pap's place; but before anything emerged, the door swung closed, producing a familiar clank. During the prior invasion, the door had been damaged, so the slightest breeze swayed the door open and closed, creating a horrifyingly scary clank. It was the most relieving discovery Dod had ever made.

Once inside, Pap's house was dimly lit by moonlight, as it had been before. Dod tiptoed down a cluttered hall that led him straight to a recognizable spot: the entrance to Pap's office. He slid inside and walked across the dark room until a pile of swords clattered under his feet.

"Now, where did I leave that candle?" muttered Dod. He bent down and began to carefully feel around for the one he had left during his abrupt exit. "I've got it!" he said triumphantly, as his hands found the precious light.

The buster candle was easy to ignite; all it required was a decent strike against something solid. And with Pap's sword collection littering the floor, he had the candle lit as soon as he found it.

Shortly thereafter, Dod selected a sword from the pile. He felt like he was probably the only one in Pap's house at the time, yet the pounding of his heart insisted he take proper precautions. Next, he emerged from the office and made his way down the familiar hall, through the entry room, and to the front door. If Buck and Boot had accompanied him, he would have lingered, but without them, the lure of interesting objects was diminished.

Dod exited Pap's house and entered the long corridor to the shaft; it reminded him that all of the rappelling equipment was at the bottom, waiting for a ride up. He turned around and tried to reenter, to search for a spare harness, however, the door was locked.

Without hesitation, Dod began exploring the hall and pleasantly found there were items hung on the walls, offering a selection of parts to choose from in manufacturing his own rappelling gear. It was a much different experience than the time before, where he had been forced to scurry in the dark while escaping. There were a couple of coats, shovels, wooden poles, buckets, brooms, and coils of twine.

Below the coats, Dod found something else—a six-inch metal hook. He almost skewered himself on it accidentally. And he wasn't the only one that had missed seeing it. The hook was covered in long, silky black hair, the likes of which he had never seen before; and when he looked closer, he found dried blood on the hair. It chilled his blood to see it. Possibly the hair was from the dreadful creature that had followed him during his last escape. He couldn't be sure, but thinking about it made him hurry in selecting an old coat to aid his descent. Also, using a strip of twine, Dod lashed the candle to the end of his sword and then tied a loop of twine to the other end, making it possible to wear it around his neck like a sling.

"I'm keeping the lights on this time," said Dod proudly as he slid down the rope, using the coat for friction.

At the bottom, finishing his task was almost too easy. Before his feet had even touched the ground, candlelight reflected off Pap's keys. They dangled from his broken necklace that was caught on the side of a large wooden basket. One of the edges protruded like a finger, holding the chain hostage.

Relief washed over Dod. The keys hadn't been taken by anyone, and he had successfully recovered them.

Dod tucked the priceless treasures into his pocket and grabbed for the door when memories of Jibb confronting him flooded his mind. They were enough to persuade him into hiding the sword behind a pile of blankets before leaving the shaft. After all, the Drat Patrol was guarding Raul Hall, twenty-four seven, following the skunking; and though he didn't plan on being caught by them, he knew their suspicions would be much worse if he were carrying a sword.

When Dod emerged, Boot, Buck, Sawny, and Dilly were standing at the entrance to Green Hall, waiting for him, busily talking and laughing. Their commotion made it easy to join them without being noticed by guards—which was very lucky. With Zerny and Jibb gone, the flow of drats walking the halls was almost constant. They had been told something that left them on high alert, and they intended to do their job, detaining anyone who looked remotely suspicious. And by morning, it was clear their worries were not without merit.

A SURPRISING ATTACK

"To the tents, men!" ordered a large drat soldier, doing his best to vacate a majority of his troops from the Twistyard halls. "We need most of you right now. Leave one guard; and the rest of you hurry to the tents!"

"Are we under attack, sir?" asked Jibb's cousin Dolrus, who looked similar to Jibb, but younger—about sixteen years old. His eyes showed concern at the request to hustle anywhere by command.

"Not exactly—" snorted the senior officer, twisting the end of his long white beard. "Now hurry! Raul Hall will be fine for a couple of hours with one guard babysitting the door."

The young soldiers looked at each other, somewhat fearfully, and lagged, as though they each thought they ought to be the lucky one left behind with the plush job of monitoring Raul Hall.

"You!" blurted the commanding officer, noticing the confusion and therefore inserting his authority. He pointed his crooked finger at a strapping drat that looked mid-twenties and alert. "Stay put! The rest of you, follow me to the tents. We have some pest control to attend to."

Dilly and Dod stared in amazement. They were sitting on a bench in the main, next to Green Hall's door, waiting for Sawny to come out, when they overheard the yelling and witnessed the troops marching past. It was shocking to see the soldiers jogging down the hall, alarmed by something they referred to as 'pest control.'

"What do you think pest control means?" asked Dod, looking at Dilly.

"I don't know. It sounds to me like a code name for some sort of attack. They don't want the rest of us panicking, so they're trying to be clever."

"But who would attack their tents?" asked Dod, perplexed by the strangeness of the situation.

"Maybe 'the tents' is also in code," said Dilly eagerly. "It could mean the barns, or the eastern forest area, or the pastures above the bluff. Regardless, it doesn't really matter; today is sure to be exciting!"

Dilly's eyes lit up with delight. She loved the idea of an adventure and wasn't picky as to the type or whereabouts of it. If there was a pending battle or dispute, she wanted to be there, preferably wearing a sword and riding on Song.

Another large band of drat soldiers ran past, soaking with concern, yet the leader at the front seemed in control. He hollered at his troops to pick up their pace and then added an interesting twist:

"Rush along or you'll deserve what you get—and I intend to still make you wear them!"

As the men disappeared down the hall, Sawny came walking out and raised one eyebrow.

"Since when do Drat-Sprats exercise indoors?" she asked

rhetorically, shaking her head. "Bonboo's been away only one night and they've already gone freshy-mad."

"Don't worry, they're up to real action," said Dilly, jumping to her feet gleefully. "If we hustle, we won't miss a thing."

"Aren't you hungry for breakfast?" whined Sawny, lacking her sister's enthusiasm.

"Not enough to ignore whatever *they're* running off to do," responded Dilly promptly, pointing at yet another three squads of soldiers passing by. "Do you think I should get my sword?"

"Dilly!" said an exasperated Sawny. "There are plenty of drat troops to deal with whatever trouble they're facing."

Sawny caught her sister by the shoulder, attempting to win her attention away from the marching swordsmen, and begged her. "Please Dilly, let's go eat breakfast—and afterward we'll find out where they're going. Besides, maybe it's just a drill anyway."

Dod hopped up and nudged Dilly, too.

"All right," she said, gazing cleverly at Sawny. "But I'm going to hold you to the part about joining them when we're done eating."

"I didn't say we would join them," insisted Sawny adamantly, becoming aggravated. "I said we could find out where they're going."

"It's the same thing, isn't it?" said Dilly, smirking. She knew she was winding up her sister's nerves, and she shamelessly enjoyed it.

"Hardly!" snapped Sawny. She turned to Dod, rolled her eyes, and asked impatiently, "What do you think?"

Dod wasn't quite sure how to respond. Both girls waited for him to pick a side.

"I think we should be ready for anything," he finally concluded, choosing neither sister. The girls had squabbled long enough that the hall had quieted down.

"Look around," said Dod. "Drat forces have left the building with only a dribble of soldiers to man key positions. The Dread's behind this. I can feel it. He's on the move here at Twistyard."

Sawny cringed and Dilly grinned when Dod mentioned The Dread. Together, the threesome made their way to the Great Hall to eat, all the while warmly discussing what to spend the day doing. Dod mostly refereed.

At breakfast, the room buzzed with animated conversations. Everyone seemed to be talking about the strange event that was going on outside. Boot and Buck, followed by Toos, Juck, and Donshi, came and sat with Dod, Dilly, and Sawny. Boot was the first to speak, half laughing and half looking confused.

"Have you seen what's going on out there?" he said, pointing to the fields. "It's unbelievable! I've never heard of anything like it. What do you guys make of it?"

"What?" asked Dilly, beginning to slide to the edge of her seat. She appeared as if the suspense was going to overpower her any minute and she would have no choice but to run out and take a look for herself.

"I guess that's what you get for sleeping in. You're a link left out of the chain," teased Buck.

"Last night was pretty busy," argued Dilly, who had spent much of it talking with Dod after he had returned with the keys.

"I know—you did your chitchatting in my room, remember?" said Buck, before stuffing the frosted top of a giant strawberry muffin in his mouth. He then proceeded to say,

Pone-style—still chewing repulsively and giving a mischievous eye— "You could have at least dimmed the candles."

"Baby!" snapped Dilly teasingly, furnishing Buck with a friendly shove.

"Nice," said Toos, chuckling at Buck. "You've mastered Pone."

Donshi nodded, agreeing with Toos, and smiled admiringly in Buck's direction, while Juck began to lather his head with the remainder of his cup of water, attempting to flatten his hair and part it down the center like Toos's.

"Nice, Buck. You're just like Pone," said Juck, doing a lame impersonation of Toos; water dripped off his large ears and besmudged his shirt, making him look even goofier.

"You're hair is too short to pull it off," said Sawny wryly, glancing at Juck's pathetic attempt to slick down his military-tight stubble; however, feeling sorry for him when she read the disappointment in his eyes, she quickly recovered by fibbing, "But your voice was close."

Dilly couldn't stay seated any longer. Her plate of fruit and pastries was hardly enough to keep her planted. She rose to her feet, full of excitement, and begged, "What's going on outside?" She hopelessly tried to peek past the hordes of people to see through the windows.

"Crazy stuff," said Boot, enjoying how much Dilly was tormented by not knowing. He nearly delayed longer in telling her, to build the suspense, but seeing that Dilly was going to bolt away, he continued on.

"Little animals are pouring in from all over. They're chewing on the soldiers' tents and clothes, rummaging through their things, and generally behaving as wild as a flock of crowing, half-plucked Mountain Roosters. I didn't see a single critter act normally. They've completely lost their minds. Something's not right."

"Little animals?" said Sawny, raising her eyebrows. She paused in the middle of eating her bacon-and-egg sandwich with cheese sauce to join Dilly in interrogating Boot with suspicious glances.

"It may sound funny," responded Boot, tingling with amusement that the girls suspected he was the cause. "And I'll be the first one to admit that if we were talking about a few scurrying rugs, maybe twenty or thirty, you'd be right to look at me like that—it would make for a jolly prank—"

"It's not a prank," said Toos, butting in.

"Right!" said Boot, the tone of his voice shifted away from frivolity. "There are thousands of them attacking the drats' stuff, doing a lot of damage. And don't forget, the soldiers were assigned here to protect us. Who knows the real motive?"

As Boot spoke, others gathered to hear him. "After I get done eating," he continued, beginning to sound like a statesman, "I'm heading back out there to help them—and the rest of you should, too."

"What kind of animals?" asked Dilly, slowly sitting down.

"Mostly rats, mice, and squirrels, but I saw a few raccoons and muskrats, as well as a badger," said Boot. Buck and Toos nodded in agreement.

"We've been whacking them with sticks and catching them with nets for about an hour," chimed Toos. "It's the strangest thing I've ever done."

"Yes, I'd agree this whole place has gone twirling mad!" boomed Sirlonk, who had crept up behind Dilly and Dod unnoticed. "And someone's orchestrating this whole disaster, that's for certain—just like the note promised! I think it's time for aggressive measures to be taken, don't you?"

"What note?" asked Dilly sharply, spinning around in her chair to face Sirlonk.

"Oh? I assumed you of all people would have heard by now," said Sirlonk, looking shocked.

Dilly was still upset at Sirlonk for the rude comments he had made the night before about Bonboo; nevertheless, she did her best to behave civilly.

"Well, I haven't," said Dilly carefully, attempting to hide how eager she was to know every particular.

"Then I shall tell you," gloated Sirlonk. "Mercy found a note with this morning's early delivery of milk and eggs, and she quickly turned it over to Youk. In the letter, dozens of threats were made against Twistyard and Bonboo's family specifically. Since you're—well—at least seen as a very important part of Bonboo's family, I presumed Youk had informed you promptly, even before informing the rest of us."

"I would have thought so, too," said Dilly, looking disappointed. "What action do you think we need to take?"

"I'm not in charge," said Sirlonk quickly, "nor do I intend to lead all of you in doing anything—Bonboo did leave Youk in control during his untimely absence—but it seems fair to say that turbulent times like today deserve the sword exemption."

Sirlonk searched the table with his eyes, judging whether the crowd was in agreement with him or not, and when he saw that they were, he continued on.

"Why, this is just the sort of thing it was created for. Rally the Coosings, and everyone else I've taught to draw a sword, and meet me in front of the main entrance to Sword Tower. I'll see to it that you're all given the privilege of selecting a weapon from the vaults. After all, Bonboo has insisted I teach swordplay. It doesn't seem logical for us to sit around, unarmed, while the enemy approaches....Just look, the note's already being fulfilled; drat forces are scattered, exactly as it promised. Shouldn't you each be ready to defend yourselves?"

Everyone was nodding, except Dod. A cold look of disapproval oozed from his eyes. While Sirlonk had been explaining his proposal, flashes of destruction filled Dod's mind. He could smell the musty air and almost taste the dust. He could see darkness filling the cracks of space between the mounds of fallen rubble. And this time, his ears heard moans and groans coming from dozens of victims. It was horrid!

"Don't go in Sword Tower!" blurted Dod.

"What?" said Sirlonk, looking stunned.

"Nobody go in Sword Tower. That's what The Dread wants. He's waiting for us to exercise the sword exemption, and when we're all joined—every last swordsman among us—something awful will happen down there. The Dread must know that in order for us to equip ourselves, according to the rules, everyone participating is required to be present, in the vaults together, signing for the swords and swearing integrity."

"That's ridiculous!" scoffed Sirlonk, incensed. "How would The Dread know anything about our private procedures and safeguards installed by Bonboo? I'm actually somewhat surprised you know about them. You're cozier with Bonboo than I thought."

"You can't assume The Dread is a nasty outsider," warned Dod. "Even you should be careful today, Sirlonk."

"I plan on being careful, *by being prepared!*" grumbled

Sirlonk angrily. "That's why I think we should all sword-up and stop pretending the drat troops will do us any good against a well-designed assault. I'd prefer a dozen Coosing with swords than all of the drat troops and their weaponry. Besides, what's your plan? Do you even know the claims of the note?"

Dod's face flushed with embarrassment. "I haven't seen it yet, but I'm sure—" Dod began.

"Don't be!" snarled Sirlonk, interrupting Dod's defense. "You played the hero on a rocky wagon ride and pulled some nonsensical move at a Bollirse game, so I heard, and now you're the expert on tactical defense against a genius like The Dread? You're simply out of step and way out of class."

Dod didn't respond. He looked to Dilly and Sawny for help.

"What did the note claim?" asked Sawny sheepishly, seeking the truth.

"It promised to disrupt drat forces, burn buildings, overturn Twistyard hierarchy, destroy every last Coosing, and snub out Bonboo's family. From the wording, I would be surprised if Bonboo were still alive. Regardless, it's your choice what we do."

Sirlonk then turned from Sawny and looked sharply at her sister, adding, "You decide, Dilly."

"Me? Why do you say it's my choice?" gasped Dilly in agony, caught between Sirlonk and Dod. For once, she didn't particularly want to be at the center of attention.

"Because it is—factually speaking," said Sirlonk. "At this morning's surprise meeting, Youk took a consensus of The Greats' opinions, and it was split down the middle; however, the tentative decision was made to pack up the Coosings and take them to High Gate if any of the threats began to happen—and well, as we've all seen, they've begun."

"What? They plan on ordering us to High Gate?" said Boot, whose cheeks were starting to redden. "I'm not going anywhere, especially while many of my friends are left here, awaiting further attacks."

"I still don't see how this is my choice," argued Dilly, feeling greatly conflicted.

"It is, dear girl," insisted Sirlonk matter-of-factly. "I've already given my opinion to Youk, as have many others, pleading with him to see that the logical course is to utilize the special talent we have right here, by mobilizing. There's no question in my mind that Raul Coosings, and every Rauling, would rather wait with swords in their hands than to cowardly hide in a closet at High Gate—of course, they are exceptional at swordplay. But you, dear girl, have a voice that Youk would listen to. If you speak for the groups, as a representative of the Coosings, Lings, and Bonboo's family, I'm confident he would order us to sword-up. After all, Twistyard is your inheritance, your family's hope for changing the future."

Dilly and Sawny stirred in their seats. All eyes were on them. Even the surrounding tables of people, who weren't technically in the conversation, were now listening.

"Don't be a coward, Dilly," hollered Sawb from a neighboring table. He and his followers from Raul were rumbling with demeaning comments.

"That might be asking too much of her," added Eluxa tauntingly. "Swords are sharp and pointy. Her little sister could get hurt when she falls."

Sirlonk turned around and gave a sufficient scowl to quiet the jeering and then turned back to Dilly.

"I'm sorry to ruin your breakfast with this sort of decision," he said patronizingly. "I'm ready to defend myself and Juny, but I'm worried about the rest of you. What would I tell Terro if anything happened to Sawb, or what would I tell myself if anything happened to you, Dilly? You know you're like a daughter to me. I have Jilser, right here. You, too, should be carrying a sword for your protection."

Sirlonk pulled back his black cape and revealed his battle sword, Jilser, tucked neatly in its case, secured at his waist.

"When you've made up your mind, come find me. I'll be out watching the spectacle. Who knows, maybe I'll help them—pathetic drats."

"I've already decided," said Dilly with conviction. "I'll speak with Youk."

"Good girl," praised Sirlonk. "I knew you would do the right thing. You always do." He turned on one boot and whisked off to the fields.

"Ahhh," groaned Dilly. "I can't believe all of this is happening. Who would The Dread get to attack us? Who could possibly be our enemy?"

"It could be anyone," said Boot. "Didn't you say there was a sizable army that attacked our friends—you know, the night you and Dod rode off without me?"

"That's true. I almost forgot about them," admitted Dilly.

Sawny's face went white. She pushed her food away, only half finished, because her appetite was gone.

"Do you think Sirlonk's right about Bonboo?" she asked gingerly; her feelings were close to the surface.

"No. Of course not, Sawny," reassured Boot. "He didn't go alone. Zerny and Jibb went to help him out, and they're both great with weaponry. Besides, Bonboo's been around a long time. He knows how to behave wisely. He'll come back just fine."

"That's it!" whispered Dod excitedly. "Weren't Miz's two sons visiting Zerny and Jibb?"

"I think they still are," answered Boot, not sure where Dod was leading the conversation. "Joop and Skap told me they planned on staying for a few months. I doubt they've left."

Dod turned toward Dilly. His eyes held confidence that empowered the words he spoke.

"We need to do some homework, and after that you can have your chat with Youk. Everything's going to be fine."

The rest of breakfast went by quickly, without anyone saying very much. When Dilly tried to prod Dod for more information about his plan, he looked around and said, "Let's wait. There are too many ears in here."

When the group had eaten, Boot asked Toos to round up Greenlings for the purpose of aiding the drats' fight against the pests and then followed Dilly out into the front courtyard.

Mice and rats covered the ground, making the grass come to life. They all seemed to be instinctively heading toward the drat encampment, as if bound by a dark spell.

"Creepy," gasped Dilly with Sawny hiding behind her. "Where are they coming from?"

"The fields," responded Buck. "With as much grain as we grow, there are dozens of times as many more within a few miles' radius of here. Haven't you ever helped with the harvest?"

"Let's get to the point," said Boot, turning toward Dod. He looked annoyed. "What's going on? Don't you think we should equip ourselves with swords?"

Dod nodded in the direction of Lake Mauj and started

leading the group, weaving around the thicker pockets of wriggling rodents. It was disgusting. Sawny, in particular, could hardly tolerate the number of furry creatures that scurried over her shoes, and as a result, she found herself screaming and jumping erratically as she tried to follow; Dilly similarly disdained the circumstance, but strode through them without a peep; Boot and Buck weren't as concerned about the rodents as they were about Dod's silence.

After they were far enough away to speak without being heard by anyone else, Dod began his explanation.

"I had another flash at breakfast," he said, looking cautiously over his shoulder. "It happened when Sirlonk mentioned getting the swords from Sword Tower. I think we all suspect that the basement of Sword Tower is the spot we have been searching for, the location I keep seeing in my weird images of destruction. It all fits together. What if The Dread is trying to lure us down there, to destroy us while burying the reserve of swords?"

"So, you're not against the idea of staying here to protect Twistyard?" asked Boot.

"No. Of course not," insisted Dod. "I'm all for carrying swords and sticking around—I just don't like the idea of going to the basement of Sword Tower to get them. Maybe a few people could go down and bring them up for the rest of us."

"Is that all?" asked Dilly, showing disappointment. Sawny looked mad; she didn't appreciate having walked through the waves of rodents to hear what he could have so easily told her within the safe confines of the castle.

"No," said Dod, chuckling as he read Sawny's face. "I thought of something else." Dod pointed in the direction they were headed. It was straight for Zerny and Jibb's house.

"We need to have a chat with Joop and Skap," he said. "They know a few things about maylers, don't they?"

"Dod! You don't think they did this, do you?" scolded Dilly defensively, glancing back at the crawling fields. "Even if they knew how, they wouldn't! Trust me. Joop and Skap are as nice as you'll ever meet."

"The best way to find out is to talk with them," argued Dod. "If they did it, we might be able to detect their guilt, and if they didn't, they'll likely have some insight on how we could stop the problem, right? It never hurts to ask for the help of a mayler's sons when being attacked by animals."

Boot entered the large house first, followed by the others. It was silent. Ornate carvings of beasts hung on the walls, staring ominously at the group as they searched for Joop and Skap. Embers glowed dimly in the fireplace, signifying someone had been there recently. Finally, Sawny found a note, propped against a twig arrangement on the kitchen table. She read it out loud:

We've gone fishing for a couple of days. A dear man lent us his boat, so we intend to roam the islands of Lake Mauj. Don't be alarmed if we stay a while, for we have plenty of supplies. To our luck and your arrival,

Pooraah,

Joop & Skap

"Pooraah?" said Boot. "I didn't think anyone used that word anymore. To hear it, you'd surmise they were stuffy-in-the-cap aristocrats. I guess they've been spending too much time with the likes of Youk and not enough with their hosts, Jibb and Zerny."

"I like the word," said Dilly, smiling. "Besides, maybe they're just trying to fit in here. You can't blame them for that. Since they're known as Miz's sons, most people quickly peg them as farm-hatted mountain men. After all, not everyone respects the unorthodox education of a mayler."

"Fishing," groaned Buck enviously. "That's where we should be right now. On a day like today, I bet they're catching some big ones."

"But who did they write the note for?" asked Dod, puzzled.

"Zerny and Jibb," answered Dilly. "Who else would they be expecting in this house—*us*?" Dilly laughed at Dod's foolish question.

On the way back to the castle, they crossed paths with drats driving loaded wagons to the lake. Ascertainy had counseled the troops to wash their supplies thoroughly, citing an obscure study that claimed rodents had responded predictably to certain smells; she therefore surmised that the most likely cause of the furry guests' tenacity was in actuality their uncontrollable response to a malicious spraying of the encampment during the night.

Ascertainy was right. To prove her point, she insisted, in the name of science, that one troublesome tent be kept unwashed and placed in an outer wheat field, beyond the buildings, while the rest of the soldiers' supplies be soaked and scrubbed with water. When the camp was fully uprooted and cleaned, the pests retreated. And by evening, no mice or rats remained to torment the soggy equipment; however, the lonely tent in the wheat field was completely destroyed.

After dinner, Dilly tracked Youk down to have a chat with him, though she wasn't planning on just arguing Sirlonk's case.

Her strongest reason for the meeting was to read the dreadful note for herself.

Dod, Buck, Boot, and Sawny all waited close by, wanting to hear the results of the conversation as soon as possible. Aside from the awful rodent infestation, nothing else had distressed Twistyard all day. An hour passed slowly before Dilly emerged from Youk's quarters. She came out smiling and nodding.

"Thank you. I will," she said respectfully.

"What did he tell you?" asked Boot, rushing her, even before Youk's door was all the way closed.

"Not much," answered Dilly.

"Not much?" complained Boot. "We spent an hour waiting for you, and you say *'not much?'* You're going to have to do better than that."

"Well, I think Sirlonk made a bigger deal out of the note than it really is," said Dilly. "Youk explained that they've been receiving threats for weeks, quite regularly, and that Bonboo hasn't done anything differently—just continued to be careful—utilized drat troops for safety patrolling and guarding."

"What about being forced to go to High Gate?" asked Buck.

"Youk did say that he thought it would be good to be ready for an escape to High Gate, but only if things looked horrifyingly bad; and he doesn't see that happening any time soon. He thinks one or two people are responsible for the problems we've been having, like today's rodent festival, so he cautioned me to be careful and to stay in groups, but not to worry."

"And the threats against us and Bonboo?" asked Sawny.

"I won't lie to you. The note does specifically claim threats against us and the Coosings, but, the last six, over the past three weeks, have too — it's nothing new. There were only a couple of original aspects in the message: one was that drat troops would be scattered, and the other was a threat against Sirlonk. That's probably why he was so worked up this morning."

"No wonder," said Dod. "I thought he seemed unusually annoyed at breakfast; and that's saying a lot for someone who's always annoyed anyway. Which reminds me, did you talk about the sword exemption?"

"Yes, I did," said Dilly. "Youk agreed he would be fine with having a few drat soldiers retrieve swords to equip us, so long as the rest of the procedures were carried out as prescribed in the exemption — perhaps in the open field. Although, at the present time, he doesn't see the need to do it unless circumstances change and it becomes essential. And I must admit, it's probably a good idea for now — with all the trouble swords could cause."

"That's easy for you to say," joked Boot, trying to hold back a chuckle. "You already have half the vaults' contents under your bed."

"Then you better be nice to me," replied Dilly playfully.

"Or stay away from you," added Boot.

"I don't think you could," said Dilly, pleasantly glowing.

DREADFUL NEWS

For a week, Youk was right about the attack. Nothing happened. After the rodents disappeared into the fields, drat soldiers went back to their regular posts, which had been assigned by Bonboo and Zerny, with the small exception of adding a few more men at the entrance to their camp.

Sirlonk didn't like the decision to hold off on distributing swords, so he continued to use his powers of persuasion, attempting to convince his pupils that they should insist on swording-up. For that purpose, he reopened training and held unusually long hours, welcoming everyone that had studied under him before. He even included Boot, despite their running conflict, and he had his subjects dueling with spar swords, working to make them feel confident in their abilities. The swordplay bonanza was as encompassing and contagious as the Bollirse binge had been.

Other areas of Twistyard also felt an increase in participation. By demand, Tinja held three practice classes daily in Hatu, Strat held an intense course in defense and mobility with shields, and Ascertainy was constrained to begin a lecture series on the history of traditional attacking methods. Pots, Lings, and Coosings all felt an increased need to be prepared in the event of an assault, for the rodent episode had shown them that with ease, an enemy could create enough chaos to dismantle the guarding drat forces—not to mention, it proved someone or some group of people were engaged in mischief against Twistyard, beyond idle threats.

Dilly loved the extra time spent practicing swordplay. She felt it was useful in preparing for a possible meeting with The Dread, while also serving her primary purpose of improving her skills, hoping to make a mark against Raul in the upcoming tournaments. Sawny was even persuaded to join in. She decided that things were bad enough to justify taking a momentary break from books in order to revamp her fencing abilities.

Boot, Buck, and Dod also took part in the exercises; however, Dod purposefully avoided all dueling and mostly engaged his practice against trees and fences on the outskirts of Sirlonk's large classes. He knew he had a long way to go before he would be prepared enough to not make a complete fool of himself in a real duel, so he worked hard on being as invisible as possible. Eventually, though, he couldn't hide. There was sufficient bad blood between him and Sawb's mob of followers from Raul that a confrontation was inevitable.

"Hey, come back," yelled Sawb, late one morning when he noticed Dod was heading out of the crowd. "Let's see if you're as good as everyone says you are….I challenge you!"

Dod froze in his tracks. Sweat began to form on the sides of his brow. He was holding the slender limb of an elm, because there were so many students in Sirlonk's over-inflated classes that everyone had to rotate with the spar swords in shifts.

"Sorry," Dod responded without making eye contact. "It's my turn to use a stick. You'll need to find someone else to fight. I'll be over here, practicing with the bullrish bush."

"Did you hear that, Joak? Dod needs a sword," said Sawb condescendingly to his friend. "You've made a pig of yourself already, go stick for a while—or better yet, watch me jilt the boockards out of Dod. You'll learn a few things."

Sawb grabbed Joak's sword and, in the process, pushed a number of people out of his way. It caused commotion that turned heads instantly.

"Get him, Dod," yelled Toos. "Show him how Pap would've done it."

Another boy, named Scott, a Sooshling twig that resembled Jim, was big-eyed with excitement when he hollered, "Everyone come and see. Dod and Sawb are striking a duel. Now Raul can swig a cupful of their own poison."

"You wish!" snarled Kwit, leaving Sawb's side momentarily to shove the boy to the ground. With Kwit's giant frame, it was like a professional wrestler picking on a twelve-year-old.

"The day anyone from Green beats Sawb," said Kwit gruffly, "is the day I fancy up and prance the halls like Eluxa."

"Then go find a skirt!" said Scott defiantly, scurrying across the ground on his knees. He didn't dare rise until he was safely at Dod's side.

Eluxa, hearing her name, climbed on a stump to see better and posed with her spar sword over her shoulder.

The crowd stopped slicing and whacking; and in a remarkably short period of time, they formed a large circle around the feud. Even Sirlonk, The Great Sword Instructor, had to push in order to have a front row spot.

Sawb tossed Joak's sword to the ground at Dod's feet and said, "Show me what you've got." He then glanced at his followers and grinned, raising his own sword in the air, evoking cheers.

"I don't feel like it right now," said Dod quietly. He turned his back on Sawb in an attempt to retreat into the crowd, but couldn't find an opening. The wall of people was teeth-tight.

"What? You don't *feel* like it?" mocked Sawb loudly. "You're scared to duel against me—and it's only practice. We're using spar swords. You can't possibly get hurt. What are you afraid of, coward?"

"What are *you* afraid of?" demanded Dilly, who stepped into the circle behind Sawb. "I've been asking for a match all week and you've hid like a snake in a rat's hole. If you're finally able to duel, Dod's going to have to wait in line behind me. I'm first!"

Dilly was a rescuing angel. She alone knew Dod's weakness—how poorly he handled a sword—and she cared enough to help him keep it a secret.

"Step aside!" said Dilly to Joak and Kwit, who jumped between her and Sawb. "You might want to make yourselves comfortable. I plan on a full match. We're going to need some space."

Dilly turned her head for just a moment, pointing the way for Joak and Kwit to exit, when something horrible happened.

SMACK!

In a cruel act, lacking any sportsmanship, Sawb struck the broadside of his retractable sword across Dilly's right hand, while she wasn't looking. It made a strident sound, followed by Dilly's wailing. The point of impact was against her four fingers that held her sword, and the blow was hard enough to incapacitate her from dueling. She dropped to her knees and grabbed at her throbbing fingers.

"Get this baby out of the circle," said Sawb to Joak and Kwit. "I don't have time to hear her whining. Dod and I have unfinished business to attend to."

Sawb spoke with arrogance, as if he were the greatest of swordsmen, yet the act he had just performed was anything but great; it was a cheap, low down, scoundrel, scumbag, maggot-sucking, unfair blow—or at least those were some of the thoughts that ran through Dod's mind.

He looked to Sirlonk for intervention, hoping what Sawb had just done was deplorable enough to have Sawb be disciplined on the spot; however, to Dod's astonishment, Sirlonk seemed to enjoy the riotous atmosphere and didn't show the slightest indication of objection. On the contrary, he appeared to be proud of his brother's son.

It was the last straw! A moment Dod had considered many times had come. He had planned on being abused by bullies to the extent that physical contact was imminent, since they ran their mouths constantly in his face, threatening to do plenty; but now that the moment had arrived, it was filled with more emotion and conviction than he had ever imagined.

It was Dod's worst case scenario: Hitting Dilly with a blind shot, while she was trying to stick up for him, and then having Sirlonk condone it was infuriating. It made the blood run so fast through Dod's head that he could hear it pounding in his ears, and the noise it caused was loud enough to entirely drown out the crowd of shouting people.

Without saying a word, Dod scooped Joak's sword from the ground and marched straight for Sawb.

"It's nice to see that you've changed your mind," said Sawb, gloating. "Here now, let's test what you know."

Sawb raised his sword and swung it around in the air, giving a fancy show of ability, and then pointed it directly at Dod. When the move didn't even register a response in Dod's undeterred eyes, Sawb uncomfortably added, "I'll have you for lunch. You're a nobody."

Dod continued to march forward. He didn't hear what Sawb had to say, nor did he care, for his rage was beyond reasoning.

The encounter was brief enough to be missed by anyone who blinked. When Dod was within striking range, Sawb leaned in and jabbed with his sword, poking Dod's right shoulder. Fortunately, the spar sword retracted, as expected, causing no more harm to Dod than a pinch—but that was only a side note to the real action.

Sawb was so busy concentrating on proving how good he was at swordplay that he entirely missed the serious nature of Dod's intent. When Sawb struck, Dod was lifting Joak's sword with his right hand, pretending to duel; however, rather than focusing on blocking the jab, Dod put all of his attention into swinging a powerful left punch. It connected solidly with Sawb's arrogant nose, sending him to the ground.

Over the years, Cole had prepared to defend himself with his fists, and though he had always hoped he would never be forced into a position where he would actually need to use them, he had practiced a quick left hook, reserved exclusively for such a day. In his plan, if he were ever attacked, he would distract with his right fist, while hitting hard enough with his left to stop the conflict cold, or at least give himself time to retreat—and with Sawb, it worked perfectly.

Blood ran down Sawb's face from his nose as he struggled to

pull himself up to a sitting position. His eyes were angry, showing he wanted to fight back, yet they also revealed he was too scared to stand up—partially because of what had just happened, but more than that because of Dod's reputation. After all, Dod was Pap's grandson, and he was mad.

"I thought I made myself clear," growled Dod in his roughest voice, glaring sternly at Sawb. "I don't feel like dueling right now—maybe some other time."

Dod threw Joak's sword into Sawb's lap and added, shaking his clenched fist at him, "If you ever treat a girl like that again—*ANY GIRL!*—you'll be sorry! Mark my words. I want to see you start showing some respect for women! Do I make myself clear?"

Sawb stared, cold and glazed, fighting the urge to rise up. He didn't nod or say anything to Dod, but the swooning of a dozen girls from Raul, who found Dod's words heroic, left Sawb the pathetic loser.

Even Eluxa played her best eyes in Dod's direction, flipping her silky hair out of her face, hoping to attract his attention.

Dod, on the other hand, had someone else on his mind. He walked over to where Dilly was still whimpering, holding her fingers. Joak and Kwit saw him coming and abruptly let go of her, vanishing into the crowd of spectators as quickly as they could, making it clear that they didn't want to be the next in line to feel Dod's wrath.

"Come on, Dilly," said Dod, putting his arm around her. "I think it's lunch time."

Boot, Buck, Sawny, Toos, and all of the other Green Coosings and Greenlings rushed to surround the twosome as they left the class, like a swarm of bees, protecting their queen.

"Make sure you come back later," encouraged Sirlonk in an

exalted voice. "All of that hot energy is ideal for swordplay. Good show to you all."

In the Grand Kitchen, Mercy and Sawny attended to Dilly's fingers with ice, while the others from Green Hall went to save the best tables for lunch. Dilly's fingers had swollen up and were starting to show a black-and-blue line where Sawb's sword had struck.

"What a weasel," responded Mercy, when she heard what Sawb had done to Dilly. She pulled a tray of roasted chickens from the oven and set them out to cool, all the while shaking her head in disgust.

"Sawb's been afraid to duel you fair-and-square ever since you made it a priority to be the best," she continued loudly, gaveling the daylights out of a slab of raw beef. "He knows you're going to beat him in the tournaments this year, if it's an equitable match. That's why he uses deplorable moves, like the trash he pulled today. He hopes you'll stay clear of his title—"

Mercy waved her wooden hammer in the air, plugging in forcefully, "—and mind you, I expect you won't!"

"He's better than you think," lamented Dilly somberly, rotating the ice across her fingers.

"Sawb? Sawb? Are we talking about the same Sawb?" blurted Mercy, getting worked up enough that many of the kitchen helpers grabbed at loaded platters and headed out of the room.

"Yes, Mercy. He's a rat—but he's good at swordplay. Nobody would dispute that he's the best in Raul Hall, and they're the best in the castle."

"Don't forget about The Greats!" chimed Mercy, throwing a fifty-pound, well-tenderized hunk of beef onto a flaming grill using two giant forks; the juicy meat sizzled and sent smoke billowing up to where a tuba-sized duct remarkably sucked it all out of the room.

"Of course some of The Greats are better—" admitted Dilly. Sawny nodded, too.

"And I see you as one of them!" interrupted Mercy passionately, grabbing at a leg's-length spoon with a top nearly the size of her head; she bent down and stirred vigorously a bathtub-like cauldron of soup that bubbled over a pit-in-the-floor flame. "Don't forget that you're Bonboo's great-granddaughter," she added, beginning to huff and sweat, "and he calls you great for more than one reason."

"I know. I know," said Dilly, wincing a little as Sawny inspected the bruises that were darkening across her fingers. "He says that a lot," continued Dilly. "But it's candy talk, not real."

"I beg to differ!" insisted Mercy adamantly. She stomped her foot on the floor and poised for emphasis, holding up the dripping spoon, and bellowed, "THIS IS YOUR HOUSE, GIRL! Sawb and the rest of those disrespectful smuggies of soot are not welcome if they insult the very princess of the palace... well, princesses—you too, Sawny."

Including Sawny in the conversation led to the rest of the story. She smiled ear-to-ear and then said with delight, "I suppose Sawb won't need any lunch since he's already had a bite to eat."

"He has?" asked Mercy, sensing there was more.

"Yes, we forgot to tell you," Sawny continued, "Dod gave him a knuckle-sandwich. It was solid on his nose—made the blood run and everything."

"I should like to have seen his face," chirped Dilly, starting to revive as the ice numbed the pain. "He was, unfortunately, facing away from me. You'd think Dod could have flipped him around when knocking him to the ground. What kind of gentleman is he, anyway?"

Dilly and Sawny both chuckled pleasantly. Mercy was also pleased, having heard the beginning of a tale she knew they would need to dwell on.

As the story unfolded in its every particular, Mercy continued to listen and add her plentiful thoughts, while cooking for thousands and directing the dispersal of food through men and women under her charge. At one point, Boot poked his head in the room to ask why the girls weren't coming to join the rest of the group, since lunch was already underway, yet when he saw Mercy holding them hostage—and the girls did look amused by the things she said—he silently slipped away before being trapped with them.

The Great Hall was bustling with working people. In addition to the lunch-time rush, many drats were climbing ladders to hang ornate decorations from the ceiling. They were preparing for the following morning's celebration, observing Rainfall Day.

All of Green showed respect for Rainfall Day as much or more than Americans show for Thanksgiving. The two holidays actually had a lot in common. They both revolved around giving thanks for the blessings of life and friendship, and they both celebrated the abundance of food by feasting.

When Boot returned to eat his lunch, he found his spot was taken by a drat who was steadying one end of a giant A-frame ladder. The man apologized profusely to Boot for interrupting and then promised they would hurry as fast as they could.

"Don't think another thing of it," said Boot cheerfully, reaching around the ladder and man to grab a bite of lunch. "I can eat standing as well as sitting. I'm talented that way. There's no need to relax my lower end in order to digest properly."

The drat thanked Boot and smiled, though he appeared uncomfortable.

"Can I help you with that?" asked Boot, noticing the ladder was starting to sway. "I'm not too bad at posting up."

"Except the time you sent me flying in Gramp's apple orchard," said Buck, reminding Boot of his poorly-executed prank.

"I was only joking around—no harm done."

"Actually, my broken leg and I didn't find it very funny," said Buck, grinning.

"That's because you jumped," said Boot, grabbing at more of his lunch. "I was just making the ladder shake, like a little burp in the ground. If you would have held on, you'd have been fine."

"I did hold on," blurted Buck, his voice cracking momentarily. "I held on tight to a twenty pound bucket of apples—and it didn't help me stay perched very well."

"Don't listen to him," said Boot to the worker. "Let me help you with that."

Boot grabbed the ladder firmly and the swaying stopped. A muscular tredder was climbing the other side with an unusual leather ornament. It was large and painted bright red, with a few white streaks.

"That's the biggest apple I've ever seen," said Toos, pointing to the strange object. It was three feet in diameter.

"Then you've never seen the 'Big Apple' before, have you?" joked Dod.

"What big apple?" asked Donshi sweetly, turning her bright-blue eyes on Dod. Apparently, the scuffle with Sawb outside had spun Donshi's favorable gaze in Dod's direction; she was hopelessly crushed-out, like a lost puppy who had just discovered a pair of loving, safe arms and a warm meal.

"A city I know of has the nickname, 'Big Apple,'" responded Dod quickly, blushing; it had nothing to do with what she had said and everything to do with the way she had said it.

"Oh," said Donshi admiringly, doing her best to weasel her tray of food closer to Dod's.

Small talk and eating continued as the tredder on the ladder attempted to hang the gigantic ornament; it dangled precariously over Boot's head.

"Boot, I'd move if I were you," recommended Pone from a table away; he was filling his mouth with a chicken leg. Boot grinned at Pone, thinking about Buck's impersonations of him.

"What?" asked Boot, pretending he hadn't heard. Boot hoped to draw Pone into saying more with a stuffed mouth. He glanced at Buck and raised his eyebrows.

"You should move," said Pone.

"What?" asked Boot, putting his hand up to his ear.

"That apple might not stick," said Pone loudly, chewing away. He plopped a clump of grapes in with the half-a-roll he was already working on and, while spinning his hand in the air, said through his food, "Perhaps you could steady the ladder from a different angle."

Toos, Juck, and many of the other Greenlings laughed; they recognized what Boot was doing.

"He's right," interjected Dod, feeling uncomfortable. "You really should move." Dod noticed that the strong man, hanging the ornament, appeared to be groaning.

"Oh, I'm not afraid of a leather apple," snickered Boot, perfectly relaxed. He jammed a handful of carrot sticks into his mouth and did his own impersonation of Pone, making a crunching sound as he said calmly, "It's just a decoration."

The Greenlings and Coosings roared, very amused by Boot's table-side entertainment.

Pone, recognizing Boot's play, joined in the laughter and then did a perfect impression of Boot, with a flawless display of his posture and speech, which made the crowd go wild. Pone was a fun-loving master of the masquerade.

Suddenly, disaster struck. As soon as the tredder at the top of the ladder had hitched the apple to a metal loop, it broke free and came crashing down.

Boot didn't flinch when he heard Pone yell, "WATCH OUT!" Instead, full of the fun atmosphere, he stood up straighter, to make a point of his fearless nature and to continue pleasing his spectators. After all, it was only a leather ball of sorts.

The apple fell thirty feet from the ceiling; however, before it hit the crown of Boot's head, Buck jumped to his feet and vigorously tackled his brother, sending them both flying.

CRASH!

When the ornament hit the ground, it burst open and rocks littered the Great Hall floor; a gaping dent scarred the polished stone where the apple had struck.

"Rocks?" gasped Boot, completely shocked. "That could have killed me! Who put rocks in that thing?"

"I'll be bush-trimmed to the roots!" muttered the drat who had steadied the ladder. "No wonder we were having such a hard time. I'm going to personally find out who's at the bottom of this prank! It could have seriously injured someone—"

The workmen left the ladder in place and the shattered ornament on the floor while they went to investigate.

"Thanks Buck," said Boot in a very serious and grateful voice. "You're the best brother anyone could ever ask for!"

"I'm just protecting my space," said Buck teasingly. "If you were gone, Dod and I would eventually give in and our bedroom would be filled with half-a-dozen other Coosings; but with you around, I know that won't happen."

"Right," said Boot, "I'm sure that's why you did it."

A crowd of people started gathering around them. They left their own lunches to come over and see what had caused the loud crashing sound. Even Mercy, followed by Dilly and Sawny, came running; their chitchatting could wait.

"How did this happen?" asked a large, red-faced drat named Scuttle, who was the Chief Gardener at Twistyard. His spiky hair and well-trimmed beard were graying white, and his massive chest stretched his shirt tight in the center as he breathed in and out, trying to calm down. At six-and-a-half feet, he towered above the other workers and commanded a great deal of respect.

When nobody came forward to explain, he searched his personnel with his mud-brown eyes, glancing around the room at everyone wearing the purple-collared uniforms. "Zerny's not going to like this," he muttered under his breath.

"I SAID, HOW DID THIS HAPPEN?" barked Scuttle. This time he was loud enough to be easily heard by all of his subordinates. They came scampering to him, looking nervous.

"While they were hanging the decoration, it fell," responded Boot, feeling awkward that he hadn't said anything yet. "It almost hit me on the head—and I didn't wobble the ladder, I promise! You can ask anyone."

Boot was so accustomed to being in trouble, when trouble happened around him, that it was strange to honestly retell the event without taking the blame.

"Would you please identify the men who were working this ladder?" said Scuttle firmly.

"Sure, it was—let's see," said Boot, scanning the crowd of faces. Scuttle's men stood ready for inspection and instruction.

When Boot didn't readily see the twosome, he pushed Buck's lunch to the side and climbed on the table to get a better view. Still, the men weren't in sight.

"There was a large tredder on the ladder—" Boot began, when Scuttle jumped in.

"Tredder? We're all drats!" said Scuttle, wearing a most peculiar expression. "Are you sure it was a Tredder?"

Boot instantly noticed that he recognized the other members of the decoration crew; they were Twistyard gardening hands and stablemen.

"Didn't you hire any outsiders to help with today's preparations?" asked Boot.

"No, we certainly didn't," said Scuttle. "If you saw a tredder on the ladder, we've got a problem. This was done on purpose."

"He was a tredder," said Buck, adding his testimony to his brother's. "And I don't believe I've ever seen him around here before. Did anyone else recognize him?"

The crowd stayed silent, wagging their heads side to side.

Rigorous attempts were thereafter made to apprehend the mystery men; sadly, nobody was able to find them. Their escape had been well planned. Drat forces doubled their efforts and increased precautions after the event, but it was too late to catch the perpetrators.

Youk was concerned with the disruption and breach of security, so he, too, became actively involved in the investigation, interviewing Boot, Buck, and Dod separately, as well as riding his beloved mare through the neighboring forests, trying to find the fleeing criminals. All of the efforts were in vain.

By dinner time, messengers were sent to surrounding villages, warning them of trouble causers and canceling their prior invitation to join at Twistyard for a breakfast party to celebrate Rainfall Day. If unknown faces brought danger, the safest way to avoid further attacks was to monitor all guests carefully. Even the current visitors at Twistyard, especially the short-stay diplomats and nobles, were all accounted for, noted, and warned, leaving no room for an uninvited guest to slip into the crowd without being identified.

Also, in light of additional, secret news, Youk held a private meeting concerning another issue. He refused to make the information public; nevertheless, it seemed to stir things up amongst The Greats that were present. Directly following the brief gathering, a group of four people, including Youk, Sirlonk, Strat, and Tinja, headed for the barns, leaving in such a rush that they didn't stop to eat dinner.

When Dilly and Sawny saw them hurrying, they left their food and followed.

"What's going on?" asked Dilly, chasing a spiffier-than-usual Strat; he had a fresh haircut, his customary chin and lip stubble were gone, and he wore polished, new boots that matched his splurgy outfit. To look at him, you would think it was the night he was being honored as the best Bollirse coach in all of Green.

"I wish I could tell you, but I can't," said Strat, moving

with purpose. "If you want to know, you'll have to ask Youk directly. He made us all promise to keep it a secret."

Dilly looked around and couldn't see Youk.

"Where is he?" she begged, jogging to keep up.

"His mare is out in the overgrown pasture—you know, the one where we used to keep the spring colts," said Strat, pointing to a field just beyond the row of barns. Trees and bushes hid Youk and his horse from view. "He wanted her to get fresh feed after returning from today's search," he said.

"Come on, Strat. Please just tell us," nagged Dilly persistently. "We won't share it with anyone else. We promise."

Strat stopped and shook his head, his solemn brown eyes penetrating to the girls' hearts. "If it were only a matter of keeping a secret, I would tell you both; but because of the promise I've made, it's now a matter of my honor. You know I can't change that."

Dilly and Sawny followed Strat into the barn, wishing he could at least give them a hint. Sirlonk and Tinja were leading in the front, a few paces ahead of Strat, so they were already rigging their horses.

"You don't need to tell us," said Sawny nervously. "You'll make sure we're secure, right? If it were a matter of our safety, you'd find a way to warn us, right?"

Strat looked at the girls sympathetically when he reiterated, "I wish I could tell you—I really do."

Without any more words, he jogged across the large barn to the far end and started getting his horse ready. Dilly and Sawny watched for a few seconds and then turned around to walk out.

"Pssst."

Dilly spun in surprise. Sirlonk was signaling to her, though he held one finger up to his mouth, suggesting they be quiet.

"Pssst."

The girls walked over and stood by Sirlonk's horse.

"What is it?" whispered Dilly.

"I think it's dreadful that they intend on keeping the two of you out of the loop," said Sirlonk quietly. "It's not right, so I'll tell you. But I expect you'll maintain tight lips."

Dilly and Sawny nodded their heads and leaned in to hear the news.

"Bonboo told Youk his journey plans before he left. He anticipated being back two days ago and said that if he weren't home by dinner today, Youk should send out a search party—something was surely wrong. So here we are, heading off to find out why Bonboo hasn't returned."

Tinja led his horse down the middle of the barn, heading for Sirlonk, which caused a quick change in the volume and content of the conversation.

"I'm sorry girls. As I just said," grumbled Sirlonk in a loud and seemingly annoyed voice, "I can't tell you any more than Strat just did. Youk made us promise, and that means something to me."

Sirlonk winked at the end, for only Dilly and Sawny to see, before mounting his horse.

"Are you about done?" hollered Tinja to Strat.

"I'm coming," he bellowed back. "I may be slow on a horse, but I can rig one in a flippy."

Moments later, after watching the horsemen disappear out of sight, Dilly and Sawny broke into tears. They went back into the barn and hid behind Song, sitting upon a pile of freshly-cut grass. With the new information that Bonboo was possibly in trouble, neither of them had a sufficient appetite to finish eating dinner; and having nodded to Sirlonk that they would keep the news a secret made things difficult. If they went back inside while crying, people would want to know why.

Finally, hours later, when the sun began to set and there was still no sign of Bonboo, the two girls marched inside the castle and went to bed early. On their way, however, just as they had forecast, Boot, Buck, and Dod all tried to find out what was wrong; yet to their bedroom door, and inside, they refused to speak a word of what distressed them, other than to frankly state through their tears that something felt misplaced.

A heavier than usual darkness cloaked the castle. Boot, Buck, and Dod sensed it, even though none of them said anything about it until around midnight, when the boys were preparing for bed. Boot was the first to speak up.

"I think Dilly's right," he said. "Something is misplaced or wrong. I don't know what it is, but there's a bad feeling about tonight. What do you think, Buck?"

"Same."

"What about you, Dod?" asked Boot, giving him a nudge.

"Yeah, I feel it, too. So what should we do?"

"Go to sleep and forget about it, I guess," said Boot. "There's not much we can do in the middle of the night—especially with drat troops patrolling like they are."

Dod walked to the window and looked out. He saw in the distance five little flashes, torches in the night, riding toward the barns.

"We've got company," he said. "I can't tell who it is. Come take a look."

Boot and Buck dimmed the lights in the room and moved to the window, next to Dod.

"You're right," said Boot, straining his eyes. "I wonder who would be coming to Twistyard at this time of night."

"When was Bonboo expected to return?" asked Buck.

"That's true," admitted Boot, interpreting Buck's question to be a suggestion of the riders' identities. "Maybe he is coming in late with Zerny and Jibb—and those friends from High Gate's border town—in order to be here for tomorrow's celebration."

"Bonboo wouldn't ride on a moonless night," said Dod. "It has to be someone else. Let's go and find out who."

"Are you kidding?" asked Buck. "We'll never make it past the drats in the hall."

"We don't need to," replied Dod. He walked out of the bedroom for a moment and then returned, hefting a large coil of rope. "That hall closet has a lot of neat stuff."

"Out the window?" groaned Buck.

"We're only fifty feet up, if that," argued Dod. "Besides, since the drats relocated their tents, our part of the wall is somewhat hidden from their view. We'll be fine in the shadows."

Dod tied one end of the rope to his heavy oak bed frame and dropped the rest out the window.

"You can stay here if you want, but I'm going," said Dod, slipping his shoes on his feet and a black cloak over his pajamas. "It'll only take me a couple of minutes. I'll be right back."

In a flash, Dod disappeared out the window. Boot fidgeted back and forth, watching him descend the rope to the ground. Shrouded by darkness, Dod was barely visible.

"I guess I'll go with him," said Boot sportingly. He walked over to his bed and sat down to put on his shoes. "Someone needs to keep an eye on that kid. Besides, I haven't put my pajamas on yet."

When Boot noticed Buck's apprehension, he added firmly, "You stay here and pull the rope up once I'm down; and when we come back, lower the rope—savvy?"

"I'll watch for you," sighed Buck, relieved that he had been given an easy out.

By the time Boot finished getting ready to enter the night, Dod was gone; and even after he descended the rope, there was still no sign of him.

"Dod?" whispered Boot, walking quietly in the direction of the barns. "Dod, where are you?"

A rustling sound drew Boot's attention, veering him off his original course.

"What are you doing over here?" he said quietly, approaching someone who was seated by a thicket of bushes.

"Who's there?" said a grumpy drat soldier, lighting his candle and drawing his sword.

Boot turned to run when his foot sunk into an unusually muddy spot, sending him to the ground. He hid his face with the top part of his cloak and started crawling; however, the voice of the grumpy soldier, insisting he stop or be skewered, was convincing enough that he obeyed.

"Who are you?" said the drat, approaching Boot. "Speak up right now!"

But before Boot could answer, the light went out and a scuffling sound ensued.

"Run! Run! Get up and run!" said Dod. He had surprised the soldier from behind, ambushing him. With one hand, he had taken the soldier's light and snuffed it out, and with his other, he had swiped the soldier's sword. Of course, it was easier than it might have been. The poor young drat, keeping a lonely night watch, had been dozing off near the hedge and wasn't fully with himself, so the surprise disarmament sent him running rather than fighting.

"There goes our top-notch guard," whispered Dod. He set the sword and candle on the ground, next to the drat's over cloak.

"I'm sure he'll be back in a hurry," complained Boot, staggering to his feet.

"I know," responded Dod. "But when the soldiers return with him, they'll find his sword and candle, nicely positioned right here with his cloak. Don't you think it will indicate a wild dream rather than loose bandits?"

"Maybe," agreed Boot hesitantly. "Either way, let's split from here."

At the entrance to one of the barns, Dod and Boot hid in a large hedge, eavesdropping on the conversation of the men inside.

"I s-still can't b-b-believe it," said one of the men. It was Zerny's voice. "W-we did everything w-we could."

"And we're just lucky to have escaped with our own lives," said Jibb.

Dod and Boot looked at each other. The incident Zerny and Jibb were discussing sounded fascinating, even if the men were no longer a mystery.

"You were right," whispered Dod to Boot. "It's just Bonboo and his men. I guess I should have listened to you and we wouldn't be in this mess." He directed Boot's eyes to the area where they had encountered the drat soldier. There were at least fifty torches burning. It looked like the men were searching the whole region, bushes and all, including right below where Buck was waiting to drop the rope for reentry.

"That's fine," joked Boot. "You'll learn to believe me. I'm usually right."

A few of the torches in the distance stopped meandering and headed straight for Dod and Boot.

"We'd better dig down," groaned Boot quietly. He shuffled back and forth in the hedge, getting as low to the ground as he could; and when he couldn't lay flatter, he proceeded to push dead leaves on top of himself.

"It looks as if you've done this before," whispered Dod.

"Lots of times. I've learned that hedges like this are thick enough to hide a person, unless someone's looking. If you're not down like a worm, you get caught."

Dod mimicked Boot's actions and the two became virtually invisible. Shortly thereafter, drat forces surrounded the bush, standing on the dirt roadway in front of the barn doors.

"Jibb, we're glad to see you've returned," said a drat soldier, positioned only a few feet from Boot's nose. Six other soldiers accompanied him. Boot and Dod hid so deep in the leaves that they could barely see the outline of the men's boots well enough to count numbers.

"I wish we had better news," answered Jibb. "Bonboo's been assassinated!"

The awful words hung in the air like black storm clouds. Dod and Boot lay motionless. They couldn't believe what they had just heard. It was so shocking that even after all of the men had left, Dod and Boot continued to remain still—paralyzed by those three simple words.

This was the kind of bad news that changed everything.

THE RACE

While Dod lay thinking, covered in leaves, his heart began to pound faster and faster. *"Promise me, Dod, promise me,"* echoed in his mind. Bonboo's pleading eyes haunted him. The answers to so many questions—so many secrets Bonboo wanted to share—were hidden; and the key word, to acquire the two pieces of the map, was entrusted to Dod alone: Dossum.

"We've got to go to Lower Janice," said Dod, breaking the ten minutes of silence.

"What?" asked Boot, answering in a choked-up voice that revealed he had been crying.

"We need to go to Lower Janice—first thing in the morning. I promised Bonboo I would do something when he passed away."

"The carriage ride—right, you need to get the maps," said Boot, gaining composure. "Are you going to share the secrets with me? After all, I know the word, too—Hoppas."

"He changed it," responded Dod cautiously, not really wanting to go into detail on how he knew and Boot didn't. "It's not Hoppas anymore, although I'm sure I'll be able to share many of the secrets with you—"

Dod's voice then altered as he attempted to lift the tragedy from Boot's mind with a subdued joke. It was awkward. "—of course I'll need to look them over first. Maybe there's a reason he doesn't want very many people to know them—they could be all sorts of bad things about me."

Dod and Boot crawled slowly out of the dirt and leaves. Guards no longer stood anywhere near them, but a few glowing torches glimmered in the distance. Soldiers were stationed along the castle wall, making a return through the bedroom window impossible.

"It's just as well that we can't go back," said Boot, sounding like a boy with a skinned knee who was trying to shake it off or at least hide his sore feelings. "If I'm going to Lower Janice with you to visit Higga, we'll need to leave in a couple of hours anyway, before the sun rises, because under no circumstance will I be caught missing Mercy's morning banquet."

"That's easy for you to say," replied Dod. He opened his cloak.

While Boot couldn't see very much, he knew exactly what Dod was complaining about. He was wearing pajamas.

"Don't worry about it," assured Boot. "We'll look good together—you in your pajamas and me in my muddy get-up."

"A sleeper and a slob," mumbled Dod.

The two friends crept into the barn and found a soft bed of straw in the loft. Both of them were still sad inside, dreading the reality of Bonboo's passing—especially Boot. Bonboo had been like a father to Boot for over thirty years, so once he thought Dod was asleep, he began to cry quietly again.

In the morning, when the farthest corners of the sky were starting to turn a light bluish orange, and while the rest of the canopy was a sea of dimming stars, Boot awakened Dod and helped him onto a saddled horse.

"Won't Dilly be mad?" asked Dod, noticing through his half-opened eyes that the horse Boot had selected for both of them to ride was Song.

"She'll understand," said Boot confidently. "If my horse hadn't run off, we'd be riding him. Besides, this is jungo."

"Jungo?" said Dod.

The word sounded vaguely familiar, yet slipped Dod's sleepy mind.

"We're out for revenge," grumbled Boot. "Whoever did this horrible thing to Bonboo will pay; and since I'm nearly his blood, jungo would apply. I'll see things are made fair for the family, even if it's the last thing I do! I'm not afraid of The Dread, or any of his filthy friends, so let's meet them. Jungo! Jungo! Jungo!"

By the time Boot got to the chant of jungo, at the end of his disclosure, a shining sword waved in the air.

"Where did you get that from?" gasped Dod, wondering how Boot had managed to secure a sword, saddle a horse, and plan for a family's revenge, all in the dark while Dod slept.

"I'm borrowing it," replied Boot. "Sirlonk has a small cache of half-a-dozen of them in a little box he hides under the back log-lining of his horse's stall. I once saw him resort to it when trouble came knocking six years ago. Anyway, we can return them before he ever notices they're gone."

"We?"

"Here," said Boot, pointing at a second sword he had stowed in one of two sheaths that dangled from the front of the saddle. "I assume you'll join me in any fancy fighting."

"Sure—count on me!" said Dod boldly; however, his insides didn't feel as confident in his own ability to use a sword as his voice seemed to indicate. But Boot's zeal for jungo appeared big enough to handle anything, so Dod determined that the least he could do was to speak the part of a faithful friend, even if he didn't have the skills to pull his fair weight.

"Last night I couldn't sleep much," said Boot, nudging Song into a trot. "I thought and thought until my brain hurt. At first I was mostly sad, but after a while, my sorrow turned to anger. How dare someone take Bonboo from us—and for what?"

Boot glanced at Dod with determined eyes. "That's when it dawned on me," he continued, "The Dread knows about the map and the secrets, and he wants to claim them for himself. The kind of things Bonboo has kept hidden would be devastating if The Dread got his hands on them. I bet he'll magically show up today in Lower Janice, trying to trick Higga into giving him her half of the map; and when he does, we'll be there, waiting. He'll pay for what he's done!"

Dod had never heard Boot speak with such conviction. It was almost as if Boot had aged a few decades during the night. His plan for meeting The Dread was genius and his courage to confront him was noble.

"I'll follow whatever you've got planned," said Dod. "Just let me know what you want me to do."

"First things first," responded Boot, giving orders like a general. "When we get to Lower Janice, you go in and get the map, bring it out, and we'll hide it in the woods. After we know it's safe, we'll keep an eye on Higga the rest of the day. When someone comes for the map, it'll be time to *interrogate*." Boot patted his sword. Jungo was filling his mind.

"So it won't bother you if we miss Mercy's morning celebration of Rainfall Day?" asked Dod with surprise.

"Jungo is more important than fancy food," said Boot, taking a deep breath of morning air. "Justice needs to be served, and I'm more than ready to dish it out! Besides, family honor requires it."

The ride to Lower Janice took less time than Dod's first encounter with the road. As they passed the spot where Bonboo's carriage had almost launched off of Drop's Cliff, memories flooded back. Dod shook his head in unison with Boot.

"If only Bonboo had taken the attempts more seriously," groaned Dod.

"Then he wouldn't have been Bonboo," sighed Boot.

The two rode in silence. It was fitting. The world around them was peaceful. Even the pastures and barnyards surrounding Lower Janice seemed respectfully quiet, as if they were soldiers paying tribute to their fallen captain.

In the city, early morning mist filled the air, awaiting sunrise. Dogs and kids were still asleep, and the only sounds that could be heard were coming from a few barns where cows were being milked. After trotting through the streets for ten minutes, heading toward Higga's house, Boot broke the silence.

"Bonboo's not the only one this town will be mourning today."

Boot pointed at piles of rocks, positioned on porches and front steps of homes and businesses. Dod hadn't noticed them before, yet when Boot brought them to his attention, he remembered they were a symbol of respect, honoring a newly deceased loved one. Higga's dwelling had two piles of rocks on her front stairs and another large pile on her porch.

"When you're in there, make sure to ask Higga who died," said Boot, helping Dod off Song. "I'll wait here for you."

"Shouldn't we hold back awhile?" asked Dod uncomfortably. "It looks as if she's still asleep, like the rest of this town. I would hate to wake her up early on a holiday—and with bad news. Maybe we could rest in the park over there."

"Not until we have her half of the map. She'll understand. And don't scare her about The Dread coming to visit her. We'll keep an eye out for him. There's little need of her worrying all day. It will be bad enough for her to hear about Bonboo. Perhaps you could tell her we're not exactly sure how he died. That could soften the news."

Dod's knees knocked together as he climbed Higga's stairs. He wasn't afraid of Higga, but delivering such bad news and then promptly needing to ask for the map seemed rude.

"Are you sure you don't want to tether Song to the front post and join me?" asked Dod, pleading with his eyes.

"Nope," responded Boot. "I need to keep a close eye on Dilly's horse—and what about The Dread—and besides, Bonboo's system was specifically set up with one recipient. If we both approach her—and I know she's a rule keeper, to the smallest detail—she might not give it to us. You need to do your part, do what you promised Bonboo."

Boot's statements were scattered and sounded like excuses. Nonetheless, they were the truth, and Dod knew it.

KNOCK. KNOCK.

The sound echoed into the street. If it were any other time of day, the knocking may have gone unnoticed; however, with the stillness of the morning, even a butterfly's flapping would be audible.

"Yes?" said a voice through the door. "Come on in. It's not locked."

Dod entered the house and found Higga propped up by pillows, her portly frame was stretched out on an oversized dripchair in her disorderly entry room. Dod uncomfortably eyed the scene.

Higga's parlor had walls that were covered with misaligned paintings of important people, including Bonboo and Sirlonk. Two intricately-worked oak bookshelves, which leaned precariously away from each other, held medals and awards of every shape and size, as well as a number of statues that were likely gifts of appreciation for her remarkable service. In the corner, a glass case was encrusted in dust and filled eccentrically with medical apparatuses that looked outdated and barbaric. Stealing the bulk of the room, a disproportionately large coffee table was buried under stacks of books and piles of papers which drooped in every imaginable direction and, consequently, littered the floor with educational debris. It was a cluttered room that matched perfectly Higga's disheveled appearance.

"I'm sorry for the way I look," apologized Higga, pulling at her crumpled curls and glancing down at the wrinkled outfit she wore; most of it was hidden by a sea of colorful cushions. Her face was reddened and puffy, especially below her eyes.

"I should have gone up to sleep last night, I just never did," sighed Higga.

"You're fine," said Dod softly, not showing the feeling of panic that was growing inside. "I'm the one that needs to apologize. I'm sorry for bothering you so early in the morning—and on a holiday."

"It's a holiday?" squeaked Higga sleepily. "Oh yes, now I

remember. I can't believe I forgot. Today's Rainfall Day, isn't it? I'm not much good this morning." She shifted in her chair stiffly, knocking some of her pillows to the jumbled floor where they nearly concealed a half-rolled, dirty map of Soosh.

"After yesterday's painful news," continued Higga with a frog in her throat, "I cried hard enough to forget about most everything else."

"Who died?" asked Dod cautiously.

"You don't know?" gasped Higga, looking shocked. "Oh lad, where have you been? I hardly expected to be the one telling you of such sorrow. Bonboo's been killed. Messengers, bearing his ring, came from Twistyard last night, as the sun was setting."

Dod dropped to his knees in bewilderment. The Dread had already done his work. Dod knew Higga had given up the map—his heart told him—but he had to ask.

"Higga," said Dod quietly, and then he paused to think of the right words to say. When none came to his mind, he finally blurted very clearly, "Dossum!"

"What son?" asked Higga.

"Dossum! I'm here at Bonboo's request," said Dod, cringing because he sensed it was hopeless.

"I'm sorry, son, but I don't understand what you're asking," said Higga, squinting down her nose at Dod; she shifted, knocking more pillows to the floor.

The air in the room felt heavier than when Dod first entered, making it hard to speak.

"Dossum!" sputtered Dod. "It's Bonboo's secret code word—so you'll know I'm the one he's chosen to pick up your half of the map—the one he entrusted to you."

"My goodness, son!" exclaimed Higga defensively. "The

word's not Dossum!" She sat up straight in her chair, revealing brownish stains on the burgundy riding outfit that she wore, and looked concerned for her life. "Why are you doing this?" begged Higga keenly. "He didn't choose you!"

"Yes he did!" protested Dod. "I promised him I would ask you for your half and Dilly for hers."

"How do you know so much?" muttered Higga, scowling callously. "What have you done to Bonboo?"

"Me?" wheezed Dod, completely stunned. He felt like a fist had just punched the air out of him, so he took a huffing breath and fought back.

"I haven't done anything!" argued Dod, his voice trembling. "I might well ask you the same question. How did you find out about Bonboo's passing before anyone at Twistyard? And why are you sleeping down here, dressed, and all dirty from who-knows-what mischief?"

"It seems like you knew early enough to come trotting up here in the dark of the morning," said Higga, drenched with bitterness. "If all of Twistyard doesn't know—"

She paused while her eyes narrowed to slits. "—then how did you find out? And the messengers—I heard them with my own two ears—all of us did. They were sent from Twistyard to declare the unhappy tidings of Bonboo's passing."

Higga jumped to her feet, unbelievably agile for her body type, and grabbed for a sword that was concealed behind her chair. She pointed it in Dod's direction and said coldly, "Now tell me everything you know, or I'll mush you out—I promise I will!"

"I'm telling the truth," choked Dod in disbelief. The very woman who had helped to save his life now appeared determined to end it.

Higga moved closer, unconvinced by anything Dod had said, and whistled a shrill peep. Two black, snarling dogs, as big as mountain lions, thundered down the stairs and came to stand, one on each side of her, right on top of the books and papers that littered the carpet.

"I don't know what's happened," cried Dod, wishing Boot would burst through the door to his rescue. He mustered his strength and looked her in the eyes, hoping his face would draw sympathy. "If you've already given the map to anyone else," he said slowly, "you've been tricked."

"I WASN'T TRICKED!" Higga roared like a horrendous beast. She was scarier and louder than the dogs that now barked ferociously. "YOU'RE LYING! — YOU BETTER CONFESS! — NOW TELL ME THE TRUTH!"

"I am!" said Dod, hardly able to be heard over the noise. He jumped to his feet and made for the door when one of the Devil Dogs blocked his way, showing its sharp teeth; and when Dod spun around to plead for help, a cold blade pressed at his throat. The tip nearly drew blood. With little effort, Higga could finish him off—mush him out as she had promised.

Dod raised his weaponless arms in the air and begged, "You're making a huge mistake, Higga. Bonboo made me promise him that I would go after the map. I don't want it! I'm just doing this to keep my word—and in hopes of stopping whoever killed him. He actually made me promise twice—once in Pap's house, when he told me he had changed the word to Dossum, and once before that, while on a carriage ride. The word originally was Hoppas."

Higga lowered her sword slowly and looked puzzled. The dogs went silent, instinctively reading her actions.

"You know Hoppas?" whispered Higga.

"Yes, I know Hoppas," said Dod, nodding. "I'm telling you the truth."

Higga whistled a low-pitched chirping signal and The Guards of The House scampered back upstairs, their tails between their legs.

"He never told me he had changed it," said Higga mournfully.

"Maybe it was on his long list of things to do," suggested Dod in a frenzied voice; his nerves were shot. "You know how busy Bonboo's been lately," he added, trying to force a friendly smile.

Higga dropped her sword and started to cry. She became the Higga Dod had expected.

A few minutes passed with Higga blubbering and Dod trying to comfort her. She was so consumed by grief, over letting Bonboo down, that she couldn't speak more than two words without sobbing loudly and shaking. It was a challenge to Dod, who wanted to leave, but wasn't about to go until she could answer his questions.

Finally, after Dod had distracted her attention to the shelves filled with honors she had received — reminding her that everyone, including Bonboo, was proud of all the good she had done — her weeping slowed enough to broche the issue of the night before.

"Can you tell me who came for the map?" asked Dod carefully; it was like he was tiptoeing on a bridge of eggs.

"He was…well…it was dark, and I was out on my front porch — " mumbled Higga between tears.

"Okay," said Dod, prodding her gently. "Good. That's good. What else can you remember?"

"Two men rode up, and one came and whispered Hoppas quietly—"

"What did they look like?" asked Dod, jumping in too quickly.

"I don't know!" barked Higga, beginning to sob harder again. "It was dark—or I wasn't looking—or I was crying. I just don't know!"

"Can you remember anything about them?" begged Dod, feeling discouraged. He knew Boot would be terribly disappointed if Higga couldn't at least point them in the right direction.

"The man that approached me and told me Hoppas—he comforted me with a few kind words about Bonboo. He knew all sorts of things, memories and stuff—"

"So he was close to Bonboo," said Dod.

"I think," admitted Higga, almost containing her tears. She reflected back momentarily and then burst out again. "Oh why did I give it to him? I didn't even see who he was!"

"Don't be sad," said Dod sympathetically. "We've all been tricked by the same deceiver. It's The Dread!"

Dod patted Higga on the shoulder and smiled. A burst of inspiration filled his mind with a straight course of action. "Everything's going to be all right," he said. "Your half's no good without the other half, and I know for a fact that Dilly hasn't given up hers yet. We'll stop him."

"Dilly?" said Higga, momentarily less sad and more pensive. "She has the other half?"

"Right," said Dod. Without further conversation, he slipped out the door, sped down the stairs, and rushed across the road to where Boot was standing next to Song, beneath a giant willow.

"We've got to hurry," said Dod breathlessly.

"Do you have it?" asked Boot.

"No, that's why we need to hurry—we've been played!"

"WHAT?" gasped Boot. "Then why were you going through all that chanting and yelling. I thought you were doing some proof-of-rights to get the map."

"Hardly," said Dod. "You don't even want to know what *that* was."

"Then who has it?" demanded Boot, mounting Song with a leap.

"The Dread!" said Dod. "He came last night—had some accomplices announce Bonboo's passing, showing a ring—"

"Like the family ring means anything!" groaned Boot. "Dilly has two or three of them, and I even have one!"

"Well, it worked for him," said Dod. "Shortly after the announcement, which supposedly came from Twistyard messengers, two men rode up. One asked Higga nicely, giving the old word, and she was grieved enough to hand it over without any questions."

"Who were they?" demanded Boot, getting agitated; he looked like he couldn't decide whether to ride away or bolt into Higga's house for some advanced interrogating. "She must have recognized them," he said red-faced.

"No," replied Dod. He put his hand in the air and had Boot help him to his place on the back of Song. "That's the most frustrating part. She didn't get a good look at the people. It was too dark and she was too upset."

Boot groaned loudly. His plan for identifying The Dread was already foiled; and despite his quick actions, the master of deception was one step ahead. But before Boot could say another word, Dod spoke up, fighting to hold back his enthusiasm.

"Let's see how fast Song can run," suggested Dod nonchalantly.

"To where?" asked Boot in a hopeless voice, still pondering his failed plan.

"To Dilly!" said Dod, smiling big. "We need to protect her. She's got the last half of the map. The Dread will seek her out next; and we need to be there, waiting—Jungo, right?"

Boot bubbled with pride and rapped Dod on the shoulder, saying, "Good man, Dod. Good man."

Mud flew in the air as Song ran back toward Twistyard. Boot and Dod spoke about the various people they suspected, citing clues that pointed one way or another. In the end, however, notwithstanding most of the evidence suggested The Dread was someone they knew, he still remained a mystery.

With the sun up, Boot felt comfortable taking shortcuts. He left the main road many times, trotting through fields and forests. At one point, a particular thicket became bothersome enough that Dod pulled his legs up and crossed them behind Boot, Indian style, to prevent bushes and trees from tearing through his thin pajama legs. It would have been a good idea if he had also increased his grip on Boot, but not wanting to create an uncomfortable situation by holding him tightly, Dod lost his place and tumbled off the horse.

GRRRRMP.

On the way to the ground, one sharp branch grabbed the bottom of Dod's cloak and tore it straight up the side, three-fourths of the way to his collar. An inner pocket also burst and sent small supplies flying everywhere.

Boot promptly stopped Song and came back to help Dod up, yet when he saw a four-foot pine tree, wearing a myriad of things from the broken pocket, he couldn't help reverting back to his typical, though more somber, teasing self.

"You'd give all of that to the tree and none to me?" jabbed Boot. "At least let me have the chouyummy. That pine wouldn't appreciate it the way I would."

Dod grinned when he noticed the sapling. It looked like a poorly decorated Christmas tree.

"You can have it—it's my present to you," responded Dod, handing up the chocolate-like treat.

"Thanks. Chouyummy's just what my stomach is growling for," said Boot, hopping out of the saddle. He began picking things off the branches and handing them to Dod: a white-and-blue handkerchief, a small ball of twine, a Bollirse globe, a strand of red ribbon, a half-eaten cookie, a couple of sugar sticks, a bright-blue sock, a well-used candle, a lucky feather charm, and a mostly-eaten block of chouyummy.

"Really, you can eat the chouyummy," insisted Dod when Boot tried to hand it to him. "Besides, I don't have enough room to fit all of this stuff in my other pocket." Dod ate the rest of his cookie as a show that he had split the food fairly, so Boot didn't need to feel bad eating the chouyummy.

"You sure packed supplies," remarked Boot, helping Dod to his feet.

"You never know when it will come in handy," said Dod. "As a matter of fact, it says right here—"

Dod paused while he produced from his overstuffed, remaining pocket the book Commendus had given him. He flipped through the pages, trying to find a particular quote.

"Here it is: '*You never know what junk from your pockets will become treasures.*' See, we're proving this book right; a half-eaten cookie and bit of chouyummy taste better now than they ever would have tasted at the castle."

"Gaaaaaah!" gagged Boot. "Except for the hair!"

"Sorry about that. My pocket has been crawling with them ever since I carried Dilly's hairclip, and I've tried to clean it out, honestly."

Dod looked down at the pages of his book while closing it up. Suddenly, the way the morning sun caught the paper revealed something amazing: indentations! Pap had written a note and used the book as a table; and since the paper was soft, marks were left, disclosing parts of the sentences where Pap had pressed harder.

"What a clue!" exclaimed Dod. "You have got to hear this, Boot!"

BONBOO,
I FEAR THAT WE MAY HAVE A . . . TRAITOR AMONG
US . . . . THE DREAD, SO I AM
WRITING TO ALLOW YOU . . . . GETS TO YOU, PLEASE
BE CAREFUL. . . . . . DON'T TELL ANYONE ELSE ABOUT
. . . . BUT, BY KNOWING, YOU MAY AT LEAST WATCH
HIM MORE CLOSELY.
PARTICULARLY, BECAUSE YOU HAVE TRUSTED HIM WITH
TWISTYARD . . . . VERY DANGEROUS. . . . . . . AND HIS
SON, TOO. I HOPE THAT I AM . . . .
EVER YOUR FRIEND, PAP

"Who is it?" asked Boot. "Who is Pap writing about? Did he include the name of the person he suspected to be The Dread?"

"Not that I can see," said Dod, twisting the book every-which-way. "You take a look."

Boot and Dod turned the book back and forth in the light, trying to glean a few more words from the indentations. They particularly hoped to find the name of the person Pap was describing. Unfortunately, it wasn't readable.

"I bet this note cost Pap his life," said Dod, shaking his head.

"You're probably right," agreed Boot. "Somehow, The Dread knew Pap had figured him out, and so he killed him."

"At least this gives us a few clues," said Dod, putting the pieces together in his mind. "The Dread is someone at Twistyard—someone with a son—and—"

"It's Zerny and Jibb!" blurted Boot.

"What? Are you sure?"

"It has to be Zerny," said Boot confidently in his angry voice. "And he's working with his son, Jibb. I remember Bonboo saying that he trusted Zerny with Twistyard. He's been Bonboo's Head Keeper of the Grounds for…well, it seems like forever; and you've seen the way Dilly and Sawny trust him."

"I know," said Dod, nodding.

"Not to mention," blurted Boot, his neck muscles tightening, "is it just a coincidence that Zerny and Jibb are the ones that came back in one piece, announcing Bonboo's death? Why didn't they bring his body back with them, or at least have wounds to prove they fought valiantly? I'd have been bloody and tied to a flat before deserting Bonboo like they did."

"I've been saying it all along," said Dod, tucking his book back into his pocket. "Zerny gives me the creeps. He acts nice and polite around Bonboo and Dilly, but believe me, he was a completely different person when he bailed out with the horses and left us to die. He's definitely the man with the scar, the one that locked the carriage and cut the riggings."

Boot reached up and drew a sword from its sheath.

"Jungo! Jungo! Jungo!" he chanted. "The race is on! We shall make things right before the sun sets today!"

Dod pulled the other sword and echoed Boot's chant. Magic filled the air. The Dread was known, and although he wouldn't be easy to stop, Boot and Dod were ready to confront him.

Song ran faster than usual, almost like he, too, sensed the urgent task that lie ahead. Dod and Boot were on a mission to stop Zerny and Jibb before they finished their dirty deeds at Twistyard; unfortunately, as Song entered the open courtyard, crowds of people, scurrying around the grounds, seemed to indicate that calamity had already struck.

SMELLING TROUBLE

"What's going on?" inquired Dod of three drat soldiers who were heading on horseback away from Twistyard. One of them looked up for a few seconds, but didn't reply.

The entire grounds in front of Twistyard Castle were covered with thousands of people, filling the lawn and spilling onto the streets and between buildings. One cluster, near the main road, had a hundred horses, saddled and waiting, and another five hundred or more harnessed to carriages that bustled with activity.

Boot took his cloak off and covered the two swords that dangled from the front of his saddle as they approached the throng.

"Let's keep our swords a secret," whispered Boot over his shoulder to Dod. He directed Song toward the jam of wagons.

"Boot!" cried a voice from the crowd. It was Youk, wearing his fanciest white hat and a dapper, shiny-buttoned suit, with an expensive, gold-and-ruby-handled rapier sheathed and hung at his side. "I have been looking all over for you. Is that Dod on the back?"

When Song pranced to the side of Youk, Dod wished he could disappear for a few moments or have his regular clothes magically replace his pajamas and torn cloak.

"You aren't planning on going like that, are you?" gasped Youk. His question was directed to both Dod and Boot.

"Going where?" asked Boot, glancing down at his soiled clothes. Dod did a similar assessment of his own horrendous appearance, while casually tugging at the fraying ends of his ripped shroud; it was clownish to wear next to Youk's elegance.

"To High Gate, of course," said Youk, waving his hand officiously in order to direct a carriage past the loggerhead to a spot he designated.

"What—" began Boot, who had hoped the crowds and wagons were people coming to pay respect, not leaving out of fear; however, Youk briskly cut in.

"Haven't you boys heard the news?" he said, looking surprised. "Bonboo was assassinated. Most of the nobles and dignitaries, as well as many of the Coosings and Lings are leaving for High Gate in a few minutes. I assume you will be going with them."

"Oh, we've heard," responded Dod, noticing how the back of Boot's neck was turning red. The pleasantries with Youk were too pleasant for Boot, considering the circumstance. "It's such a nightmare, isn't it?" said Dod, attempting to extract a twinge of sorrow from Youk.

"Right—I know!" said Youk cheerfully. "Look around at all this! I've got to somehow make order out of chaos." He didn't mention Bonboo's passing, which irritated Boot all the more.

"So he's dead and life goes on without him, huh?" added Boot, glowering as he watched Youk imperiously direct another wagon, this time, having them move to a parking slot that was no better than the place they were already occupying.

Youk glanced up and read Boot's face. "Bonboo was the oldest living tredder!" he contended, looking annoyed. "He had a full life—and some beyond that! At this point, there's not much we can do about *him*. We need to think more of what to do about *us*."

"Are you heading up to High Gate with them?" asked Dod, smiling at Youk while carefully poking Boot in the back, reminding Boot to tone it down. Youk was in charge. They didn't need him angry at them.

"No, I'll be overseeing things around here—at least for now," said Youk, blotting sweat from his forehead with an intricately-embroidered handkerchief. "Mercy is still planning on a feast in an hour or so, but you, Dod—you certainly should be heading to High Gate with the rest of this bunch or you won't make it in time for the dropping of the barrier at noon—"

Dod began to explain, when Youk continued, with a raised, authoritative voice, "—you'll miss the honor banquet Commendus is hosting. I've heard he has something special for you. We wouldn't have you miss that, would we?"

Mentioning Commendus reminded Dod of his evening engagement. He had completely forgotten about the award ceremony and the fancy suit that hung in his closet.

"Right," mumbled Dod, flushing pink with embarrassment from the looks he was getting; Eluxa and three of her friends had come along, strolling through the crowd, and had made quite a stir, pointing at his pajamas and laughing.

"Actually," said Boot, "as you can see, we are—well we appear—discombobulated. It's a long story. In a nutshell, we're like this because of a little prank Zerny and Jibb played. Have you seen them?"

Boot knew he was stretching things—in truth, what The Dread had done was not a prank—yet stopping Zerny and Jibb, without the added entanglement of Youk's scrutiny, was top on his list of things to do.

"It's about time someone got you back," chuckled Youk, pointing at Boot's mud-splattered outfit. "Though I must protest, they're not likely the ones. They had the displeasure of accompanying Bonboo—with the attack and all—so after everything they've been through lately, it doesn't seem logical that they would be up to pranks this morning."

"Perhaps," confessed Boot casually. "All the same, have you seen them?"

"I have," said Youk. "About an hour ago. They were consoling Dilly in the Great Hall, eating breakfast. But you really should go and get ready. This group will be leaving for High Gate in the next few minutes. Rush now! I'll attend to Song."

"That's a nice offer," said Boot, looking genuine as he watched Youk take hold of the reins, a matter of inches from the concealed weaponry. It was a disastrous predicament.

"Yes, you're too kind," said Dod, really dying inside and wondering how they would fair when the contraband swords were discovered; he had given up on blushing, even with Eluxa's continued giggling, for fear takes precedence over embarrassment.

"On second thought," added Boot cleverly, gently tugging the leather straps from Youk's hands, "it'll be faster if we tie him to the post by the entrance. But thanks anyway, Youk. You're a fine leader and a great friend."

"Always glad to help," said Youk, tilting his head suspiciously.

Boot didn't waste another second. He had Song cut through the crowd at a quick walk. When Dod and Boot were out of Youk's hearing range, they both sighed heavily.

"That was close," said Boot, wiping sweat from his brow with his sleeve.

"I'd say," added Dod, patting Boot on the shoulder. "His hands were inches from the swords. *You* almost had a lot of explaining to do."

"You mean '*we*,' don't you?" asked Boot.

"Nope. I'd have run like the wind and left you to do the job," said Dod teasingly.

At the castle entrance, Dod tied Song's reins to a metal hitch while Boot carefully wrapped the swords in his cloak. The two boys practically flew to Green Hall when they learned from Toos that Dilly and Sawny were in their bedroom.

"Dilly! Sawny!" called Boot and Dod, banging on the door to the girls' portion of Green Hall. "We've got to talk!"

"We'll be out in a minute," answered Sawny.

The silence only lasted a few seconds before Buck noticed Boot and Dod. "You're back," he called from the entrance to their bedroom.

"Did you sleep well?" responded Boot, smirking.

"Probably better than you," said Buck, laughing at Boot's muddiness and Dod's disrepair. "But I worried all night. I kept listening for a pebble to hit the window."

Dod and Boot walked down the hall and joined Buck in their room. They closed the door and began changing their clothes while explaining the situation.

"I've been wondering about Zerny and Jibb," said Buck when Boot revealed the mystery letter. "It has seemed suspicious to me that they were always near the location of The Dread's strikes. They were at High Gate for the poisoning, but supposedly weren't at the castle, so they didn't get poisoned. And Zerny was driving the wagon when you and Bonboo were almost killed, but he magically rode off unharmed."

"It looks pretty obvious, doesn't it?" said Boot. "And it's a tragedy. You would think you could trust the people closest to you. Zerny's whole clan has worked for Bonboo for so long that they're practically family."

"I've seen it happen before," blurted Dod without thinking.

Boot and Buck turned in surprise. It was then that Dod realized he had only seen it happen on TV, so his statement about witnessing deceitful friendships did seem unusual.

"Well, I've heard stories of people who purposefully got close to someone because he was their enemy," added Dod. "You know, 'keep your friends close and your enemies closer.' That's something people say."

Boot and Buck still looked puzzled.

"At least that's what people commonly say where I'm from."

"No wonder you saw through Zerny's deception right away," said Buck. "We should have listened to you the night you arrived at Twistyard. Around here, it's bad form to attack unless you've declared yourself as an enemy. A man's word is good, foe or friend. I guess that's why The Dread is so unusually successful—his word isn't worth much."

"Knock, knock," said Sawny through the door.

"Just a minute," responded Boot, still searching for a clean shirt. He had neglected his laundry duties for long enough that finding something acceptable was challenging.

"Can I wear this one—please?" groaned Boot to Buck as he

held up Buck's favorite, a royal blue with a fancy, bright-white collar.

"I guess, but you better be careful—no more mud stains!" stressed Buck, regretting it the moment he agreed.

When the door opened, all three boys gasped. Sawny's hair was a mess and her face was red and swollen. She looked worse than ever.

"Haven't you been crying, too?" she asked with a frog in her throat, holding back tears.

"I have," said Boot, trying to sound sympathetic. "We just don't like to let anyone see us cry."

They took turns giving Sawny hugs and telling her that everything was going to be all right. Eventually, Boot managed to ask Sawny where Dilly was, of course assuming she was still in her bedroom.

"She had to hurry off," replied Sawny. "She was late for a private meeting with Zerny."

That was all Sawny had to say. The boys jumped into action. Time for mourning and comforting was over.

"Where's the meeting?" insisted Boot. He grabbed his cloak of swords and tucked them under his arm.

Dod scurried to his bedside and retrieved Pap's sword, which was hidden underneath a pile of clothes.

"What's going on?" asked Sawny.

"We can't explain all of the details right now," exploded Boot, talking ninety-miles-an-hour. "You need to trust us. Zerny is The Dread! Dilly needs to stay as far away from him as she can—and Jibb, too."

"We ate breakfast with them this morning—"

"I know he seems nice," blurted Boot, "but it's a cover. Trust me."

Dod handed his sword to Boot, who wrapped it tightly in his cloak with the others.

"Please help us save her. Where were they planning on meeting?"

"Down by the old dock," said Sawny dismally. "—behind the castle, I think. He said he had something to tell her that would raise her spirits."

"Sure he does," muttered Boot sarcastically. "That's a bunch of boosap!"

The three boys left Green Hall in a flash. They ran so quickly, hoping to catch up with Dilly, that a clump of drat soldiers suspected something and insisted the boys stop. And when they didn't, the soldiers began to chase after them. It was a debacle of sorts. If the boys paused long enough to explain, the soldiers would likely lock them up, both for breaking orders and concealing contraband swords; but if they continued running, the next band of soldiers would stop them for sure, even if the ones trailing directly behind couldn't catch up.

"Quick, over here," ordered Boot to Dod and Buck. He led them off the main hall and toward the library.

"What are we doing?" asked Buck desperately.

"I have a plan. Don't worry," said Boot.

When they entered the library, running like mad, Boot firmly shut the giant door and propped his foot against its base.

"Put your weight into it," he commanded, leaning in.

Dod and Buck followed, pushing with all of their might—which was necessary, considering the drat soldiers on the other side were giving it their best efforts, too.

When it seemed the soldiers were about to win the push-a-war, Boot took his bundle of swords and clanked them against the lock.

"There, it's locked up. They'll need to go around," said Boot loudly.

Buck started to let go of the door when Boot shook his head profusely.

"Keep holding on," he whispered.

After a few seconds, the pressure from the other side of the door ended. The bluff had worked.

Boot then led them up a small staircase, two floors, and wound them around and through a catacomb of bookshelves. In a distant corner there was a door that opened up to a small hall, lined with doors.

"And I thought I had seen every inch of this place," said Buck in amazement. "You're the best, Boot. How did you know about this spot?"

"I occasionally read," he said.

Boot counted doors quietly under his breath. When he got to thirteen, he grabbed for the handle. Inside was a supply closet, filled with book-cleaning instruments, tools for fixing shelves, and piles of shelf parts. The only light in the room entered from the hall through the doorway.

Buck and Dod waited while Boot went in.

"You want us to hide?" asked Dod, confused. "What about Dilly? We should at least try to reach her, and if the drat soldiers stop us, we'll convince them that they should accompany us to the old dock. Don't you think so, Boot? We don't have time to waste in this closet."

Boot held up one finger and continued to search the room. He obviously knew something the others didn't. After pacing back and forth, staring at the floor, he got on his knees and felt the boards carefully.

"Here it is. I knew they didn't get rid of it."

Dod continued to hold the door open, for light, while Buck helped Boot slide a heavy cabinet out of the way. A three-foot square of the flooring came up easily.

"A secret passage," mumbled Dod, feeling guilty that he had begun to doubt Boot's motive for spending time in the closet.

"Not exactly," responded Boot. "But it will do." He took a large coil of rope from a shelf in the corner, grunting as he hefted it, tied one end to the door handle, and threw the rest down the hole.

"Ladies first," joked Boot, pointing for his brother to enter the shaft.

"Then you ought to be getting along while I wait," suggested Buck.

When neither of them budged, Dod broke the stalemate; he shut the door and made his way to the hole, holding the rope for direction. The room became dark, with only a streak of dim light, leaking in through a crack.

At the bottom, piles of rotting garbage were waiting. Buck and Dod descended rapidly, landing on their knees in a massive vat of waste. However, Boot knew better, so he climbed down carefully at the end.

From the garbage room it was easy to exit into the front field. A large metal door opened up to a stone patio, where a monstrous fire pit filled the middle section and a pleasant-smelling, flowering hedge surrounded the exterior. From there, a little path wound through the thicket of bushes and led straight to the bustling, grassy courtyard.

Their timing was not a minute too soon!

"Dilly!" yelled Boot across the crowd. He had spotted her right away, but cutting through the mob of people, without losing sight of her, was going to be difficult. "We need to talk with you. Dilly. Dilly! DILLY!"

There were hundreds of people chatting, between Boot and Dilly, so it didn't matter how loud Boot got, the chatter was still louder.

"I don't want to lose her," he said to Buck and Dod, pointing her out. "One of us should stand here on this rock, keeping an eye on her, while the other two go and retrieve her."

"I'll stay," volunteered Buck, not particularly wanting to fight his way through the noisy crowd.

"Okay," agreed Boot. "—and hold these," he added, handing Buck the cloak filled with swords. "If she moves, point in the direction she's headed."

Dod and Boot merged with the sea of people and hurried to catch Dilly. It could have been more difficult, but they were lucky. Dilly hadn't gone far before she was greeted by Sirlonk, who stopped her momentarily; and by the time she was ready to continue, Boot and Dod had caught up.

"Where's your suit?" asked Sirlonk, looking down judgingly at Dod. He particularly seemed fixated on the messy part of Dod's pants, where the rotten garbage had left a stinky grime.

"I'm not sure if I'm going to be able to make it tonight," answered Dod. "Boot and I have some things we still need to do."

"What a shame," said Sirlonk. "Of course, I understand it's hardly a time to be celebrating. I would stay here myself, to join you in mourning, if it weren't for my responsibilities. Youk's insisting I safely deliver these guests to High Gate."

Sirlonk pointed over his shoulder at a large crowd of dignitaries and nobles. Saluci's uncle Neadrou happened to look up, so he tipped his hat and rolled the ends of his slightly-graying brown mustache, curling it upward on both sides.

"If I'm to spend the night at High Gate," said Sirlonk, in a melancholy voice, "I suppose I'll attend Commendus's banquet, though it won't be much of a celebration for me. I've got dozens of memories of Bonboo in that palace. Are you sure you won't join me, Dod? I'm terribly lonely mourning Bonboo's passing by myself, and Juny's set on staying here. You should go and receive your award. I'll accompany you while we mourn together."

"I've got to excuse myself," muttered Dilly, interrupting Sirlonk's request to Dod. She didn't act like her usual self. It was clear she was overcome with grief.

Dod turned to stop her when Boot put his hand down and signaled that he should wait. Their eyes momentarily met, communicating the plan.

"Sirlonk," said Boot in a confidential voice, looking over his shoulder to make sure Dilly was out of hearing range, "Would you please take Dilly with you to High Gate?"

"I couldn't take her right now. Look at how grief-stricken she is. The ride alone would be difficult for her. And the party tonight—well, it's more than she could handle right now. The best thing for her is to stay here and get some rest. After a couple of days, I'm sure she'll come around."

"No Sirlonk, you don't understand," said Boot. "I need you to take care of Dilly for the next little while. She could be in real danger! If you ever had the slightest warm feeling toward Bonboo, you would honor his memory by protecting Dilly. Please!"

"I think she would be safe enough here with all the drat soldiers around. You're overreacting."

"Maybe we are," said Dod, "but Dilly is so important to all of us and to the continuance of Twistyard, we want her to receive the best protection; and you're the best, Sirlonk. Please."

Sirlonk straightened up and smiled when hearing his praise. It was a statement he didn't plan on refuting, and so out of arrogance he allowed himself to become encumbered with the task.

"You do have a point. I am the best," said Sirlonk, patting his sword Jilser. "I guess I should protect Dilly. She's practically my daughter."

"And if it were anyone else," added Boot quickly, "she'd decline. I'm sure you're clever enough to convince her she should go with you."

"Yes. I'll do it," said Sirlonk proudly, marching off in the direction Dilly had gone. Boot and Dod followed at his heels, hoping he would be successful; and when they caught up to Dilly, they weren't disappointed.

"Dilly, if I may have a word with you," said Sirlonk carefully. "I should be honored if you would mourn with me. Let's remember Bonboo for the great man he was. Accompany me to High Gate, where I'm told Commendus will be rendering tribute to him at the grand banquet. I'm hardly one for parties at a time like this; nevertheless, we need to do our part—yes our duty—to give Bonboo the proper respect he deserves!"

"I'm sorry, Sirlonk," said Dilly somberly, beginning to turn around, "I need to meet someone for a few minutes, and by the time I'm done, you'll be gone."

"No, I'll go with you; and when you're done, we can leave for High Gate. So who were you planning on meeting?"

"Zerny."

"Aren't you running late?" asked Sirlonk.

"Yes, I am, but I'm sure he understands."

"Well, My Dearest Dilly," said Sirlonk patronizingly, putting his hand on her shoulder. "Of course he understands why you couldn't make the meeting."

"I'll try to hurry," said Dilly, starting to tear up.

"It's too late—I saw him ride off on his horse, down by the lake shore. I suppose he couldn't wait. You can talk with him when we get back, assuming he's not at High Gate this evening. If I know Zerny, and I think I do, he's planning on going to High Gate. You'll see. Perhaps he could hitch his horse to my wagon for part of the ride and you could speak with him while journeying."

"Dod and I will get on a horse and go fetch him for you, Dilly," said Boot.

"But it was supposed to be a private, secret kind of meeting."

"Why, yes," blurted Sirlonk. "I wouldn't dream of being part of your special conversation. He probably wants to share with you his personal memories of Bonboo, or something tender like that. I'll tell you what, though, if you'll do me the favor of coming along—and you'd be saving my life, I really mean it—I'll ride up front with the driver and clear the cart for you and Zerny, all the way to High Gate if you wish. You could talk with him and, when you're done, honor Bonboo at the banquet tonight. Besides, I know you'd feel better in a new outfit from Commendus."

"And Sirlonk will let you wear a sword," added Dod spontaneously, trying to seal the deal. "Please go with him to High Gate. I'd feel safer knowing you were there, armed and ready, when I accept my commendation. After Bonboo's assassination, it seems an honor banquet, hosted by Commendus, would be a prime location to have a chance meeting with The Dread. Regardless, I'm confident The Dread will be revealed today."

Mentioning The Dread dried Dilly's tears. Something sparked inside her. She, like Boot, had a feeling of desire for jungo, and it couldn't be ignored.

"Do you really think The Dread will attend Commendus's banquet?" asked Dilly.

"I don't know about that," said Sirlonk, looking embarrassed by Dod's assertions.

"I do!" said Dod. "I feel it inside. It's hard to explain. Maybe it won't happen at the banquet, but something's going to happen—and soon."

Dod wasn't lying to Dilly. When the moment came, he spoke what he felt, though it also fit the purpose of getting Dilly to agree to be watched closely by an expert swordsman. At the same time, Dod was hoping he could help Boot and Buck capture Zerny and Jibb fast enough to deliver them to the proper authorities at High Gate, which meant moving quickly if they were going to arrive before the dropping of the barrier.

Within a few minutes, Dod and Sirlonk had escorted Dilly to Sirlonk's carriage and secured her within, while Boot went to retrieve Song and Buck.

"Promise me you'll leave a message for Sawny," said Dilly through the window to Dod. "I know she still wouldn't agree to go—she mourns best with her books—regardless, she should be informed of my whereabouts."

"I'll try to tell her myself, and if not, I'll at least pass the word along," promised Dod.

"Don't forget your suit," added Sirlonk, waving to Dod as he climbed up the front of his wagon; however, before Dod had walked far enough to join Boot and Buck, Sirlonk slipped up behind him and added a few more messages, outside of Dilly's view.

"See Dod, I am the best!" he gloated. "And if you don't make it in time for the banquet, shall I receive your commendation for you?"

"I guess so," replied Dod. "Just make sure you keep a close eye on Dilly *all* of the time—especially if Zerny is around!"

"Zerny? I hardly think Zerny will be making it to High Gate. Don't you suppose he'll be too busy waiting by the old dock—that foolish drat!"

"You didn't see him riding by the lake?"

"Goodness, my boy! Do you always need to be so nit-picky? He and Jibb passed me on their way to the old dock, and they were riding on horseback, so I think it's fair to say I saw them riding down by the lake."

"Oh, I see. You stretched things to convince Dilly."

"It was your idea!" snapped Sirlonk angrily. "I'm just doing you a favor. Some people are never grateful."

"No, I didn't mean it like that."

"Well, if you do happen to see Zerny or Jibb," added Sirlonk, "let's keep it a secret that Dilly's with me. I don't trust them right now."

Sirlonk hurried back through the crowd, ducking down as he approached his wagon, to elude Dilly's view, and then started a chain reaction of movement by ordering the other carriages to load up and drive.

Shortly after Sirlonk's wagon pulled out, Boot and Buck rode up.

"Climb on," said Buck, lowering his arm to help Dod.

"Three on one horse sounds impractical."

"Not for Song," responded Buck, "especially considering the short distance. Horses cut through crowds better than people. Besides, while you and Boot were helping Dilly into the cart, I saw two men in the distance, on horses, riding away from the dock. They were probably Zerny and Jibb."

At the water's edge, two sets of fresh tracks followed the beach line of Lake Mauj, confirming Buck's claim.

"Let's check the dock first," said Dod, countering Boot's attempt to direct Song to follow the two horsemen.

"We have. It's right there. I don't see anyone."

Boot pointed at two hundred yards of half-rotten wood, meandering in and out of the lapping water. Not a single boat was docked. It was easy to see that nobody was near the lake.

"Don't you think we should check a little?" asked Dod, pointing at a portion of the dock that merged with the castle; some parts were concealed from view.

"Why would he be waiting up there?" asked Boot, getting impatient.

"I don't know. Give me a few minutes," said Dod. He hopped off the back of the horse and asked for his sword.

"Here you go," said Buck, passing it down. "Hurry! We need to get moving if we hope to catch up. Song's strong, but he'll tire quickly if he's carrying all three of us."

"Maybe you could go and get your horse while I'm looking around," suggested Dod. He knew Boot and Buck were eager to start tracking, yet something about the dock begged for attention.

"It's not an option," responded Buck. "Youk borrowed my

horse and Sawny's too, to help pull carriages to High Gate. The barns are practically empty right now; and as you know, Boot's horse hasn't been returned. We're lucky as it is to have the use of Dilly's horse today."

"I'll hurry," said Dod, feeling apologetic for slowing the others down. He wouldn't have even asked to check if it weren't for the haunting impressions he felt about the location.

On the dock, the wood under Dod's feet creaked and squeaked as he walked across the old planks. Years of stormy waves and sand had aided the dilapidation to the extent that it was obvious why Bonboo had constructed a new shipyard, a mile up the shore.

The back of the castle was much different than Dod had expected; it was actually a large stone that towered upward out of the sand, forming a cliff-like, thirty-story wall. It was a formidable bulwark against occasional big waves on Lake Mauj and hid much of the building. The natural setting was only interrupted by a stairway in the middle at the base, which led from the rotting dock to a sheltered cavern. It appeared to be an entrance to the deepest basement of the castle, or possibly caves below it.

"Now that's a hideout if I've ever seen a hideout," mumbled Dod to himself. He made his way toward it, only veering off course slightly to get a closer look at something red that was stuck to the dock and blowing in the morning breeze. It was an old, discarded, piece of a torn shirt, pinned down by two heavy stones; and written on the fabric was the following message:

Dilly,
We're sorry we couldn't wait. The matter we are attending
to is most urgent. We'll track you down, no matter where

you are, the moment we get back. Please try not to shed
tears, for they are certainly in vain.
Your friends,
Zerny & Jibb

Dod held the cloth in his hands and read the note over and over. By the third reading, his ears began to turn crimson with anger. Even though the words sounded congenial, the message was honest and evil. They had every intention of tracking Dilly down; and crying about it, or about Bonboo, wouldn't do any good—so they thought!

"Boot! Buck!" shouted Dod, turning back to his friends, but they were out of hearing range and riding away!

It was disappointing to be left at the lonely dock; nevertheless, it consoled Dod to know that his friends had a better chance of catching Zerny and Jibb without him—less weight on poor Song. Not to mention, it was just as well that they not depend on him as a swordsman.

"Good luck," said Dod into the wind as he watched Song trot the shoreline. Before long, they were out of sight.

Other than the soft whistling of the morning breeze and the musical sloshing of water under the dock, everything was quiet. Not even the slightest peep of a human voice could be heard, which was surprising considering the mobs of people filling the front courtyards—or at least they had been when Dod left them. Still, nobody was visible from the secluded water's edge.

"What would you do, Pap?" asked Dod to the sky, and the wind, and the rocks, and the gentle waves. A response didn't come bellowing back, but Dod felt peaceful enough to stroll up and down the planks, talking about his circumstance with himself and thinking of what to do next. In the end, he decided to return to the castle for Mercy's feast, which wasn't a terribly difficult decision with his empty stomach growling loudly.

The Great Hall, where the feast was to be held, was positioned on the farthest end of the castle; and by following the road, which meandered around thickets of bushes, the distance was more than twice what it would be as the crow flies. Assessing the situation, Dod decided to utilize the spare candles in his pocket and attempt the basement entrance.

When he had climbed to the top of the worn staircase, no doors met him. Instead, a vast cavern opened upward, going deeper than the light of his candle; and the wide antechamber was lined with side corridors, branching off of the main.

"Hello," called Dod.

"Hello, hello, hello," echoed back.

"Is anyone in there?"

"...in there...in there."

It was almost foolish to ask. The darkness of the cave seemed to explain perfectly that Dod was all alone. Suddenly, a draft of air blew in his face and the smell carried him away. Without question, this was the spot he had been looking for. This was where The Dread was going to do great mischief. This was the place Dod had seen in his flashes. He knew it, and the smell proved it.

Curiosity drove him into the cave, deeper and deeper, searching for anything unusual; and the question kept coming to his mind, 'Why would The Dread be interested in anything down here?'

The main cavern had a dirt and rubbish-rock base at the opening; however, fifty feet inside, the floor turned to neatly fitted stones, like the castle, and the walls were structured with columns and support beams.

"This must be part of the basement," whispered Dod. But it didn't make sense. With Boot and the others, Dod had thoroughly searched the basement, and they had never entered the portion he was seeing.

"Or is this below the basement?" he mumbled. "Perhaps. The Dread could strike down here—like right here," said Dod, patting a monstrous column. "If this tumbled, it couldn't be good for the castle above."

Another draft of air filled his nostrils; it gave him goosebumps until the hair on his arms prickled like the spines on a cactus. Glimpses of destruction ran through his mind. He could see piles of fallen beams, mingled with rock and debris, and the broken components in his mind matched perfectly the well-set walls around him.

"Hello," Dod yelled into the darkness.

"Hello, hello, hello," echoed back. It wasn't as loud of an echo as it had been at the opening of the cavern, but it still revealed that the wide hall went on for some distance.

A muffled noise, barely audible, continued after the echo ended. Dod probably would have missed it all together if it weren't for his close attention to the tail end of his own echo.

"Hello," Dod yelled again. This time he yelled even louder than he had before; and feeling uncomfortable about being alone, Dod clenched his sword and made ready for the strangest of encounters. Yet despite preparing himself mentally, what he finally saw, when he ventured down the hall, was unexpected. He had certainly been smelling trouble!

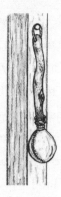

THE RESCUE

"He's already struck!" gasped Dod as the light of his candle flickered against a distant backdrop of rubble. "No wonder Zerny and Jibb felt pressure to leave in a hurry."

Dod moved quickly down the hall to where twisted beams and rocks blocked one of the side corridors. The ceiling and walls had collapsed, completely filling the entrance and spilling over into the larger passageway; halfway up the pile of debris, Boot's bag was positioned, just as Dod had seen it in his mind—or so he thought. When he climbed the wreckage to have a closer look, the bag was empty, and it wasn't Boot's.

"Hello," shouted Dod. "Is anyone in there?"

This time, instead of hearing an echo, he completely tuned his ears to a faint cry for help coming from behind the barricade.

"I'll get you out. Don't worry," yelled Dod frantically. However, after he had spoken, he realized the extent of the task; it was a mountain of large pieces, the smallest of which were far too heavy for Dod to move on his own.

"Wait here. I'm going for help," he said to the mound. He felt foolish after he had spoken. The phrase 'wait here' was ridiculous since the people who were trapped within had no alternative but to wait. Regardless, Dod turned and ran back the way he had come, not feeling nearly as adventurous as before.

While jogging up the road he had ridden down with Boot and Buck, Dod found a bushy, brown thicket of Hercoil Tangle shrubs and took the opportunity to conceal his sword. It was perfect timing, since shortly thereafter, he bumped into three drat soldiers patrolling the lane.

"I found a collapse in the cave above the old dock," said Dod, breathing heavy from running. "Some people are trapped inside, and the wreckage is big enough that it will take a dozen horses or hundreds of men to move it."

"Did you see it happen?" asked one of the soldiers, looking at Dod suspiciously. Another drat, with a shaggy beard and beady, distrustful eyes, clutched the hilt of his blade and waited for Dod's response.

"No, but if we free the people inside, we'll know more," said Dod, panting. He accompanied the soldiers to the Great Hall where he found it was full. Despite the exodus, many remained at Twistyard, enjoying Mercy's feast.

It didn't take long before a group of nearly two hundred men, equipped with candles and ropes, were following Dod back to the cavern. All of the soldiers, stationed at Twistyard, went on highest alert, preparing for an attack.

Youk dropped everything else, on his lengthy, newly-inherited list of duties, to personally oversee the effort. As he followed Dod to the rubble, he explained that the grotto had been used for a number of different purposes over the years, but lately had only served as a large closet for stockpiling emergency supplies. It was baffling to him why anyone would have interest in the location, which led him to believe that the debris had to have come from an accidental collapse.

Once in the cave, many lit candles and the chatter of friendly companionship made Dod feel better about the circumstance. He knew, as a team, they were going to save the trapped people. Everything felt right. As a matter of fact, Dod became so inspired by the atmosphere of camaraderie that he almost told Youk about Zerny and Jibb, though at the very moment when he opened his mouth to explain, something in the back of his mind stopped him; it was a murky feeling of uncertainty.

"You were saying?" prodded Youk eagerly. He momentarily turned away from directing the affairs of the rescue to give Dod his full attention, sensing Dod was holding back important information.

Dod's insides ached to share his suspicions. He wanted to have as many people working on stopping Zerny and Jibb as had been summoned to dig out the trapped people.

"I was just going to say," said Dod, stumbling along, "that it seems interesting…that something like this would happen today." He fabricated on-the-fly a different answer to replace what he had almost shared. He silently hoped it was good enough to pass Youk's scrutiny.

"You mean after Bonboo's assassination?" asked Youk, urging Dod to continue with his thought.

"Yes…I guess that's what I mean," said Dod haltingly, looking away from Youk's probing eyes.

"It's a good thing you…*happened* upon this, isn't it?" said Youk, still waiting for Dod to explain himself. "Now tell me, why were you down here instead of careening to High Gate?"

For the first time in the discussion, Dod realized that Youk suspected his involvement in the collapse was more than as a passerby. "I, uh…thought this was a shortcut to the banquet," answered Dod. It was the truth, even if it lacked his reason for being at the dock in the first place rather than suiting up and heading to Commendus's engagement, as Youk had ordered him to do.

"Everyone, take the line and pull," yelled a drat soldier, who had accepted the responsibility of coordinating the manual labor. Dod conveniently left the conversation with Youk where it was and joined vigorously in pulling the giant rope.

"Heave, pull…Heave, pull…Heave, pull," called out the line of people who were drawing the cord, synchronizing their tugging efforts by chanting. Bit by bit, a colossal wooden post emerged from the rubble, knocking stone blocks around. After it completely dislodged, a cry of victory roared through the cave.

"We have more where that came from," ordered the head soldier. "Tie the rope to another one."

Dod stole a glance over his shoulder and noticed Youk was still watching him. It was disconcerting.

The rescue process continued for hours of heaving and pulling. When each object was removed from the pile, celebrating would ensue, followed by a moment of silence—listening to see if the captives were free.

After three hours, Sawny appeared, looking much nicer than she had earlier that morning and carrying a leather bag.

"Mercy suggested you might be hungry," she said to Dod. "Why don't you take a break and eat?" She pulled back the top flap and revealed a banquet feast in the satchel. It effectively tempted Dod away from the rope. The smell alone was heaven sent.

"Thanks. I'm famished," admitted Dod, wiping his dirty hands on his pants. His arms trembled from fatigue and hunger.

"So, what's happened here?" asked Sawny curiously. She appeared in much better spirits than before, and her face was less swollen.

Dod looked around at the crowd—especially Youk, who buoyantly critiqued the effort, while keeping his white gloves clean—and decided to take his lunch break outside.

"We're still trying to figure it out," responded Dod after he and Sawny were out of the cave and, more importantly, out of the other people's hearing range. "Boot and Buck are tracking down Zerny and Jibb. They went up the coast. I'm starting to get worried about them because they haven't returned yet."

Sawny looked out at Lake Mauj. The water stretched for as far as the eye could see, with a few islands dotting the shimmering glass, like low-hanging clouds. She took a seat on the steps and turned back toward Dod, who was still eyeing where Boot and Buck had disappeared, as if he expected them to materialize if only he gazed harder.

"Do you really think all of this was caused by Zerny and Jibb?" asked Sawny. She pulled Dod's lunch out of the bag and arranged it next to her. He quickly plopped down and reached for the food.

"Maybe," said Dod, pausing to take a hungry bite of his steak-and-onion sandwich, followed by gulping a swig of grape juice. "They were down here this morning—that's a fact!"

Sawny looked nervous. "Regardless of who did this," she said, "Dilly's not trapped in there, is she? Have you seen her lately?"

Dod felt stupid; he hadn't remembered to tell Sawny of Dilly's message, even after promising.

"She decided to accompany Sirlonk to High Gate for the

party," he began apologetically. "I meant to tell you earlier—and then this happened. They plan on honoring your grandpa tonight. Sirlonk begged her and she went along."

"I thought she'd decide to go," said Sawny. "Sirlonk's so persuasive."

"You knew Sirlonk wanted her to go?" sputtered Dod, choking on his food.

"Oh, yes," said Sawny, picking at Dod's lunch until she settled on his dessert. She sampled a corner of the hand-sized blueberry tart and smiled sweetly. When Dod continued to stare, pensively, she went on. "He woke us up early this morning, banging on our door, and told us about Bonboo...then he tried to insist we go with him to High Gate."

"Really?"

"Yes. He was quite bent out of shape when Dilly said she wouldn't—he rubbed it in about his favor last night."

"What favor?" asked Dod, feeling his insides lurch uncomfortably; and it wasn't his lunch.

"Sirlonk twisted the rules to tell us what was going on—that Bonboo was missing and that they were going to look for him. It was a secret."

Dod remembered there had been five riders at the barn the night before and therefore asked eagerly, "Who went along?"

"Sirlonk, and Youk, and...let's see," said Sawny, pausing to recall who else had gone. While she was thinking, she stole another taste of his pastry.

"There was one more...who was it?" asked Dod impatiently. His heart began to pound.

"Actually, there were two: Tinja and Strat."

Dod quieted down and ate his food as he thought the puzzle

over. Something wasn't right. Four men had gone out looking for Bonboo, however, only three of them had returned with Zerny and Jibb. That left one of them missing.

"HOOOORAAH!" rumbled from inside the cavern. Dod and Sawny jumped up and ran to see what had happened.

To everyone's great astonishment, Doochi came crawling out of a newly-made breach in the mound. He was dirty, whiskery, and looked greatly disheveled.

"Doochi?" said Youk, raising his eyebrows in amazement. "When did you get here?"

"I-I don't know what you mean," said Doochi, scratching at his matted, filthy hair. He squinted as he surveyed the crowd of rescuers.

"When did you return to Twistyard?" responded Youk, dumbfounded, looking at Doochi like he was a ghost.

"I never left!" he said adamantly.

Youk blinked in disbelief.

"I've been trapped behind there for who knows how long—" insisted Doochi, pointing at the remaining heap of rubble. "It's been since whenever I disappeared. I've lost track."

Youk's looks weren't the only ones that conveyed doubt, so Doochi explained, all the while holding back tears, "Days and nights jumble together when you're trapped alone like that—I mean, everybody, look at me!"

His appearance was the most convincing piece of evidence he had; his clothes were worn ragged and grimy to the extent that they barely hung on him; and his pathetic, spotty facial hair clumped haphazardly like a molting chicken that just emerged from a dust bath; and his head was crowned with such a horrendous 'do' that it would likely need to be shaved clean before hoping to grow anything worth leaving; and his eyes alone, nearly drugged with the fullest gamut of emotions, seemed to prove he was telling the truth.

One Rauling, a tidy, sharp-dressed boy rushed to Doochi's side and exclaimed, "I told them all you hadn't written the note; your handwriting's far worse than that." He stayed a few paces back, not wanting to dirty himself, but appeared to care.

"Note?" asked Doochi. "What do you mean, Remmy?"

"The note you supposedly left, telling us all you had quit the Coosings," said the boy, taking a step back; he could smell Doochi's poor hygiene.

"I wouldn't quit the Coosings!" retorted Doochi, furrowing his brow. "Sawb really stretched when he appointed me last year—my family, you know; we're not chauss or toting gold. It's taken me fifteen years as a Rauling to earn my way in. What kind of sick person would prank a note like that?"

Doochi paused, then his face lit up; he knew what had happened.

"I have some important news for Pap!" he exploded, talking so quickly that he fell over his own words. "Where is he?"

"Don't you know what happened to Pap?" asked Youk, prodding more with his eyes than he did with his questions.

"No! They didn't, did they?" blurted Doochi, looking devastated. "Was Pap poisoned?"

"He was," said Youk, approaching the trembling boy. "What do you know of it?"

The smaller conversations in the cavern went silent. Remmy and the other rescuers looked spellbound, hanging on Doochi's every word.

"I was exploring down here one night, after curfew,"

confessed Doochi, not afraid to face Youk squarely. "And you may punish me as much as you want for doing it—but while I was in here, searching among the supplies, I overheard mumbled parts of a conversation. At length, I realized two or three men were discussing how to poison Pap. They had already tried twice and failed. It startled me to hear it; and unfortunately, I bumped a rack of metal hitches to the ground. When the men came running, I hid in the back of this hall, under a pile of blankets on a shelf."

"Were you alone?" asked Youk.

"Yes. It has been driving me crazy. I lay still, under the blankets, until a crashing sound shook the hall; and when I finally dared to crawl out, the corridor was pitch-black and the air was filled with dust. I was trapped."

"And you survived all this time?" replied Youk with a heavy dose of skepticism in his voice. Even if he believed the boy, he was going to make him earn clemency.

"I certainly did," said Doochi, nodding his head and gazing about at the crowd of mesmerized listeners. "The hall's probably three hundred feet deep, thirty feet wide, fifteen feet high, and lined with survival supplies on every shelf: I'm physically fine, it's my brain that's nearly bonkers. And ten lifetimes from now is too soon to drink apple juice or chew a beef strip again."

Doochi leaned in, close enough to rap Youk on the shoulder, and added bravely, "Bonboo should look into a bit of variety with the supplies."

The cave rumbled with subdued chuckles.

"Right," said Youk slowly. He searched for any sign of intentional deception.

"So, tell me what happened to Pap?" asked Doochi. "Did you catch them?"

"He was poisoned while en route to Soosh," said Youk, backing away from Doochi as Remmy had done.

Dod and Sawny stared in horror: Doochi had never gone home—which made Sirlonk a big liar!

Youk continued to question Doochi, with the crowd watching intently, but not Dod; he bent over and studied the ground, fearing he was possibly about to retch. He didn't want to hear or see the truth—not after personally instigating Dilly's trip to High Gate—however, the clues were staring him in the face: Half buried in the rubble, right between Dod's legs, was a shiny button bearing Sirlonk's family insignia!

"Sirlonk!" whispered Dod to Sawny. He groaned while holding the proof in his hand. "Dilly's in danger! We need to warn her!"

The rescuers were so driven by their curiosity for Doochi's comments that they didn't even notice when Sawny and Dod moved to leave, including Youk. Once again, Dod wanted to get other people involved, and Sawny certainly did, too, but a muggy, suffocating feeling set in the moment they tried, which sent them racing away to solve the problem on their own.

"I guess Pap was wrong about his suspicions, unless Zerny and Jibb are working with Sirlonk," said Dod.

"Why do you say that?" puffed Sawny, trying to keep up as they ran.

"He wrote a note, and it mentioned The Dread having a son—possibly working with him."

"Sirlonk has a son," said Sawny, her light-brown curls bouncing with each leap.

"Not at Twistyard," said Dod confidently, keeping the pace fast.

"Yes he does: Tonnis."

Dod glanced sideways, shocked.

"You're kidding me! Tonnis is Sirlonk's son?"

"Yup," said Sawny, puffing heavier. "You'd never guess by the way Tonnis acts. He's probably the only decent occupant of Raul Hall I can think of; 'course Doochi's had a good enough shake down that he may be nicer now—assuming Sawb lets him back in."

Dod slowed his pace to a jog and then stopped. He looked up at the sun, high in the sky, and frustration filled his eyes.

"We've already missed the dropping of the barrier, haven't we?" groaned Dod.

"I'm afraid so," said Sawny, doubling over to catch her breath. "But that's not exactly the end of it," she added, peering up at Dod, who was also winded; he grimaced and stretched like a runner who had just lost a race.

"What do you mean?" he asked, coughing to clear his dry throat.

"Well, there's always an exception to rules," said Sawny, holding back a smirk. The way she said it proved she was Dilly's sister.

"I happen to know of an exception created for dropping the barrier," she continued matter-of-factly. "I read over it once with Bonboo."

Dod looked at Sawny with hopeful eyes.

"I can't guarantee anything," Sawny added quickly. "It may not work for us; and even if it does, they could throw us in jail for doing it."

"That sounds exciting!" said Dod. Incarceration was preferred to the mental agony he was stewing in over accidentally sending

Dilly off with The Dread. The guilt was written on his face and ate at his insides; he couldn't imagine thinking of anything else until Dilly was safe.

"If we dong the waiting bell and signal properly with mirrors," said Sawny, looking into the air, "the guards have instructions to do an emergency dropping of the barrier—unless other circumstances prevent them. But we'll still need to make it before the sun sets."

"We can do that," said Dod.

"Of course, only Bonboo should be signaling," said Sawny cringingly. "—which he won't be—but I am his great-granddaughter. I could tell them that I have an urgent message for Commendus, and once I've informed him of Dilly's danger, even if they had to lock us up, Commendus could stop Sirlonk."

"Don't forget I'm a specially invited guest at Commendus's palace for tonight's honor banquet," said Dod, beaming. "That should make the guards listen to us. If we're dressed the part and I show them my invitation, don't you think they'd let us in?"

"It's at least worth a shot," urged Sawny, gulping. "If Sirlonk is The Dread—"

"Oh, he is. I'm sure of it now," interrupted Dod.

"A few minuets ago you said it was Zerny," replied Sawny, still holding some doubt.

"I know, and maybe he and Jibb are somehow involved, but Sirlonk had to be the instigator of Doochi's trapping. I've got his button right here." Dod held it up. "This implicates him in Pap's poisoning, which means he—"

"And he totally lied to us about talking with Doochi," blurted Sawny, beginning to get hot in the head. "Not to mention, lying does seem to be a theme with Sirlonk. After all, he had no problem breaking his word last night to provide me and Dilly with the latest news on Bonboo's circumstance."

"He's evil. I've sensed it all along," said Dod.

"You have not," snapped Sawny, shoving him off the trail into a Gazandra bush; the needled branches looked prickly, but were softer than pine.

"Yes I have," insisted Dod, crawling out.

"At least Sirlonk seems to fancy Dilly," said Sawny gingerly, poking her foot at a slumping, grayish weed. She was trying to stay positive. "I don't think he would hurt her."

"Did you think he would poison Pap or kill Bonboo?" blurted Dod. "He's already acquired Higga's half of the map to Bonboo's secrets, and he still needs Dilly's. What are the chances of her giving it up without a fight?"

"None, if she's still breathing," groaned Sawny anxiously.

Dod and Sawny picked up their pace, hurrying to retrieve Dod's sword and suit, and to find mirrors to signal with and a horse to borrow. They flew through the first three items, but the fourth was practically impossible. Nobody's horse remained at Twistyard. In total, over nine hundred of them had left for High Gate that morning, most of which were temporarily taken to pull carriages.

With little time to spare, Dod suggested they stop asking for permission and start searching the barns. " — even if there's only one horse remaining," he said confidently, "we'll take it. Dilly's life is at stake."

The first four barns Dod and Sawny looked in were completely empty, as were a half-dozen fenced fields that usually brimmed with mares. It was disheartening. The rejections from everyone had been honest excuses, for all of the horses were gone.

Dod reassured Sawny that the last barn would have at least one. He knew it. Twistyard wouldn't sit without a messenger horse. It would be too imprudent; however, shockingly, the final stalls were as empty as the others in the previous barns.

"This is outrageous!" said Dod in frustration. He walked over to the stall where Dilly usually kept Song and flopped down on the soft straw in the back. "I can't believe all of the horses are gone. It's crazy. It makes you wonder what might be coming. How long would the drat forces last against an assault without being able to send for reinforcements? Why would Youk allow it?"

"Maybe he's involved?" offered Sawny. She was starting to tear up; and logically so, for it seemed everyone in the world was out to get them.

"Wait! That's it! Would Youk give up his favorite horse?" said Dod, remembering the treachery of Coyote Trail. "Last time he loaned her out, things didn't go very well. If he were trying to hide her—make sure no one would touch her—where would he put her?"

Sawny thought for a minute and then led Dod toward the little, overgrown field, hidden by trees, where Youk had kept his mare out to pasture the night before.

It appeared deserted. The bushes, weeds, and young trees towered twelve feet in many places, making a thorough search impossible from the fence line.

Dod and Sawny split up and scoured the brush, jogging from one open pocket to the next. The pasture had been abandoned for long enough that it appeared more wild than fallow.

Finally, Dod let out a cry. "Over here!" he yelled with excitement. "Come over here! You're brilliant, Sawny! You're brilliant!"

In the middle of the thickets, a half-acre of grazed grass was inhabited by two horses, each loosely tied, giving them freedom to roam just far enough to eat. One of them was Youk's favorite mare, and the other was Shooter.

"We'll leave Brown Sugar," said Dod, thinking about his nasty experience climbing Coyote Trail. "Let's ride double on Shooter. He's strong enough to get us to High Gate before the sun sets."

In a flash, the horse was saddled and the duo set off running. Nothing could stop them, not even the seven drat soldiers that saw them riding and ordered they halt, suspecting the horse was illicitly borrowed.

Every shortcut was employed to reduce riding time, even the dreaded Coyote Trail. They recognized that each minute drew the sun further across the sky, reducing their chances of successfully bringing the triblot barrier down.

When Dod and Sawny finally arrived at the entry to High Gate, it was like finishing a horse race after the crowd had gone home. Where mobs of people had waited to get in the first time Dod had been there, only a lonely sparrow hopped about, eating pieces of wheat that someone's load had leaked under a scorching, noonday sun.

Now the sky was different. Across the distant horizon, faint clouds turned red and orange. Only half of the sun was still casting rays; the other half hid behind a mountain.

"At least it's over there," said Sawny, trying to build up enough courage to follow through. "For much of the year, it sets directly behind that larger string of mountains. If it had today, it would already be too late."

"Let's do it," said Dod, dismounting Shooter and walking over to the giant bell. "Now how do I dong it?"

Sawny pointed at a large stick with a leather clump secured to the end. It hung six feet up a post and was covered with dust. From every indication, it had never been used.

"All right. I feel privileged," said Dod, his heart pounding rapidly. He drew the rod down and positioned to strike. Just then, an elementary school memory entered his mind. It made him sweat. In fourth grade, Cole had been blamed for pulling the fire alarm, which he hadn't done, and had narrowly dodged getting expelled for it.

Now, holding the special stick and ready to trigger a real alarm of sorts, Dod felt the embarrassment all over again.

"Here's to Dilly," he said, striking the bell firmly three times.

Sawny nudged Shooter into the middle of the road and pulled out two mirrors. She flashed them back and forth, catching the light with one and sending it in the direction of High Gate with the other, hoping the last rays of sunshine would still convince the soldiers to react positively.

Nothing happened.

Dod struck the bell three times again, which was followed by Sawny's systematic flashing with the mirrors. It was all in accordance with the regulations, yet still nothing happened.

One last time, Dod and Sawny repeated their procedure, however, the only thing that responded was the sun: It finally set. And since rays were no longer able to reach the mirrors, trying again wasn't an option.

"We did our best," mumbled Dod. He hung the stick in place and joined Sawny on the back of Shooter. Together, they waited quietly for what seemed like an eternity—about five minutes.

"I guess it didn't work," admitted Sawny, her voice quivering. "I'm sorry I dragged you into this."

"No, I think it's the other way around," said Dod, trying to swallow tears. They had given it everything and failed.

DONG

The distant pavilion's bell rang out.

DONG, DONG.

DONG, DONG, DONG.

"It's working!" cried Sawny. "We did it! It's really working!"

The bells pealed, from one tower to the next, just as they had the first time Dod visited High Gate, though some of the towers took longer to respond. It was the most wonderful music; not because of their sound, but because of what they represented.

When the process was over, Dod and Sawny knew it for certain by the approach of a troop of soldiers, who stormed the wide road and headed to meet them.

"I hope they let us enter," winced Sawny, realizing the moment of truth was quickly nearing. She liked her theory of entry as a topic of discussion; actually following through with it was scary.

"I'm sure everything's going to work out just fine," said Dod, not very convincingly. "If you were them, you'd send soldiers to greet us, wouldn't you? Besides, they could have ignored us if they didn't plan on helping us, right?"

Dod attempted to reassure Sawny, but most of his statements ended in questions. He, too, dreaded the approaching confrontation and had plenty of doubts.

"What's your business and who ordered this?" demanded a large tredder soldier; he was well decorated with medals and marks of commendation, indicating he was a battle-tested general. Obviously he was in charge of the other fifty men who rode with him and, probably, the three hundred that waited on horseback by the entrance to High Gate.

"We did, sir, under the seal of Bonboo Tillius," said Dod confidently.

"That's impossible! You'll need to come with us," said the general stiffly. He glowed reddish-purple with agitation at having been summoned to great lengths needlessly. "Men, surround them!"

"Hold on, we're telling the truth!" pleaded Dod. He didn't sound as confident anymore. "This is his great-granddaughter Sawny Tillius, from Twistyard. She bears an important message which is only for the ears of Commendus."

"And you couldn't wait until tomorrow?" asked the incensed commander. He scowled angrily.

"I doubt you're truthful," he grumbled, raising one hand in the air while ordering, "Men, take them to the binding hall for interrogation, and if they resist your assistance, kill them!"

"Why would we lie to you, sir?" begged Dod. He felt the pressure of two horses pushing on either side of Shooter, mounted by men with drawn swords. "Don't you think we knew the seriousness of requesting a special dropping of the barrier? And yet we did it anyway, to be faithful to our charge."

"Then what message does the girl bring?" barked the general. He was beyond furious, calculating the thousands of men that were affected, currently waiting at attention in towers and holds all around High Gate, with swords and spears and bows ready for an ambush, all unnecessarily working so two very simple-looking people could make an evening entry. "I'll be the judge of whether it's worthy of the mountainous trouble you've caused," said the chief officer, glaring coldly.

Royal feelings flooded over Dod like a wave overtaking the beach. He could see Pap in his mind, standing for truth, holding the very sword that was now stowed in a sheath, attached to his waist.

"SIR!" Dod insisted in a regal voice, commanding everyone's full attention. "I am the grandson of Pap, the very hero who was murdered within your walls. I carry his sword at my side, and am, by virtue of my own acts, as much as by blood, his rightful descendant. The lady has a message for Commendus—and him alone. If you were to hear it, I would need to dispose of you forthwith. That is my charge!"

"OUTRAGEOUS!" yelled the commander, his tredder ring pulsating with blood. "You're nothing but a common boy!" His fingers fidgeted with the silver-and-brass handle of his sword, as though he desperately wanted to end the argument with his blade.

But Dod didn't back down. "See us through!" he said courageously.

"Not tonight," said the general, who was working to stay in control of his temper. "Commendus will hear of you tomorrow, when I personally tell him of your ludicrous claims."

"Then perhaps at the same time you may explain to him *this* as well, for I am confident he will request your rationale." Dod drew the invitation from his suit pocket and held it up for the men to see. "I delayed my coming in order to protect Sawny."

"Is that authentic?" asked one of the soldiers who was close enough to read the invitation.

"Regardless, his weapon is familiar," blurted a different soldier in a gruff voice. He pointed at Dod's sword from Pap. "I recognize the insignia on the handle; it's Pap's, all right. And his sheath bears the name Bonboo Tillius. He must be Pap's grandson, as he says."

Sawny beamed, grateful she had borrowed a sheath from Dilly's collection that bore her grandfather's noble name.

The general's face cringed noticeably when he drew his horse close enough to read Dod's invitation from Commendus.

"You're Pap's grandson," he said, forcing an apologetic tone. "You're the one who helped Tridacello recover our triblot, right?"

"Yes, I am," said Dod, nodding.

"I'm terribly sorry that I didn't recognize you," said the commander, still red-faced, but submissive. The words burned like fire on his tongue as he awkwardly made excuses for his behavior.

"Perhaps the night air has affected my eyes," he stumbled, "and my temper, too…and with all the trouble we've seen lately here at High Gate, everyone's concerned about suspicious behavior."

Dod continued to stare, unbendingly, until the general finally confessed, in a tortured voice, "Please forgive me and my men for our ignorance. We'll step aside."

The man nudged his horse, and all of his men quickly followed. "Oh, and accept my personal condolences," the commander called out, this time sounding almost genuine. "Pap was the greatest of men—and Bonboo, too."

"Thank you," said Dod pretentiously. "Very well, then. We'll be on our way." He felt snobbish with his response and posture, but he didn't dare act his normal self, for he feared the tide of doubt would return to the soldiers and they would have another go at him.

Once in High Gate, Dod and Sawny rode as fast as they could to Commendus's estate. Something inside them cried out that Sirlonk was making a move on Dilly; and unfortunately, that foreboding something was right!

CONFRONTING THE DREAD

Discommo Manor was beautiful at night. By the time Sawny and Dod approached the entry, torches blazed brightly, licking the night air. Guards stood ready, as they had at the entrance to High Gate; however, the soldiers here reviewed Dod's invitation and then quickly admitted him with pleasant words of greeting.

"Don't you think Commendus should post his guards closer to the lake?" said Dod to Sawny jokingly, trying to relax the tension they both felt over Dilly's predicament.

"You mean you're scared of his pets?" asked Sawny, brushing hair out of her face.

"Not me—for others less brave," said Dod in a mannish voice. He puffed his chest and grinned. "I'd actually prefer his pets right now over ever having to request the triblot barrier be dropped again—one or two sets of fangs instead of fifty swords. What could a little snake do?"

"Little?" gasped Sawny. "Hardly!"

"Besides," continued Dod, amused with the subject, "it would be fun to see a diasserpentous at night, don't you think? I hope one pops out of the water as we stroll by."

"Don't say that!" chided Sawny, becoming serious. "Bad luck will get us."

Shooter was trotting along the lakeside, nearing where they had seen the diasserpentous before.

"Oh, you think so?" said Dod, smiling even bigger.

"It happens all the time," explained Sawny, pushing the pestering lock of hair once more from her face. "The moment you mock something troublesome, you're the one facing it. Bad luck, I tell you. Don't say another word about that beast until we're safe inside the palace."

Sawny's voice reminded Dod of his mother scolding him. But no one could blame Sawny for being nervous. By the entry gate to Discommo Manor, the area was well lit, especially around the soldiers; on the other hand, along the lakeshore, where they were riding all alone, the path had more spaces of darkness between torches—and the mist rising from the water didn't help create a comforting ambiance, either.

"So, you don't want me to sing about the wee-little, black pond-snake?" joked Dod.

Despite concern for Dilly and anticipation of the coming confrontation, Dod was enjoying the moment; it was much like the pleasure of going on a date to a haunted house.

"Dod!" scolded Sawny.

"Snaky—little snaky," mocked Dod playfully, brimming with satisfaction.

"Dod! I'm warning you!" scolded Sawny, bristling up as she glanced toward the murky water; she instantly looked away, trying not to dwell upon the creepy tree-shadows that danced on the glasslike surface.

"Where are you little snaky?" called Dod, puckering to whistle; but before he could conjure so much as a peep, he was thwarted.

WOMP!

Sawny hit Dod squarely across the side of his head.

"I told you to stop teasing me," she said defensively. "I'm serious about bad luck. It's funny until it happens to you. Keep in mind, we're *both* on this horse by the lake."

Dod rubbed his cheek, mostly for show, and grumbled, "Sorry."

"During the day is one thing," continued Sawny, feeling driven to explain herself. "But seeing that creature at night, with its deathly-cold eyes and its wriggling body..." Sawny shivered. "It would be...well...over the line for me. I can assure you of that. I think I'd pass out!"

Dod rode in silence for a few moments, feeling his right ear tingle from being pounded by Sawny. For half-a-second he even considered not teasing anymore, however, the lure of an approaching spot, where the road was only a few feet from the water's edge, was too much temptation.

PLOP!

Noise from the surface of the water sent Sawny into near convulsions; her hands grabbed Dod from behind so tightly that her fingernails almost drew blood through Dod's suit; and she screamed so loudly that Dod knew it would be at least a week or two before he would be capable of hearing the mellow chirp of a bird or trickling of a small stream.

"Shhhh," said Dod, trying desperately to quiet Sawny. "I'm sorry. Shhhh."

But Dod's efforts were in vain; Sawny was terrified.

"MOVE! MOVE!" yelled Sawny, getting louder. "MAKE THIS HORSE MOVE! IT'S COMING!"

She kicked her feet frantically into Shooter's sides until he bolted.

"We're fine. Quiet down," begged Dod, tugging back on the horse's reins. "People are watching."

"I heard it!" Sawny screamed. "That thing is coming!"

Dod did his best to calm Sawny while slowing the horse enough to avoid appearing distressed. Of course, the screaming drew attention anyway. However, when his efforts to convince Sawny didn't work, he finally confessed: "I flipped a nut in the water...*I* made the noise."

WOMP! WOMP! WOMP! WOMP!

Dod took four blows to the head before the beating ended.

"And Boot said Dilly was the physical one," whined Dod.

"I warned you!" argued Sawny, trying to catch her breath. "I could have died back there. My blood nearly curdled."

"Sorry," whimpered Dod. He was sincere this time; his distance from the water made it easier to apologize without worrying about repeating the act; and his face stung enough that he had learned his lesson.

A few minutes later, near the wonderfully lit castle, a man wearing an all-white suit and a stiff-rimmed black hat stopped Dod and took Shooter by the reins, saying, "Ninety-seven." It was the number of the stall where he intended on putting Shooter.

"Thank you," said Sawny, quickly hopping off the horse. She was still mad about the pranks, though she felt better when she took a few steps and looked back at Dod: The right side of his face was red, and one distinct handprint showed on his cheek.

"Thanks," said Dod to the barn hand, following Sawny. "Ninety-seven, right?"

"Yes, sir," said the man, purposely looking away from Dod's cheek to save him embarrassment. "When you're ready for your horse, we'll fetch-and-saddle if you remember that number."

"Dod," blurted Sawny with surprise. "Look at that!" She spoke as if all had been instantly forgiven and forgotten.

A handsome, large brown horse with a charcoal-black mane and an unusual spot on one haunch was tethered to a post by the steps which led to Commendus's front entrance.

"It's Grubber!" said Sawny.

"You recognize that horse?" asked the man who was ready to lead Shooter away.

"Definitely. It belongs to my friend Boot. His steed was taken a few weeks ago."

"I'm sorry to hear that," remarked the barn hand. "That horse showed up last night by the pond. We tied it to the post this morning, hoping one of the guests would recognize and claim it."

"I'll return it to Boot," offered Sawny. "He lives at Twistyard. If you want to make sure that it's his, check the horse's front left leg, on the inside by the hoof: Grubber has a three-inch scar."

"Certainly," said the man, still holding the reins to Shooter. He walked over and examined Grubber's leg and then said, "What a stroke of luck for Boot. He has a beautiful friend, willing to return his horse to him. Ninety-eight, my lady."

After the man was gone, walking the two horses to their allotted stalls, Sawny looked at Dod and apologized for hitting him.

"That's okay," said Dod, taking strides up the massive staircase. "I deserved it. I shouldn't have teased you the way I did. My aunt's always on my case for going too far with stuff like that."

"Here," said Sawny. She pulled a glowing-rock necklace from her purse and insisted, "I want you to have it, Dod. You might need it tonight—for good luck if nothing else. I've used it for good luck before."

"You and your superstitions—so did it work?" asked Dod, pausing to let Sawny put Bly's wonderful invention around his neck.

"Sort of…well, not really," confessed Sawny flatly.

At the top of their climb, Sawny and Dod paused on the patio to catch their breath. In front of them, double doors, fifteen feet high, were held open by posh greeters, boisterously welcoming people to enter the palace. A few guests strolled around the granite porch, taking in the night air while enjoying the company of others. All of them were dressed in stylish clothing, which made the setting picture-perfect.

"Neadrou, good evening," called Dod to one man who was sitting alone by the entrance. He looked healthy, early sixties (though likely one hundred and sixty), and very affluent. His clothes were not only elegant, they clearly aimed to prove his wealth, for the rims of his jacket lapels were bedazzled with glittering diamonds and his cummerbund sash around his waist was laden with such jewels as would tilt the head of a queen.

"I saw you this morning," answered Neadrou, tipping his head in recognition, "but I don't think we've had a chance to formally meet." Neadrou rubbed his smooth chin, then twisted the ends of his mustache until they curled.

"I'm Dilly's friend Dod, and this is her sister Sawny," said Dod, straightening his back to look as dignified as he could.

"It's a pleasure to meet you both," said Neadrou officiously. "I'm Neadrou of the Zoots, Saluci's *famous* uncle." He stood and casually pulled back his coat, making sure to show off that his display of gems went all the way around his waist, not just in the front. In so doing, he flaunted his formidable frame and magnificent sword; it was no wonder he had been such a successful general and the subject of Youk's praise.

"It's a shame Saluci and Youk weren't able to make it tonight," he said in a hollow, regretful voice. "If they could only prioritize better, perhaps they would create more room in their schedules for engagements like this." Neadrou lifted his left hand and sipped something purplish-green from a gold-rimmed, crystal goblet that had his name etched in the side.

Dod and Sawny glanced around, looking for Dilly.

"Commendus understands people like us, doesn't he," said Neadrou dramatically, smiling as he raised his fancy cup. "Ramsey's Jubulous is my favorite. It's nice he's remembered to have it shipped from the other side of the world to please my taste."

"Yes, right," rushed Dod, not quite sure what to say. "Have you seen Dilly and Sirlonk?"

"I have," said Neadrou slowly, then he took another pleasant sip of his brew. "I saw them this evening about half an hour ago—around the time of that unusual dropping of the barrier. Did you hear it? With the sky fading, I found it rash they dared pause our protection for anything. Perhaps troops were sent to Twistyard or somewhere else, I suppose."

"Right," said Dod, hiding what he knew. Sawny poked him to redirect Neadrou, who was beginning to talk about the necessity of timeliness when positioning soldiers for attack.

"You're absolutely brilliant at such things," said Dod, barging into Neadrou's explanation. Dod hurriedly glanced at Sawny and added, "So where did her sister go?"

Neadrou blinked.

"Her sister Dilly…with Sirlonk," said Dod hastily.

"They were heading on a walk around back," responded Neadrou, reeling from Dod's compliment yet confused by his unwillingness to listen patiently. "It's enjoyable to watch the stars come out, isn't it?" he continued, relentless to a flaw at insisting on a mannerly style of conversation that better suited the occasion than Dod's rush-rush.

Sawny tapped at the ground impatiently with her foot as Neadrou looked heavenward and, in a melodramatic way, sighed "—not that I can see very many from here, with all the torches lit. I'd imagine they're fortunate enough to have a better view from wherever they are. If I weren't so averse to the dark, I'd take a stroll, too—of course, my eyes! After the Battle of Hermounts…"

Dod and Sawny didn't know anything about the encounter he referred to or the accident that had affected his sight, for Youk hadn't gotten around to sharing that one, nor did they have time to listen to Neadrou's leisurely retelling of it.

"And have you seen Commendus?" asked Dod, looking expectantly at Neadrou, doing his very best to hasten the conversation along. It was more than bordering on rude.

"He's probably inside," said Neadrou bluntly, offended that they didn't show proper interest in chitchatting with him. "His party hall is filled with guests. They're beginning to sample the pre-platters…"

"That sounds tempting," interrupted Dod, cutting him off abruptly. "Come on, Sawny, let's go taste the snacks." He grabbed at Sawny's hand and whisked her off.

Neadrou watched, feeling affronted, as the junior duo scurried away.

Once inside the palace, Dod changed gears quickly. It was troubling to hear that Sirlonk had already been alone with Dilly for half an hour, yet in front of other guests, he had to contain himself. He knew people were likely working with Sirlonk, as Doochi had claimed, so he didn't want to give them the advantage. In his most confidential whisper, Dod shared with Sawny his plan.

"Go and find Commendus. Inform him about Dilly and Sirlonk. Request he discreetly send soldiers to apprehend him—"

"But I'm coming with you," argued Sawny, not nearly so quiet. "We need to stop Sirlonk right now!"

"If you want to help Dilly," said Dod, finding it hard to speak softly and quarrel, "you need to get Commendus involved. We don't know who's helping Sirlonk."

Dod's anxious face whittled at Sawny's persistence. "We know someone facilitated the poisoning!" he added pointedly, causing his throat to grow raspy from forcing emphasis into a whisper. He paused as a cluster of women, whose gowns draped to the floor, pranced by, decked in opulent jewelry. "And he's probably got many more," continued Dod, undeterred. "You know how terribly influential Sirlonk is. Who knows the number of people we're dealing with? We need backup."

Dod's eyes begged. "Besides," he said, "who could beat Sirlonk in a sword fight better than fifty men?"

Sawny exhaled noisily before responding. "Okay," she muttered. "I'll go search for Commendus—but promise me, Dod, that you'll find Dilly and make sure she's unharmed."

"I'll protect her with my life," said Dod, shivering as he felt a sudden chill, "though it won't be worth much without your soldiers coming."

Dod quieted considerably at the end when he sensed the approach of others.

"Dod! It's great to see you," boomed a familiar voice, overtaking their conversation. Tridacello strode up behind them with Bowlure at his side. "I thought you weren't going to be able to make it tonight," continued Tridacello cheerfully; his tone was happier than Dod had ever heard him.

"I'm here," said Dod, spinning around.

Bowlure stared.

"Are you all right?" he asked, pointing with one of his giant fingers at the red handprint on Dod's face; all six-foot-ten of him appeared genuinely concerned.

"I'm fine, thanks," said Dod restlessly. He pulled an uncomfortable smile and claimed, "The bugs by the lake were horrible, weren't they?"

Sawny blushed a guilty-pink.

"Oh, I didn't notice," said Bowlure honestly, tucking his tie back into his vest. In a suit, he hardly looked like Bowlure. "Maybe it's my fur; it's so thick they don't usually bother me, except on my face, where I'm nice and smooth like the rest of you." He smiled and nodded courteously at Sawny, attempting to flirt, before rapping Tridacello on the back.

"Well, My Good Sage," he said, "this just proves it once and for all, fancy buttons and dozens of awards don't make people right, even if they're wonderful at swordplay and wearing all white." Bowlure enjoyed the rhyme, and it showed on his face.

"Sirlonk said he didn'd know," grumbled Dungo, contradicting Bowlure as he came bustling up, wearing an unusual, custom-made outfit that allowed for his four arms and tail. He looked completely out of place and miserable in the relatively homogenous crowd around him—Bowlure included; for with a full suit and shoes on, Bowlure appeared like an immensely well-built man. Dungo, on the other hand, didn't; his bulk and hunch, and four-armed, big-footed, poky-horned look, made him stick out wretchedly—a clumsy brown bear among the dainty white sheep. Even Dod felt bad for him.

"Perhaps it was the way Sirlonk said it," suggested Tridacello, mediating the squabble. "I, too, recall he seemed confident Dod wouldn't be coming tonight."

Bowlure grinned at Dungo, justified by Tridacello's memory, while Dungo shook his head, disagreeing.

"Look at you," said Dod, trying to express that he thought Dungo cleaned up nicely; he worked hard to hold back his laughter, for seeing Dungo in clothes was like looking at a pet that was poorly dressed by a little girl for a tea party, and knowing his personality made it all the more funny.

"Look ad you self, puny, ugly worm!" grumbled Dungo sullenly, all the while squinting callously at Dod. He hated the circumstance.

Dod would have taken offense if he hadn't already met Dungo, but since he had, he was prepared for debauched and spiteful comments, filled with pessimism and selfishness. Sawny, however, had never seen him before, and therefore looked horrified. She poked at Dod's calf with her shoe, reminding him to hurry.

"What Dungo's incapable of saying," said Bowlure, looking brilliant in his attire, "is that you, Dod, appear sharp...I mean, *voila*, you're accompanied by beauty!" He pointed at Sawny and then gazed cleverly into her eyes, adding in his most debonair voice, "Your lady-friend, here, looks simply radiant!"

"This is Sawny, Dilly's *little* sister," said Tridacello, helping Bowlure out with introductions.

"Oh, I see the family resemblance," began Bowlure. He forthwith hung his head in respect and said, in a somber, hushed tone, "My deepest condolences, my lady. Bonboo was the greatest, most wonderful man I've ever met. We all mourn with you."

"I knew I should have stayed with them longer—" added Tridacello, showing remorse for having returned to Green early, before Bonboo, Zerny, and Jibb.

"It's hard on all of us, isn't it, Sawny?" said Dod, glancing sideways. Sawny was dutifully bound by her driving desire to help Dilly, so she hardly allowed herself to think about Bonboo's passing. She caught Dod's eyes with a *"Save Dilly!"* look.

Seeing the strength of his three friends gave Dod an idea. "Would you quickly give me a hand with something?" he asked.

The moment the words escaped his lips, an overflowing feeling of regret set in. And Sawny looked mortified, struck with disbelief; Dod had just told her to watch out for others, yet trusted the likes of the bulky-man and strange creature who accompanied Tridacello.

"We'd be happy to help," said Tridacello politely. "What would you like us to do?"

Somehow his kind words didn't erase the ominous feeling.

"I—I actually meant help Sawny. She wanted to speak with Commendus alone, and I need to run for a minute—the bathroom. All that riding cramped me up. I may be awhile. Would you escort her, please."

"It's nothing to be ashamed of," said Bowlure, misreading the embarrassment on Dod's face. "You're probably still recovering from your injuries. How long did Higga have you out?"

"Excuse me," blurted Dod, not answering Bowlure. He turned and ran down the hall. He didn't slow his pace when he passed crowds of people, or even when two guards specifically instructed him to stop running. Dilly needed his help immediately! He could feel it as clearly as he could feel the weight of Pap's sword jangling at his side.

On the back patio behind the palace, a few giant torches burned in a circle with moths darting at the dancing flames. Over thirty people stood in a clump, talking and enjoying the magnificent view of the city. Also, at least a hundred more were strolling around the yard, following a stone path that was lit with occasional torches.

"Where is she?" mumbled Dod to himself. "Think! Think! Think!"

Dod frantically scanned the area and struggled to know where to go. He suspected Sirlonk wouldn't want to be near other people, so he wasn't likely on the patios, yet if he were in the vast yard, where would he hide? There were so many places to choose from: in the orchards, or by the lake, or with the cattle, or somewhere beyond the out buildings…and the list went on and on.

Suddenly, inspiration came. He saw a drat family running from an army. They were being pursued vigorously while trying to escape; hiding in bushes, then running—hiding in a forest, then running—hiding in a hole, then running—finally hiding by a waterfall and finding safety. The key was the water: It was loud enough to drown out the crying of their little ones.

Dod instantly knew where Dilly was. She had to be near

the trickling of water he could hear, coming from the darkened, lower portion of the patios where Commendus kept his exotic fountains.

Following his ears, and wearing Sawny's glowing-rock necklace for light, Dod ran into the night toward a flight of stairs. The sound of water became louder and louder with every step. After descending to the lower level, all of the guests and torches were left behind.

BOOM-BOOM, BOOM-BOOM, BOOM-BOOM, BOOM-BOOM!

Dod's heart began to pound in panic like the clomping of a galloping horse. With no moon in the sky, all of the stars cast an eerie light, which caused the rising water in the fountains and the gently swaying trees in the planter boxes to come to life. Even the night breeze seemed to be the breath of a hidden enemy.

"Where is she? Where is she?" demanded Dod of himself, moving between the fountains as a lion would, stalking his prey. He was becoming impatient. A few more minutes would be too late! His eyes searched for movement and light, and his ears tried to ignore the splashing water while refocusing on the smallest of other detectable sounds.

After passing the first two fountains, Dod noticed a third, throwing water twenty feet in the air. He instinctively knew it was the spot, the place where he'd find Dilly and Sirlonk, because the gnawing pit in his stomach said so. It was terrifying to consider what he would see and face; however, without hesitation, he bolted toward it in answer to destiny.

As he approached with speed, he recognized two people, obscured by the spray, struggling on the other side of the thundering water.

"SIRLONK!" yelled Dod at the top of his lungs, hurrying around the fountain as fast as he could. "SIRLONK! DILLY!"

To his horror, Dod approached in time to see Sirlonk pointing Jilser at Dilly's throat.

"If you take another step, she dies!" shouted Sirlonk in a depraved voice.

"Run, Dod!" cried Dilly, her tears marring her words. "Run while you still have a chance. Get away from here as fast as you can!"

But Dod stood still, momentarily paralyzed; his feet were like the rooted, stubborn stumps of trees, not able to retreat as Dilly bade nor attack in her defense.

Sirlonk exploded in anger; he pressed the sharp tip of his blade closer to Dilly's throat, until it touched, and yelled, "SILENCE!"

"I can't leave you, Dilly," sobbed Dod, standing motionless.

"Run!" begged Dilly, feeling her life was at an end. "Save the secrets!"

Dod didn't understand. It was all too confusing. She was the key to the secrets, not him; her life was important, not his. Without Dilly and her part in Bonboo's plan, Dod couldn't obtain the secrets, even if he did run, which his legs forbid him to do anyway.

"He has Higga's half," yelled Dod bitterly. "It's no use!"

"Trust me and run!" pleaded Dilly urgently; her voice was failing her as she winced under the uncomfortable prick of Sirlonk's encroaching blade. She had resorted to a crumpled position upon the ground, tearfully holding injuries she had sustained from dueling.

Sirlonk let out an atrocious cackle as he looked toward

Dod triumphantly. "He has the keys, doesn't he?" said Sirlonk, turning back to face Dilly, who lay at his feet. "You gave *him* the keys? You foolish child!"

"DILLY!" roared Dod. But she couldn't speak.

"You're as imprudent and irrational as your bumbling great-grandfather," continued Sirlonk mockingly. "His stupidity cost him his life, Dilly! He could have lived so much longer, so much stronger, with more power than this world's ever seen. And what did his integrity buy for him? A lousy death at the hands of cheap labor!"

"Run!" squeaked Dilly pathetically, begging Dod.

"Not likely," chided Sirlonk. "Dod won't run; not with you here, Dilly."

Sirlonk bent down and stuffed a handkerchief in Dilly's mouth as she tried to explain the situation to Dod; and with the flick of one wrist, he spun Dilly's face to the ground.

"You're a lady—die like one!" screeched Sirlonk, his voice cutting the night air as he raised Jilser to strike.

"NOOOOO!" yelled Dod, leaping forward and drawing his sword. His movements forced Sirlonk to stop his assault on Dilly in order to defend himself.

"Simply pathetic!" responded Sirlonk, easily deflecting Dod's attack. "You can't save her. I'll kill you—and then I'll kill her. It's what I do best!"

Dod swung his weapon in the air and began to back up slowly, drawing Sirlonk farther and farther from Dilly. And when he had lured him far enough, he yelled, "Run, Dilly! Run!"

But Dilly didn't say anything, and she didn't move.

"If you've killed her," sobbed Dod, "I'll cut your heart out—I swear I will!" Dod used his left hand to wipe tears from his eyes. The farther he backed up, the less he could see of Dilly, so he watched in vain for any movement from the glowing rock she wore around her neck.

"That will be hard to do when you're dead," taunted Sirlonk cruelly. "But look at the bright side, I'll put you out of your misery quickly if you share a little secret with me."

Many unspeakable words rolled through Dod's mind as he chose wisely the ones he used.

"You putrid, loathing, degenerate snake! I would die a hundred times before bending to tie your shoes, so if you're asking for my help, the best I can offer is to teach you a lesson with *this*!" Dod lunged forward, jabbing viciously with all his might.

"Are you going to punch me, too?" asked Sirlonk, laughing at Dod's weak attempts to strike. "I'm the best, Dod. Accept it and give in. If I wanted you dead right now, I could kill you this instant, or the next, or the next, or the moment after that; I'm playing with you, Dod. You're a toy to me—and not a very clever one, either."

Sirlonk dipped his sword to the ground and held it between his legs; he leisurely pulled his gloves off—first one, then the other.

"Dilly made me get these wet, while I was trying to persuade her into telling me where she put *my* keys. What a pity. I loathe wet gloves."

Sirlonk threw them at Dod and smiled wickedly as he held up his right hand, near his glowing stone. A jagged scar—the same scar Dod had seen in his mind—zigzagged across Sirlonk's hand.

"Do you recognize this? Your grandfather gave it to me, and a whole lot more! Oh, silly me. I forgot, you haven't read his books, or any of Humberrone's."

"You stole them!" cried Dod angrily.

"They're amusing to read. Everyone has a handle or price, and their writings have done a marvelous job of filling me in—and it's the least Pap could do for me after what he did. He practically killed me! The night we fought, he got lucky, five against one; and after I was worn down from defeating the other four, my disguise got in the way of our swordplay. If it hadn't been for that, I'd have ended it there. Pap was no match for me."

Sirlonk shifted his weight and grimaced. "Do you know it took me eight months of therapy to learn to walk normally again? Me, The Great Sirlonk! Who would have thought? Never before and never again! I need the secrets, Dod. They're rightfully mine—so this sort of folly won't happen again. Pap deserved what he got. I only wish I could have seen his face when he died."

"You poisoned him, you coward!" blurted Dod, gripping the handle of his blade so tightly that his knuckles turned white.

"Not without help," said Sirlonk factually, as calm as the night's gentle breeze. He still held his rapier between his knees, teasingly, as he rubbed his hands and explained the way a professor would.

"Pap was on to me," he said, holding one finger up, "so someone else had to offer the toast, someone cozier." Sirlonk crossed his fingers and pulled them down, into a fist, signifying a close friend had poisoned Pap.

"Of course," he quickly added, drenched with arrogance, "if I could have chosen, I would have waited for a chance to duel with him again—man to man—and I'd have beaten him horribly."

"In your dreams, maggot!" yelled Dod, lunging toward Sirlonk, attempting to take advantage of his weak position, while his sword was down and his mind was on the conversation; but the move ended abruptly, with Sirlonk slicing the shoulder of Dod's suit. Sirlonk was impenetrably good at dueling.

"I'm telling you the truth when I say I could end this right now," mocked Sirlonk, momentarily covering his eyes with one hand and recklessly waving Jilser around with the other, impersonating Dod's clownlike moves. "I'm always one step ahead of you," Sirlonk gloated. "You name it. One of my personal favorites was watching how wretchedly you all acted in dealing with your pest problem. Oh, and in case you were wondering, I first invited Miz's two son's on a one-way fishing trip, so they couldn't help you out. They're stranded and starving to death. Isn't that nice?"

"I should have let you die when I had the chance," blared Dod angrily, feeling a surge of energy. "I saved your life and you don't even know it—the night you rode with Zerny and Strat. I was the one defending you with stones. And what did you do? You blundered around with your torch, like a walking target. They'd have finished you off if it weren't for me." Dod shook his sword in the air for emphasis.

"You simple fool," laughed Sirlonk proudly. "You see with your eyes, but you're still blind as a gopher-pup. It's almost pointless to explain. I planned that ambush to incite conflict. The only people you saved were as pathetic as yourself—not worth much. I signaled the attack by holding my torch up, while entering the tent. And when I continued to hold it, the hirelings knew to not shoot me. It was easy faking an injury—and to think I was that convincing! I'm always one step ahead. Always. Always! Why do you think people call me *The Dread*?"

Flashes of Pap rushed through Dod's mind, as well as bits and pieces of conversations with his mother, and Josh, and Alex, and Aunt Hilda; it was empowering to recall them; it gave him fresh courage to stand boldly, even if only to fall.

"I think they call you The Dread because your face is so ugly," said Dod defiantly, rubbing his shoulder where Sirlonk had glanced him. His tongue was the only good sword he knew how to use.

"Very funny," snorted Sirlonk.

"And because you're *dreadfully* jealous of people who possess *real* influence, like Bonboo," mocked Dod, backing up slowly, smiling as Sirlonk scowled. "—and your brother, *Terro!*" he added bravely.

"Terro's nothing without me!" snapped Sirlonk, losing his cool. "I made Terro!"

"And don't forget about your son," chided Dod. "He acts *dreadfully* weak. He's a shoe-shiner for Sawb and his pals."

"HE'S YOUNG!" boomed Sirlonk, yelling so loudly that spit flew out of his mouth. "He'll learn his place or else!"

"And then there's your *dreadfully* sorrowful name—*Chantolli*."

"I didn't invite you to use my family name!" growled Sirlonk, turning impishly evil, dark as the hands of the devil. The volume of his voice was no longer peaking with his emotions, for he was past red-hot; his eyes burned ferociously like white-coals; his chitchatting had come to an end, for it was no longer enjoyable, now that Dod held a mirror to his face.

"*Chantolli! Chantolli! Chantolli! Chantolli!*" screamed Dod 'til his throat hurt, feeling the rage of indignation bubble to the surface.

CLASH, CLANK—CLASH, CLANK, CLANK.

Dod and Sirlonk jumped in and out, swashbuckling like pirates. It was a unique feeling for Dod. The training and instruction he had received suddenly flowed freely through his sword, making him almost equal to the task. He lunged and darted, slicing and jabbing, then ducked and dodged as Sirlonk pressed upon him. It was back and forth for a few brief minutes before tragedy struck.

SWIPE!

Sirlonk's sword gouged into Dod's left shoulder, forcing him to cry out in pain. He staggered back, feeling defeated, until he remembered Dilly's special move—*disaster*!

Unfortunately, when Dod tried the move, it really was a disaster! Sirlonk easily deflected it, knocking Dod's sword from his hands, and then mocked the action, acknowledging gleefully that it hadn't worked for Dilly, either.

"Just give me the keys and I'll let you live," said Sirlonk, not even winded from the fight, for he had only been playing. He pushed at Dod with Jilser, backing him up against a knee-high stone wall that dropped off on the other side.

"YOU'RE A LIAR!" yelled Dod, holding back tears. "Even if you were telling the truth for once, I still wouldn't give you the keys. My integrity can't be bought!"

Sirlonk swung his sword casually, forcing Dod to trip backward in order to avoid being hit.

"Everyone has a price," said Sirlonk, bearing a wicked smile. "Everyone! What if I were to offer you Dilly—I could do a lot worse than dip her in water and poke her with my blade. Now tell me where *my* keys are!"

Dod fidgeted on the wall, reaching deep inside, gaining the inner strength to respond. "I won't tell you where they are. You don't scare me."

Dod groaned, feeling triumphant in defeat. He was lying

on his back on the rock ledge like a deathbed, but still true to himself. It was his final stand.

Sirlonk prodded at Dod's suit with Jilser and smiled. "I suppose you don't need to tell me," he said slowly, "I see them!" His eyes filled with greed and power as he looked at Dod's chest and pointed; the three keys on Dod's chain were dangling in plain sight, next to his glowing stone, having jostled out of his shirt when he fell.

Air from the darkness below wafted up to Dod in his moment of despair. It smelled wonderful and he instantly knew where he was.

"You win. Here are your stupid keys," whimpered Dod, faking submission as he plopped his hand over them.

But rather than handing the keys over, which Sirlonk fully expected, Dod tore the lucky glowing rock from his neck and threw it at Sirlonk's face, while rolling sideways off the wall.

"You can't hide from me!" bellowed Sirlonk viciously. "I'm coming down to get you, to hurt you, Dod!" It was almost as if he had turned into a horrible creature, overcome with desire for the keys.

Meanwhile, Dod scurried into the safety of Dr. Shelderhig's overgrown garden, which was at the bottom of the twelve-foot drop.

"It's just a matter of cat-and-mouse," said Sirlonk, throwing Dod's glowing stone down to measure depth. He then followed, landing in a fighting position with his sword in hand. "Do you know why I like cats?" he continued, hunting for Dod with his eyes, "because they play with their prey before they kill it. We enjoy that sort of thing, Dod."

When Sirlonk spoke, his voice echoed throughout the garden, magnified by the walls. "If you give up now, and throw me the keys, I'll leave you and Dilly alone—I give you my word....I only want the keys....Come out and let's talk....Besides, you don't really think I want to hurt you or Dilly, do you? She's practically my daughter.... And you're such a smart boy, you deserve to live....You're more like Pap than I thought. How did you know I was planning on a little accident in Sword Tower? Be good and come out, so we can strike a deal...."

Sirlonk pleaded his case, lying through his nose as he crept about the garden, systematically moving Dod toward one side—to corner him. Each pause was calculated to better track his prey. And unfortunately, it was working, due to Dod's poor landing when coming off the wall; he had injured one leg bad enough that he moved faster on all fours, which created the additional problem of producing more sound, becoming an easier target to follow.

"Dod, let's be friends," persisted Sirlonk, still stalking him. He was getting close. "I was good friends with your grandpa....I know what happened was awful, and you blame me, but it wasn't entirely my fault. There's so much more to the story than you know....If you give me the keys now, I'll tell you the other half of the story—why your grandpa had to die, and who killed him."

"YOU LIAR!" blurted Dod. He didn't mean to cry out, it just happened in anger.

"Ah ha! I've got you!" said Sirlonk, dashing through the bushes and vines to where Dod was.

In an attempt to hurry away, Dod pushed too quickly with one foot and snagged his thick-hide shoelace on a troublesome root. It stalled his movement long enough to leave him caught like a fish on a hook, waiting for the fisherman.

"You should have listened to me, Dod," said Sirlonk gloatingly. "Now you'll never know what really happened to Pap!"

Still trapped, Dod turned to face his accuser for the last time.

He knew it was the end. Time slowed down, like it had when he fell off the wall near Pap's place, and everything around him came into focus; the stars were more beautiful than ever before; the smell in the air was intoxicating and so wonderful that he wished to live at least a little longer if but to enjoy the pleasure of smelling; the foliage under him was softer and more pleasant than his bed at home; and beyond the chatter of Sirlonk's voice, Dod could hear crickets and night beetles playing a magnificent symphony.

Amidst everything wonderful for the senses to enjoy, Dod could also see clearly Sirlonk's baneful face, laughing with pleasure as he approached close enough to discover Dod's misfortune. Sirlonk's eyes brimmed with hate, visible by the light of the rock around his neck, and his tredder ring turned purple, filled with blood from his dark heart.

"Say goodnight," cackled Sirlonk gleefully, pointing his sword to attack.

It was the last thing he said before the tables turned. In an instant, all of the vines surrounding Sirlonk came to life, and like a storm of rattlesnakes, they struck. The Night Devil was no enemy to Dod: It had found prey that was as evil as its own name.

"HELP! HELP!" pleaded Sirlonk, struggling to free his arm that held his sword, though it was completely hopeless; the Night Devil had at least fifteen squirming vines, wrapping tightly around Sirlonk's limbs, while its pods struck viciously at his glowing stone, latching onto his neck and chest.

Within seconds, The Dread was silent.

BITTER-SWEET JUSTICE

"Dod? Are you down there?" croaked Dilly from the patio as she peered over the wall.

"Dilly! You're alive!" gasped Dod, overjoyed; his voice revealed he was out of breath, struggling to make his way through the thick greenery.

"Are you okay?" asked Dilly, straining to see Dod. She wondered where Sirlonk had run off to.

"Here," grumbled another voice from behind Dilly. A bright light immediately filled the patio and cast some of its rays down into Dr. Shelderhig's garden. It was Dungo, holding a buster candle he had just lit. His size dwarfed Dilly.

"I'm sorry I passed out," called Dilly apologetically toward the seemingly empty garden, "or I would have helped you. When Sirlonk shook me, it sent me off like a fading dream." She craned her neck side to side, still unable to see Dod, but she could hear the sounds of his movements.

"It's a good thing your friend, here, came along," continued Dilly, glancing respectfully at Dungo. "He's the one who saw you go over the wall."

"Dungo?" said Dod in surprise as he came crawling out of the foliage, arduously pulling Sirlonk's body behind him. Dod's hair was tousled hippity-hack, his clothes were tattered and dirty, and his left shoulder was sliced and bloody, peeking out of a hole in his fancy coat; but Sirlonk looked worse, for his white suit showed the mess better.

"What?" stuttered Dilly in disbelief, completely astonished. She thought her eyes were playing tricks on her. "Is that really Sirlonk?" she asked, leaning over until she almost toppled off the wall. Her muscles were still shaky from fighting, and she shivered uncontrollably, wet to the bone from her unpleasant dunking in the fountains.

When Dod made his way into the full light, Dilly sighed, "It is Sirlonk. You got him." She was nearly speechless with shock, for she knew how well The Great Sword Instructor dueled; and first-hand she had just barely, narrowly, survived her own encounter with him—and that, too, by default, he having chased after Dod without finishing her off.

"Actually," said Dod, "the Night Devil got him. It attacked the light around his neck—hence the mess you see." Dod pointed tiredly at Sirlonk's shirt, vest, and jacket that were splotched. "I was going to leave him there," continued Dod, huffing noisily as he worked his way toward the wall, "you know, let the vines have their fill of his blood—until I thought of the map—Higga's half. I didn't want to risk it getting destroyed, so after Sirlonk was incapacitated, I cut him free."

"With what? Your weapon's up here," said Dilly in a dazed-like trance. She pointed at his sword that lay a few yards away from her; though she didn't look where she pointed, for she couldn't take her eyes off Sirlonk's limp body; it felt surreal. Jungo had been served, despite the odds.

"I used—well, a special knife," said Dod, patting his vest. "When Sirlonk stopped kicking, I took it out and cut the vines at their base, far enough down that they didn't get me."

Dod almost said which knife it was—since it was the lucky one from Boot that he had stowed in his suit pocket—nevertheless, before it slipped out, he remembered he had promised Boot he wouldn't reveal to anyone how he got the knife, so instead, he kept that part of the story a secret. He also held back another important piece of information: The real reason he had risked his life to save The Dread was because he wanted to know more about Pap's death and who else was involved.

"Oh! Dod, you're hurt!" exclaimed Dilly, finally becoming aware that Dod struggled on all fours; she had been so mesmerized by the scene of Sirlonk that she hadn't truly noticed anything else, including Dod's pathetic condition.

"Probably not any worse than you," responded Dod, looking up at Dilly's bedraggled state; she hunched and slumped unladylike in pain and shivered continually; and her beautiful hair was sticking out in matted clumps, half dried from the evening breeze; and her wet dress had smudges of dirt and blood on it, attesting to the fact that she had seen more than enough of Sirlonk's dark side.

Dilly looked up at Dungo and begged, "Can't you help him?" Her frazzled emotions were close to the surface.

"Yeah, id would be normal fur me do bail him oud," responded Dungo sullenly. He turned and handed Dilly the candle before jumping down into the garden. His body was perfect for the task. His four strong arms easily carried both Dod and Sirlonk; and with one leap, he sailed high enough to grab the top of the wall, sufficient to pull himself up to the patio, without ever letting go of his load.

"Dry dad some dime," gloated Dungo, setting Dod and Sirlonk on the ground.

"Thank you, Dungo," said Dod, feeling embarrassed that he had originally asked for his help, while in the castle, and then had changed his mind.

"Id's all righd. I happy do help," said Dungo, blinking at Dod. He had a puzzled look on his face. "So, is Sirlonk gonna die, you dink?"

"No," responded Dod. "I'm sure he'll spend a long life in prison, paying for all of the deeds he's committed as The Dread, or possibly I've only delayed his parting, depending on what your courts will allow."

Dilly helped Dod to his feet, and the two of them steadied each other feebly.

"We did it," said Dod to Dilly, exhausted, looking her squarely in the eyes. "But I do have a question for you. When were you going to tell me the importance of these two keys?"

Dilly let out a garbled chuckle. "I planned on telling you," she said, wiping a clump of mud off his lapel, "that is, if you needed to know."

"Thanks," said Dod sarcastically, grinning in a jaded sort of way. He pulled a leather scroll from his pocket and held it out for Dilly. "This is Higga's part of the map. It was on Sirlonk. Where's your half?"

"My half is right here," replied Dilly, patting the keys which dangled around Dod's neck. "My half of the map is actually just the keys—"

Dod raised an eyebrow.

"As far as I know, anyway," said Dilly, bending to rub her sore leg. "The keys were it. I had Pap keep an eye on them for me, though he only knew they were special to me—he didn't know anything about their secret purpose, or their origin."

"Oh," sighed Dod. "I guess we'll see."

Suddenly, clammy fingers seized around Dod's and Dilly's necks at the same time.

"Dank you, ugly worms!" muttered Dungo, snatching the map and keys away from Dod. "Der for us now."

"You, too?" choked Dod, straining to speak. It was a nightmare. He and Dilly were both exhausted and weaponless.

"No dime do dalk, jus dime do die," mumbled Dungo.

After tucking the map and keys into his pocket, Dungo took his two spare hands and covered their faces, blocking their noses and mouths; and no matter how hard Dod and Dilly struggled, neither of them had the strength to overpower him.

SWOOSH, WHACK, WHACK, WHACK, WHACK!

Out of the darkness appeared Bowlure and Tridacello. No sooner did they begin their military magic than Dungo was forced to release his captives and attempt an escape; but his efforts were foiled by fifty soldiers, who cut him off in his retreat, led at the front by Sawny.

"How did you know where we were?" asked Dod breathlessly, looking up at Tridacello and Bowlure. "Your timing was perfect."

"I have a good nose for smelling trouble," responded Bowlure happily. "I can smell Dungo's stench from a mile away; and when he left the palace, right as Commendus was ordering the banquet to begin, I knew something was up. We would have come faster, but we stopped to redirect the soldiers Sawny had misled into the backyard in search of you."

"Dilly!" cried Sawny, leaving the soldiers and running to her sister. They embraced tightly and didn't let go for a long time.

In luxury, Dod and Dilly were both cleaned up and attended to by Commendus's personal medical team, with Sawny at their side and Bowlure and Tridacello close by. Fortunately, neither Dod nor Dilly had any major injuries, just minor lacerations and a sprained ankle.

The banquet was fabulous. Dod, Bowlure, and Tridacello all received their commendation medals for recovering the stolen triblot; however, Dungo lost his privileges once it was determined that he was involved with The Dread and had likely participated in helping to originally steal the triblot in the first place.

After that round of medals, a special set of medallions were given to Dilly, Sawny, and Dod for having finally discovered the true identity of The Dread and, more importantly, for stopping him. The crowd of guests applauded loudly and could hardly be contained for joy when it was announced that The Dread was locked up, for everyone present had been plagued in some way or other by his wicked deeds.

When the awards portion of the evening was over, wonderful tributes to Bonboo were given, first by Commendus and then by Dilly. Following their comments, guests mingled in the hall, taking turns speaking with Dilly, Sawny, and Dod. It was a decent ending to a very, very long day.

The next morning, Dod arose early, feeling like a child on Christmas. The string of events that had happened the day before left Dod overwhelmingly grateful they were over. The cloud of corruption was lifted and the man who had killed Pap and Bonboo was securely incarcerated. Dod had known for some time that he would have to face The Dread, it had plagued him day and night, so now that it was over, Dod was relieved that he had accomplished the task and survived!

For two quiet hours, Dod sat and put pieces together in his mind. They mostly made sense, however, one pressing question bothered him: Was Sirlonk lying when he said there was another half to the story—some other half which included someone else—someone who possibly made the decision to have Pap killed, despite Sirlonk's desire to wait for an opportunity to do the job with his sword?

It was puzzling. Dod knew many of the things Sirlonk had said were lies, but it made sense that Sirlonk, as the egotistically self-named The Dread, would want to finish his rival off in a duel. After all, Sirlonk was the best swordsman Dod had ever met; and if Pap had beaten him sorely—so bad that it took months for him to recover and walk—Sirlonk would feel such a burning desire for revenge that even jungo would seem light by comparison.

With these thoughts in mind, Dod took a trip to the deepest basement before breakfast, seeking answers from someone who knew. As he descended the last leg of the castle's winding, stone staircase, he felt a chill that nearly touched the center of his bones; the torches that burned brightly, hanging off the walls along the way, did little to cast light on why.

In the dungeon, dozens of soldiers, armed with weapons of every kind, were standing rigidly, in three rows, all stationed near one particular cell. It was not difficult to guess who occupied their attention.

"I'm told you saved me," muttered Sirlonk, greeting Dod through a thick matrix of bars. He glanced past Dod's face at the troops, crossly, and then down at his own clothes, disapprovingly. He was dressed in a tacky, used outfit that had obnoxious yellow polka dots on the sleeves, and his hands were gloveless and dirty, cuffed together and to an iron post. It sucked the life out of him to be mangy and common-looking.

"I dried do save you!" groaned Dungo from a different cell, nearly buried in piles of chains; his strength called for extra precautions.

"I bet!" snorted Sirlonk sarcastically in Dungo's direction. He still kept his airs about him, despite everything, including attempting to straighten his back and tip his nose snobbishly before asking, "Why did you do it, Dod? Why did you save me?" His cold eyes did their best to prod intrusively.

"Because I couldn't let you die," fibbed Dod, looking down at the ground; he wasn't very good at lying, and despite Sirlonk's restrained condition, it was creepy to even look at him, especially after everything Sirlonk had said and done the night before.

"There must be something else—some other reason," pressed Sirlonk. He said it like he already knew the answer. "Speak up, boy. I haven't got much time before they're escorting me to Driaxom—Driaxom! They're taking *me* to Driaxom! I'd rather die than be jailed at Driaxom, you buffoon. You consigned me to a worse torment than death and you didn't even know it. You lucky, ridiculous fool."

Sirlonk's whining brought on a burst of indignation. Dod had spent half of the last evening listening to grateful people say their thanks, along with hearing their stories of The Dread's wicked acts; and so, with such a trail of crimes to Sirlonk's credit, it was irritating to hear his pathetic cries.

"After what you've done, Driaxom is hardly the beginning of what you deserve!" said Dod, finally mustering enough mettle to look directly at him.

"Then why don't you deliver the rest yourself!" snapped Sirlonk arrogantly, followed by a chuckle. "Of course…I see in your eyes what you're wondering. You're hoping my capture is the end—and that the deeds will stop—and that what I said last night about Pap was all a lie. You're hoping, but you must already know the answer or you wouldn't be down here right now. This is not the end, dear boy—oh, goodness no! Search your mind. This is just the beginning!"

"Tell me the rest!" shouted Dod. "You owe it to me!" He was frustrated with the calm, evil look in Sirlonk's eyes. It wasn't fair; no matter what horrible fate awaited Sirlonk at Driaxom, it wouldn't change the fact that Dod was wrongly bound by ignorance, a nagging, pestering, irksome demon of sorts that had to be faced, that had to be conquered before life could continue the way it was before.

"Tell me!" blared Dod. He grabbed the bars and shook them furiously.

"I can't," said Sirlonk in a composed voice. "That would ruin the surprise, *My Little Mouse*." He winked cleverly at Dod.

"Tell me!" begged Dod, beginning to feel hopelessness accompany the fuming anger he already felt; there was nothing he could offer Sirlonk, and he knew it.

"I won't," laughed Sirlonk, looking around the room at the crowd of militia men and then back to Dod. "Not now—not here—but who knows, maybe someday."

It was pointless to try to force Sirlonk. He was already consigned to the worst fate men could offer and still unbending.

"Enjoy Driaxom," said Dod, finally giving up on his games. "I hope you live a long, long, *long* life!"

Dod left with his hands over his ears. He didn't want to give Sirlonk the pleasure of having the last word.

At breakfast, Dilly and Sawny both lifted Dod's spirits. It was amazing how well they looked, considering the night before; not to mention, it had only been one day since they received word of Bonboo's assassination. Completing jungo, mixed with gratitude for their safety, made the darkness of their circumstance fade away.

"I bet Boot will die when he finds out he was chasing the wrong person and we caught the right one without him," said Sawny, delicately slicing her ham into perfect squares.

"And I can't wait to see the look on his face when I ride in on his horse, Grubber," added Dilly, bubbling over with anticipation. "We'll have to rub it in really good." She slowly picked at the last remaining pieces of fruit on her plate, full from the mountainous breakfast she'd already eaten, and politely waited for Sawny.

"You girls certainly enjoy tormenting people," joked Dod, glad to see the sisters were happy.

"Like you don't?" responded Sawny. She then recounted to Dilly the folly that had happened the night before by the lake, making sure to emphasize how embarrassing it had been to be seen with Dod at the party, while he was wearing a handprint on his cheek.

Dilly laughed until she nearly fell off her seat. When she finally was able to speak, albeit haltingly, she confessed that she had thought poor Dod had been slapped silly by Sirlonk, for she wondered how else he had received such a printing on his face.

Shortly after breakfast, Dilly rushed her comprehensive good-byes to everyone at the palace and then joined Dod and Sawny by the stables. Grubber pawed at the ground, anxious to get going, while Shooter calmly chewed down a patch of taller grass by the barn doors.

Leaving Commendus's palace was especially easy this time, since the vast troubles caused by The Dread were being left behind. The only pause they took was at the lakeside, when Dod wanted a brief moment to look at its beauty. Something unusual whispered to him, not audible, yet meaningful all the same; it told him volumes through feelings; they were shadows of the days ahead, and somehow the lake held a clue. But Dod knew his searching for that part of the mystery would need to begin some other day. It was time to celebrate the defeat of The Dread.

Back at Twistyard, word spread quickly of the great news. Boot and Buck congratulated their friends, begging to hear every detail of The Dread's downfall after only offering a few lines of explanation concerning their own misguided attempts to stop Zerny and Jibb. Apparently, Boot and Buck had caught up with them at Higga's house, where Zerny planned to catch The Dread. It didn't take long, especially with Higga's help, to sort out that Zerny and Jibb were as oblivious about The Dread's identity as were Boot and Buck.

Dilly kept her word and made Boot squirm, teasing him fiercely about losing his horse and needing Dilly and Sawny to do everything for him. The very act of teasing was therapeutic for all of them after the rough days they had recently experienced.

Twistyard still appeared somewhat shattered, not quite

ready to face the world without Bonboo. In an attempt to seize upon the good in life, Youk and Zerny insisted on a second celebration, to be held the following day. It would honor all of the good people who had been affected by The Dread's craftiness and, more particularly, the people who had fought to stop him. In their words, "Let's remember the good and discard the bad."

So it was fitting, and more than a little bit surprising, when an old friend showed up just in time to be the head speaker of the feast: It was Bonboo! He had been sequestered away, for his safety, by Zerny and Jibb, after a failed assassination attempt.

Great lengths had been taken by Zerny and Jibb before finally resorting to hiding Bonboo in order to smoke out The Dread; and though they didn't catch him themselves, their plan had worked in bringing Sirlonk forward. For them it was a great success to have someone capture The Dread at the end of their long, secret investigation. They had journeyed many places and done countless things trying to track him down, including breaking into Sirlonk's quarters, skunking out Raul Hall, and accidentally starting a fire in the little ribble-barn.

Everyone rejoiced! There were so many things to be happy about. The Dread was in jail, Bonboo was alive, Doochi had been rescued, and even Miz's two sons, Joop and Skap, were retrieved from an island safe and sound.

Dod especially felt at peace. He had faced his own fears and, in doing so, had discovered an inner strength he hadn't known before. Not to mention, his efforts spent apprehending Sirlonk didn't go without a reward. As a token of gratitude, Dod was given Shooter. If he could have selected anything himself, he would have chosen Shooter over all of the other possible rewards; that is, unless he could have had one of his hopeless wishes — that his father or grandpa could come back to life.

Yet strangely, spending time in Green, and seeing everything Pap had done, was almost like bringing him back. The world went on, and within the prevailing freedom, Pap's memory was preserved.

Back at Green Hall, after the wonderful celebration feast, Dod couldn't sleep. He thought of the events that had happened and finally concluded many important questions still remained unanswered. At the top of his priority list — apart from the secrets Sirlonk and Bonboo wouldn't tell — Dod wanted to know more about Zerny: The wagon experience haunted him. And then there was Youk: Despite his friendliness, he appeared to be hiding something.

Multiple loose ends deserved further research; fortunately, with The Dread on his way to a torturous stay at Driaxom, Dod breathed freely knowing he and his friends would have plenty of time to discover all of the answers. He even made a mental list of tasks to begin in the morning.

As Dod lay in bed, feeling glad that things had worked out favorably, he stared up at the ceiling until his thoughts carried him away. In an instant, he no longer saw a wooden canopy, nor shadows and moonlight. Instead, he saw an unusually large drop of water on the outside of his bedroom windowpane. He was back at home, and it was still raining! Just as Bonboo had suggested, it was as if time had completely stood still.

"That was the craziest thing," muttered Cole to himself.

He looked around his room, happy to be back, yet suddenly skeptical of whether anything had actually occurred or whether it was simply a dream. It was too weird. But before he could doubt any more, he reached for a picture of Pap, framed on the wall, and felt a strange pain; and when he stretched the neck of his shirt to see what hurt, the gash on his shoulder stopped all controversy within. The unusual adventure had really happened, and Cole instantly knew Sirlonk's words held more meaning: It was just the beginning!

Book 2

THE ADVENTURES OF DOD

DARK HOOD AND THE LAIR

AVAILABLE FALL OF 2011

Download free chapters at
www.TheAdventuresofDod.com

At home, Cole thinks the world of Green is known only to him, but when trouble comes knocking and his medallion is stolen, he discovers the opposite is true! Increasingly, the destinies of Green, Raul, Soosh, and Earth are becoming intertwined, as dark forces move closer to their bone-chilling goal.

With The Dread in Driaxom, an unknown villain emerges, possessing an unbreakable, crimson sword. His identity is shocking; and he's not alone! The forces of evil are more prevalent and determined than Dod and his friends would have ever imagined. So the adventure continues, filled with fun, intrigue, and betrayal. Some people will stop at nothing to get what they want!

Thanks for being part of the adventure!

We would really love to have you come and visit us at **www.TheAdventuresofDod.com** for free downloads: free e-books, free audio-books, free maps, free comics, and more! It's the site for all things Dod related. Make sure you tell your friends that they can read this book for free if they download an e-version of it from our website. We hope everyone gets a chance to enjoy it.

Questions for Discussion

1. Cole isn't very good at baseball, yet he continues to play in order to keep a promise he made to his grandpa. Have you ever been teased for keeping a promise? How important is it that you keep your word?

2. Cole's younger brother Josh was caught fighting after a bully picked on Alex. What would you have done if you were Josh and somebody was being mean to your sibling? What could you do to stop a bully without getting in a fight?

3. What do you think Bowlure meant when he told Dod, "Why be mad when you can choose to be happy?" How does your attitude affect the way you feel? Have you ever made a bad situation better by trying to think positively?

4. Bowlure and Dungo were both very different looking than everyone else, so their appearances scared some people. As a result, how did Dungo respond to others? How did Bowlure respond to others? Have you ever felt like you didn't fit in?

5. When Dod first meets Boot, he thinks he knows just how Boot will act based on the way Boot looks. Was he right? What things did Boot do that proved Dod was at least partially wrong? Have you ever judged someone incorrectly based on their looks?

6. Many of the characters in this book like to tease each other, with Boot being the king of pranks. Do you ever tease your family members or friends? When is teasing okay, and when is teasing bad? How do you feel when people tease you?

Questions Continued

7. In chapter 11, Bonboo tells Dod, "Too much truth in the hands of a liar is more dangerous than a world of lies told to the truthful. When people like The Dread are mostly honest, they're more deadly." What do you think he meant? How could a few small lies be more harmful than lying all the time?

8. In chapter 14, Boot says that it would have been a tragedy if Shooter had lived out his life lazily roaming through fields instead of doing hard things. What possible tragedies are around us today? How would it be a tragedy if kids skip class regularly to have fun with their friends? Or if they don't graduate from high school? Or if they don't go to college? Or if they spend all of their time playing video games?

9. In this book and in life, some people like to build others up, while some people like to tear others down. Which one is Bonboo? Sawb? Boot? Bowlure? Sirlonk? Dilly? The others? Can you think of examples from the book that support your answers? Can you think of people in the real world who build others up? Which kind of person would you like to be? Why?

FOR MORE COMICS, GO TO

www.TheAdventuresofDod.com

Pet Contest

"I heard you say you'd rather take a bath in red ants
than sit in a pit of Glantor-Worm slime...
Well, happy birthday Tridacello!"

About the Author

Thomas R. Williams grew up in Utah, roaming the mountains and fields with his best friend, Kyle, in search of snakes and lizards. To this day, his mother shudders when she recalls a large reptile that was cleverly placed near her face, and one of his sisters is convinced that Santa should have annually brought him coal! Now, decades later, Thomas lives with his patient wife and twelve children. Together, they roam the mountains and fields looking for lizards and snakes, and to the chagrin of many people, Santa still leaves them presents every Christmas.

To learn more about the crazy author of this book, or if you want free downloads, or if you're interested in laughing at stuff, or if you're just bored, please visit our website at www. TheAdventuresofDod.com. Also feel free to email the author at Tom@TheAdventuresofDod.com.